"An exciting blend of techno-thriller and spy fiction, Flannery's new book exploits a near-future setting. One of the novel's most exciting episodes involves an aerial duel conducted entirely by electronic simulation. His new book is a winner in fact as well as title."

—*Publishers Weekly*

"Flannery takes his rightful place among such masters as Tom Clancy and Clive Cussler."

—Ed Gorman, *Mystery Scene*

WINNER TAKE ALL

Sean Flannery

A TOM DOHERTY ASSOCIATES BOOK
NEW YORK

This is a work of fiction. All the characters and events portrayed in this book are fictitious or used fictitiously, and any resemblance to real people or events is purely coincidental.

WINNER TAKE ALL

Cover art by Joe DeVito

A Forge Book
Published by Tom Doherty Associates, Inc.
175 Fifth Avenue
New York, N.Y. 10010

Forge® is a registered trademark of Tom Doherty Associates, Inc.

ISBN: 0-812-52288-5

First edition: March 1994
First mass market edition: April 1995

Printed in the United States of America

0 9 8 7 6 5 4 3 2

This novel is for the men and women of all navies who risk their lives sailing above, upon, and beneath the unforgiving sea.

PART ONE

1

T-AGOS *JOHN HOPKINS*

Three hundred twenty miles northwest of the Rybachi Peninsula, the T-AGOS *John Hopkins* was making fifteen knots through the angry chop of the Barents Sea. The 2,285-ton U.S. Stalwart-class ocean-surveillance vessel had been on an ELINT (electronic intelligence) gathering mission off the Russian coast for the past ten days. She had been ordered not only to monitor the numerous radar and missile bases that dotted the region and any submarine activity in the area but also to take a close look at a new naval air station at Polyarnyy. They were operating, as normal, under the guise of an ocean-floor sonar-mapping mission. They had not been bothered, even though they were so near to sensitive Russian waters. A few minutes earlier, however, that had changed. The *John Hopkins* towed the UQQ-2 SURTASS, which was the latest in passive-sonar equipment. They had picked up the footprint of a Russian submarine.

"Bridge, sonar."

The skipper, Lieutenant Commander Newton Peters, picked up the phone. "Bridge."

"I've got a positive now on that sub."

"Go ahead."

"Looks like an Alfa. One of the older varieties, I'd say, from the noise she's making."

Peters wasn't surprised that they'd picked up a shadow, just irritated that it had come so soon. He'd been up against the small, deep-diving Alfa boats before, once on a mission in the North Sea, and again a few years ago off the coast of Newfoundland. In both instances the titanium-hulled submarine had dived to three thousand feet, literally disappearing from his sonar as if a magician had pulled some trick.

The Alfa was noisy as long as she remained above any thermocline, but she was extremely deadly. Even the skippers of the much larger, much deadlier U.S. Los Angeles-class attack submarines were wary of the Alfas.

"What's he doing, chief?"

"He's coming to the same course as us, sir. Making about the same speed. Depth as just under one hundred meters."

Peters, a large, harsh-looking man whose friends thought he looked a lot like a younger Gary Cooper, pondered this information for a moment. "Keep an eye on him."

"Should we flash him?"

"Not for the moment. Just keep us posted if he changes course, speed, or depth."

"Aye, aye, sir," the sonarman said.

Peters felt edgy. He put down his telephone and motioned for his executive officer, Lieutenant Ronald Lindsey, and his ELINT officer, Lieutenant John Christiansen, to follow him back to the wardroom.

When they were settled and the door was closed, the skipper turned to his exec. "What do you think, Ron?" His voice was soft.

"Well, he knows we're here, all right, no doubt about that. The question is, does he know *why* we're here?"

Peters studied his ELINT officer. "How soon before

we're in range to find out what we've come to find out, Chris?"

Lieutenant Christiansen looked at his watch. It was a few minutes past 0230 local. "Not for another nine or ten hours. Let's say around noon."

"Depends on what that sub down there is going to do when we get close to the coast," Lindsey said, clearly nervous. "He might shoot."

Peters, who'd joined the Navy when his exec was still in grade school, was an old enough hand not to be too excited when the enemy came sniffing around. "He's not going to start a shooting war unless he gets jumpy, or we do something stupid."

"He could try to jam us. Their ECMs are fairly sophisticated these days," Lieutenant Christiansen said. He was even younger than the exec.

"How effective would that be?"

"Not very, but he might think it would work."

"So," the skipper said, "we either forge ahead and see what the sub will do about us, or turn tail and head home."

"We could radio for . . ."

Lieutenant Commander Peters shook his head, cutting off his exec. "Radio silence, Ron. You read the same orders I read. We either do what we've been sent out here to do, or we make a one-eighty. Let's go for it."

"I agree," the ELINT officer said. "We're here to do a job, let's do it."

Lieutenant Commander Peters paused again. There were just as many aggressive skippers at the bottom of the ocean as there were collecting pensions. But what the hell. He nodded and got up from the table. "Let's go active and ping the bastard half a dozen times so that he damned well understands we know he's down there."

SSN *POGIN*

The Russian-built nuclear-powered attack submarine *Pogin* did not bother to mask its reactor or propeller noises as it shadowed the American surface vessel. She had been on patrol in the Barents Sea north of Polyarnyy for thirty days with nothing to do until now. The crew was grateful for the diversion, although most of them had no real idea what was going on.

Captain Second Rank Mikhail Badim had just returned from speaking with his navigator in the next compartment when the first sonar pings hit them. He, as well as the other forty-five men and officers, looked up reflexively. It was a sound that every submariner respected. They had been found.

The pinging went on for ten seconds and then stopped.

"Sonar, what's his status?" Badim asked.

"Still on course two-nine-five, making fifteen knots, Comrade Captain."

"Range?"

"Three thousand meters, relative bearing one-six-five."

The American ship was behind them and off to the right. "Come right five degrees to three-oh-oh, reduce speed to one-fourth."

"Aye, aye, Comrade Captain," the helmsman replied.

He was a farmboy. But so were they all. A good crew, Badim thought, but with no combat under their belts, and not even any shadow work these days with American warships. Well, all that was about to change.

His *starpom* (executive officer), Valeri Melnik, standing behind the ECM (electronic countermeasures) console, looked up, a knowing expression on his face. Only he, their navigation officer, Kirill Karpovich, and their *zampolit* (political officer), Aleksei Grichakov, had been advised of their real orders. The rest of the crew didn't even know they'd left the Black Sea eleven days ago. The *Pogin* was a Ukrainian Navy vessel, not Russian.

Badim had served in the submarine service for seventeen

years, working his way up the hard way, by dogged persistence. He had no father or even an uncle who had been a high-ranking military officer, no politburo connections, no one to give him sponsorship. But then with the breakup of the Soviet Union he had transferred to the Ukrainian Navy's Black Sea Fleet. There was no love lost in Kiev for Great Russians.

"They know we're here," Melnik said.

Badim managed a tight smile. "So it would appear."

Karpovich looked up from his chart table. "We have seventeen minutes to intercept on this course and speed, my Captain."

"I want a range on the beam of one thousand meters within the next ten minutes. You have the conn."

"Aye, aye, sir."

Badim motioned for his exec and *zampolit* to leave the bridge with him. They went back to the cramped officers' wardroom. Grichakov was last in and he drew the heavy curtain.

"Well," the *zampolit* said. "It seems that we've gotten lucky."

"Or unlucky, depends upon your point of view," Captain Badim said.

"We have our orders, Comrade Captain," the political officer said, bridling.

"Yes, and we will carry them out, Aleksei. The question is, just how far are we going to take it?" As often was the case within the new military establishment, there were orders and then there were *orders*. The more vague a military unit's instructions, the less likely they would be carried out properly, but the more insulated were the commanders and planners should the mission fail. The *zampolits* called this the "initiative" factor. Badim called it asinine.

"He knew we were here before he pinged us." Melnik said softly.

"I don't think so . . . ," the *zampolit* started, but Captain Badim overrode him.

"Valeri is correct, of course. He is towing his passive sonar, we have already established that. And of course we are making our usual noises."

"But he believes we are Russian," Melnik said. "Why did he go active?"

"To let us know that he knows we're here."

"I don't understand this," Grichakov said. He was a naval officer, but he was also Ukrainian KGB. He wasn't a bad sort, but often, like now, he tended to get in the way. He took up precious time for unnecessary explanations.

"He doesn't want us to make a mistake," Badim explained patiently. "He wants us to believe that he is simply working on a bottom survey in these waters and not spying."

"But he is spying!"

"Yes, of course, and we have our orders, Aleksei. But as I was saying, just how far do we go?"

"We shoot," the *zampolit* said without hesitation.

Melnik leaned forward. He had served with Badim now for three years, since the Ukrainian Navy went active. They knew and trusted each other. But this was a dangerous game they were playing.

"Do we blow him out of the water? Do we damage him? Do we surface and challenge him to turn around and go home? What?"

"Sink the bastard," the *zampolit* said with feeling. He was a much younger man than either Badim or Melnik. A graduate of Moscow State University and the old KGB's School One, he had spent barely three months at the Frunze Academy, so he knew nothing of military esprit de corps. This was his first submarine assignment. But he was Ukrainian.

"If the Americans send another ship out here in response, what then?"

"Sink it as well. Our orders."

"Perhaps they might send another submarine."

Grichakov hesitated a moment. "Then we call BLACK-SEAFLEET for help."

"We have been ordered to maintain radio silence until we have actually engaged the enemy. Our signals are monitored. And we have to surface to send them, thus inviting further detection and attack, not only by the Americans but by our Russian friends."

Grichakov threw up his hands in frustration. "I, too, have read the orders. Here we have the perfect situation. Do you mean to tell me that you are going to run away?"

"No," Badim said, suppressing a smile. "I merely wanted to hear from my ... officers."

"Well?" Grichakov asked.

The sonarman had identified the surface ship as a Stalwart-class ocean-surveillance vessel. It carried no armaments except for what was in the crew's small-arms locker. The *Pogin*, on the other hand, carried twelve acoustic-homing antisubmarine torpedoes, free-running antiship torpedoes, two of which were fitted with nuclear warheads, and the SS-N-15 nuclear-tipped antisubmarine missile. There was no match between the two vessels. The *John Hopkins* above was at the *Pogin's* mercy.

Badim glanced at his watch and got to his feet. "Let us commence, then, comrades." He left the wardroom and went back to the bridge.

"Navigator, status," he called.

"Coming up on our point," Karpovich answered.

Badim hesitated, conscious of the eyes of his crew on him. He had his orders, dangerous as they were. He shrugged.

"Bring us to periscope depth. Battle stations."

T-AGOS *JOHN HOPKINS*

"Trim tank noises, she's on her way up," the sonarman called.

"Same course and speed?" Lieutenant Commander Peters asked.

"Yes, sir. She's still on an intercept with us. She can't be more than twelve hundred meters out."

"What the hell does he think he's doing?" Lieutenant Lindsey growled.

Lieutenant Christiansen stood in the doorway from the ELINT compartment, his eyes wide. "We told him that we knew he was there, and now he's coming up to take a look? ECMs?"

"Not yet, Chris," Peters said. "Sonar, give him one more ping. I don't want him coming directly under us."

"Aye, aye, sir."

SSN *POGIN*

Everyone aboard the submarine heard the single ping.

They were making barely ten knots now, the diving planes set to bring them up smartly, but nowhere near normal attack speed. Badim was watching the big depth gauge over the helmsman. Melnik was carefully pumping water from the trim tanks to maintain their even speed of ascent.

"Sonar, any change in the target's course or speed?"

"*Nyet*, Comrade Captain."

The moment of decision was coming soon, Badim told himself, careful to keep the expression on his face and the tone of his voice neutral. He'd been warned.

"You're on the front line, you understand this clearly, Mikhail Ilich?"

"All of us will be on the front line, Comrade General, the moment I shoot."

"It will come and you shall have to defend yourself and your boat. Is that such a terrible burden?"

"No, of course not. But how can you be so certain that such an incident will materialize?"

General Pavl Ivanovich Normav, chief of Ukraine Army-Land, a portly man, smiled indulgently, as a father at a child who doesn't understand something simple. He glanced at the chief of BLACKSEAFLEET Command, Admiral Nikolai Gavrilovich Dyukov.

"You explain it to our cautious captain."

"One of their ships will be there and you will engage. Leave the worries to us."

"If we are detected by Polyarnyy . . . ?"

"Dive deep and leave the area. Another opportunity will be arranged for you."

"To do what, Comrade Admiral? Exactly?" Badim asked.

"Engage an American spy ship."

"Sink it?"

"Yes."

"The incident will be blamed on the Russians. There will be casualties."

"That is our intention," Admiral Dyukov agreed. He sat forward. "These will not be innocent men you will be engaging. They will be spies. The blame will cut both ways—to our Russian friends for attacking an American ship, and to the Americans for spying."

"Tensions will be increased," Badim murmured, thinking it out. General Normav still had many contacts in the Russian military establishment. Especially among the old guard, many of them hotheads. The situation would somehow be bent to his purpose.

"Yes," Admiral Dyukov said. "There will be those in Moscow and in Washington who will become nervous."

"PIT BULL will be called off."

"No," Normav said, shaking his head. "Follow your orders, Comrade Captain. Leave the rest to us."

That was in person. Their written orders were much more vague.

Badim hit the comms switch. "Torpedo room, bridge."

"Aye, aye."

"Load one and two tubes. Mark Cs. Standard HE load."

The Mark C was a wire-guided 533mm antiship weapon loaded in this case with standard high explosives—not nuclear-tipped warheads.

"Thirty meters, Comrade Captain," the helmsman called out.

"Up periscope." Badim stepped forward into the attack

center, turning his cap backward as the attack periscope rose to pierce the surface chop above.

T-AGOS *JOHN HOPKINS*

The port lookout shouted to the bridge, "I have a periscope at eighty degrees off our port beam."

Peters was at the forward windscreen. He raised his light-enhancing binoculars to his eyes, searching the heavy dark chop of the sea, and suddenly he had it as a creamy white phosphorescent trail through the black water.

"Anything from him, Chris?" he asked.

"Negative, Captain. No electronic emissions across the board. No ELF and no comms buoy."

Lindsey was at his elbow looking through binoculars. "What the fuck is he up to?"

"That's not his search periscope," Peters said softly.

Lindsey lowered his binoculars and looked at the captain. "He can't be getting ready to attack us, can he?"

"Let's hope not," Peters said. "Sonar, keep a sharp ear. I want to know if and when he floods his tubes."

"Yes, sir," the passive-sonar man said, obviously impressed.

Peters raised his binoculars again. The submarine was still traveling at in inbound angle which would bring him a perfect beam shot. He would just have to turn sharply to the right and his shot would be set up. Actually, he thought, the sub wouldn't even have to do that. It could just as easily fire from the present angle.

"At this range he couldn't miss," Lindsey said.

"No," Peters replied. "Prepare a message for direct transmission to CINCLAN by high-speed burst. I want it loaded and ready to go the instant I give the word."

"Yes, sir."

"Tell them that we're under attack by a Russian Alfa-class sub. Give them our coordinates, and tell them that we are destroying our crypto gear."

Lindsey wanted to say something, but Peters held him off.

"Show it to Chris, make sure he understands. Do it now, Ron, there may not be time later." Peters looked out again to port. "I'm giving him two minutes maximum to come within one-hundred-percent no-miss range."

"Right." Lindsey hurried off the bridge back to comms.

SSN *POGIN*

"Range on the target one thousand one hundred eighty meters. Elevation angle two degrees," the fire-control officer called out.

Badim was watching the American surveillance ship through his attack periscope. Because of the heavy seas, he'd been forced to raise the scope head an extra meter to get a clear sighting. He knew that the captain of the other ship had spotted him by now, and would almost certainly have identified which periscope was up.

"Send up the snoophead," he ordered.

"Aye, aye," the *michman* (warrant officer) replied. He hit a switch sending up a complex array, on a mast just forward of the attack periscope, that consisted of a number of electronic-countermeasures sensing devices that would automatically monitor electronic emissions from the surface ship.

"Keep a sharp eye now, I want to hear anything he sends off," Badim said.

"I have a solution on the target," Melnik, his *starpom*, said.

Badim continued watching the surveillance ship. How had those old bastards in Kiev known it would come to this? And why had they selected him?

"I have a solution . . . ," Melnik started.

"I have ears," Badim interrupted gently. Even so mild a reprimand must have stung.

The angle remained the same.

For a full thirty seconds Badim was still.

"Range on the target one thousand meters, mark," the fire-control officer called out.

"Prepare to fire," Badim said.

"I'm flooding tubes one and two," Melnik said. He nodded to the chief petty officer handling the controls. "Outer torpedo doors are opening."

T-AGOS *JOHN HOPKINS*

"Christ, she's flooding her tubes," the sonarman called out nervously.

Everyone on the bridge tensed.

"Range and bearing on the bogey?" Peters asked.

"Range is one thousand meters, target bearing is two-seven-three."

Which was eighty-seven degrees off their port beam. Peters could feel it in his gut now: As incredible as it seemed, the Russian submarine was going to fire.

"Sir?" Lieutenant Lindsey called from the comms door.

Peters held up a hand. "Hold off just a minute."

SSN *POGIN*

"I have a confirmed solution on the target," the *starpom* said.

To every officer sooner or later comes the moment of truth. Badim had heard that line somewhere in his distant past. His moment had arrived.

"Fire one, fire two," he ordered.

The *Pogin* shuddered as both torpedoes were launched.

T-AGOS *JOHN HOPKINS*

"I have two high-speed screws incoming," the sonarman called.

"Full speed ahead, full left rudder," Peters said, bracing himself for the sharp turn.

The helmsman cranked the *John Hopkin's* wheel all the way left and the ship responded immediately.

"Sound general quarters." Peters glanced over at his exec. "Send the message now, Ron, and have Chris destroy the crypto gear."

"Yes, sir."

The port lookout called in. "Two torpedoes incoming, bridge."

"Brace yourselves!" Peters shouted.

SOSUS CONTROL

SOSUS Atlantic Control is located outside of Keflavík, Iceland, and is connected via cable to a broad-reaching series of seabed sonars ringing the northern Atlantic basin. The explosion was picked up, processed by computer, and displayed on one of three dozen consoles.

The technician at that console, Petty Officer Charles Denkins, brought up the incoming data on his search-and-comparison screen, overlaying the information with known Russian and U.S. naval ship movements in the region.

"Jesus," he muttered. He punched up his comms console. "Watch commander."

"Yes?" a voice came over his headset.

"I have an apparent incident in sector two-five-four-seventeen."

2

THE PENTAGON

It was 0900 Washington time when Admiral Norbert Thompson, CINCLAN, charged out of his office like a oneman freight train and took the elevator down to the Command Center in the subbasement. He was a short, swarthy man, built like a locomotive. He'd graduated number two in his Annapolis class in time for Vietnam, where he'd distinguished himself under fire on the battlefield. His superiors, as well as his subordinates, called him "one tough son of a bitch."

The twixt from the *John Hopkins* had just been relayed to him through Atlantic Fleet Communications, and it was nearly beyond belief. Now, of all times. The stupid bastards!

His operations officer, Admiral Del Franklin, who looked like a foot soldier, was there along with the J3, Admiral David Maxwell.

"We were on our way down when you called, Bert," Admiral Maxwell said. Outwardly he was a mild-mannered man, with thinning gray hair, but his resolve was as hard as platinum.

"You've heard, sir?" Thompson asked.

"Yes, George called. The question is, what the hell is going on out there, and what the hell are we going to do about it?"

George was George Vincent, chief operations officer at the National Security Agency in Fort Meade. The *John Hopkins* was on a joint Navy-NSA mission, so the agency had been automatically cut in on all comms and especially ELINT from the operation.

"We've got a possible confirmation from SOSUS," Franklin said. "They picked up a single explosion in the region, within moments of Peters' message. Didn't have time to call you, sir, sorry. But we knew that you were on your way down."

"No sweat," Thompson waved off the apology. "Newt Peters is a good man. He wouldn't go off half-cocked."

"That was going to be my first question," Admiral Maxwell said. He was looking at the situation board. They stood on the second tier. Below them in the well were the communications and radar technicians at their consoles. Directly across was the big board that showed an electronic map of the entire world, all known naval vessels shown, along with the tracks of U.S. and Russian surveillance satellites. It was a busy map.

Behind them was the glassed-in conference room where the Joint Chiefs normally sat. It was empty now, and Thompson wanted to keep it that way for as long as possible.

As he had wanted to explain, this was an Atlantic Fleet problem. Nothing more. Peters had evidently strayed too close, been warned off, and then been fired upon when he'd ignored the threat.

"There's been no further comms from the *John Hopkins*, has there?" Thompson asked his operations officer.

"Negative."

"Send a request for a clarification."

"If they're actually under attack, sir . . ."

Thompson softened a little. "As soon as you get that message off, send out one of our Orions from Bear Island to take a look-see."

"Yes, sir." Franklin started off.

"And Del?" Thompson called after him.

Franklin stopped and looked back. "Sir?"

"Plenty of time to start worrying later. No one is going to start a war over this. Not now."

"Yes, sir."

Thompson turned back to Admiral Maxwell. "Did you see this?" He held out the message flimsy.

"No," Maxwell said, taking it.

```
Z101349ZJUL
T O P  S E C R E T  F L A S H
FM: USS JOHN HOPKINS
TO: CINCLAN
INFO: NSA-OPS
1.  AM UNDER ATTACK BY SUSPECTED ALFA-
CLASS SUBMARINE.
2.  AM DESTROYING MY SENSITIVE EQUIP AND
DOCS.
3.  PRESENT POS. 71-DEG. 52.3-MIN. N . . . 35-DEG.
15.2-MIN. E.
4.  REQUEST IMMEDIATE ASSISTANCE.
X X
END FLASH
JOHN HOPKINS SENDS
101050Z
```

"Was he getting too close, Bert?" Admiral Maxwell asked.

"If his navigation is accurate he's two hundred miles off their coast," Thompson growled. "No reason for them to have fired on us, unless they wanted to provoke us into replying."

"The *Hopkins* is unarmed."

"Yes, sir. But we've got the *Phoenix, Boston,* and *Norfolk* up there just now. Within striking range. That sub skipper has to know we have the hardware in the vicinity."

"It doesn't make a lot of sense," Admiral Maxwell said, glancing across at the big board. "Not now, of all times. What could they hope to gain?"

"Could be that sub driver has just gone over the edge."

Admiral Maxwell turned back, his eyes narrowed. It was everyone's nightmare. The rogue submarine skipper with a boat full of nuclear weapons. Welcome World War III.

"We'd better get Don Horvak up here from Norfolk."

Rear Admiral Donald Horvak was the commander in chief of Atlantic Submarine Service. The man knew more about submarine warfare than any officer in the Navy.

"I've already called him. He's on his way in."

"How about Mooreland?" Admiral Maxwell asked softly, looking toward the glassed-in conference room. Air Force General Thomas Mooreland was the Chairman of the Joint Chiefs of Staff.

"I'd like to keep this as an Atlantic Fleet problem, at least for the moment, Admiral," Thompson said. The part he left unsaid was that this was a *Navy* problem, and the chairman, who was Air Force, might not understand the full ramifications.

Admiral Maxwell nodded. "I'll stick around, but I'll keep out of the way."

"It's your call, Admiral," Thompson said.

"Yes, it is," Maxwell replied thoughtfully. He went over to his desk and sat down. "Take this one with care, Bert. Something about it doesn't smell right to me."

OLD SENATE OFFICE BUILDING

Montana Senator Patrick Wood was just leaving his office for an early meeting with one of his colleagues on the Senate Armed Services Committee when his executive assistant, Randy Turner, motioned frantically for him to remain. Turner was on the telephone speaking in low tones, and when Wood gave him a questioning look, the younger man held up one finger and nodded back toward Wood's office. The senator hesitated a moment, then went back inside. Turner joined him a minute later, closing the door behind him.

"Something's come up, Senator, and I think you're going to want to hear it before you leave."

Wood, who was serving his third term as "the have-gun, will-travel senator," as the media liked to call him, trusted the judgment of his assistant almost as much as he trusted his own instincts. Turner's advice had been strident at times, but never wrong. In this town, over the past few years, the man's homosexuality had proved to be a definite plus.

"What's up, Randy?"

"I just got off the phone with a friend of mine who works on the JC's staff at the Pentagon. About an hour ago a Russian submarine attacked one of our research vessels in the Barents Sea. The place is locked up tighter than a drum."

"Research vessel?" Wood's right eyebrow arched. Along with his narrow, sharply defined face and hawk nose, the gesture was the one most exaggerated in the political cartoons. It fit his acerbic personality.

"That's the official line, Senator. But true or not, it doesn't matter. Our ship apparently is in international waters, unarmed, and at least ostensibly minding its own business. It's the timing, sir. What are they thinking?"

Wood sat down behind his desk, his thoughts churning. There was an advantage here. He could almost smell it. The same political instincts that had brought him to this office, and continued to keep him here, were rising. "How good is this source of yours, Randy?"

"Very. But don't ask his name—you won't have to lie about it later."

Wood waved off the suggestion. "Did he give you any details? The name of our ship? Casualties? Has the god-damned boat sunk up there with American boys aboard?"

"Just that she's the *John Hopkins*. Designed to map the floor of the ocean, and measure undersea currents and temperatures and shit like that." At thirty-six, Turner was a handsome, urbane man who dressed off the pages of *Esquire*, drove a Porsche, and took in vacations to Prague, Moscow, and Paris—the capitals. Four years ago he'd attached himself to Wood like a remora to a shark. "Look, Senator, the President's press conference tomorrow would be a perfect time to stick it to him with this."

"I agree, but it's going to have to be played just right or it'll backfire in our faces," Wood warned. "We'll feed this to the *Post* and the *Times*, maybe Jennings over at ABC, but we're going to have all our ducks lined up, do you understand what I'm saying, Randy?"

Turner nodded, a faint smile creasing the corners of his mouth. "My friend is coming over from the Pentagon to have lunch with me at my apartment. But I think you should talk to Jules and get a reading from him. Without Guerin Airplane Company's Space and Weapons Systems Division we don't have much of a case."

"They're walking a tightrope."

"I agree, but the purpose of this exercise is jobs, Senator. The President is all wrong trying to help the Russians out of trouble this way. Waiting for them to catch up is insane. We need to upgrade our own forces. Now!"

"If the Russian officer corps goes on strike because their military machine is falling apart at the seams, the entire country will fall apart."

"We would deal with that eventuality. In the meantime let's be perfectly clear that we should come first."

Wood picked up the telephone and got his secretary. "Darla, get me Jules Joslow at Guerin Space and Weapons Systems Division in Billings, will you? And hold any calls or visitors for the next hour."

Wood held his hand over the mouthpiece. "Get back here right after lunch. We'll go over this in detail. Maybe we can slip something to Jennings in time for tonight's eleven o'clock."

"PIT BULL is ours, Senator," Turner said with a triumphant grin. "And when the rest of the country sees what you've done for Montana, maybe it'll be your turn on Pennsylvania Avenue."

Wood smiled at the retreating figure of his assistant. The bastard would stab his mother in the back if he thought it would do him some good. But he was the perfect assistant.

Guerin's Space and Weapons Division military liaison came on the line from Billings. "Pat, good news or bad? We can use some good. Stan is going to announce the latest round of layoffs."

"How many this time?" Wood asked. Stanley Schade was vice president in charge of the division.

"Five thousand."

"Tell him to hold off for a couple of days. I think I might be able to find a way for you to get into the Rio war games."

"This round?" Joslow asked excitedly.

"If not this round, then the next. The F/A-22 Starfire will fly, my friend."

"South Korea, Taiwan, Brazil, and Chile will be watching. There's a lot of money on the line."

"Billions," Wood agreed. "It's just what this country needs."

3

T-AGOS *JOHN HOPKINS*

The *John Hopkins* listed ten degrees to port. She had been hit twice, but both torpedoes had been set high, just a few feet below the waterline, so as not immediately to sink the ship, but merely to disable her.

Lindsey and Christiansen were aft destroying their crypto gear and their most sensitive documents. Rosario, the sonarman, hurried forward to wreck their sonar heads. It seemed that they were in no immediate danger of sinking.

The ship's comms were still working. Peters hit the switch. "Damage-control party, bridge."

"Aye, bridge."

"What have you got down there, Scotty?"

Chief Petty Officer Randy Scott was their chief engineer. He had gone below immediately after the explosions.

"I can give you two hours at best, skipper," he radioed.

At this high latitude, dawn came early. At least it would be light when they abandoned ship, unless the sub attacked again.

"No chance of saving her?" Peters asked.

"No. We've got three bulkheads out. No way for our pumps to keep up with it. Two hours tops."

"Any chance she'll roll?"

"Not in these seas, and not unless those sonsofbitches hit us again. If that happens, skipper, all bets are off."

"I'll keep you advised. But listen, Scotty. If I tell you to get your people topside on the double, there'll be no screwing around. You got that?"

"Aye, aye, skipper."

Peters released the comms switch and again studied the still-dark sea off to port. Nothing had happened since the attack. What little fire there was had been quickly extinguished. One man had been killed, and two others slightly injured. They had been lucky, so far. But Lindsey had said they'd received confirmation of message from CINCLAN. And SOSUS would have heard the hits. Help was on its way. If they could just hang on long enough.

SSN *POGIN*

"Sonar, what have you got for me?" Captain Badim asked.

"Her engines stopped, Comrade Captain. I hear flooding noises, and pumps . . . at least three."

"Put another fish into her side," the *zampolit*, Grichakov, said, his eyes bright.

Badim ignored him, returning to the attack periscope. The American ship was listing heavily to port now. By the looks of her she would not remain afloat for very long. To this point everything was going according to plan.

"You are certain she got off a message, Valeri Pavolich?" he asked his *starpom*.

"A very brief message, but he got one off."

Badim thought about it for a moment. "Surface the boat." He lowered the periscope into its well.

"They will have already destroyed their classified equipment," Grichakov said.

"I'm sure."

The *zampolit* looked at him through narrowed eyes. "Do you mean to take prisoners, then? This was not in your orders."

"I mean to do exactly that, Comrade Political Officer. And yes, you are correct in your terminology; this is *my* boat, they were *my* orders."

"We will almost certainly have company from Polyarnyy. Russian company."

"Yes. But I am no murderer. It is our duty to pick up the survivors."

They were coming up. The angle on the bow was steep enough so that the crewmen had to brace themselves.

"How close do you want us, Captain?" Melnik asked.

"Fifty meters. I want a boarding party over the side as soon as we establish communications."

"What if they don't reply?"

"Then put a flare across her bow. They will reply. Their captain is no fool. He has already established that."

NATIONAL SECURITY AGENCY

Bill Lane got out of his XJ6 Jaguar sedan, crossed the parking lot, and entered the east door of NSA's vast Fort Meade complex hidden in the thick woods behind an electrified double chain fence. Just inside he had to open his briefcase for inspection and then step through an electronic scanning arch before he was allowed to proceed up to his office on the third floor.

At forty-five, Lane was a dapper dresser, his tastes running to British-tailored three-piece suits unless he was out for a night on the town, in which case it was Italian silk. He'd returned from England in 1970 as a Rhodes scholar, his specialty in comparative political systems. Directly out of school he had joined the Air Force and had been sent to Saigon on embassy duty as a special advisor to the ambassador and the CIA chief of station. He had been one of the last out of Saigon in '73, and two years later had gone to work for the NSA as an analyst and expert on Soviet Russia. For some reason even he couldn't explain, he had developed a "feel" for the Russian mentality. He knew how they thought. He could predict with reasonable accuracy what an individual Russian might do in any given circumstance. He'd been right more often than wrong, and his opinion was much sought after even though he did have distractors who felt what he was doing was nothing short of witchcraft, and was therefore unreliable.

He had been raised in a German-Jewish neighborhood of Milwaukee. And the trick he had learned was that if you wanted to understand a Russian, first you had to understand a Jew. The Jews had suffered for two thousand years as a people; the Russians nearly as long. The Russians had an old saying: Life is unbearable, but death is not so pleasant either. The Jews had always been acutely conscious of how the world viewed them, and for Russians, saving face was everything.

It was simple, but it worked. And Lane had made a career of it.

The office of the director of the Russian Division was at the end of the broad corridor, a half dozen doors down from Lane's office. The door opened as he was coming down the hall, and Tom Hughes, the assistant DRD, stepped out.

"Your desk loaded this morning, Bill?" Hughes asked his friend. Whereas Lane was divorced and lived alone (in splendid isolation, as he called it), Hughes was married, with six children, a dog, and two cats. Despite himself, Lane was fond of the hours he spent at the Hughes' house.

"The usual, Tommy. What's up?"

"Lewis wants you on the double. Do you recall the *John Hopkins*?"

"A naval surveillance ship, isn't she? Up in the Barents Sea taking a look at the new station on Polyarnyy?"

"Right. Seems that a Russian submarine took a potshot at her this morning."

"Good Christ," Lane said. "Did we stray too close?"

"Two hundred miles out. Doesn't look like it. The Pentagon wants some answers. They've sent out an Orion P-3C from Bear Island to take a look."

"How are the Norwegians taking it?"

"They're going along with us, for the moment. At any rate, he sent me to fetch you. You're to drop everything."

"It's the timing, sir," Lane said to Benjamin Lewis, director of NSA's Russian Division.

"It's got us all worried, Bill," Lewis said. He was a huge man, with thick black hair, a massive head, and a barrel chest. His birth name was Lebedev. He, too, understood the Russian mentality.

Lane sat across the big desk from him. Large windows opened onto the pleasant wooded countryside below. The sky was perfectly clear and blue. The agency's antenna farm in the distance looked like something out of a science-fiction movie.

Hughes poured them some coffee. Lewis quickly gave his briefing.

"They wouldn't be risking the entire enchilada unless they had something else going on. A strike?"

"Maybe at Polyarnyy, but not nationwide. Not yet."

"About what you've been predicting for the past three weeks. I was about to put a muzzle on you, but now . . . I'm not so sure."

Lane sat back in his seat. He needed more information, of course. Yet his own assessments of what the Russians were up to just now had been based on data a lot less concrete than the attack on a U.S. surveillance vessel by a Russian Federal Navy submarine. He had been going on hints, suggestions, trends, and possibilities, and little else. The Russian military establishment was fractured, on the verge of total collapse. If that happened there would be no way of predicting what individual unit commanders might take it in their heads to do. There were a lot of nuclear weapons still in service over there.

Another possibility was the old guard. Lane had tried to convince his superiors, Lewis first. Sooner or later Russian President Nikolayev would be sidestepped, if not assassinated. The seeds of dissention, especially amongst the remainder of the older generation, that had been sown in the beginning were starting to bear fruit. Lane had been waiting for it from the moment the new moderate Russian leader had taken office and consolidated his power.

But this now. Why attack a U.S. surveillance ship unless she had strayed into Russian waters? Especially now, practically on the eve of PIT BULL.

"Could be a maverick operation," he said.

"I thought the same, but it seems to be too controlled for some hotshot adventure."

"How long before the Orion is on station?"

"Another half hour."

"In the meantime you want me to put something together, is that it?" Lane asked.

"I know I'm asking you to stick your neck out ... again, but there's nothing else for it. I'll let you call the shots on this one. In other words, this either stays in house, or we take it to the President. Your choice. I can't get inside that skull of yours."

Was this the old guard's move? Lane wondered. He would have thought that if anything was going to happen, it would happen during Operation PIT BULL when the opportunities for mischief would be uncountable. Why now? Why in the Barents Sea?

Lane could think of only two possibilities: either the Russians had more to hide at Polyarnyy than we'd suspected, or this action was one element of some sort of a plan to wreck PIT BULL or use it to some special advantage. The operation was to be a very high-tech war game between elements of the U.S. and Russian Navies. A mock battle would be staged in the South Atlantic Ocean off the coast of Brazil— waters neutral to both countries. President Reasoner had pushed for the "Rio Games," as they were also being called, in an effort to help stay off a total collapse of Russia.

"As expensive as the exercise might be, the cost will be far less than dealing with a disintegrated nation ripe for takeover by another Stalin or Hitler," the President had explained.

His detractors, and there were plenty of those, called the Rio Games a "dangerous boondoggle" despite the sophisticated safeguards that had been built in.

Every contingency had been planned for, every eventuality covered by a series of interlocking controls.

But this move by the Russians in the Barents Sea would put a different spin on PIT BULL. He wondered just how far they were going to take it.

"I'll need a direct pipeline to CINCLAN as well as the Pentagon," Lane said.

"You've got it."

"No holds barred downstairs either. I'll need full access to our archives—all of them."

Lewis nodded.

Lane tried to work it out here and now, but there simply wasn't enough information to go on. It would be easy to jump to conclusions, he thought.

"We don't have a lot of time, Bill, so I'm going to want you to work fast. Cut corners if you have to, but I want something on my desk yet this morning. Can you do it?"

Lane got to his feet, a slight smile on his lips. "Can I borrow Tom for the duration?"

"You've got him," Lewis said.

"Then we'll get started," Lane said, and he and Hughes left the office.

Lewis stared at the closed door for a time after they had left. Lane was a good man, one of the best in the business, in his estimation. But he was a wild card. Telling a man such as him to cut corners was like telling a fish to swim. His nature was to do things his own way. He usually got fine results. But when he failed, he failed spectacularly. This time, their backs were against the wall. They had run out of time. PIT BULL was only days away; so what in hell were the Russians up to?

ORION P-3C

The sun was coming up in the east as a faint blotch of light on the overcast horizon. The Lockheed Orion was outbound from the Norwegian Air Force base on Bear Island at twenty thousand feet, following the electronic pathways toward the last reported position of the *John Hopkins*. The Orion had dropped down out of the clouds fifteen minutes ago and came in at barely five hundred feet above the light chop on the ocean's surface.

"There she is, skipper," the copilot, Lieutenant j.g. David Dralle, said, pointing off to starboard. "About two o'clock."

The pilot, Lieutenant John Alexander, leaned over Dralle to see out the starboard window.

A couple of miles away, the *John Hopkins* lay dead in the water, her list pronounced. No lights were showing, nor could they see any activity on deck.

He hauled the big prop-driven plane to the right and throttled back to drop another hundred feet.

He keyed his microphone. "Listen up, guys. We're coming in over the target. I want you to look sharp for that Russian sub."

"Skipper, we're tracing him now," Chief Petty Officer Stew Hansen, their ELINT officer, replied. "Definitely an Alfa. Dead in the water, about thirty meters submerged."

They were coming in low over the *John Hopkins*, and Alexander searched the water for the sub's outline. But the chop was too big and the light was wrong.

"George, try raising our people, and then message CINCLAN that we're on station, the *John Hopkins* appears to be sinking, and that we're painting the Russian sub standing by."

"Aye, aye, skipper," Chief Petty Officer George Byron said. He was their radio officer.

The *John Hopkins* flashed past below. Alexander started his long lazy turn to the right, a smile on his face. All he wanted was an excuse to drop his fish. The *John Hopkins* was an unarmed surveillance vessel. The P-3C, on the other hand, was an ASW (antisubmarine warfare) aircraft, armed with four Mk 46 torpedoes, six mines, and two nuclear-tipped depth charges.

Any excuse, he thought. Any excuse at all.

MIG-31 FOXHOUND

One hundred twenty-five miles out, the lone MiG-31 Foxhound was outbound at Mach 1 from its base at Polyarnyy at the mouth of the Tuloma Karaginskiy River when his radar illuminated the American P-3C.

In the rear seat, the fire-control officer, Lieutenant Boris Ivanovich Trishin, studied the data displayed on his JTIDS (joint tactical information distribution system) screen, which showed that the P-3C was flying at barely three hundred feet above the surface on what appeared to be a station-keeping flight pattern.

But what was he doing here?

Trishin transferred a simplified version of the data to his pilot's HMD (helmet-mounted display).

"Does he know we're here?" the pilot, Lieutenant Sergei Vladimirovich Vasilyev, asked.

"No ECMs so far, but they're probably in a passive mode."

"I'm activating my look-down, shoot-down radar."

They were too far out, Trishin thought, but he said nothing to Vasilyev, who was young and eager. The Foxhound's primary missile, the AA-9, had an effective range of between twenty-five and forty nautical miles. It would be another six minutes before they were in range.

But if the Americans were on the ball, they would detect the weapons-radar lock long before Vasilyev fired. It would give them time to think.

ORION P-3C

"Jesus H. Christ," Hansen's voice came over Alexander's headphones.

"What have you got, Stew?" Alexander radioed back to his ELINT officer. "Talk to me."

"We're being illuminated by a weapons-control radar system, skipper . . ." Hansen cut himself off in mid-sentence. "There he is, the sonofabitch."

"What have you got for me?" Alexander called back, his gut tightening.

"An incoming, relative bearing two-seven-five, speed of approach just over Mach 1, at about thirty thousand feet."

"Can you say aircraft type?"

"Looks like a Foxhound to me, skipper, probably out of Polyarnyy, and he's hauling ass. We're locked. I think you should get us the hell out of here."

"Hold on," Alexander said, forcing a calmness into his voice. "What's his range?"

"Just over a hundred miles. But at his speed he'll intercept us in something under seven minutes, and he'll be within firing range within four."

Why is he illuminating us so goddamned early? Alexander asked himself. He glanced at his copilot, who was clearly getting nervous. "We've got some time yet."

"Aye, aye, skipper. But I think this sonofabitch means business. Just like his buddies down below."

"George," Alexander called his radioman.

"Aye, skipper."

"Message base what's going on out here. We need an immediate response."

"Will do," Byron replied.

Alexander thought for a moment. "Meanwhile we head northwest, away from the coast."

He hauled the big plane around to a heading away from Polyarnyy and the approaching MiG, and increased their speed to just over four hundred knots. But he remained low, well under five hundred feet, where wave clutter in the Foxhound's radar might confuse them.

MIG-31 FOXHOUND

At a speed of nearly thirty miles per minute, the Foxhound quickly closed to firing range.

Their orders had been precise. There'd been an explosion aboard an American spy ship, which was possibly a diversionary tactic. Shortly afterward an American warplane had been sent south from Bear Island. Polyarnyy was too sensitive to allow the Americans—anyone—to come close. They were to be turned back. No matter the cost.

"I have a positive lock," Trishin said, punching up the final weapons pulse-Doppler radar information to Vasilyev's HMD.

"That's a confirm," Vasilyev said. He reached down and armed a single AA-9 missile.

"Hold it," Trishin said excitedly.

Vasilyev's thumb poised over the weapons launch button.

"The target has turned away," Trishin said. "The target is definitely moving away from our coast."

Vasilyev hesitated a moment, then caged his firing switch, his heart hammering with excitement. This time it was very close.

"Let's show them our appreciation," he said. He hit the afterburner, dumping raw fuel into the jet's tailpipes, and it was as if a gigantic hand were pressing against their chest as they quickly accelerated through Mach 2.

The big fighter/interceptor shuddered as Vasilyev pointed its nose downward while continuing to accelerate.

Two minutes later they passed less than two hundred meters over the Orion, and Vasilyev hauled back on the stick, standing the Foxhound on its tail as he did two eight-point vertical rolls.

"I think we got their attention," Trishin said dryly.

SOSUS CONTROL

The morning shift was in full swing. The command staff all the way down to the sector supervisory level had been advised that something had happened overnight north of the Rybachi Peninsula. But only a few technicians put it together and they were keeping their mouths shut.

Petty Officer Charles Denkins, the first to realize something was going on in that region, had stuck around after his shift was over, with the permission of the incoming watch commander. Denkins was one of the better "ears" on the team.

Just like a good sonar operator, a good SOSUS (sound surveillance system) operator could tell more from an incoming signal than even the Cray-2 supercomputers could. Experience and intuition—Denkins had both.

He sat at one of the spare supervisory consoles behind the watch commander, Lieutenant Commander Barney Fitzgerald. His uniform blouse hung over the back of his chair, his tie was loose, his shirtsleeves were rolled up, and his feet were propped up on the console desk.

To all the world it looked as if he were sound asleep, leaning back in his chair, his eyes closed. But his mind was alert. The sound of the ocean through his expensive earphones, he would tell anyone who would listen, was like a combination of whale songs, the noise you got from a seashell, and Bach. But more. Buried in the mush were messages. Footprints, they were called, of everything that sailed upon or beneath the sea.

Something big was happening up there. The explosion had been identified as a torpedo attack on an unarmed U.S. Navy surveillance vessel by an Alfa-class attack submarine.

When he had seen the incoming report earlier this morning, Denkins had been intrigued. Why, he asked himself, would a Russian submarine bother with an unarmed surveillance vessel, unless of course it was believed that the *John Hopkins* was on a mission?

But even then, the Russians would not have sent out an attack submarine to do the job. That was overkill. Unless something else was going on up there. Unless there were reasons that none of them could understand yet.

So he went searching. Using the command-override controls of his supervisory console, he plugged into the listening sectors, which were chunks of sea forty nautical miles on a side, sliding north and south, east and west, in ever-expanding circles out from the *John Hopkins* position.

Two hundred miles to the south-southeast, back toward the Norwegian mainland, he got his first break, picking up what was obviously a Los Angeles-class nuclear attack submarine.

He punched up the display possibilities, which immediately identified the sub as the USS *Boston*, passing out of her assigned station. From her sounds, she was heading northeast at a good clip.

A few minutes later he picked up the second L.A.-class sub, a little farther to the south and west, this one the USS

Phoenix, also headed toward the *John Hopkins*, and just behind it the third, the USS *Norfolk*.

So, whatever had happened to the *John Hopkins*, the U.S. Navy was interested enough to send three attack submarines into the region with no regard to stealth. Their footprints had all been loud and clear. They were hauling ass and evidently not in the least bit concerned if the opposition detected them.

Again Denkins went searching, this time to the south and east. He didn't think the Russians were going to make their presence so obvious. They would be looking for the advantage of surprise.

Southeast, perhaps 180 miles from the *John Hopkins*, he heard something. Possibly just clearing the coast. But then it was gone.

Denkins pulled his feet down from the console and sat forward. He pressed the earphones against his ears.

Lieutenant Commander Fitzgerald turned around in his chair and looked questioningly at him.

Denkins held up a hand for silence.

There it was again, faint, far down in the background noise. There were two of them . . . no, three submarines. At least one of them a Kilo class, all diesel-electric. He recognized the characteristic *whoosh-whir* of the footprint.

The other two seemed farther away. Check that—not farther, just quieter. Definitely nuclear, in a stealth mode.

Definitely Sierra-class, nuclear-powered attack submarines. Two pressurized, water-cooled reactors driving geared steam turbines. One shaft. Big nine-bladed prop.

Denkins motioned for Fitzgerald to plug in, and he shoved one of his earphones off. "Two-fifty-three-twenty-four. But you're going to have to listen close."

Fitzgerald donned his earphones and punched up the proper sector. He stared at Denkins as he listened. At first there was nothing but ordinary sea sounds, then one of the Sierras came up from the mush.

A glint of recognition crossed Fitzgerald's face. Moments

later the second Sierra came up, and then the Kilo right in front of it.

When they faded at last, Denkins took off his headset, and Fitzgerald followed suit.

"I hear a pair of Sierra-class attack submarines," the watch commander said. "And a third, I think. But I couldn't make out her type."

"Kilo class."

"Of course," Fitzgerald said. "All on their way to the *John Hopkins*."

"I think I'll stick around a while longer, sir," Denkins said.

"You do that," Fitzgerald replied, bright with excitement as he picked up his telephone.

NATIONAL SECURITY AGENCY

Bill Lane was back in his boss's office by 10:15 A.M. He had sent Tom Hughes downstairs to work up the graphics of their presentation, which would be needed if they took this beyond the NSA.

"You don't screw around, do you?" Benjamin Lewis said.

"No," Lane said. "I don't think we've got the time. Not in view of what has been happening this morning since we last talked."

"The Orion is back on Bear Island, the crew shook up but safe."

"Polyarnyy is sensitive. They wanted no company. But it fits."

Lewis looked owlish, his eyes wide. "It's time you earned your money, Bill. Tell me, what's going on."

"I've been plugged into SOSUS Atlantic Control all morning. They've picked up three of our Los Angeles-class attack submarines heading toward the *John Hopkins* at a high rate of speed. The Pentagon had to respond . . . or at least CINCLAN did. And there are two Sierra class and one

Kilo incoming as well. But they're running quiet, trying to hide."

"Why the stealth? It's their coast."

"I'm not sure," Lane said slowly, gathering his thoughts.

"The Alfa has one of our surface ships and apparently means to hold her. In the meantime there's a lot of firepower gathering up there. Again, Bill, the timing is damned curious."

"We should go to the President with this," Lane said. He was getting an odd feeling that he knew what was going on, even though he could barely admit it to himself, let alone share his idea with anyone. All the signs were there. He'd begun seeing indications as early as four months ago, but until now he'd had nothing concrete to go on.

"We'll see Murphy first," Lewis said sharply. "But before we do anything, you're going to have to convince me, Bill. And convince me good, because just now the stakes are too damned high for my liking."

Traditionally there had been the same rivalry between the National Security Agency and the Central Intelligence Agency as there was between the old KGB and the Soviet Military Intelligence Service (the GRU), or between the Mossad and the AMAN, the Israeli Military Intelligence Service. However, since General Roland Murphy had become Director of Central Intelligence, that interservice rivalry had diminished. Murphy and Lewis had been friends since boyhood. Neither agency did much these days without the other's input—which made for higher quality in U.S. intelligence data.

"If I'm reading this right, the Russians no longer maintain much of a submarine presence off that coast," Lane said. "They don't think it's necessary."

"I've seen your evaluations. But that is an Alfa up there. No doubt about it."

"It may be Ukrainian. Black Sea Fleet."

Lewis sat back, stunned. "Go ahead."

"Colonel General Pavl Normav. I believe he and his old-guard cronies could be behind this. If not directly, certainly indirectly."

"He's Chief of the Ukrainian Army, not the Navy."

"He's de facto chief of the entire Ukrainian military establishment. Nothing of any importance comes out of Kiev without his stamp of approval."

"The Rybachi Peninsula is a long way from the Black Sea."

"If that sub driver was sharp, he could have broken free without detection. There's a lot of traffic through the Bosporus and the Dardanelles that he could have hidden under."

"Why?" Lewis asked.

"PIT BULL. I think it was just the sort of thing Normav has been waiting for."

"But that's still days ... and oceans away, Bill. Where's the connection?"

"There may be no direct connection," Lane said, although he thought there might be. "All I'm making are assumptions, discussing possibilities."

"Don't hide behind that academic bullshit. This is me you're talking to. If you want me to take this to Murphy and then the President, you're going to have to lay all your cards on the table in plain sight."

"By the time PIT BULL begins, General Normav wants us and the Russians to be uptight. Accident prone. Like the old days when our forces faced the Russians across the wall in Berlin. There were a lot of incidents. A lot of casualties."

"But PIT BULL will be different. Christ, between Rio and the DOMEs ..."

Lane shook his head. "Nearly one hundred thousand men and officers will be involved."

"Blank rounds. Laser aiming and targeting. No one will be armed. We've gone all over this."

Lane took a moment before he answered. "I think this is just what Normav and his advisers want."

"You're talking about shooting match, Bill."

Lane had brought a single file folder with him. He

opened it, withdrew the three sheets of paper stapled together, and laid them on Lewis' desk.

For a long moment the director of the Russian Division made no move to reach for the report.

"It's a special report from the Kiev Science Institute to the director of the Ukrainian KGB."

Lewis glanced at the cover letter. "It's dated five years ago."

"That particular copy, from what I'm led to understand, came from General Normav's staff eight months ago."

"Hammerstrike," Lewis said. It was the name of the study that Lane had instituted in December last year, subtitled, "First Strike Possibilities." In it Lane explored the possibilities of a Ukrainian nuclear strike upon the Russians. His conclusions had been frightening enough so that the entire report had been swept under the carpet at the DCI's level. The White House had never seen the document. The philosophy was that, so long as the confrontation was contained on that continent, we would be better off staying out of it.

"They may believe that by wrecking PIT BULL we'll do their dirty work for them."

"Then why attack the *John Hopkins*?"

"To get us involved," Lane said. "Our people up there still believe that the attack was Russian. And just maybe the attackers want us to look one way while they pull something off in another direction."

"Get your coat, Bill," Lewis said. "It's time we got over to Langley."

CIA HEADQUARTERS

It was 11:05 A.M. by the time they were ushered into the DCI's vast office on the seventh floor at Langley. Also present at the meeting with the DCI were the deputy director of

Central Intelligence, Lawrence Danielle, and the CIA's general counsel, Howard Ryan.

After the introductions, Lewis got right down to it. "There is a developing situation in the Barents Sea that I believe is going to require some fast action, General. I thought we'd start with you before we took it to the President."

The Director of Central Intelligence, General Roland Murphy, looked from his old friend to Lane. He was a bull of a man with a reputation to match. He was fond of saying that while the buck might stop at the Oval Office, the "bullshit" stopped at his desk.

"Last night a Russian-built Alfa-class sub attacked one of our surveillance ships, and when we sent an Orion out for a look-see it was chased back to Bear Island."

"Has this anything to do with that operation you were running with the Navy? Polyarnyy?"

"Yes," Lewis said. "The *John Hopkins*. But she was still two hundred miles off the Russian coast when she was hit. It doesn't make any sense from where I sit . . . or at least it didn't until now." He glanced at Lane.

"General, I think this incident has something to do with PIT BULL," Lane said.

General Murphy eyed him thoughtfully for a moment, and finally nodded. "You'd better tell me what you've got in mind, son, and what cards you've got to back it up."

"Yes, sir," Lane said. He withdrew the report he'd shown Lewis from his briefcase and handed it across the desk. General Murphy glanced at it and then tossed it over to the Agency's general counsel.

"That's old news, son," General Murphy said.

"Sir, that report was taken from Colonel General Normav's office in Kiev eight months ago. It was marked 'Most Secret.' "

"I would have thought they'd have buried this by now," General Murphy said.

"Apparently not," Lewis said. "Hear him out, General."

"The Ukrainians—or more specifically General Normav

and his supporters—apparently believe that a nuclear war is winnable," Lane said. "It's as simple as that. Carl Sagan, in their estimation, was wrong when he predicted that a nuclear winter of catastrophic duration would result from an all-out exchange of nuclear weapons."

"According to you, he's engineering a situation in which we would attack Russia—not Ukraine."

"Kiev is close enough to Moscow that the Ukrainians would have to worry about fallout. They believe that it couldn't get much worse for them than what they're going through now."

"A dangerous assumption," Murphy growled.

"Yes, sir. But they survived Chernobyl and other such accidents."

"What about Ukrainian President Myakotnik? He's a moderate."

"He'll be sidestepped. Sir, I've watched Normav's staff appointments over the past year. The man has been gathering hawks around him. From what I've been able to gather, he's put together a first-rate war staff."

General Murphy's eyes narrowed. "He started this a year ago?"

"At least as early as that. Perhaps he was at it before I noticed what was going on over there."

"Before PIT BULL came up."

"Yes, sir."

General Murphy exchanged glances with his deputy director, who nodded.

"It fits with what we've been hearing, Roland," DDCI Danielle said.

"Sir?" Lane asked.

"Eighteen months ago we believe there was an attempt to assassinate Myakotnik. At the time, our sources were not all that reliable, and when nothing seemed to come of it, we let the matter slide. But what's significant is that the rumors came out of the Normav camp."

"He failed, so he's decided to try something else," Lane said.

"Perhaps," General Murphy said. "What connection does this have with PIT BULL?"

They were all watching Lane. "I think the Ukrainians mean to try something next week. Sabotage. I don't know."

"During PIT BULL?"

"Possibly."

"What about the incident in the Barents?"

"It may be serving two purposes, if I'm correct. The first would be to test our resolve. And the second to distract our attention from something else."

"But you don't know that for a fact. You're guessing."

"Yes, sir. But I think they'll try to delay PIT BULL."

"Long enough for them to slip in as many submarines, undetected, as possible before the opening of the exercise," Lewis finished the thought.

"Yes, sir, I think that's possible," Lane said.

"We're going to the President with this one, General," Lewis said.

"I agree," the DCI said, not taking his eyes from Lane. "But first I want to know what you're proposing we do about it."

"Cancel or at least delay PIT BULL until we can stabilize the situation and find out how much of the Ukrainian Navy is actually left in the Black Sea."

Now Lewis and Murphy exchanged glances. "I'll talk to him," the DCI said. "But with the built-in safeguards there won't be much the Ukrainians could do to us even if they did break loose down there."

"The President should talk to President Nikolayev in Moscow and tell him what we know."

"What *you're* guessing," Murphy corrected. "Let's keep that straight. Because at the moment that's all you're doing. No hard facts here, only interesting speculation."

Lane had expected as much, and he could not blame the DCI. His speculations were thin. "Then send me up there. To the Barents. Let me talk to that sub driver."

"They've apparently got the crew off the *John Hopkins*," Lewis said. "The recon aircraft, before she turned tail, reported that the ship was lying dead in the water. No sign of any life rafts. The only place they could be is aboard the submarine."

"Good Christ," General Murphy said.

"Yes, sir," Lane said. "If for no reason other than that, may we go to the President?"

"Immediately," Murphy said, reaching for his telephone. "Because unless I've missed something, that Orion was challenged by a *Russian*, not a Ukrainian jet."

THE WHITE HOUSE

They used the Situation Room in the basement because of the audiovisual equipment Lane needed for his presentation. There was a handful of people in the small wood-paneled room, among them the Chairman of the Joint Chiefs, General Thomas Mooreland, and the President's National Security Adviser, Bill Townsend. Most of the others were Navy men in uniform whom Lane did not recognize.

"The President will be down in a minute," Townsend told Lane. "If you just want to get set up."

"Go ahead, and don't be nervous," Lewis told Lane. He and the DCI went over to speak with General Mooreland, who looked like he was in a foul mood.

Lane went to the back of the room where he loaded the slide projector with the carousel that Hughes had hastily put together for him. He was arranging his notes at the lectern when the President came in and everyone stood.

"You're Bill Lane?" he asked, coming to his chair at the conference table.

"Yes, Mr. President."

The President glanced at General Murphy and then Benjamin Lewis before he sat down. "I understand there's some trouble in the Barents Sea. Let's proceed."

"Thank you, Mr. President." Lane dimmed the lights and brought up the first slide, a map of the northern coast, in-

cluding the Rybachi Peninsula. "At approximately 0300 local time at the scene this morning, our ocean-surveillance
vessel the *John Hopkins* was attacked by what we believe
was an Alfa-class Russian-built nuclear submarine. A few
hours later, an Orion P-3C patrol aircraft was dispatched
from the Norwegian Air Force base on Bear Island, and it
was challenged in the vicinity of the disabled *John Hopkins*,
most likely by a fighter/interceptor aircraft from the
Polyarnyy naval air station that the *John Hopkins* was sent
to look at."

Lane used the pointer to show the present position of the
John Hopkins and the submarine that was still standing by.

"At this moment, three of our Los Angeles-class nuclear
submarines are in route to the *John Hopkins*. The *Phoenix*,
Boston, and *Norfolk*." Lane pointed out their positions. "The
Russian Navy has responded in kind, sending a Kilo class
and two Sierras to the scene."

"What has the NSA got to do with this?" the President
asked Ben Lewis.

"The *John Hopkins* was on a joint NSA-Navy mission,
Mr. President."

"That's right," General Mooreland said. "I agreed to it.
We needed some close-up info on Polyarnyy."

"Any word on causalities?" the President asked.

"Not yet, Mr. President," Lane said.

"What's happened to them?"

"We believe they were taken off their ship and brought
aboard the submarine."

"As hostages?" the President demanded, but before Lane
could respond he went on. "So we've got a Mexican stand-
off developing up there. Our three subs against their four.
I'll call President Nikolayev. We'll defuse the situation."

"No, sir," Lane said. "There's more to it than that."

The President looked at him for a long moment. "You
wouldn't have come over here this morning if you didn't
think so, correct?"

"Yes, Mr. President."

"Then go ahead."

Lane switched to the next slide, which was a photograph of a Ukrainian Army general coming out of a large building. "Colonel General Pavl Ivanovich Normav, chief of Ukraine Army-Land. This photograph was taken about eighteen months ago, when the general was emerging from his office just hours after what we learned was a possible assassination attempt on Ukrainian President Yuri Myakotnik.

"That's speculation, isn't it, Roland?" the President asked the DCI.

"A little stronger than that, Mr. President. But there is no proof forthcoming."

"I see," the President said.

"There has been no connection made between the assassination attempt and General Normav," Lane continued, "but shortly after that incident the general began making drastic changes in his staff, including his key line officers."

"To what purpose?" the President asked.

"To make war against Russia, Mr. President. It's taken all this time to put something together, but in each case the staffer who was removed was a moderate, and his replacement a hawk. In each case inexperienced men were replaced with experienced officers, some of them even brought out of retirement."

"And this has been going on for how long?"

"For the past year," Lane said. He flipped through the photographs of a dozen old-guard officers, some of whom General Mooreland and the other military men recognized.

"Okay, Mr. Lane, you've told us that General Normav has rearranged his staff. What bearing does that have on the incident this morning?"

"I'm coming to that, Mr. President. If you will just bear with me."

The President nodded, but there was a dangerous look in his eyes.

"Eight months ago a document was taken from General Normav's office and made its way here to us," Lane said, switching to the next slide, which showed the cover page of the warfare summary report in Russian with a translation to

English next to it. "This is an old report, one that we know the Ukrainians developed nearly five years ago. The important fact is that it is apparently being given prominent play in General Normav's office now."

The mention of the timing was not lost on the President, or on anyone else in the room.

"Get on with it," the President said.

"If PIT BULL succeeds in the way we hope it will, the Russian military may pull away from the brink of collapse. The danger of another Kremlin coup would diminish."

The President stared at Lane. "You understand that stabilizing the Russian military is not the only object of this exercise, Mr. Lane. There are jobs in this country on the line, as well as the combat readiness of our own Navy. PIT BULL will pay dividends."

"Yes, sir. But if something were to happen . . . some accident, some act of sabotage . . . the situation would be different."

The President turned to General Mooreland. "Is something like that possible, Tom?"

"Certainly, but it wouldn't affect the overall outcome of the exercise, Mr. President." The Chairman of the Joint Chiefs leaned forward for emphasis. "We've built into our safeguard systems what we term Super Redundancy. Accidents can and will happen, that's inevitable in any operation of this size. And we could be vulnerable to an individual act of sabotage. But PIT BULL is so large, so well coordinated, and so well controlled that any trouble would be localized—perhaps to one section of one ship or unit."

"Mr. Lane?" the President asked.

"There are two possibilities General Normav may be working toward. Wreck PIT BULL, which might edge the Russian military a step closer to disintegration."

General Mooreland shook his head.

"Or create an incident during the games in which we would go to war for real against Russia."

"That's ridiculous," Mooreland said sharply. "You're not looking at the facts. Speculation, nothing more."

"Assuming one or the other scenario is correct, why did the Russian Navy attack our surveillance ship?" the President asked. "What did General Normav have to do with it?"

"That submarine may not be Russian Navy. It may be a unit of the Ukrainian Black Sea Fleet."

"But our search airplane from Bear Island was forced off by a Russian jet fighter, isn't that so?"

"Yes, Mr. President. Or at least we believe that to be the case. But the situation up there is confusing at best. We're getting a lot of conflicting reports. No one can be sure at this end what's really going on."

"General Normav would have a lot to lose if he got into it with the Russians at this time."

"Yes, sir. But he may believe that the incident up there might start something between us and the Russians at Polyarnyy. We were spying on the base—or intending to do so."

"We've intercepted some Russian military communications between Polyarnyy and Fleet Command in Moscow," Lewis said. "Seems as if they believe that the *John Hopkins* had an on-purpose accident so that we could bring up resources for a rescue operation."

"They believe our intention was to spy?" the President asked.

"Yes, sir. And they are correct. But there is no mention of the submarine in any of the traffic we've listened to."

"But the submarine could be Russian?" the President asked.

"Yes, sir," Lane said. "Russian or Ukrainian. However, the Russians would deny any knowledge of it."

"But you believe that the *John Hopkins* crew may have been taken aboard that submarine?"

"I do, Mr. President."

"How would you like to go up there and defuse the situation for me? Talk to the captain of that submarine and tell him that we know what he's up to. We don't want to escalate the situation, but we *will* have our people back. If the submarine is Russian, they will back down. They do not want to jeopardize PIT BULL. If the submarine is Ukrainian, find out what they want. Tell them we'll join forces with the Russians, if need be, to hunt them and kill them."

"That would be a dangerous move, Mr. President. The Russians would be very suspicious of us. They believe we're spying."

"This is a dangerous world we live in, Mr. Lane. Will you do it for me? Will you bring the crew of the *John Hopkins* home?"

"Yes, sir. I'll give it a try."

"That's all I can ask of anyone."

want to jeopardize 107 BULL. Killin submarine is Ukrain-
les, then out what they want. Tell them we'll join forces
with the meeting, if need be if won't be about that which

within the first, they said.

5

SSN *POGIN*

Captain Badim tightened his hold on the search periscope's
grips as the *John Hopkins'* stern rose into the air, seemed to
hang there, and then began the slide down into the sea.

"I'm picking up displacement noises, Comrade Captain,"
his sonarman said. "Sounds like one of her engines broke
loose."

The stern disappeared in the midst of a big wave, the last
of her air flooding out, making the surface of the water boil.
And then she was gone.

For a time Badim remained at the periscope staring out
at where the American spy ship had disappeared. One
man was dead, his body gone down with the ship. The
other thirty-eight men and officers were aboard the *Pogin*
... nearly the same number of Americans as Ukrainians
aboard.

They were terribly cramped for room, but, as it had been
explained to the Americans, there was no alternative.

"We cannot bring them aboard, Comrade Captain," his

zampolit, Grichakov, had argued. "In the first place there is not enough room . . ."

"Then which of them shall we bring aboard, and which shall we leave to drown or die of exposure, Aleksei? Can you tell me this?"

" . . . and in the second place, this is a warship. Our configuration, the equipment aboard, all of it is classified."

Badim had smiled at this last. "This is a very old class of submarine, Aleksei. Since 1972. By now I think the Americans know at least as much about her as we do." He shook his head. "No secrets here, except for our communications equipment. And I promise not to invite any of them into our communications center."

"We are a Black Sea Fleet vessel, not Russian."

Badim swung his hand around. "Where does it say that, my Comrade Zampolit? Even if a Russian officer were to come aboard, he would not easily be able to determine which flag we sail under."

"Then what do you mean to do with the Americans?" Grichakov had demanded. They had stood within the attack center, Melnik and Karpovich the only others there besides the helmsman.

Badim had stepped forward so that he was practically on top of Grichakov. "Once again let me remind you that this is my vessel. You are here as an observer and adviser . . . nothing more. And now you have observed the situation and you have given me your advice. I suggest that you have done your duty and that you now keep out of my way."

Badim lowered the periscope into its well. In the past hour Grichakov had made himself scarce. Even when they had brought the Americans aboard, and had distributed them throughout the submarine, he hadn't shown himself. It was just as well, because there was a lot of work yet to be done.

He hit the comms. "Sonar, I want you to keep a sharp ear now. We may be getting some company."

"Aye, Comrade Captain," the sonarman replied. "I have nothing yet, other than the American spy ship. She's beginning to break up now, her bulkheads are collapsing one by one . . ."

"Spare me the details," Badim said. "Ivan, anything from the snoophead?" he asked his *michman*, Ivan Yudkin.

"Some chatter out of Bear Island about the Orion, Comrade Captain, but no one seems to be doing anything about it."

"They will," Badim said. "I want you to keep an especially sharp ear out for anything, anything at all. This is very important. The moment something comes up, you must inform me. Immediately. Do you understand?"

"Yes, Comrade Captain. But do you think they will send someone else out here?"

"Most assuredly," Badim said. General Normav had been wrong about nothing so far. The man was in league with the devil. There was no reason to suspect he would be wrong about the rest of it.

Releasing the comms switch, he turned to his *starpom*, who stood with Karpovich at the chart table. "Take the conn, Valeri. I think it's time I have a chat with the American captain."

Melnik was a full head taller than the captain. He lowered his voice. "How long are we going to stay here like this, Captain?"

"Not long now, Valeri. Are you getting nervous?"

"Fuck your mother, but we're beginning to smell each other. And it is not a pleasant odor."

"There'll be plenty of time for bathing later, believe me. But for the moment this is where we shall remain."

"Why, can you tell me this? None of this part was in our orders. We have stopped the American spy ship. Why is it we remain here? Are we waiting for the Russian Navy?"

"Someone is going to come out here to claim their crew, Valeri. We're going to be here to greet them."

"Do you mean to give them back?"

Badim managed a slight smile. "That depends upon how badly they want them. We'll see. For now you have the conn. Anything, absolutely anything comes up, I want to be called."

"Rest assured, Captain, you won't miss a thing if I have anything to say about it," Melnik said with much sincerity.

"Good." Badim clapped him on the shoulder. "That's very good."

The *Pogin* was small as submarines go. At something under 270 feet, with a beam of little more than 30 feet, she displaced only 3,700 tons submerged. Her normal crew complement was forty-five men and officers, and with the addition of the thirty-eight men and officers from the *John Hopkins* every square meter of space aboard was crammed with human bodies.

The *Pogin*, however, was remarkable in one respect. She was constructed of titanium, instead of steel, which allowed her to dive more than three thousand feet—twice as deep as any other submarine. And she was exceedingly fast. Her submerged speed was over forty knots, which made her one tough sonofabitch. There were no attack submarines in any fleet against whom she couldn't give a good account of herself.

It was why an Alfa had been picked for this mission.

Badim had to wonder why his particular crew had been selected. General Normav had not explained, nor had Badim asked.

A young machinist's mate was standing guard duty at the door to Badim's cabin, where the American captain and his executive officer had been placed. He looked up, his eyes wide, when Badim came back.

"Everything has been peaceful?" Badim asked.

"Yes, Comrade Captain."

"Good, then go to the galley and get yourself something to eat. I'll call you when I need you."

"Are you sure, my Captain? I mean, I don't mind staying . . ."

"Go on."

Reluctantly the young man went aft. Badim knocked once and entered his own tiny, cramped cabin.

Lieutenant Commander Newton Peters sat at the tiny folddown desk, while his executive officer, Lieutenant Ronald Lindsey, perched on the edge of the cot. They had been talking intently, and both looked startled as Badim entered.

"I'm told that you have been fed?" Badim said.

"Yes, we have. What about my men?" Peters asked.

"They have been fed and bedded down as well. No harm has come to them."

"What do you mean to do with us, Captain . . . ?"

"My name is not important. And what is to become of you and your crew will depend in a large measure upon yourself, as well as your superiors."

Peters' eyes narrowed. He got to his feet. "I'm listening," he said.

"You were in command of a spy ship, Captain. Please tell me the target of your search."

"We were an ocean-surveillance vessel, as you well know. An *unarmed* ship, as you also know."

"You were mapping the seafloor."

"That is correct."

"And the ocean floor just here is so vitally important to your government that you were moved to destroy your . . . mapping equipment rather than let it fall into our hands." Badim gave a thin smile. "I think you are in a very difficult position, Captain. I'll give you more time to consider your options . . . all of them, including the well-being of your crew."

"Don't threaten me, you sonofabitch."

"Not a threat, Captain," Badim said coldly. "But in my country we shoot spies. Think about it."

Badim turned and left his cabin. The young machinist's mate stood at the hatch to the galley, drinking a cup of tea and wolfing down a piece of dark bread. He hastily put down his cup and rushed forward.

"If they try to get out of there, shoot them," Badim said.

The young man nodded and swallowed hard. "*Da*, my Captain."

KIEV

It was eight o'clock in the evening but since Kiev was on the same latitude as Newfoundland, it was still light outside. Colonel General Pavl Ivanovich Normav stood at the window of his eighteenth-floor apartment looking down at the traffic on busy Kirov Ulitskey toward the Dnieper River, a glass of vodka in hand.

He was tired. But then he had every right to be. He had passed his seventieth birthday six months ago, and he had seen all there was to be seen . . . or nearly all.

At times like this, alone at the end of a busy day (his wife of forty years had died eight years ago), he often thought back over his life, which had had its real beginnings in 1942 when at the age of fifteen he had joined the tank corps as the youngest squadron commander in the service.

"You were born to lead men in battle, Pavl Ivanovich," his commanding officer had said to him.

Normav had remembered that exact moment in great detail, and whenever he was troubled or faced a crisis, he would recall their conversation and it would give him strength.

Very soon now, he told himself, the old glory would return. There was nothing so tragically beautiful as a young man falling on the field of battle. He had an almost mystical feeling about it.

"A nation's true and correct destiny can be determined only in time of war," he had told the graduating class of Frunze. "Peace is honorable only if it happens naturally, and not at the expense of the strongest nation."

For too many years he had seen the power of the Soviet Union being eroded by the silly fools in the Kremlin. And for the past dozen years, first that upstart Gorbachev and then Yeltsin had nearly emasculated them. *Perestroika, glasnost*, and democracy, the three-headed snake they had lived with, were a shame and a blight on the land and her peoples. Ukraine was now their only salvation. Their only hope for restoration of the old order.

Normav's hand tightened on the glass, and with a great effort of will he forced himself to calm down as he turned away from the window, crossed the room, and poured a second drink.

After the near disaster last year, when their assassin had failed to get President Myakotnik, he had worked day and night gathering his forces; in some cases gathering the old names around him. The men of like spirit and mind, who were willing to do whatever was necessary to preserve the old idea of the *Rodina* . . . the motherland.

In the meantime they had been looking for just the right situation to arise, never dreaming that it would be handed to them on a silver platter. Operation PIT BULL it was being called. What a joke! A farce!

Those fools in Moscow wanted an excuse to gather their forces into one cohesive unit. Well, PIT BULL had provided just such an excuse, and they were taking full advantage of it.

Nikolayev and those old women in the Kremlin, including Marshal Leonov (the Russian counterpart of the Chairman of the Joint Chiefs), had Operation PIT BULL, while Normav and his Ukrainian loyalists had their own operation, which they called KEENSCHCAL (Dagger Point). And in a few days the entire world would feel the razor-sharp point of the Ukrainian dagger.

The telephone rang, startling him out of his thoughts. He put the glass down and crossed the room to answer it. Admiral Leonid Aleksandrovich Ryabov, chief of naval operations, was on the line.

"I am on my way over, Pavl Ivanovich," the Navy man said.

"My door is always open to you, Comrade Admiral," Normav said carefully. Both of them supposed that their telephones were tapped. It was a fact of life even in Kiev, one that neither man questioned.

"I'm just a block away, I'll be there in a minute or two."

"I'll instruct security," Normav said, hanging up.

Something had evidently happened. Something so important that Ryabov could not trust it to the telephones, and something that demanded their immediate attention.

Normav's old heart began to accelerate, the adrenaline beginning to pump as it did at the start of battle. Let it begin, he whispered to himself. One last time. He wanted to be involved with the ultimate conflict. The war to end all wars. He had to smile. There would never be an end to war. Conflict was in man's basic genetic makeup; strife was in his nature.

He went into his small study at the rear of the apartment where he turned on the overhead fluorescent lights, which contained white-noise generators that would foil any electronic eavesdropping equipment, then informed Security downstairs that a guest would be arriving. After the near miss on Myakotnik they all were cautious. Normav was certain that the President's people suspected him of complicity in the assassination attempt.

He brought the bottle of chilled vodka and glasses back to his study, along with a small plate of blini. He and Ryabov were definitely of the old school, where vodka was never drunk without something to eat as an accompaniment.

The admiral arrived a few minutes later, hanging his coat in the hall, and he followed Normav back to the study. In contract to Normav's bulk, Ryabov was a thin, wizened old man with parchment skin and deep-set milky eyes. But his brain was still sharp and he was a fine commander. Except for the political upheaval that had split the Union, it would have been he instead of Leonov sitting in the marshal's chair in Moscow.

"I came as soon as I heard," Admiral Ryabov said. He accepted a drink from Normav, tossed it back, and picked a blini off the plate. "Nikolai called me. It has begun."

Admiral Nikolai Dyukov was commander in chief of Black Sea Fleet.

"It's our Captain Badim?"

"Yes. He's sunk an American spy ship in the Barents Sea. An air response was ordered out of Polyarnyy when the

Americans sent out one of their reconnaissance aircraft. The American aircraft was forced off."

"Did the air crew get off a message?"

"Yes," Admiral Ryabov said. "Nikki was very specific about that. Both the ship and the aircraft messaged the Norwegian base at Bear Island that they were under attack by *Russian* forces. Moscow will view the messages as a ruse, of course."

"Good," Normav said, his thoughts racing ahead. "Anything from the Americans?"

"Nothing."

"How about the Kremlin? Did they detect our sub?"

"Nothing from them either," Admiral Ryabov said. "But it's coming, Pavl Ivanovich."

"Yes, and when it does we will be ready for it," Normav said with a smile. He finished his own drink, ate a blini, and then poured them each another. "Now, tell me what is happening with our good Captain Badim in the Barents Sea. He is waging a successful war against the *Amerikanskiy spion*?"

"A very successful war," Admiral Ryabov said. "But then he is sharp . . . just like a dagger point."

THE KREMLIN

Marshal Yakov Borisovich Leonov, chief of all Russian Armed Forces, rode the elevator down to the Situation Room buried deep beneath the grounds of the Kremlin. He'd left his bodyguard upstairs, and his briefcase had been scanned. All sensible precautions, but this evening he thought that meeting down here was carrying things a bit too far.

But Leonov was an officer (actually an Air Force general) and he knew how to follow orders.

It had taken him the past hour and a half to sort out just what sort of nonsense was occurring off their far northern coast in the Barents Sea. At first he had suspected that some meddling fool of a local commander had made a mistake. The most damning piece of evidence, of course, was the fact that so far the Americans had not responded. There had been nothing, not so much as a peep from them.

"What are they trying to do to us out there?" Defense Minister Anatoli Tsarev had demanded.

"I don't know yet."

"Well, you'd better find out, and very soon, Comrade Marshal. We are expecting you at nine sharp in the Situation Room, and we want answers."

"Of course," Leonov had said.

It was nine now, and he had the answers . . . or at least he had some of them. The problem was that every answer raised a dozen new questions.

He was met at the bottom by another FIS security detail, who checked his briefcase and person again before he was allowed inside.

President Gennadi Nikolayev sat at the end of the long conference table. With him were seven members of his cabinet and Defense Minister Tsarev, who beckoned Leonov over to an empty chair at the far end of the table.

"Good evening," he said, opening his briefcase. He withdrew several thin file folders, which he passed down the table before he sat down.

He was, at fifty-five, a relatively young man, as were the others around the table. None of them had seen duty in the Great Patriotic War so they all spoke the same language.

"Before we begin, Mr. President, has there been any word from the American President?"

Nikolayev's left eyebrow rose. "There has been no word from him. Should there have been?"

"I expected it," Leonov answered. "But the fact that he has not communicated is in itself significant." No one had bothered to open the report he'd passed down the table. "Mr. President, as you are aware, there is an incident developing at this moment off our coast in the Barents Sea."

"Have there been any casualties?" Nikolayev asked.

"Unknown at this time."

"I see," Nikolayev said heavily. He was a moderate. He had spent the past decade proving that. Since their withdrawal from Afghanistan, Russian troops had not fired a single shot on any major battlefield anywhere in the world. "Get on with it, then, Marshal Leonov. Perhaps it is I who should be telephoning the American President."

"I think not, Mr. President, except perhaps to cancel or delay PIT BULL."

Nikolayev's broad eyes narrowed. He shook his head. "That is totally out of the question. The exercise *will* proceed as scheduled." His eyes bored into Leonov's for a long second or two, then his gaze swept the table.

Leonov wasn't going to back down. "I am paid to give advice, Mr. President . . ."

"Military advice, Marshal Leonov, not political."

"The Americans are spying on us."

Nikolayev actually smiled. "So, what is new, Yakov Borisovich? Is that what is happening up there?"

"It is an incident that must not go unpunished."

"Let's decide that together. Tell me what is brewing in the northern sea."

"An American Navy spy ship, the *John Hopkins,* was detected by one of our Rybachi radar units three hundred kilometers from Polyarnyy. Evidently there was an explosion aboard. Or it was made to look as if the ship was experiencing grave troubles."

"This is definitely a spy ship?"

"Yes."

Defense Minister Tsarev broke in. "American satellites have overflown Polyarnyy, of course, but we've been expecting something like this for some time now."

"What was done about it?"

"The *John Hopkins* sent a message to the Norwegian Air Force base on Bear Island, and subsequently an American reconnaissance aircraft was sent to the scene. Supposedly to help the disabled vessel. But the aircraft's electronic spy equipment was aimed at our Polyarnyy installation."

"Yes?"

"A very capable squadron commander dispatched a fighter/interceptor out there, and the young crew forced the American aircraft back to its base."

"No damage?" Nikolayev asked. "That was dangerous."

"None, Mr. President. But the action was justifiable in light of a subsequent development."

"Which is?" Nikolayev demanded coldly.

"As I reported, the American spy ship was heading toward our territorial waters when she stopped, but so is at least one American nuclear submarine. A Los Angeles-class attack boat."

Again Nikolayev's eyes narrowed. "What are you saying to me, Marshal Leonov?"

"It is my belief that the Americans deliberately provoked us into either responding or standing down in an effort to test our resolve."

"Why would they do such a thing so close to the beginning of PIT BULL?"

"Because they felt that we would not respond for that very reason ... that is, for fear that the war games would never get off the ground. It would have given them the perfect opportunity to gather the information they want on Polyarnyy."

"But it did not work," Defense Minister Tsarev said.

"No. We have the crew of the MiG to thank for that."

"Or damn," Nikolayev said. "The supposedly disabled American vessel is in international waters, is this correct?"

"Yes, Mr. President."

"Is it in position to spy on us? On our Polyarnyy installation?"

"Not now."

"Then we shall do nothing. Nothing, that is, unless the Americans send another aircraft or vessel to spy on us." Nikolayev sat forward. "If the Americans send a rescue vessel, we shall do nothing unless they ask for our help."

"Mr. President, we've had a long-standing agreement with the Americans not to place our submarines anywhere within five hundred kilometers of each other's coastline.

But at least one Los Angeles-class submarine is already well within that limit."

"In a position to spy on us?"

"Not unless she surfaces."

"This will remain at the command level, Marshal Leonov. PIT BULL will proceed as scheduled."

But not without precautions, Leonov wanted to say, but a warning glance from Defense Minister Tsarev caused him to hold his tongue. Yet riding the elevator back to the surface and his waiting bodyguard, Leonov was struck with the notion that they were all being used somehow. That the situation was somehow contrived, but by whom or for what purpose he could not guess.

No matter what, though, the Polyarnyy commander's orders would be clear. He was to defend his base at all costs.

GEORGETOWN

Bill Lane went directly to his apartment after briefing the President. Arrangements were being made to get him up to Bear Island in the Barents Sea (a distance of some 4,900 miles) as soon as possible, and from there out to the last known position of the *John Hopkins*.

The only thing he was told was to pack light, pack warm, and pack quickly.

He was stuffing a few things in a nylon overnight bag when Tom Hughes showed up from the NSA with a briefcase full of files and a six-pack of beer.

"So how's your stomach?" he asked.

Lane zippered up his bag and set it down by the front door. Hughes opened one of the beers and handed it to him. "What do you mean?"

"How does traveling at Mach 4 about twenty miles up strike you?"

"The SR-91 out of mothballs?"

"Bingo. Flight time a little over three hours to Bear. From

there you're to be choppered out to the *Marvin Shields*. She's a Knox-class ASW frigate on her way out to the *John Hopkins'* last known position."

"That's shaping up to be a busy piece of ocean," Lane said, taking a drink of the beer.

"There's more."

"Did you get something off the wire?"

"You bet. We monitored two high-speed-burst transmissions from REDFLEET Command beamed to Polyarnyy."

"Is the sub one of theirs, after all?"

"Probably not. The messages were directed to the base commander at Polyarnyy, or at least we think they were. We haven't decoded either message yet, but we did manage to pick out the acknowledgment of receipt and the identifier."

"Nothing about the sub?"

"Doesn't look like it. But the last KH-15 satellite pass showed what appeared to be a disturbance in the water where the incident took place. And the *John Hopkins* is gone."

Lane had grabbed his jacket and was pulling it on. "Sunk?" he asked.

"Their emergency radios went off the air, and photo analysis seems to think they can make a good case for it. Some debris in the water."

"Jesus."

"There's more," Hughes said. "Ten days ago, the Black Sea Fleet SSN *Pogin* disappeared while on a routine training mission off the Crimean Peninsula. We got this from the CIA. Navy Intelligence confirmed it. The *Pogin* is an Alfa-class boomer. Crew of forty-five men."

"If they've got the *John Hopkins* crew aboard, they've got to be bulging at the seams, and straining the hell out of their stores. Anything on the Ukrainian crew?"

"Captain is Mikhail Badim. One of the best in the fleet, but something of a maverick."

"Any tie between him and General Normav?"

"Nothing obvious, nothing that we or CIA have been able

to come up with. But it's a big world out there, Bill. New alliances happen all the time."

"What have you got on him?"

"He fits the profile. He's commanded three boats in the past nine years. He, like everyone else, knows that every assignment now is lateral. He's risen as far as he's going to rise."

"Why?"

"Like I said, he's a maverick. Apparently he's been on the carpet more than once for failing to report maneuvers before actually carrying them out. And he's got no family, no patronage."

"Unless Normav decided to pick him up."

"It's possible," Hughes said. He glanced around the apartment. "You about ready? They're waiting for you at Andrews."

"Yeah."

"I've brought your reading material. Dossiers on the *John Hopkins* crew, and of Badim and as many of his people as I could come up with."

WATERGATE APARTMENTS

Navy Lieutenant Doug Hatcher, glass of champagne in hand, stood at the bedroom windows of Randy Turner's apartment in the Watergate Complex. He could see the small-boat traffic far below on the Potomac River, and he thought bitterly that this was as close as he'd ever get to shipboard duty. Homosexuals were no longer banned in the Navy, they were simply sidestepped. His education and training were going to waste, and it made him so angry that sometimes he could barely control his emotions.

Hatcher's grandfather and father had both served aboard aircraft carriers, and his brother, Stewart, was XO aboard the USS *Ingersoll*, a Spruance-class destroyer. But he had risen as far as he'd ever rise on Admiral Norbert Thompson's staff. It wasn't fair. He wanted duty aboard a ship, and he was qualified for it. But it would never happen.

"Hey, sailor, if you're going to mope, do it on your own time," Turner said, coming out of the bathroom.

Hatcher managed a smile as Turner took him into his arms. "I was just thinking about sea duty."

"Don't you wish. You and five thousand studs."

"It's not that at all, Randy," Hatcher shot back.

"I know, and I'm sorry. If there was something I could do, I'd do it in a New York minute." Turner led the more slightly built man back to the bed. "We've still got a half hour."

"Sounds like I'm whining, but I'm not. I'm just pissed off."

"I know," Turner said soothingly. He took the champagne glass from Hatcher, set it aside, and eased the Navy man down onto the sheets.

"I know my job. I could be a real asset to them."

Turner brushed the younger man's hair off his forehead. "It's hard to believe that the *John Hopkins* has disappeared. What about her crew?"

"Probably aboard the Russian submarine. But the National Security Agency is sending someone up there to take charge."

"Who?"

"Bill Lane. He's supposed to be pretty good. He briefed the President this morning, or at least that's the scuttlebutt."

"What do you think is going on, Doug? So soon before PIT BULL, what do the Russians think they're doing up there? How do the JCs read it?"

"I don't know. God only knows what'll happen, Randy." Hatcher looked into his lover's eyes. "If it wasn't for you, I think I'd kill myself."

Not yet, Turner thought. "Don't be silly," he said. "I need you."

SSN *BOSTON*

Two hundred twenty-five miles to the north-northwest of the final resting place of the *John Hopkins*, the Los Angeles-class nuclear-powered attack submarine *Boston* was making nearly forty knots on a course of one-three-zero. She had been on a routine patrol when she had been ordered to head southeast. There was some trouble between an American surface-surveillance ship and a Russian sub. Possibly an Alfa class.

The *Boston*'s skipper was annoyed only by one fact: that he was going to have company. Evidently the *Phoenix* and *Norfolk* had been ordered southeast as well. He knew both of their skippers. In fact, the three of them had been dubbed the "rat pack" at more than one officers' club around the Atlantic rim. If those bastards had half a chance they would steal his thunder. But this time he was going to beat them to it.

"Sonar, conn," Lieutenant Commander Howard Armstrong radioed.

"Sonar, aye."

"What have we got out ahead of us, Lee?"

"We've got a frigate almost dead ahead, skipper. Sounds like she's making turns for twenty-eight, maybe thirty knots."

"Any ID?"

"She's one of ours, sir. I'd say she's probably a Knox class, though I'm not a hundred percent."

Armstrong released the comms button. His executive officer, Lieutenant Steve McGill, was looking at him.

"We're coming up on our scheduled comms rendezvous, skipper. We've got to stop and put up a buoy before we go any farther. Orders, remember?"

"What was that? Full speed ahead?" Armstrong grinned.

"You got it." He turned back to the comms. "Engineering, conn. Smitty, how about a few more turns?"

"Skipper, we're at max. You've got all she'll give."

"You sure?"

"I'm sure," the chief engineer said.

McGill lowered his voice. "We're going to be in a world of shit unless we make our comms schedule, Howard."

"That sub up there doesn't give a damn about our schedule. Steady as she goes, Steve."

They looked at each other for a long moment, until McGill finally nodded. "You're the boss."

6

THE PENTAGON

Admiral Norbert Thompson, CINCLAN, had been in the basement Command Center all morning monitoring and directing the developing situation in the Barents Sea. Along with Rear Admiral Don Horvak, COMSUBPLANT, and George Vincent, the chief operations officer at NSA with whom they had a direct communications link, he felt they were on top of the situation.

All of the Joint Chiefs were in, including the chairman, General Mooreland, who had just returned from the White House. They had stayed out of the fray so far, closeted for most of the morning in the chairman's glassed-in conference room.

The conference room door opened, and from inside, the JC2, Army General Horace Walker, beckoned to him. "Shit," he said to himself. But he'd known it had been too good to last.

"He doesn't look too happy," Horvak said.

"None of them do, Don," Thompson said. "Mind the store, I'll see if I can keep the ball in our court."

"We're not going to have a lot of time for decision-making on this one, Bert, you know that. Last we heard, Armstrong was driving the *Boston* damned hard. And God only knows what'll happen if he comes head-to-head with that sub driver."

"No luck reaching him?"

"Not yet."

Thompson hurried across the upper tier and entered the chairman's conference room. General Mooreland was seated at the end of the conference table, Admiral Maxwell on his right, and General Walker was perched on the edge, a cigar clenched firmly in his teeth. None of their aides or operations people were with them.

"I want you to spell it our for us, Bert," the chairman said without preamble. "The President is getting nervous."

Thompson closed the door behind him, but didn't bother to take a seat. "This is an Atlantic Fleet problem, General. Don Horvak is on top of it."

"Don't hand me that, Bert. With PIT BULL just around the corner, the President isn't the only one getting nervous. Horace wants to fully arm the fleet, just in case. I'll be damned if I can find any fault with his logic."

"It's going to be a Navy operation from start to finish," Walker conceded. "But if it were my ass on the line, I sure as hell would want a loaded gun for backup."

"I've got to go to the President with that," Mooreland said. "Now, what the hell are the Russians doing? Is this just a maverick operation?"

"There's no way of knowing that until we can get our people in place."

"What assets are you throwing into it?"

"We got three Los Angeles-class subs. The *Boston*, the *Phoenix*, and the *Norfolk* on their way now. The *Boston*'s ETA is within the next hour."

"That's four to three," Admiral Maxwell said.

"One of the Russian subs is a Kilo. She'll be pretty well outclassed."

"She's got torpedoes, Bert. The sting is the same."

"Yes, sir. If she can find her target and get off a shot before she herself is sunk."

"What else are you sending in?" Mooreland asked.

"The *Marvin Shields* should be on the scene within the next hour or so."

"What about Polyarnyy?"

"We're in luck on that score, General. NSA has one of their satellites in position now to watch the base, and Deke Adams' Tomcat squadron was doing land-based exercises at Keflavik. That's nearly a thousand miles out to Bear Island, two hundred or so to where the *Hopkins* went down, but I sent them on ahead. Thurber gave us the in-air refueling operation, and they should be touching down on Bear just about now and ready for turnaround within another fifteen minutes."

"Which would put them on-site within a half hour."

"Sooner if need be," Thompson said.

Mooreland shook his head. "Still leaves us with the question: What the hell do they want? We're nowhere within their two-hundred-mile territorial limit."

"But our submarines are within the five hundred klicks. And we can't say this was a transit operation."

"The fact of the matter is, gentlemen," Maxwell said, "that the *John Hopkins* was indeed on a spying mission. Which means that sub driver was within his rights."

"We don't do things like that to each other any longer, David," Mooreland said angrily. "If they didn't want us there, he should have surfaced and told us to turn tail and get the hell out."

"In the meantime, we have a developing situation which I'd like to get back to," Thompson said.

"Just hold on for a moment," Mooreland said. "Do you know Bill Lane from NSA? He works for Ben Lewis in the Russian Division."

"I might have heard the name, General."

"He's on his way up there right now. On the President's direct orders. He seems to think that sub is Ukrainian."

"Black Sea Fleet?" Thompson asked incredulously.

"That's what he says. He's apparently got some information on the sub's captain. The President wants Lane to try to talk the man down. Thinks it's possible."

"Goddammit, it was a Russian MiG that forced our Orion off. Now Lane is trying to tell us that the sub is Ukrainian? In any event, Lane won't get there before it's all over."

"He's hitched a ride on one of our SR-91s. At a hundred twenty thousand feet she'll do better than Mach 4. He'll be landing on Bear, where he'll be choppered out to that ASW frigate." Mooreland sat forward. "I want your sub drivers to put on the brakes until Lane has a chance to try his hand. PIT BULL is going forward as scheduled, and no one wants this thing to develop any further."

"That may not be possible, General," Thompson said softly.

"Why not, Bert?" the chairman asked.

"We've lost contact with the *Boston*."

"Who's driving that boat?"

"Howard Armstrong," Thompson said. "I know him personally. He's a good man, but he can get a little hotheaded at times."

Mooreland and Walker exchanged glances. "Bert, I don't normally interfere with your fleet operations. But I want that submarine stopped, and I don't care how you do it. That's a direct order."

It used to be that each of the Joint Chiefs was fairly autonomous, the Navy taking its orders directly from the Navy JC. But ever since Congress passed the Goldwater-Nichols Act in 1986, the chairman was senior, by law, to the other chiefs. He was the boss.

"Yes, sir," Thompson said, and he turned on his heel and left the conference room, as Mooreland picked up his direct line to the Secretary of Defense.

BARENTS SEA

Flying at 120,000 feet, Lane could see very little of anything below, and the sky above them was the deepest blue that he had ever seen.

The delta-wing SR-91 spy plane was state-of-the-art. Its rubber-coated titanium fuselage and wings were practically radar-invisible even to sophisticated look-up systems aboard Russian air-launched missiles that were capable of reaching that altitude. Her top speed was well over three thousand miles per hour, and she could fly nearly one-third of the way around the earth without refueling.

This 4,900-mile flight up to Bear was a piece of cake to the pilot, Air Force Captain Zachary Taylor, who'd overflown the Atlantic so many times now he had lost count.

Lane sat in the rear seat, the oxygen mask strapped so tight to his face that he could barely move his lips to talk. But all during the hour-and-forty-five-minute flight, Taylor kept up a running commentary about the territory they were flying over, about the fact he didn't have to worry about the enemy or ECMs or his cameras on this mission, about his family (married, four children) and what it was like being the only black SR-91 pilot in the service.

"The Russians ever got hold of my black ass they wouldn't know what to do with it," Taylor laughed.

Bear Island, he said, was of volcanic origin, was almost treeless despite a year-round moderate climate, and was almost always socked in with fog.

They had been at altitude for what seemed only like minutes to Lane when the pitch of the engines decreased, and they started down.

"Is something wrong?" Lane managed to ask into his mask.

"No, sir," Taylor said. "But if you want to land at Bear we're going to have to head to the deck."

"We can't be close already."

"We're about eight hundred miles out, sir. It takes a little room to get this thing down."

The spy plane's nose dropped another few degrees and they headed down toward a thick blanket of white that stretched from horizon to horizon.

Somewhere down there, to the northwest, was a Ukrainian submarine driver who was holding them all by the balls. Question was, what was it going to take to make him let go?

They had flown into the sun, so it was afternoon. And although the trip had taken less than two hours, it seemed like they had flown through the thick white fog for days when suddenly runway lights appeared ahead of them and seconds later they were touching down, the wheels barely bumping on the runway. It was the smoothest landing that Lane had ever experienced, and he told Taylor so.

"We aim to please, sir," the man replied with a chuckle. "But I don't think you're going to be so happy on your next leg."

At the end of the runway, they turned onto a taxiway, slowly bumped along the tarmac for about a hundred yards, and then stopped. To this point Lane had not seen so much as a hint of a building, another aircraft, or in fact any sort of vehicle or sign that this place was inhabited.

"What's going on?" he asked.

"This is where you get off, sir. The fuel truck will be coming along momentarily to fill me up, and then I'll be towed over to a hangar, where I'll stick around until you get back."

The canopy opened, the cockpit instantly filling with cold, damp air that smelled of the sea and dead fish. A ground crewman helped Lane undo his four-point retaining system and get his helmet off.

"Welcome to Bear Island, sir," the young man said. "Your chopper is standing by for you."

Taylor was looking up at him. They shook hands. "Good luck out there, sir," he said.

"Thanks for the ride."

On the tarmac, Lane followed the crewman into the dense fog to a waiting jeep. Someone had already gotten his single overnight bag out of the plane's belly and tossed it in the backseat.

A Navy lieutenant commander was driving. "Deke Adams," the man said. He was large, his face red. He looked like the rawboned Texan he was. "Got the *Marvin Shields'* LAMPS-I standing by for you. We'll have you aboard that ship in under two hours, and you'll be on-site shortly after that."

The LAMPS (light airborne multipurpose system) helicopter was the Seasprite, which carried fifteen sonobuoys, the ASQ-81(V)2 magnetic-anomaly detector, and a pair of MK 46 torpedoes. She was standard equipment on the Knox-class ASW frigates.

"You the pilot?"

"Not me," Adams said. They were passing along a row of parked F-14D Grumman Tomcat fighter/interceptors. "Those are mine," the man said. "I'm the squadron commander. We just came out from Keflavík to provide you a little support in case Polyarnyy gets a bee in their bonnet."

"Enough firepower to start a battle here, Commander," Lane said.

"And finish it," Adams replied. "My orders are simple, sir. You're to call all the shots until or unless the situation gets out of hand, in which case I'll be coming in with everything I've got."

"Fair enough, but I want you to give me a decent chance. My orders are simple too, and they come direct from the President. He wants our people off that sub in one piece, and he wants to avoid a shooting confrontation."

"I read you loud and clear, Mr. Lane. Just understand that we'll be keeping a close watch from this end as well."

"You do that," Lane said.

A minute later they came to the Seasprite squatting on its own pad. Bag in hand, Lane hurried across to where a crewman helped him aboard. Within the next minute the engines had been started and they were lifting off into the dense fog, nothing visible beyond the windshield.

OLD SENATE OFFICE BUILDING

"Jules Joslow has evidently let the cat out of the bag, because you've got a backlog of calls big enough to choke a horse," Senator Wood's secretary, Darla Johnson, said.

"The word is out on the Hill that we're gunning for the games," John Gustafson, one of the Senator's research assistants, put in.

The staff meeting in the senator's office had started when Turner had returned from lunch. It was more like a council of war. Wood checked his watch.

"In a little less than thirty hours the President is going on national television to give us his world vision—quote unquote. It's up to us to make him see the light."

"Amen," one of the other research assistants, Ursula Rebke, commented. "But it's the opposition you're going to have to convince, sir."

Wood smiled patronizingly. "Wrong answer, recruit. We're going to let the President convince the people that we're right and he's wrong, tomorrow night on ABC, CBS, NBC, CNN, and PBS."

Turner was grinning and the others waited expectantly. The previous President had called Wood, then a freshman senator, a "goddamn chickenshit." But the Montana Democrat had outlasted that administration and gave every indications that he'd outlast this one.

"What would it take to change this administration's notion that staging a shooting war between two long-term enemies would somehow ease world tensions by helping Russia?" Wood asked.

"By showing them how much money is being wasted?" Gustafson suggested.

"The White House is aware what's happening to our industries."

"Half the weapons-systems-industry lobbyists are camping on our doorstep, or are about to show up," Darla said.

"What'll do it is public pressure," Wood said with enjoyment. "Brought on by a groundswell of outrage when the

President goes on television and admits that the Russians are sinking American ships and killing innocent sailors."

No one said a thing, but Turner's grin widened.

"Rio will be a disaster unless we do something to protect American interests." The senator jumped up. "By God, if America is slapped on the cheek, we sure as hell aren't going to turn the other. No, sir. We're not ready for that form of suicide yet."

"What's happening, Senator?" Ursula Rebke asked.

"Death on the Barents Sea, and it's up to us to make sure the same thing doesn't happen in the South Atlantic. Our military forces need to be modernized before it's too late."

7

SSN *BOSTON*

Howard Armstrong had stationed himself at the situation table for what seemed like days. A couple of hours ago, passing beneath the *Marvin Shields*, they had picked up a part of what they took to be a message for them, transmitted from a sonobuoy. But they had passed so deep and quickly that they had not been certain what the message contained. It was logged: Unknown.

In any event, everyone aboard the boat knew by now that Armstrong wasn't about to stop for anything or anyone.

"Skipper?" Steve McGill said softly, breaking him out of his thoughts.

Armstrong turned to his exec, who stood at the chart table with Pat Williams, his navigation officer.

"We're coming up within ten miles of that sub's last reported position."

Armstrong glanced at the clock. "Fifteen minutes tops, then, at this speed."

"Captain, we don't know if he's moved or not," Williams

said. He was the boat's mathematical wizard. Some calculations he could do in his head faster than their BC-12A battle-control computer.

"He's there, he's waiting for us," Armstrong said.

"Yes, sir. But where is *there* exactly, sir?"

Armstrong saw his point.

"I don't think I'd care to crash into him at this speed," McGill said.

"You're right. But I don't want to ping him, not yet. I want to get right on top of him first." Armstrong looked at the plot on the situation table, which was transferred electronically from the chart table.

"I suggest we go into a run-and-drift mode, sir," Williams said. "At least until we pick him up."

"I agree," Armstrong said. *Phoenix* and *Norfolk* were at least six hours behind him if they had slowed down like FLEET wanted them to do, and perhaps two or three hours back if they, too, had ignored orders. Either way he figured he had plenty of time to find the Alfa and let her know who was boss of this part of the ocean. "Ring for all stop," he said. "Rig for silent running."

"Aye, skipper," McGill said, pleased with the decision.

Armstrong hit the comms button. "Sonar, conn."

"Aye, sonar."

"Lee, we're coming within a twenty-mile circle of where that sub might be hiding. She's probably at or just below scope depth."

"Want me to ping her, sir?"

"Not yet, Lee. First I want to see if you can find her on passive. Unless she's running silent like us, she'll be making some noises."

"We'll have to make turns so that I can be sure she's not hiding in our baffles."

"We're going in slow."

SSN *POGIN*

Captain Mikhail Badim stood just within the sonar compartment, a pair of headphones half on his ears.

"There," his sonarman, Leonid Zhernov, said softly.

Badim heard it, deep within the mush of normal sea noises. It sounded like water gurgling in a pipe.

"It's her cooling pumps," Zhernov said. "She's rigged for silent operation, but she's damned close, Captain."

"How close?" Badim asked.

The sonarman shrugged. "A couple of thousand meters, perhaps a little farther. She was booming in here loud and fast. It would have taken her a while to slow down. I suspect she's still making a couple of knots drifting."

"A Los Angeles class?"

"Definitely."

"And there's been nothing else in the vicinity?"

"Not so far, Captain. But if that boat has come snooping after our tail, there will be others."

Badim handed his headphones back to the young officer. "Keep a very close ear now. I want to know if the American submarine comes any closer. And keep a watch for any other ships."

"What are we expecting, Captain? Anything specific?"

"A surface ship, I think. Probably one of their ASW craft. They will want their countrymen back. We'll see just how badly they do. And maybe some of our Russian cousins."

Badim went back into the cramped attack center where his *starpom*, Valeri Melnik, was studying the charts.

"I want you to prepare the boat for an emergency dive," Badim said gently.

Melnik nodded. "Is it an American submarine, then?"

"Yes, and she's very close. Maybe two thousand meters."

"She'll pick us up sooner or later."

"Possibly," Badim said, "but we will be prepared. In the meantime I would like to stay here to see exactly what she will do, see just how good she is."

Melnik nodded. "How deep do you want to go, Captain?"

"One thousand meters."

Melnik's eyes widened. That was nearly one hundred meters below the Alfa's maximum safe-diving limit of three thousand feet. But the *starpom* merely nodded and turned back to his instruments to ready the ship for such a dive, his movements deliberate and very quiet. No vents would be opened until the actual moment of the dive. With the American submarine so close they could not afford to make any kind of a noise.

Suddenly there was a loud crash somewhere aft, metal against metal, as if someone had dropped a cooking pot or hammered a wrench on the hull.

Badim spun around. "What the hell . . ." There was a second crash, and a third, and finally a cacophony of crashes and bangs as if the entire percussion section of a symphony orchestra had somehow gone mad within his boat.

FF *MARVIN SHIELDS*

It was still overcast two hundred miles out from Bear Island with a ceiling of two hundred feet. The Seasprite pilot, Lieutenant j.g. Tom McLagan, was good, pushing his machine to the limits barely fifty feet above the whitecaps developing in the rising wind.

They had given Lane a crash helmet with a built-in comms set, and had showed him where to plug in at the third crewman's position in the back.

"Are you strapped in and secure back there, sir?" the pilot radioed.

"Right. Are we coming in?" Lane asked.

"Yes, sir. We'll be touching down in just a minute now, but it might be a little rough, we're getting some weather."

Lane could see out the side bubble window. The waves below looked sharp and steep. "How soon before it's forecast to get impossible, Lieutenant?"

"Impossible for what, sir?"

"To transfer our men from that sub onto the *Marvin Shields*?"

"I would expect we've got a few hours left. Here we come, sir, hang on."

Lane grasped the handrails so tightly his knuckles turned white.

The helicopter seemed to drop forever, which was impossible, Lane thought, because they had flown in at nearly wave-top height. He saw the ASW ship out his starboard window, riding up and down on the swells.

They were directly over the middle of the helipad and Lane could see nothing but water out either side, and finally they were down hard, the machine bouncing twice, before it came to a stop. Lane popped off his seat belts as the rear hatch was slid open by a crewman. He pulled off his helmet, grabbed his bag, and followed the man across the helipad to an open hatch in the ship's superstructure. Before he went in he turned to wave at the chopper crew, but the Seasprite was disappearing into the deck as it was lowered below on the elevator.

"This way, sir," the crewman said. "The captain is expecting you."

"Right." Lane hurried behind the young man who led him upward through a maze of corridors and hatches. The 415-foot ship was moving up and down and side to side on the swells as she made twenty-five knots toward the *John Hopkins'* final resting place.

The interior of the ASW ship was spartan by comparison to some of the carriers and even the one battleship Lane had been aboard. But this was an older class of ship. All of them had been launched from the mid-sixties to the early seventies, and, of course, had undergone repeated retrofits when more sophisticated sub-hunting gear had been developed.

It was ironic, Lane had thought, that both the Russian and U.S. Navies still spent the bulk of their budgets on the development and construction of submarines, while their subhunting equipment lagged far behind. But it was a matter of priorities. The submarines were more important. They waged the wars.

The skipper, Lieutenant J. Willis Ryder (Red to his friends), was a big lumberjack of a man with flaming-red hair and freckles. His eyes were wide and blue and guileless. His smile was infectious, though he said he wasn't smiling much these days.

Lane and Ryder met on the bridge and, with Executive Officer Lieutenant j.g. Tony Adamo, went back to the captain's cabin.

"The ship's all yours, Mr. Lane," the captain said.

"The name is Bill."

"Fair enough," Ryder said. "I've got just one question for you. Am I going to get a shot at that sub?"

Lane hoped he wasn't another hotshot like the skipper of the *Boston* was said to be. "I sincerely hope not," he said. "If you do, I will have failed at my job."

Ryder exchanged glances with his exec. "Well then, Bill, I guess it's up to us to make sure you do your job right the first time so this thing doesn't escalate."

Lane breathed a sigh of relief. "Good enough. What's our ETA on his last known position?"

"We should be in the vicinity—at least close enough to detect the sub if she's still there—within the next forty minutes," Adamo said.

"That sub is still there," Lane said. "Her driver is waiting for us to show up."

"Why?" Ryder asked.

"He wants to talk to us. He wants to give our people back. By now it's got to be getting damned uncomfortable aboard that boat."

"Then why'd he sink the *John Hopkins* and snatch her crew in the first place?" Adamo asked.

"He's trying to get us to shoot back, which we're not going to do for reasons I'm not going to get into right now. But we've got another problem."

"Oh?"

"One of our subs—the *Boston*—is likely already on station. Our first job is going to be stopping him from doing anything."

"Christ," Ryder groaned. "That's Howie Armstrong. I know him. If anyone will shoot, it'll be him."

"Is he good?"

"Yeah," Ryder said, shaking his head. "The only consolation is that if Howie starts a shooting war with that Alfa, he'll win."

"The problem is," Lane said grimly, "Armstrong does not know that the crew of the *John Hopkins* is aboard that boomer."

SSN *BOSTON*

"Holy shit." Chief Petty Officer Lee Joiner yanked the sonar headphones off his ears and hit the comms button. "Conn, sonar. Skipper, I got something. You'd better come back and listen to it yourself, otherwise you'd think I was nuts."

Armstrong shrugged and went back to the sonar compartment, where Joiner held up a set of earphones for him. At first he could make no sense of what he was hearing. But gradually the clattering, clanking noises began to die down and he was able to pick out individual noises.

"Sounds like someone banging on something," Armstrong said.

"More like beating on the hull and bulkheads of a submarine with pots and pans and wrenches and pipes and anything they could get their hands on."

"Range and bearing?"

Joiner fiddled with the dials of his equipment. "He's two thousand yards aft, bearing one-eight-three."

"We passed him."

"Sir?"

"It's that submarine. He's back there."

"But what about the noise?"

"He's trying to confuse us," Armstrong said, excited now. "Ping the bastard. I want a lock on him."

"Aye, skipper," Joiner said.

Armstrong raced back into the attack center. "Sound general quarters," he snapped. "We've got the bastard."

"The Alfa?"

"Looks like it," Armstrong said. "Secure from silent running, one-fourth forward. Come right to one-six-seven." He hit the comms button. "Torpedo room, load tubes one and two with Mark 48s."

"Loading one and two, aye, skipper."

"We don't have the orders, Howard," McGill said tensely.

"And I haven't shot yet," Armstrong said from the situation table, where he started to work up the solution himself.

SSN *POGIN*

As the last of the American crewmen was silenced, everyone aboard heard the three pings from the *Boston*.

"They have found us," Melnik said.

"How could they help but find us?" Badim grumbled. "Emergency-dive the boat." He hit the comms button. "Sonar, give me a range and bearing on that target."

"Aye, Comrade Captain," the sonarman replied.

"Torpedo room, load all six tubes. But I want four of the tubes loaded with our subsurface acoustic homers, and two tubes rigged for a surface target."

"Aye, Comrade Captain."

Their own sonar signals reverberated through the hull as the *Pogin* gathered speed and her bow suddenly angled sharply downward so that everyone had to hang on. They were heading to where the American submarine could not follow.

"Conn, sonar."

"Conn, aye."

"I have the target. Range one hundred twenty meters,

bearing zero-one-eight. She just turned onto a course of one-six-seven."

"Bringing her around to us," Badim said to Melnik.

"He's bringing up his own shooting solution."

"Apparently," Badim said. "Sonar, what's her depth and speed?"

"She's at two hundred meters, fifteen knots."

That put her ahead and below them. It was time, Badim decided, to see just what the American skipper was made of.

"Come right fifteen degrees to zero-one-eight," he told his *starpom*.

Even the helmsman looked up in surprise. That angle put them on a collision course.

"Captain?" Melnik started to ask, but Badim cut him off.

"Turn now!"

"Aye, Comrade Captain," the *starpom* said, and the *Pogin* came right.

"Sonar, conn. As soon as we're on our new course I want you to ping the target for a final firing solution."

"Sonar, aye."

"Torpedo room, conn."

"Torpedo room, aye."

"Flood tubes one and two," Badim said.

"Flooding one and two, aye."

SSN *BOSTON*

"Conn, sonar. That sub has flooded at least two tubes."

"Roger," Armstrong said. "Give me a final range and bearing to the target."

"Coming up."

"All right, look sharp, people," Armstrong said. He hit the comms. "Torpedo room, flood one and two, prepare to fire."

McGill came across the attack center to where Armstrong stood at the situation table.

"Howard, you cannot do this!"

"Watch me," Armstrong snapped back.

"Conn, sonar. Range eight hundred meters and closing fast on our starboard beam. But, skipper, he's above us and diving fast. Sir, he's on a collision course. That boat is heading right for us!"

"He knows we're here," Armstrong said half to himself. "The stupid sonofabitch has our range and bearing. He knows he'll hit us."

"Which means he won't fire his torpedoes," McGill said. "It would be suicide."

This wasn't making sense. Something about the pots-and-pans noises they had heard earlier. That sub driver was trying to tell him something.

The firing lights on his weapons-control board winked green for tubes one and two. They were ready to go, the outer doors opened.

"He doesn't want to shoot," Armstrong said, everything suddenly coming clear to him. "He never did want to shoot. He was just testing us." He looked at his exec. "Break off, come up seven degrees."

"Aye, skipper," McGill said, obviously relieved. He spun around to relay the orders.

"Come left to zero-seven-seven," Armstrong ordered, "and give me full speed ahead."

"Coming left to zero-seven-seven, full speed ahead, aye," the helmsman responded.

"Secure the torpedoes from firing," Armstrong said.

"Torpedo room, aye. Securing tubes one and two."

"Sonar, conn. What's he doing, Lee?"

"Still coming, skipper. Same course and speed, same depression on the bow."

"Is he going to miss us?"

"Not by much, Skipper."

SSN *POGIN*

"He's turned away and is heading up," Zhernov, the so-narman, called out. "His new course is zero-seven-seven."

"He's not going to shoot," Melnik said softly.

"Apparently not," Badim said. He had to wonder if the American skipper would have made good his threat to shoot had he not heard the banging of the pots and pans.

Everyone was looking expectantly at him.

"Secure from emergency dive," he said. "Level off at five hundred meters."

"Aye, Comrade Captain," Melnik said.

"Come right twenty degrees to zero-three-eight." He hit the comms button. "Torpedo room, secure all tubes from firing. Close outer doors one and two."

"Torpedo room, aye. Do you want us to off-load the tubes?"

"Negative," Badim said. "We'll just leave our fish in place for the moment. Keep a very close watch on that American submarine for us, Leonid Andreievich."

"Yes, Comrade Captain, but we have more company. A surface ship, bearing zero-five-two. It looks like an American Knox-class ASW."

"What's she doing?"

"She's slowing down, Comrade Captain. Turning now to the left. It sounds as if she's towing something. Most likely a passive-sonar array."

"It's the ship you were expecting?" His *starpom* asked.

"Yes," Badim said thoughtfully. The question was how his own moves would be interpreted by the American submarine captain. There was only one way to find out. "I have changed my mind, Valeri. Keep on this rate of turn, and bring us up to periscope depth. Very slowly."

"Do you want us to turn toward the surface ship?"

"Negative, away from it, Valeri. Away from it. This time I wish to alarm no one."

SSN *BOSTON*

"She's turning to the right, skipper," the sonarman said. Armstrong sighed with relief.

"But, skipper, she's slowed her rate of descent. It looks like she's on the way up . . . Hold on, I've got another target, this one on the surface."

"Talk to me, Lee."

"Knox class, skipper. One of ours. Sounds like the same one we passed a while back. She's on a course of three-five-four . . . belay that. She's turning to the left, and slowing."

"What's her bearing relative to that submarine?" Armstrong asked, another thought occurring to him.

"Stand by," Joiner said.

"He's not going after our surface ship knowing we're down here," McGill said.

"He's up to something, Steve, that's for damned sure."

"Skipper, their relative bearings are changing. The sub is definitely on his way up, but he is turning away from our ASW ship."

Armstrong hesitated. "All right, bring us right again to . . ." He hit the comms button. "Lee, you're going to have to feed the numbers on that sub into us on a constant basis. I want to turn us into him as we come to periscope depth, so that we'll have a continuous firing solution on him without jeopardizing our surface vessel."

Joiner whistled. "That's one for the books, skipper, but can do. Give me a second or two to set it up."

"No mistakes now, Lee. This has to come off clean. We can't afford a miss."

Armstrong faced McGill. "All right, Steve, level us off at periscope depth, but nice and easy. We don't want to make that sub driver nervous."

FF *MARVIN SHIELDS*

Bill Lane was on the bridge with Lieutenant Ryder and his executive officer, Tony Adamo. They were watching the surface of the choppy sea through binoculars as their sonarman fed them the relative bearings and depths of the two submarines.

"The crazy bastards were actually going to shoot at one another," Ryder mumbled.

"Then we would have had ourselves a full-scale shooting war up here," Lane said without looking away from his binoculars. The sea was strewn with whitecaps. It would be difficult picking out a periscope in all that.

"It could have been contained," Ryder said.

"There are three other bogie subs incoming, as well as two of ours just a few hours back."

"Jesus. They've got their naval air station on Polyarnyy as well."

"And we've got a squadron of Tomcats on Bear just waiting for a chance to take to the air," Lane said.

Ryder finally lowered his binoculars. "That boomer'll be at periscope depth any second now. What do you make of that?"

"The driver wants to talk, I hope. And your pal Howie seems to be using his head. Are we ready on the sonobuoy?"

"It's programmed with the three groups you asked for."

"Bridge, sonar."

"Bridge, aye," Adamo replied.

"The Alfa has just leveled off at periscope depth three hundred yards off our port beam."

"Terry, what about our boat?" Adamo asked.

"Still coming up, about three hundred feet. But she's put herself just aft of that Alfa, between them and us."

"Gallant," Ryder said.

"Dump the DLC buoy overboard now," Lane said. "*Boston* will pick out the message on the way up."

Ryder looked at him. "So will the Russian."

"That's exactly what I want to happen, Red," Lane said.

SSN *BOSTON*

"Conn, sonar. We've got a DLC buoy in the water." It was a downlink-communications buoy by which aircraft or surface ships could communicate with submerged submarines.

"Where'd it come from?" Armstrong asked.

"Our ASW ship, I think. Unless an Orion made an overflight."

Armstrong thought for a moment. It was the ASW vessel, little doubt of that. She had tried to communicate with them earlier. He hit the comms button. "Is it transmitting?"

"Aye, skipper. Three groups. Are you ready to copy?"

"Go ahead, Lee."

The sonarman repeated the three groups and Armstrong pulled down his cipher book and quickly translated.

XYP   TFS
DO NOT SHOOT   COME TO PERISCOPE DEPTH
              YYY
      PREPARE FOR FURTHER XMSSN

It was about what he had expected. Armstrong showed McGill the message.

"You can't ignore this one, Howie. They're listening to every move we make down here."

"Sonar, what's that Alfa doing?"

"Stopped at periscope depth, skipper."

"Communications, we're coming to periscope depth. We'll put up the UHF mast. Our ASW vessel will be sending us a message."

"Aye, skipper."

"Do you want the scope up?" McGill asked.

Armstrong chuckled. "Why the hell not, everyone knows where everyone else is anyway. And put up our search radar and snoophead. We might as well get some ELINT while we're at it."

SSN *POGIN*

Badim looked up from the translation of the message from the American sonobuoy. "So they want to talk," he said to Melnik, his *starpom*.

"It would appear so, Comrade Captain. Just as you expected."

"Then let them talk, and we will listen." Badim hit the comms switch. "Communications, send up our uni-mast. There will be a transmission from the American ASW vessel. And keep a sharp ear for any other electronic emissions . . . from the southeast."

"Aye, Comrade Captain."

"Raise the search periscope," Badim said. "Let's see what kind of a day it is out there."

FF *MARVIN SHIELDS*

"There's our boy," Armstrong said as the *Boston*'s UHF mast broke the choppy surface. Seconds later her search periscope popped up, along with her search-radar mast and snoophead.

"We can send our message via blinker," Adamo suggested. "That way the Alfa won't pick it up . . . uh-oh."

The *Pogin*'s stubby uni-mast broke the surface, followed moments later by her search periscope.

"Send the message both ways anyhow," Lane said.

"But the Russians will intercept it."

"That's right," Lane said.

Adamo hit the comms button. "Communications, send that message now, low-power UHF. As low as you can get it. And have someone send it out by light gun."

"Aye."

"Good," Lane said, his stomach tightening. "And now we just wait and see." He was the only American up here who knew or suspected what flag that boomer really sailed under.

8

THE KREMLIN

It was 3:18 A.M. when Marshal Yakov Leonov entered the Kremlin grounds through the Spassky Tower gate and was driven directly to his office in the Council of Ministers Building.

He had been awakened at midnight, at one, and again at two with updates on the situation in the Barents Sea that had come from their surveillance satellite, which the FIS had kindly released for them (at the Defense Minister's request).

At that point there had been nothing for him that would require his presence at his office, although some of the details had become worrisome.

For instance: The Americans had not only sent an ASW ship, the FF *Marvin Shields*, into the area, but they had also moved up a naval squadron of fighter/interceptor aircraft to Bear Island. As a countermeasure, no doubt, to their own threat from the naval squadron at Polyarnyy.

Tit for tat. Real war was still surprisingly much like the game of chess—which was Russia's national preoccupation.

It was expected that the Americans would be sending at least one submarine into the area, but Leonov was surprised and dismayed to learn that they'd sent three—all of them Los Angeles-class nuclear attack submarines. This fact had been confirmed by Russia's own version of a near-surface under-water-sound-surveillance system, called LARISSA-ONE, which even these days was still a secret tightly held from the Americans.

The last time he had been awakened, he had decided it was time to get to his office and take the situation in hand before it got completely out of control.

A message had been received by REDFLEET Command and had been relayed by natural course to his office. It had come direct from Polyarnyy, which had apparently intercepted a message from the *Marvin Shields* intended for the American submarine *Boston*.

He left his bodyguard in the outer office and went into his staff-briefing room, where his chief of operations, Captain General Pavl Rudakov, was waiting for him.

"I am truly sorry, Marshal Leonov, for having to disturb your sleep. But I believe this is of supreme importance, especially in view of your ... conference earlier this evening."

Leonov went to his seat at the end of the highly polished table. "What is this message?"

Rudakov handed him a thin file folder. "It may be an honorable way for us to extricate ourselves from this situation, while still making our point that our coast must remain inviolable."

"The American forces are willing to back down?" Leonov asked.

"Apparently, and with an apology."

Leonov looked at his chief of operations. He had too many years in the service of his country to miss the between-the-lines message he was being given.

Rudakov held his gaze. "And we will apologize to them."

"They will apologize to us for penetrating our territorial waters?"

"Yes, Marshal. At least one of their submarines is well within the five-hundred-mile limit our two countries have agreed upon. For that they will apologize and, of course, retreat once the crew of the *John Hopkins* is rescued. Apparently they are still in the water, though our satellite failed to detect them."

"I see. And us, Pavl Nikolai, we will apologize for what?"

"For not offering to aid in their rescue efforts, and for threatening their search aircraft."

"But there is no need for us to apologize. The *John Hopkins* was . . ."

"Not within the two-hundred-nautical-mile coastal limit, contrary to the preliminary reports we received."

"Ah, yes." Leonov sighed, sitting back in his leather chair. The former American Chairman of the Joint Chiefs, Admiral William J. Crowe, Jr., had once said that whenever something happens far away, at least eighty percent of the first reports and fifty percent of the second are invariably wrong. He called it his "crisis rule."

"Nor was their surveillance aircraft within the two-hundred-mile limit. It was, therefore, an unfortunate mistake on our part," Rudakov concluded.

"What were your instructions to Admiral Kozlov?" Leonov asked. Andrei Kozlov was commander in chief of Polyarnyy.

"To stand by until he hears from us."

"What have we learned from LARISSA?"

"The *Boston* is moving out of the area."

"Then we apologize, Pavl Nikolai. We allow the Americans to apologize, they rescue their crew and leave the area."

"And our other assets in the region?"

"They are to stand by," Leonov said. "After all, this could be a CIA operation."

KIEV

Now that Operation KEENSCHCAL had actually begun, General Normav had transferred his operational headquarters to the basement Situation Room of the State Administration of the Army Building.

Activity had been building up here over the past weeks, because the Army was running its own mock exercise to coincide with Russia's Operation PIT BULL off the coast of South America.

In this way, Normav had been able to hide his interest in the operation, and his covert work on KEENSCHCAL.

The encrypted telephone on his desk rang, and after he had dismissed his staff officers he picked it up. "Normav."

"It's me," Ryabov said.

"What happened?"

"The Americans will apologize and withdraw."

"Will they?" Normav asked, holding the telephone tightly in his meaty paw. "Or will they pretend *not* to understand?"

"They will withdraw, but there has been no direct communication between Moscow and Washington."

"Good," Normav said, thinking ahead. "Those fools still don't know about Captain Badim."

"No. But there is a squadron of F-14D fighter/interceptors on Bear Island. It's at their extreme operational limit, even with refueling, but they are a threat."

Normav thought a moment. "Can anything go wrong?"

"My old friend, you know as well as I do that when young men are in the field under stress, with orders that they cannot comprehend or stomach, and with fingers on triggers, the risk of accidents is very high."

"Yes," Normav said. "But not this time. Not yet. The Americans have evidently shown restraint."

"Remarkably so, under the circumstances. They want PIT BULL to proceed without a hitch as much as the Kremlin wants it. They are like starving dogs slavering after the same bone."

"If they are not careful, my friend, they will choke on it,"

Normav said. "Then our first step has been accomplished. It is time to put the next phase of our plan into effect."

There was a silence on the line.

"Yes, Leonid Aleksandrovich?" Normav prompted.

"It is a dangerous game we are playing, my old comrade."

"It is still a dangerous world that we live in," Normav said. "We cannot let everything that we have spent a lifetime working for go up in a puff of smoke."

"An apt metaphor, Pavl Ivanovich."

"Get over here as soon as you can," Normav said. "We will meet at the club and have a nice soak and we shall talk. Frankly and openly. Like the old days."

"A good idea," Ryabov said. "I'll bring some of the others along."

NATIONAL SECURITY AGENCY

In an underground communications-intercept facility at Fort Meade, a computer-generated set of conditions was met and an alarm bell rang five times signifying that human intervention was needed.

Air Force Captain Jean Small put down her coffee and brought the alarm up on her panel. It was a communications intercept gathered by their DEEPLOOK-SIX laser-reader satellite locked in a geosynchronous orbit over the northern Atlantic. The satellite's function (it was one of the first put up under the new space-shuttle program, and was still top secret) was to read supposedly secure Russian and Ukrainian fleet headquarters transmissions to their ships at sea. The downlink was done by laser beam that was not traceable from anywhere *on earth*.

This was a for-your-eyes-only, most secret and urgent message from the Ukrainian BLACKSEAFLEET Command itself to the nuclear attack submarine *Pogin*. NSA's recognitions computer had been set to pluck out any message relating to the situation unfolding in the Barents Sea.

Appended to the message on her board were special instructions that all such messages were to be immediately routed upstairs to the director of the Russian Division and over to the Pentagon's Command Center.

Jean Small read the message again, her eyebrows rising. Something pretty big was happening up there. World War III would probably start this way, she thought. And it would be lost in the details and minutiae of such an operation.

She printed out a hard copy of the message, rang for a runner to take it upstairs (urgent messages such as these were always distributed by hand), and then added the NSA prefix and shunted the message onto the Pentagon's trunk line.

THE PENTAGON

"Bingo," Rear Admiral Del Franklin said, tearing the message off the printer.

Norbert Thompson and Don Horvak had been talking. They looked up when Franklin hurried across from the comms console.

"What do you have, Del?" Thompson asked. They'd had no word, good or bad, for nearly an hour now.

"A NSA intercept from DEEPLOOK-SIX."

"Our boy?" Horvak asked excitedly.

"Direct from BLACKSEAFLEET Command," Franklin said, handing him the message flimsy. Horvak and Thompson read it together.

NSA SENDS   NSA SENDS   NSA SENDS
100102ZJUL
TOP SECRET INTERCEPT—
PROJECT DEEPLOOK-SIX

TO: PENTAGON COMMAND
    R-DIV
SUBJECT: BLACKSEAFLEET COMMAND
BDCST INTERCEPT
NSA SENDS   NSA SENDS   NSA SENDS
URGENT
MOST SECRET
10-07-92-Z0059Z
FM: BLACKSEAFLEET OPS
TO: POGIN
SUBJECT: URS 10-07-92-Z2327
NEGOTIATE IMMEDIATE RELEASE OF AMI CREW
JOHN HOPKINS.
MAINTAIN DEFENSE POSTURE, BUT DO NOT
SHOOT UNLESS FIRED UPON.
LA CLASS WITHDRAWING.
UNDERSTAND ERROR IN NAVIGATION DUE TO
INERTIAL GUIDANCE SYSTEM ANOMALY. THIS
PLACES YOU IN DIFFICULT POSITION WITH RE-
GARDS TO POLYARNYY. HOWEVER AMIS PLACE-
MENT OF NUCLEAR SUBMARINES WITHIN
AGREED-UPON RANGE HAS BEEN DETECTED.
TRUST YOUR DISCRETION.
ONCE TRANSFER IS EFFECTED, WITHDRAW.
BE ADVISED: SQD OF AMI F-14DS HAVE BEEN
MOVED TO BEAR ISLAND. LAG TIME TO YOU ES-
TIMATED TWENTY MINUTES OR LESS.
X X
EOM

Thompson whistled. "Trust your discretion. They must be
getting desperate up there." He looked at his operations officer. "Get this up to Bill Lane, Del. Looks as if they'll
want us to make the first move. But sanitize it. Pull out any
and all references that this is a Ukrainian operation. Bill
Lane knows the score. We'll leave it up to him if the crew
of the *Marvin Shields* is to be told. It might complicate the
issue for them."

Horvak read the message several times. "Pardon me, sir, but I think we missed it. We all did."

"Missed what?" Thompson asked.

"It's about our subs."

"The *Pogin* had to know we were there, they were going to shoot."

"No, sir, I don't mean that. I mean the line where BLACKSEAFLEET Command says our 'placement of nuclear submarines.' Submarines, sir. Plural. Somehow they know about *Phoenix* and *Norfolk*."

"LARISSA?" Thompson asked. The CIA had given them that little tidbit five months earlier. To date, however, it had not been confirmed.

"It's possible, Admiral. But that's a Russian operation. So how did the Ukrainians find out? And so soon? Must still be some old-boy networking going on between Moscow and Kiev."

"I think you're right, Don," Thompson said thoughtfully.

"Do we tell Lane?" Franklin asked.

"Yes, of course. He can use all the help he can get. But tell him to play it damned close to the vest when it comes to dealing with that boomer driver."

Franklin hurried off.

"What about the rest of the fleet, Admiral?" Horvak asked.

"Send out an advisory bulletin. Top secret. Captains and execs only."

"But you're having second thoughts."

Thompson nodded. "Makes you wonder, Don, what that was all about up there. I mean now, of all times."

"It was a mistake on the sub driver's part."

"I don't think so. Something was definitely supposed to happen up there, for a definite reason."

CHEVY CHASE

The Lovell Mansion had been built at about the same time as the White House, but unlike the President's residence the mansion survived the War of 1812 when most of the city had been burned to the ground.

Originally owned by a wealthy landowner, the house had been in the hands of the big moneymakers in each era: shipbuilders, lumber barons, steelmakers, railroad tycoons, and finally, since the early 1960s, by Howard Skeritt, founder and sole owner of FUTECH Corporation, "Producers of today's weapons systems and electronics for tomorrow's peace."

Two hundred people attended the cocktail party and buffet dinner. Senator Wood drifted away from the crowd in the living room and made his way to the third-floor study where some of the others he'd come to meet had already discreetly gathered. The room was smoky, and Bob Skeritt (Howard's younger brother and vice-president of the corporation) handed Wood a snifter of brandy.

"We were getting worried about you, Pat."

Wood eyed the handsome multimillionaire over the rim of his glass. Like shooting fish in a barrel, he thought. They were all his now. It was something he'd worked for most of his political career: money and power.

"Why's that?"

"You know goddamned well what he's talking about," Theodore McCann growled. "There's been no movement on our export license applications. Need we remind you that Rio is just a few days away, and we're all going to be screwed if we can't get some mileage out of it?"

At thirty-eight, McCann was a billionaire, one of the richest men in America. He'd made his fortune building military-application computer chips better than the Japanese. With the end of the cold war, and sharply reduced Pentagon contracts, his company and many others in the U.S. and in the former Soviet Union depended on doing business with foreign countries. It was something the President was inexplicably dragging his feet on.

"What if I told you that your troubles were over?" Wood asked. "Would you trust me, Bob? Theodore?" He looked at the others. The wealth in the room staggered the imagination.

Skeritt and McCann exchanged glances. "What have you come up with, Pat?" Skeritt asked.

Wood sipped his brandy. "What if I told you that Reasoner could be placed in such a position that he would have to flip-flop on PIT BULL? Tomorrow night, on national television."

"You've got our interest, Senator," McCann said. "Jules Joslow showed up in Portland. He said their weapons division would hold off announcing layoffs for a few days, but he wouldn't tell me why. Suggested I talk to you."

"I'm not going to tell you anything tonight. You're going to have to take me on faith—"

"Crap," Skeritt interrupted, but Wood held him off.

"If you'll shut your fucking mouth and listen for a change, you might come out of this sitting pretty." Wood finished his drink and set his glass aside. He had their attention and he loved it. "Something has come up that'll change everything. The thing is nobody knows that I know about it, and we're going to keep it that way for now. What you don't know you won't have to deny later."

"Are you talking congressional investigation?"

"It won't come to that. At least our involvement in the issue won't. What I'm saying is that something has come up that's so big it'll finally give us a level playing field if we play our cards right."

"There's a lot riding on this issue, Pat," Skeritt warned.

"I haven't let you down in the past. You're just going to have to trust me on this one."

The tension suddenly broke, and McCann clapped Wood on the back. "Well, I guess we'll have to do just that. You've been a friend of business in the past, no reason for that to change now."

"No reason whatsoever," Wood said. He looked at the ten men for a time. "We'll talk tomorrow night. After the news conference."

Wood left the study and entered a suite at the end of the hall. One dim light was lit in the sitting room, but the bedroom beyond was in darkness.

"Pat?" A woman called from inside.

Using his combination, Wood opened an attaché case on the sideboard. One hundred thousand dollars in hundred-dollar bills. The down payment, as promised. There would be other payments. Many others.

"Coming, darling," he called. That wasn't quite true, he chuckled, but it soon would be.

9

SSN *POGIN*

Since his cabin was occupied by the two American officers off the *John Hopkins*, Badim had to make do at the situation table, the rest of the attack-center crew standing off while he did his decryption of the message.

He had to do it by hand, so it actually took him longer than NSA's automatic machines in Fort Meade, a fact that no one outside of Washington was aware of.

Finally finished, he put away his cipher pad and beckoned his *starpom*, Valeri Melnik.

"What do they say?"

Badim handed him the decryption and then hit the comms button. "Conn, sonar. Anything in the vicinity other than that ASW? Russians?"

"Negative, Comrade Captain. We are alone to the range of my equipment."

Badim turned back to his *starpom*. "Well, what do you think, Valeri?"

"It is generous of Kiev to trust your discretion."

Badim had to smile. "No matter. At least we will be able to get rid of our passengers. Honorably."

Melnik gazed at him. "We have always been honest with each other," he said softly enough so that no one else in the attack center could hear him.

"Yes, we have."

"Then tell me, please, what are we doing here? Why didn't we merely challenge that ship instead of sinking her? And why didn't we tell our crew that we'd left the Black Sea? We are a very long way from home."

Yes, I have always been honest with you, Badim said to himself. But not this time, old friend. This time is different. Dangerously so.

Badim shrugged. "Yes, we are, Valeri, but there are some things only a captain should know."

Melnik held his gaze for another moment, but then he nodded his grudging agreement. "You are right."

"I'll speak with their captain, and then we will see what we can do to get rid of them." Badim smiled at his friend. "Easy now, Valeri, we will be done and out of here within the next few hours. Not long to wait. In the meantime, raise the search periscope again and keep an eye on them. They may try to make contact."

Badim went aft. As before there was a guard stationed outside his cabin. This time the door was open. They wanted no repeat of the Americans' earlier action.

"Leave us," Badim told the young machinist's mate who'd been assigned to watch his cabin.

"With respect, Comrade Captain, I was told not to leave under any circumstances."

"Just withdraw to the galley. You will still be within sight, and if I need you I will call."

The young man reluctantly stepped a few paces down the corridor to the galley.

Badim entered his tiny cabin and leaned up against the bulkhead. Both officers were seated as before, Peters at the fold-down desk, Lindsey on the edge of the cot. They had been captives for only a few hours, but already the strain was showing on their faces.

The compartment had been stripped of anything that could be used to bang on the hull. But Badim could see where a leg on his cot was bent slightly inward. They were evidently trying to break it off.

"I admire your ingenuity, gentlemen. And I'm sure that if I were in your position, I would be doing exactly the same thing. I came to tell you that we will be transferring you to one of your ASW frigates which is standing by. It looks as if I was just in time. Much longer and I suspect you would have destroyed my boat, piece by piece. I would like you off my boat as soon as possible." Badim looked into Peters' eyes. "And if you will entertain a suggestion, Captain: Stay out of Russian waters."

"We were not within your coastal waters, Captain," Peters said evenly.

"No, you were not. But you were headed in that direction, and within a few hours would have been in violation of our mutual treaties. Just as your Los Angeles-class submarine was in violation."

"Then you are offering us an apology?"

"Your intention, Captain, was to do electronic spying on our naval air station at Polyarnyy."

Peters started to deny the charge, but Badim cut him off.

"I'm not interested in what you have to say, Captain. It is only unfortunate for me that I shot you when I did. If I had waited another few hours, I would have done more damage to you and your vessel, and you would not be taking your crew home."

Peters said nothing.

"Stepan," Badim shouted, not taking his eyes off the Americans.

The guard rushed up from the galley, his submachine gun at the ready. Badim turned to him. "They are trying to remove one of the legs from my cot. If that continues, shoot them both."

Badim went back to the attack center, brushing past his

zampolit, Grichakov, who'd been standing in the passageway, an odd expression on his face.

FF *MARVIN SHIELDS*

Bill Lane climbed up to the bridge where Lieutenant Ryder and his exec, Tony Adamo, were waiting.

"His scope came up about five minutes ago," Ryder said.

Lane handed him the message he'd just received from the Pentagon and picked up a pair of binoculars. Even with his naked eye he could see the scope ahead in the chop. With the glasses, it leaped out of the background at him. It was the sub's search periscope, so the skipper evidently wasn't planning on attacking for now.

"Do you believe that bullshit about a faulty inertial-navigation system?" Ryder asked.

Lane lowered the binoculars. "Probably not, Red, but it would just have been a matter of timing in any event. The *John Hopkins* was heading in. Another few miles and that sub driver would have been well within his rights."

"Then why didn't he wait, sir?" Adamo asked. "What I mean is, why'd he shoot so fast? Is he a greenhorn?"

Lane had read between the lines. The fact that the *Pogin* was not Russian was being kept secret for the moment. "I don't know. But when I talk to him, I'll ask."

Ryder and Adamo both gaped in surprise.

"We want our people back, and he's been ordered to give them back. But he doesn't know that we know. So I've got to play a little poker. It'll be easier for him if I'm on his territory; he'll be less likely to make a mistake. And we all know that if he gets nervous, a lot of people could get hurt."

"And there's not a damned thing we can do about it," Ryder said. "I can come up with all the target solutions I want, but with the crew of the *John Hopkins* aboard that submarine my hands are tied."

Lane stepped a little closer. "Listen, Red, when we get

our boys off that sub, we are going to turn tail and head for home. There will be no shooting war. Is that clear?"

Ryder held his palms up. "This ship is yours, Mr. Lane."

"Sorry, I didn't mean to come on so strong. But there are three other subs near here ready to pounce, as well as a naval air squadron at Polyarnyy. You might get a shot off, you might even sink that Alfa. But you wouldn't stand a chance in hell of returning to Bear."

Ryder nodded. "You're right."

"Now, I want a man with a light blinker up here on the double. I want to send a message to that sub driver and I don't want the entire world to know about it."

"I don't have any Russian speakers . . ."

"Badim speaks English. So does his executive officer."

Both Ryder and Adamo were curious, but neither asked how he knew what he knew.

SSN *POGIN*

"There it is," Melnik said from the periscope. "They are sending us a blinker-gun signal."

Badim took the scope and adjusted the focus. It took him a moment to make sense out of what he was seeing. The blinking wasn't fast, but it was in English.

AAA AAA POGIN POGIN IF YOU CAN READ THIS PLEASE SURFACE PLEASE SURFACE WE WISH TO NEGOTIATE RELEASE OF OUR CREWMEN AAA WILL SEND LAUNCH WILL SEND LAUNCH AAA OUR THREE REPEAT THREE ATTACK SUBMARINES HAVE WITHDRAWN. AAA AAA POGIN POGIN IF YOU CAN READ THIS PLEASE SURFACE

The message would continue to repeat until something happened, Badim understood. The next move was his.

He leaned back from the periscope. By surfacing his boat

he would be losing his attack advantage, and he would be open to detection by the Russians.

But whoever had written the message understood this and had given him something in return: the information that there were three American attack submarines in the vicinity, and not merely one. Of course the Americans could not know that he already had this information. They were bargaining in good faith.

"They want to talk about our prisoners," he finally said to Melnik. "They want us to surface, Valeri. What do you think about that?"

"It will put us in jeopardy," his *starpom* said.

"We'll just raise the sail to clear the first hatch. Maybe we will be lucky."

"What do they want?"

"Their people back, of course. But they're sending a launch over. I assume they will be sending an emissary to talk to us. Which is fine. We'll talk. Surface the boat," he said.

"Aye, Comrade Captain," Melnik said rather formally.

"And Valeri, I want you to issue side arms to all officers."

Melnik suddenly smiled. "Yes, sir."

FF *MARVIN SHIELDS*

"Bridge, sonar," the comms speaker blared.

"Bridge, aye," Adamo answered.

"I have vent-cycling noises. I think that sub is on her way up."

"Here she comes," Lane said, holding his binoculars on the patch of sea that was beginning to boil. The Alfa's slender periscope mast and fatter snoophead ECM mast rose out of the sea, followed by the low, bulbous sail. Then she stopped, only the sail above the water.

She was three hundred yards off the *Marvin Shields'* port beam. Adamo studied her through his binoculars, shivering.

"First time you've seen a Russian sub close-up?" Lane asked.

"Except in photographs and films," Adamo admitted. "She's . . . awesome."

"So are ours," Lane said.

Adamo lowered his binoculars. "Permission to go along for the ride, sir," he addressed Ryder.

The skipper looked at Lane, who shrugged. "Sure."

Lane turned to him. "You will keep your mouth shut, no matter what happens, or what you think is happening. Clear?"

"Yes, sir," Adamo said.

Lane turned to Ryder. "If we run into any trouble, you're going to have to play it by ear, Red. But I'd suggest you query Admiral Thompson before you do anything. He's standing by. Our comms circuit is open."

"Yeah," Ryder said. "I'd like to take a shot at that sonofabitch. But I'd rather just get the *John Hopkins* crew aboard and get the hell out of here."

Lane smiled. "I'll see what I can do for you. I need to borrow one of your uniforms."

SSN *POGIN*

The *Marvin Shields'* main launch could carry fifteen people, including her crew of two, so it would take three trips to ferry the crew of the *John Hopkins* off the submarine.

It was like a big poker game. Lane had started the pot by giving the sub driver something: the withdrawal of the *Boston*. Badim had returned the ante by keeping his submarine in clear sonar view at periscope depth. Lane had responded by telling him that he had three submarines in the area, and Badim had answered by partially surfacing his boat.

Time now, Lane thought, to play their cards.

They crossed the three hundred yards of rough sea to the waiting submarine. A hatch just forward of the low sail was open and two men stood just within. As the launch got closer Lane could see that both of them wore side arms.

They drew up alongside the *Pogin* and their crewman threw the submarine a line. The taller of the two Ukrainians grabbed it.

"Do you speak Russian, Lieutenant?" the shorter one called in Russian.

"What?" Lane asked in English. His Russian was very good, as a matter of fact.

"In English, then. I suggest that you and your fellow officer come aboard and then have your launch stand off. In these seas I'm afraid you would damage your boat."

"Good idea, Captain . . . ?"

" 'Captain' will be just fine, Lieutenant."

"As you wish," Lane said.

He and Adamo scrambled aboard the *Pogin*. Lane had never been aboard an Alfa-class submarine. Although it was much smaller than American attack submarines, with its titanium hull it was one of the most dangerous machines in the sea.

They all shook hands. "I am Lieutenant Bill Lane, a special observer on the *Marvin Shields*. This is Lieutenant Tony Adamo, the executive officer."

Badim made no move to introduce himself or Melnik. "What is a special observer?"

"Just that, Captain, nothing more. No *zampolits* on our ships."

"Ah, then you do know a little Russian."

"Only what they taught me in school about the configuration of your ships' crews, sir," Lane said. "Which brings us to the crew of the *John Hopkins*, which was sunk, if I am correct, very near here."

"Yes," Badim said.

"In international waters."

"Yes, a terrible mistake on my part. You have my apology. I'm sure a formal apology will be forthcoming from my government."

Lane met his eyes. "That is acceptable."

"You mentioned something about three submarines, Lieutenant."

"Apparently their skippers picked up the *John Hopkins'* distress signal and came to aid in her rescue."

"That is admirable. But there is a treaty between our governments, in which our submarines will not come within five hundred kilometers of each other's coast."

Lane nodded. "A formal apology will be issued by my government. This has been an unfortunate experience. One which we all would like to put behind us."

"I agree," Badim said. "We have to clear up one last thing, you and I, and we can begin transferring my prisoners to you."

Lane had to smile inwardly. The sonofabitch did have something up his sleeves, after all.

"Tell me, what was the *John Hopkins* doing in these waters?"

"As you must know she is an ocean-floor-mapping vessel. A research vessel . . ."

Badim slapped his leg in irritation. *"This one is playing games with us, Valeri,"* he snapped in Russian.

"Send him back. We will take the prisoners to base with us. There they will be properly interrogated."

Lane didn't flinch. He figured that Badim knew he could understand Russian, and this exchange with the other officer was for his benefit.

"It doesn't matter what she was doing," Lane said. "She was in international waters."

"And heading toward our coast. To spy, I think. Otherwise, why did her crew find it necessary to destroy their electronic equipment before they abandoned ship?"

"That is standard aboard all naval vessels, Captain. It is the same in your country."

"Why were submarines sent?"

"To answer the distress signal."

"Is that why a squadron of your F-14D Tomcats was moved out to Bear Island, to effect the rescue?"

"No, Captain, to sink your boat, and to counter the threat of your naval air station at Polyarnyy. You fired the first shot on an unarmed vessel."

"A spy ship."

"The Orion aircraft that came out to take a look was no spy ship, but your naval aviator would have killed him had he not turned back. Why, Captain?" Lane stepped forward, assertively. Melnik's hand went to the gun at his side.

"Nyet, Valeri," Badim said calmly.

"My government will apologize, and so will yours," Lane continued in a softer tone. "I suggest that you release the crew of the *John Hopkins* to me, and we will all leave these waters."

"What guarantee do I have that once your men are off, you won't attack me? I am vulnerable on the surface."

"You have my word," Lane said.

"Do not trust him," Melnik said.

"I do." Badim said after a pause. He nodded. "We will get started now." He turned to his *starpom.* *"Attend to it, Valeri."*

"Da," Melnik said, and he went below.

Adamo motioned for the launch, which had been standing off twenty yards. Its engines revved up and it came around. The crewman tossed Adamo a line.

"The timing was unfortunate, Captain," Lane said while they waited.

Badim looked pensive. "Yes, I would have thought your people would retrain from such spy missions until after PIT BULL."

"And we thought your side would show more restraint."

"Ah, well." Badim smiled. "PIT BULL is nothing more than an exercise. But this, what has happened here, is the real world."

Newton Peters and his exec, Ron Lindsey, came up on deck, their faces lit up.

"Hot damn, are we ever glad to see you, Lieutenant," Peters said. He saluted and shook hands.

"How's your crew doing?" Lane asked.

Peters' smile faded. "One of our people went down with the ship. We've got two casualties aboard this tin pot. I've been told they're okay, but I haven't been allowed to see them."

"One has suffered a broken wrist, the other minor burns on his back," Badim broke in. "My medic assures me they are fine."

Peters glared at him, but Lane interceded.

"Let's get started, Commander. I'm told that the weather will deteriorate soon."

The *John Hopkins* crew emerged from the *Pogin* one at a time. Among the first batch were the two injured crewmen, their condition exactly as Badim had described. Spirits seemed high. The men were smiling.

"What the hell is that all about?" Lane asked.

"I'll tell you later," Peters said. "But we made a couple of points aboard that submarine."

When the last of the crew was loaded and the launch was pulling away from the submarine, Badim waved and called after them.

"Go home!"

Lane smiled. "You too!" he called back.

Peters glared at him. "I don't know who you think you are, Lieutenant, but I didn't very much appreciate your attitude back there."

"Sorry, Peters. But I'm not a lieutenant, not even Navy. You and I have got a lot to talk about."

"Just who the hell are you, then?"

"Someone trying to prevent a disaster."

Badim watched the launch cross the distance to the ASW frigate, Melnik at his side. The wind had risen dramatically in the past twenty minutes.

There was something about this man Lane that did not seem right in Badim's mind.

"That bastard was no more Navy than my aunt," Melnik said, as if he had read his captain's thoughts.

"What makes you say that?"

"He understood Russian. You were his superior officer and yet he offered you no salute. Nor was he deferential to Commander Peters. He is a civilian."

"My thoughts too," Badim said, watching the launch. "So what is he doing aboard that frigate?"

"He probably came in on that chopper we picked up on our snoophead to continue the spying."

"Anything is possible." Badim turned toward the hatch. "Let's get out of this weather. We will hang around awhile to see just what they're up to."

Badim dogged the hatch and followed his *starpom* aft to the attack center.

"I have a green board," Melnik said.

"Dive the boat. One-fourth speed forward. Fifteen degrees down-angle on the planes."

The boat shivered, as if she were glad to be out of the cold wind, and headed down. Badim raised the periscope as they were submerging and swept it in circle to make certain that they had picked up no company other than the *Marvin Shields*.

He turned to reach for the comms switch when the barrel of a pistol was placed at the back of his head.

"Not so fast, Comrade Captain. We must talk about your orders."

10

THE WHITE HOUSE

General Roland Murphy's title was not chief of the CIA, but Director of Central Intelligence, because all intelligence data gathered by U.S. agencies—the CIA, the National Security Agency, the National Reconnaissance Office, the Defense Mapping Agency, the Air Force, Army, Navy, and Marine intelligence units, the State Department's Intelligence and Research Bureau, and others—were collected and analyzed by the CIA.

Roland Murphy had taken over direction of this developing situation from the moment Lane had first been brought in to see him.

He sat in the Oval Office across from the President and his National Security Adviser, Bill Townsend. The Chairman of the Joint Chiefs, General Thomas Mooreland, had just arrived, clearly miffed.

"This is an Atlantic Fleet problem, Mr. President," Mooreland said. "If we allow it to escalate, and that story gets out, there'd be hell to pay. We get along just fine when it's our military head-to-head with theirs. But the moment the Agency gets involved . . . well, there is a lot of mistrust there."

Murphy listened patiently. "You know, General, that every submarine carries what the Russians call a *zampolit*—a political officer—and that he works not for the Navy, but the FIS."

"I understand all that, but Bill Lane was sent up there to defuse a potentially nasty situation, which he did. And to find out if that submarine is a Ukrainian Black Sea Fleet warship. The rest should be ours to handle."

"We've all seen his preliminary message," the President said. "He did a fine job, given the circumstances. What's your objection, Tom?"

"He is interrogating Navy personnel. I want it stopped."

"He's debriefing them, General," Murphy said. "It's the man's job."

"No it is not . . ."

Bill Townsend interrupted him. "General, the *John Hopkins* crew was aboard that submarine for several hours. They would have to know things Lane will be able to use. I agree with Murphy."

"The Navy has its own intelligence unit. I would let them handle it when the *Marvin Shields* arrives at Bear Island."

"There may be no time. Lane cabled that this Captain Badim seemed suspicious of him."

"We have the hardware still in the area to back him up . . ."

"No," the President said flatly. "I sent Bill Lane up there to get our people back. He's done that. If he needs to talk to the crew about what happened or what they were doing up there in the first place, he has my blessing."

General Mooreland stiffened. "Mr. President, I have a job to do—namely, defending this country. If I am not allowed to do it the way I was trained, the way I see fit, then respectfully, sir, you will have my resignation."

The President sighed and shook his head. "Tom, I neither want, nor would I accept, your resignation. But this situation, so close to PIT BULL, is delicate. If I thought that either our armed forces or theirs, or the Ukrainians', were planning to sabotage what I have worked for for so long, heads would roll. It's as simple as that."

Mooreland started to say something, but the President held him off.

"Hear me out, Tom. PIT BULL *will* come off exactly as we have planned, all its safeguards in place. It is our hope for a meaningful peace in this decade. A peace upon which we can build a trusting future. But without a stable Moscow, that may not be possible."

"Civilian interference . . ."

"That's how we do things." The President looked at Mooreland coolly. "That's why you are the Chairman of the Joint Chiefs of Staff, and I am the President of the United States."

"Bill Lane is to have a free hand?"

"For now, yes. He is working for me."

General Mooreland said nothing. He was an old soldier who knew how to take orders. But he was also the senior soldier in the United States, in which practicality (despite what the Constitution said) involved him in the political process. He had to walk a fine line. Not all chairman of the Joint Chiefs had been successful.

"Are you with me, Tom?" the President asked.

Mooreland met his eyes. "Of course I am, Mr. President."

THE KREMLIN

It was just after six in the morning when a worried Marshal Leonov, his aging legs hardly up to the strain, hurried down a corridor in the Presidium of what used to be the Supreme Soviet Building but now housed Central Administration.

Joseph Stalin had been an insomniac who often called his ministers and marshals on the carpet at two or three in the morning. At that hour a man's brain hardly had a chance to work properly. Nikolayev was more civilized. Yet six in the morning wasn't much better, in Leonov's estimation.

As usual, his bodyguard was required to wait in the corridor. Inside the anteroom Leonov was subjected to a body search, and his briefcase was X-rayed, before he was allowed inside.

The office was large, at least twenty meters on a side, with extremely high ceilings and ornate wall coverings, decorations, and furnishings. It was a place where affairs of state could be conducted under the glare of the international spotlight. The new Russians were definitely not *neokulturny*.

President Gennadi Nikolayev sat behind a broad desk studying a thick sheaf of papers. His secretary hovered behind him, while across the room Defense Minister Anatoli Tsarev sat in a high-backed easy chair sipping tea. The scene was almost domestic. But Leonov was on his guard. Nikolayev's tactics were not so far removed from the Russian psyche, after all.

"Good morning, Mr. President," Leonov said with more cheer than he felt.

The expression on Nikolayev's broad face was totally neutral. "So good of you to come so soon, Leonov. Let me come immediately to the point. What is happening in the Barents Sea this morning?"

The Defense Minister rose languidly from his seat and strode across the big room. "It seems that a Black Sea Fleet submarine may have been involved. Is this so?"

"It's what I have heard. It may be the *Pogin*. Captained by Mikhail Badim. A renegade."

Tsarev's eyes narrowed. "Our sensors, I am told, have lost him. This means he has shut down his reactor and is drifting in the silent mode."

"Perhaps he detected an American submarine, Defense Minister," Leonov said patiently. He had received the same disturbing reports from REDFLEET Command barely an hour ago. That Tsarev was consulting his own sources without going through Leonov's office was disturbing enough.

But the look on Nikolayev's agitated peasant face was even worse.

"Our resources in the area show that the nearest U.S. submarine is the one that may have engaged the *Pogin*. It is far to the southeast and heading slowly away. There are no others nearer."

Leonov studied the Defense Minister. "Perhaps the *Marvin Shields* went back on its word to stand down. It is an antisubmarine-warfare vessel. Perhaps it decided to hunt that boat."

"Will he shoot?" Nikolayev asked.

"At this point, Mr. President, I can only guess. But from what I am told of Captain Badim, he will not shoot now unless it is in self-defense."

"What was a Black Sea warship doing in those waters?"

"I do not know," Leonov said. "But our latest LARISSA reports indicate that the *Marvin Shields* has begun to withdraw."

Nikolayev threw up his hands. "Can someone tell me what this means?"

"Mr. President, we can hunt that boat, or you can talk with President Myakotnik," Tsarev said.

"He's a liar," Nikoleyev spat.

"An ELF message can be sent," Leonov said. The "extremely low frequency" transmitter, which could reach submarines anywhere in the world as deep as five hundred meters, had two drawbacks, however. First, it was slow. It took fifteen minutes to transmit a single code group, so detailed messages were impossible to send. And second, the ELF transmission could be picked up by every other submarine in the ocean. At any given time it had to be assumed (at least a fifty-percent possibility assigned to it) that the enemy had cracked their onetime codes.

"That would send a clear message to the Americans that we have lost control, would it not?" Tsarev asked.

Leonov shrugged. "It would send a message for any to hear that we would like to speak to that submarine in private."

"We could also send an aircraft to drop sonobuoys, ordering him to surface," Tsarev suggested.

"Respectfully, I would suggest we do not send any assets into the region until the *Marvin Shields* and those American submarines have time to clear the area."

"I agree," Nikolayev said. "Send the ELF transmission. Order him to surface or we will come after him and kill him."

"It will be done immediately." Leonov started to withdraw, but Nikolayev motioned him back.

"One last question, Marshal Leonov. Our detection equipment in the region cannot hear him, correct? Defense Minister Tsarev's people believe that is because the submarine is being operated in what is called the drift mode, silently without propellers turning."

"That's possible."

"Is there any other possible explanation?"

"Yes, Mr. President, two others. First, the *Pogin* may have suffered a malfunction and been sunk."

"Or sabotaged," Nikolayev said.

"Yes, sir. And second, the captain may have simply decided to dive very deep. Perhaps as deep as nine hundred or a thousand meters. At that depth most sonar would not reach him, nor would our ELF transmission."

"Why would he do this?"

"Only if he wanted to sneak away from the area at high speed without detection."

"The Americans' SOSUS network would pick him up, wouldn't it?"

"Yes, if he were going out into the open Atlantic. But once he broke free he would be virtually undetectable by any means."

A startled expression crossed the President's face. He looked at his secretary and Minister of Defense. "What speed is this submarine capable of, Marshal Leonov?"

"In excess of forty knots."

"A thousand nautical miles in twenty-four hours. Not fast enough to reach the operational area of PIT BULL."

"No, Mr. President," Tsarev said.

Nikolayev breathed a sigh of relief. "Still, I think it is time I call President Reasoner. It is time he and I had a chat." He looked at Leonov. "That's all. Keep us informed."

"Of course," Leonov said, and he withdrew. In the huge anteroom he was just in time to intercept the director of the Foreign Intelligence Service, Vladimir A. Krykov, who had arrived for the overnight briefing.

"Ah, Marshal Leonov," Krykov greeted him effusively. "Your people certainly are making for some interesting reading these days."

Leonov shook his head. "Whatever you do, don't mention PIT BULL while you're in there, Vladimir Aleksandrovich. The man is rabid about it."

"Yes, I know. Frankly it makes me nervous. But then . . ." The FIS chairman sighed. "What's the latest from the Arctic Circle?"

"The submarine has disappeared. Its reactor is off or it has gone deep, we don't know. I'm ordering an ELF sent out. I would very much like to talk to that captain and find out what is on his mind."

"No reason for alarm. The Ukrainians are too weak to harm us. You know what I mean."

"I do not," Leonov said directly.

"We have friends in Kiev."

"In the Black Sea Fleet?"

"On General Normav's staff."

Leonov glanced at the closed door to Nikolayev's office. "Whatever you do, Vladi, do not mention that either."

"There's no proof that Normav or his people are involved."

"Nevertheless, do not mention him. I will see what I can come up with from my end." Leonov shook his head. "The obvious solution, of course, is to cancel or delay PIT BULL. But he won't hear of it."

THE WHITE HOUSE

It was a few minutes after 10 P.M., and the President and his advisors were once again in the basement Situation Room. This time everyone was tense.

"What's the latest word from Bill Lane?" the President asked.

"We've had nothing from him since his message that the crew of the *John Hopkins* was safe aboard the *Marvin Shields*, heading back to Bear," General Mooreland said tiredly. Most of them had been on the job for the past twenty-four hours.

"And now you say that the submarine that caused all the ruckus has gone deep and is heading south?"

"It appears so, Mr. President. Our latest from SOSUS Atlantic . . ."

"I know, I've seen it. Christ, what a mess." The President ran his fingers through his hair. "He'll be one more submarine whose position we're uncertain of. There are lots of them in the Atlantic and Pacific."

"Any chance he can reach PIT BULL in time?"

General Mooreland shook his head. "He does have the range. But even at top speed, which would give him a run of something more than a thousand nautical miles in twenty-four hours, it would still take him a couple of weeks to make it."

The President looked up at the wall map of the world. "But in a week's time he could be off our east coast."

"Along with a number of Russian submarines, Mr. President," General Mooreland said. "And he's an attack submarine, not a missile boat."

"Then what the hell are the Ukrainians up to?" the President asked.

"I don't know, Mr. President. I am not a politician," General Mooreland said.

The barb was not lost on the President. "We've already established that, Tom." He eyed his other advisers. "I think it's time that I use the hot line to call President Nikolayev. Discussion?"

Townsend, his National Security Advisor, nodded agreement. "Couldn't hurt, Mr. President. Might defuse the situation."

Roland Murphy also nodded. "I agree, but Mr. President, I hope that you won't give away our advantage here. I'm speaking of their underwater listening network which we think they call LARISSA. The Ukrainians may have inadvertently given us a confirmation, if that Black Sea Fleet message was authentic."

"That's right, Mr. President," General Mooreland said.

"I'll keep that in mind," the President said.

"It's a little after six in the morning in Moscow, Mr. President," Townsend said. "A perfect time. Mr. Nikolayev is an early riser."

"Yes," the President said. The red hot line had been installed in front of him. He picked it up. A soft burring came from the instrument and continued until the handset at the other end was picked up.

"Hello, Mr. President. This is the President of the Commonwealth of Independent States."

"Yes, Mr. President, this is the President of the United States, good morning. I assume, Mr. President, that you have been advised of the unfortunate situation that has been developing in the Barents Sea."

"Yes, Mr. President. And I agree that it is a most unfortunate situation," the Russian leader said cautiously.

"Especially at this moment in time, when our ... mutual project is so near to fruition."

The Russian President hesitated, probably to give his translators a chance to come up with the word *fruition*. "Yes, you are correct," the Russian said. "I hope that this matter can be resolved to our mutual satisfaction."

"I believe it can be, Mr. President, though some of my advisers are doubtful."

The Russian leader chuckled in appreciation of the President's openness. "My problems are the same, only exacer-

bated by the state of our economy. You know. But PIT
BULL is too important."

"I agree. I extend my apologies for any misunderstand-
ings of the purpose of our ocean-mapping vessel *John
Hopkins*. I understand that she and our Orion search aircraft
came very close to Russian sovereign waters."

"Yes, Mr. President, very close, but not actually within
our waters. It was an unfortunate error on our part."

"I believe that for the time being this incident should not
be . . . shall we say, publicized."

"I agree."

This time it was President Reasoner's turn to hesitate. It
was like playing poker. "Is there any obstacle that you can
foresee to the start of PIT BULL next week? Anything that
we could work out together?"

"I do not think so, Mr. President," the Russian leader
said, almost too quickly. "But, as you know, there are a few
troublesome problems in any such massive undertaking.
Sometimes old friends become enemies out of a misguided
purpose."

"May I help?"

"I think at this moment it is not necessary, Mr. President,
although I appreciate your concern and your offer. If . . . I
do need your help to resolve a minor problem, after all, I
hope that both of our governments will show restraint."

Bingo, the President thought. Nikolayev was just as worried as he was about the Ukrainian submarine. "That goes
without saying, Mr. President. Please do not hesitate to call
on me."

"Yes. Then shall we say good-bye for now, Mr. President?"

"Yes, good-bye, Mr. President. Have a pleasant day."

"And you a pleasant evening. Good luck with your news
conference tomorrow evening."

The President hung up the red telephone. Everyone else
around the table put down his earphones. All had monitored
the conversation.

"One thing is sure, Mr. President," General Murphy, the

DCI, said. "Whatever happened up there was not a Nikolayev-sponsored event. He wants PIT BULL to go forward."

"My reading exactly. So what the hell did happen?"

"It was a maverick operation."

"You have your work cut out for you," the President said to Murphy. Then he let his eyes roam around to the other faces. "You all do. And none of us has much time."

KIEV

General Normav's Chaika limousine dropped him off at the entrance to his private club a block off Kalinin Square and Ukrainian KGB headquarters. It was 6:30 A.M., and he was tired from his long night of labors.

The morning was fairly warm. He entered the plain steel door that was guarded by two military officers.

At the end of a broad hall, he took wide carpeted stairs down into the basement, along another corridor, and then through two sets of swinging doors into a dressing room. Quickly, in anticipation of a few pleasures for his old bones, he stripped, hanging his uniform in his own little closet. Donning one towel around his waist and another around his neck, he padded out to the pool housed in a huge, steam bath of a room. Already several old men were seated around tables eating salmon, caviar, and blini and drinking chilled mineral water, sweet champagne, or spiced vodka. For many of these men this hour of the morning was actually the end of the day; others always began their day with caviar and vodka.

This place had been built in the mid 1800's by the Czar's brother-in-law, and had fallen into disuse, from 1917 until the late sixties, when it had been rebuilt as a private military club for officers.

In effect, over the past ten years or so, it had become

General Normav's private domain. He was the ranking officer on the premises.

No attendants were allowed in the baths, so the officers could talk openly about any subject. The only disadvantage was that the officers had to serve themselves.

Normav stopped at the supply bar to get a bottle of spiced vodka and a large platter of caviar and blini with lemon wedges, grated egg, and onion. He took the things around the far end of the long pool to his usual table, where a group of old, bare-chested men were drinking and eating, deep in conversation.

At the sight of the man sitting at the far side of the table, Normav was momentarily stopped in his tracks. But he recovered smoothly and approached with a friendly smile.

"Ah, Comrade Marshal Leonov, what a rare pleasure having you down here from Moscow this morning," Normav said carefully, setting his things on the table.

The others were Admiral Viskov, chief of the Ukrainian Navy; Admiral Dyukov, CINCBLACKSEAFLEET; General Ivan M. Voznoy, chief operations officer for the Ukrainian Missile Service; and General Anatoli N. Belikov, deputy director of the Ukrainian GRU, the Military Intelligence Service. All of them except Leonov were old-guard, all close personal friends of Normav, handpicked by him and dedicated to KEENSCHCAL. Leonov, in his mid-fifties, was the youngster of the group.

All of them seemed ill at ease.

"Pavl Ivanovich, we have just been having a pleasant chat waiting for you," Leonov said. He was smiling, but looked like a shark. "With all this power here, though, it is a good thing that there are no saboteurs out and about. One bomb would wipe out a very important sector of your military command."

"Not necessary, just give it a little time. We are all old and harmless men who will be dead of natural causes in a few years."

"I think not so harmless."

Normav laughed, but the others flinched. There was little doubt why the marshal had come to Kiev.

"Come," Normav said. "Let's all go in for a soak, and we can talk." He glanced down the length of the pool. The cavernous room seemed filled with shadows.

Leonov looked at him for a moment, then got up and, laying his towel aside, followed the older but larger man into the warm sulphur waters of the pool. The others filed in behind them.

"You should come down here more often," Normav said breezily. The soothing water was up to his barrel chest.

"There is so little time," Leonov said. "Usually more important things take my days." He sighed. "You know the old proverb, Pavl Ivanovich. The Russian is clever, but it comes slowly—all the way from the back of his head."

"Yes, and you are a very clever man, Yakov Borisovich. What is it that has come slowly to you, all the way from the back of your head?"

They had formed a circle, Leonov and Normav across from each other.

"The *Pogin* has disappeared."

"Do we know this ship?" Normav asked, turning to Viskov. "Do you, Admiral?"

Viskov didn't bother to answer, nor had anyone expected him to.

Leonov's eyes stayed on Normav's. "It was a very ugly incident, which could have easily escalated, and still might."

"I do not understand. Why are you telling me this?"

Leonov's eyes were strong. "Operation KEENSCHCAL . . . Dagger Point."

Normav held himself in check, though he was seething. How was it possible for the man to know about the operation? And how extensive was his knowledge?

"I've contained it to this point," Leonov was saying. "I did not want to bring it to the attention of Tsarev, or the President, because they would have had your head. You have served the *Rodina* too long and too hard to end your career down here in disgrace."

"We are an independent nation here. Return to Moscow."

"I don't know all of the details of your operation, of course. But I have learned that you are trying to sabotage PIT BULL."

"Why have you come here this morning, Comrade Marshal?" Normav asked.

"To ask you to give up this nonsense. Why else would I be here?"

Normav laughed, the low sound echoing.

"I met with President Nikolayev this morning. It is his intention that PIT BULL be run as planned. I will meet with President Myakotnik this afternoon."

"PIT BULL will be run on schedule, Comrade Russian Marshal, but not as planned."

"Is that why you sent your submarine to the Northern Sea? To play into the hands of our hotheads? You admit that . . . ?"

"I admit nothing except that I love the *Rodina*, the whole *Rodina*, and I do not wish to see her become a second-class nation because of meddling fools such as Gorbachev, Yeltsin, Nikolayev, and Myakotnik."

"In the name of the *Rodina*, then, Pavl Ivanovich, what have you done? What have you and your cadre planned?"

Normav didn't bothering answering. He could see in the others' eyes that they were frightened. But they were good and loyal old soldiers, and they were with him.

"I will get to the bottom of this."

"I told you that we were old and harmless men. But you disagreed with me, Yakov Borisovich. You were correct."

"What?" Leonov said, his voice echoing hollowly in the large room.

Normav started toward him.

"You're crazy," Leonov cried, suddenly realizing that he was in mortal danger. He tried to back up, but General Voznoy was in his way. "You all are insane."

General Belikov came in on his left, and Admiral Dyukov on his right.

"I will see that you are all shot," Leonov screamed. "All of you."

Normav grabbed a handful of the man's hair and pulled him forward violently at the same moment Voznoy kicked his feet out from under him. Leonov fell forward into the water.

He came up seconds later, sputtering and trying to shout, but now it was too late for him. The five old men shoved him back down.

He was young, and he struggled for a long time, but finally the last breath went out of him with a shuddering series of bubbles and he drifted still.

Normav stepped back. "The rest of you stay here. I'm going to my office. Keep his head under for at least another couple of minutes, and do not try to revive him for at least ten more. Then even if you're successful, and he does come around, he will be so brain-damaged from lack of oxygen that it won't matter."

"The question is, how much did the bastard know?" Viskov asked. "And who else besides him knew?"

"I think he kept it contained. He probably wasn't one-hundred-percent sure, which is why he came here. He wanted to confront us . . . me, to see how I would react." Normav shook his head. "The damned fool. KEENSCHCAL goes forward as planned. Nothing will stand in our way."

SSN *POGIN*

The liquid-metal reactor aboard the *Pogin* was a sealed unit, not designed for access at sea. Only in dry dock could technicians service it, replenish its fuel rods or lead-bismuth coolant.

They were deep, running in a drift mode to the west-southwest on a branch of the North Atlantic Current. Nearly every system aboard the submarine was shut down or on standby.

Somewhere out there were the ASW frigate on its way back to Bear Island and the Los Angeles-class submarines. Any one of them had the capability of finding them.

The American SOSUS network stretched across here too. It could detect the presence of enemy submarines that made the slightest of noises.

Russia's own LARISSA-ONE system, which was based on magnetic-anomaly detectors and not sound detection, could "see" a quiet submarine that was in the drift mode. But it would work only down to around seven hundred meters—the deepest that American submarines could dive, but well above the Alfa's diving range of one thousand meters. (The planners had never expected it would have to be used to hunt former Russian submarines!)

Badim was hunched in a narrow crawl space behind his chief engineer, Lieutenant Vasili Romanovich Sitnikov. The younger man was taking the twenty-seven screws out of a sealed access plate at the base of the nuclear reactor's core-control unit. Badim held the flashlight for him.

"The seal has definitely been tampered with, Comrade Captain," Sitnikov said.

"Take the plate all the way off and let's see if that bastard was telling us the truth," Badim said.

"Yes, Captain."

Their *zampolit*, Aleksei Grichakov, had explained exactly what he had done, as he held the barrel of his pistol against the base of Badim's skull. That was four hours ago. Since then they had been in the drift mode at one thousand meters below the surface.

Melnik had wanted to kill the bastard immediately, but it was Grichakov's manner that stopped him, stopped them all. The man was telling the truth. Somehow he had placed a powerful explosive on the reactor's core-control unit. The explosives would blow unless Grichakov punched in a personal code in a remote-control unit that he held. That had to be done very four hours on the hour. Of course that gave them plenty of time to surface, get off a distress message, and abandon the boat before she blew. But the first rescue team to get to them would be the Americans, and this crew would go home in absolute disgrace. Normav would have them shot.

"Fuck your mother," Sitnikov said softly. He looked back at Badim. "It is here, just as he said it was."

Badim looked into the space behind the access plate. An LCD was counting down the minutes until either the bomb exploded or Grichakov's code was programmed in. The counter showed that there were 209 minutes to go.

It was true, Badim thought, sitting back on his haunches. He had no choice.

"We will head west-southwest, Comrade Captain," Grichakov had said, backing off after everyone had calmed down.

"Where are we going?" Badim asked.

Grichakov had smiled. "To the Panama Canal, of course. You have demonstrated your disloyalty and your weakness, so now I am in charge."

SSN *BOSTON*

"Conn, communications."

"Conn, aye," Armstrong answered.

"It's coming in again, skipper. It's ELF, and it's of Russian origin. Four code groups. Keeps repeating itself at sixty-minute intervals."

"Does it match anything in our computer?"

"Negative. They've changed their code groups since the last time we were updated."

Armstrong thought a moment. "All right, stick with it." He released the comms button and looked across the attack center at his exec, Steve McGill.

"It's the *Pogin*," Armstrong said. "I'll bet anything on it."

"We've got our people back. The *Marvin Shields* is on her way to Bear."

"So why does REDFLEET want to make contact with a Ukrainian sub? I tell you, Steve, something is going on."

The *Boston* had herself been running slowly on a south-southwesterly course, at the depth of two hundred meters.

"Okay," Armstrong said. "Okay. Let's find out just what the hell is going on. Surface the boat. Up-angle on the planes, fifteen degrees, all ahead one-half."

THE PENTAGON

"I've got a decode on that Russian ELF, sir," one of the comms officers told Rear Admiral Don Horvak.

The Command Center was all but deserted now that the crew of the *John Hopkins* was on its way back to Bear Island. Horvak had stuck around until he could make contact with *Boston*. He had just wanted to make sure everything was okay up there. He was a worrier. His wife called him a "fuss-budget." And it was true.

Boston had surfaced five minutes ago and sent off a burst message including the four code groups from the Russian's ELF transmission to the region. Like Armstrong, Horvak had wondered about the message. Until now.

"I'll be damned," he said. He quickly scratched out a message on his standard pad and handed it to the comms officer. "Get this off to *Boston* immediately."

"Aye, Admiral."

Horvak sat back in his chair and reread the carbon of the message as he debated calling Bert Thompson in. "Later," he mumbled to himself. First he wanted to see what those bastards were up to. Was it a joint Russian-Ukrainian operation, after all?

Z120917ZJUL
T O P   S E C R E T
TO: SSN BOSTON
FM: COMSUBPLANT

1. RUSSIAN ELF TRANSMISSION FOUR GROUPS, TRANSLATED AS FOLLOWS: POGIN XXX SUR- FACE IMMEDIATELY XXX IMPORTANT REDFLEET MESSAGE FOLLOWS XXX WHITE SABLE SENDS XXX

2. WHITE SABLE IS MARSHAL Y. B. LEONOV. BELIEVE HIS MESSAGE WILL BE OF EXTREME INTEREST.

3. REMAIN IN THE AREA. FIND POGIN. INTER- CEPT WHITE SABLE MESSAGE.

X X

EOM

GOOD LUCK XXX HORVAK SENDS

11

FF *MARVIN SHIELDS*

It was still light at 7:30 when Lane opened his eyes and sat up in the narrow bunk. The seas had been building all afternoon, and the motion aboard the 415-foot frigate was getting lively.

At least he'd had a few hours sleep. He'd been going on adrenaline for what seemed like days. The crew of the *John Hopkins* had been in even worse shape, although Newton Peters admitted they'd been fed and treated decently.

Lane made his way to the head, where he splashed some cool water on his face. His eyes were bloodshot, his face haggard. He'd changed out of his borrowed uniform and was in his own civilian clothes now.

The President told him to calm the situation down and bring the crew of the *John Hopkins* home. He had done that. But there'd been something in Badim's manner that didn't quite add up.

He went topside. Lieutenant Ryder and his exec, Tony

Adamo, were in the wardroom with Newt Peters and his exec, Ron Lindsey.

"I was about to send someone down for you," Ryder said. "Coffee?"

"Please." Lane sat down at the table. "What's happened?"

"That sub has disappeared," Adamo said.

"Disappeared? How?" Lane accepted the coffee from Ryder.

Adamo shrugged. "We're towing our passive sonar, just in case."

"I didn't trust that bastard," Ryder interjected. "I still don't. We weren't out of there for more than a few minutes and she began to dive."

"We expected that," Lane said.

"Yeah," Ryder said, "but we didn't expect it to keep diving."

"How deep?"

"We lost her when she went through a major thermocline at two thousand feet. She was still going down fast. If she remains below that thermocline we'll never find her."

"Have you contacted CINCLAN? SOSUS might be reading something."

"Not yet," Ryder said.

"Why not?" Lane snapped.

"We thought we should wait until you were up. We're less than four hours out of Bear Island."

"You don't want to upset the applecart."

"Look, Lieutenant Lane, or Mr. Lane, or whoever the hell you are," Peters said, "my ship was sunk under me. One of my crewmen was killed, and two were injured. For what? If that sub driver had told us to get the hell out of there, we would have done that without a backward glance. And nobody would be dead."

"You were in international waters. We certainly are now."

Peters scoffed. "Yeah, but that sub captain was right. We wouldn't have been in international waters for long if he hadn't shown up."

"You've done this before."

"A lot. But this time was different. This time, for some reason, they decided to shoot first and talk later. Now that boomer is down there below us. If he decides to shoot again we'll be shit out of luck."

Peters had not lost his nerve, Lane reckoned. Something else was eating at the man. "What happened aboard that submarine? Are any of your people Russian speakers?"

Again Peters and Ryder exchanged glances. "I think that this discussion will wait until we get to Bear."

Lane sighed and leaned back in his chair. He lit a cigarette. "I'd like to get a message back to Washington. Encrypted. High-speed burst."

"Certainly," Ryder said. "Tony will get it off for you."

Adamo pulled out a pad.

"Mark this with a Z flash designator, and make it top secret," Lane began.

Adamo's eyebrows rose.

"To: CINCLAN, with copies to the National Security Agency, Russian Division, the Director of Central Intelligence, the Chairman of the Joint Chiefs, and the President."

"Sir?"

"Am I going too fast for you?" Lane asked.

"Do you really want to send this . . . I mean to all these people?"

"They're the ones who hired me."

Peters nodded. "All right, Lane, you've made your point. I speak a little Russian and so do a number of my crew. And you're right that something screwy was going on aboard that sub."

"Anything to do with the way she disappeared?"

"Possibly. It's even possible she's been hijacked."

"Mutiny?"

"I don't know, Mr. Lane," Peters said uncomfortably. "All I know is that one of the officers aboard that submarine, named Grichakov, has got a different idea of what that boat should be doing than her skipper does."

"Mikhail Badim," Lane said. "One of the better sub drivers in the fleet."

"So that's his name," Peters said. "At any rate, when we were brought aboard, that submarine submerged and went deep. Soon we were rigged for silent running. We figured that someone on the surface was listening to us. But Red here tells me that one of our L.A.-class subs had a firing solution on the *Pogin* not knowing that we were aboard."

"She's the *Boston*," Lane said. "Go on."

"This Grichakov came around to us and told us to start banging the bulkheads with anything we could get our hands on. He even brought some things from the galley. So we did. We made such a ruckus that I thought we were going to be shot. Shortly after that we surfaced. And not long afterward we were freed."

"Aleksei Grichakov," Lane said half to himself.

"Sir?" Adamo asked.

"He's the *zampolit* aboard that sub. If he has taken over, something is gone wrong."

"What?"

"You wouldn't want to know," Lane said. "All right, this time we really are going to send a message. This one to Admiral Thompson, CINCLAN."

SOSUS CONTROL

"They're getting heated up in Washington," Lieutenant Commander Barney Fitzgerald said.

Petty Officer Charles Denkins looked up from his console with bloodshot eyes. His face had stubble of a beard. Fitzgerald handed him a cup of coffee and the flimsy of a message that had just come in from the Pentagon's Command Center.

Denkins, wearing his earphones, sipped his coffee as he read the message. The *Marvin Shields*, now steaming back to Bear Island, had tracked the Russian-built Ukrainian-fleet submarine *Pogin* down to a thermocline at a little over six hundred meters, where they lost her.

Another Orion P-3C was being dispatched to the region, but it was felt that if the *Pogin* chose to remain below six hundred meters, she would not be found with sonobuoys or FLIRS equipment (forward-looking infrared scanner), which could detect the heat signature of her nuclear reactor.

In fact, the only methods by which the Ukrainian sub could be detected were by the SOSUS sensors scattered on the ocean floor in that region (like looking for the proverbial needle in the haystack) or by an attack submarine. After what had already happened, though, sending the *Boston* or another boat snooping around wasn't such a great idea. And what was a Black Sea Fleet boat doing in those waters, anyhow?

The Pentagon was asking if SOSUS Control could help.

"But they want it yesterday, Charlie," Fitzgerald said.

Denkins put down his coffee with a theatrical sigh and nodded sardonically, although secretly he was delighted finally to be given a real challenge. "Did the *Marvin Shields* transmit a position on that sub?"

"It's already in our machine, identified as the SSN *Pogin*."

Their "machine" was a Cray-8DX supercomputer in the basement, one of the largest and most powerful computers in the world. Denkins brought the display up on his console, which showed the *Marvin Shields'* exact position fixed within one foot by global positioning satellites, and the *Pogin*'s position relative to hers.

Before she lost herself beneath the thermocline, she had been traveling slowly west-southwest.

Denkins studied the display. The Ukrainian submarine had been traveling at about twelve knots, one-fourth her top submerged speed. If she had kept going at that rate, or had accelerated, she would have been picked up by the SOSUS sensors.

He made a quick check of the computer memory to make sure that one of the less experienced operators hadn't picked up something and simply logged it "unknown."

There had been a number of anomalies, but he brought each one up and dismissed them all.

Next, he went looking for the three Russian submarines that had been in the region; one of them a diesel-electric Kilo class and the other two, Sierras.

He found them quickly, setting their depth, track, and speed into the battle-problem program he had entered for this run. They were heading home, not bothering to mask their noises. Was the Alfa hiding somewhere below them?

He did not think so. He turned his attention to the three Los Angeles-class submarines in the region. He was trying to eliminate everything else in that piece of ocean so that the computer could erase those noises from his display. Whatever was left would be the noises that the Alfa was making. There wasn't a submarine built anywhere in the world yet that was completely noiseless.

He would find it.

The *Phoenix* and *Norfolk* were easy; they came up on his display immediately. They were still well to the southwest of Bear Island, heading back to their patrol stations. The *Boston* was a different story.

One at a time he brought up the sectors in an ever-expanding circle around the *Boston*'s last known position, listening for the telltale footprint of the nuclear submarine.

But it wasn't there.

"Son of a bitch," Denkins swore softly.

Fitzgerald heard it, but he said nothing. Denkins was oblivious to anything around him. And he was good enough at his job that no one intruded. Ever.

The problem was volume. The oceans of the world were so vast, so deep, and their bottom topographies so complex. It was impossible for any nation to lay listening devices everywhere.

Only at a few choke points in the North Atlantic, Mediterranean, and North Pacific was the U.S. listening carefully for a sign that the Russian submarines were trying to break out from their home waters.

Most of the time we were successful, Denkins thought.

Or at least we hoped so. But once the subs were out in the open ocean, unless we happened to be on their tail with one of our own submarines, we were out of luck. It was called a "breakout" and we had to assume that at any time, now that they had solved their fuel-supply problems, there were dozens of Russian attack and missile submarines circling silently off our coasts. No one had expected the Ukrainian Navy to enter the game and complicate things. But they had.

The problem, Denkins knew, was one of outthinking the sub drivers themselves. If you could figure out what the driver was trying to do with his boat, you might be able to beat him to the punch and be waiting for him when he showed up.

The *Pogin* was missing and now so was the *Boston*. The two boats had nearly slugged it out earlier, so it was possible that their drivers had a thing for each other.

Find the *Pogin*, and the *Boston* would show up. Or vice versa, which would be a hell of a lot easier, because the American sub couldn't dive so deep and wouldn't be trying to hide from SOSUS.

Denkins made one other assumption: The *Pogin* was not heading home; she was trying for the open Atlantic.

But the *Boston* would be there, too.

Denkins looked up at the world map. They'd be heading west-southwest, he expected, the natural route.

Turning back to his console, he began bringing up sectors in that direction, one at a time, listening for any kind of a noise that would tell him the *Boston* was there.

THE PENTAGON

"You're telling me that the Ukrainian submarine has not surfaced in response to the ELF message?" Admiral Norbert Thompson asked.

It was late. Yet Thompson was as crisp as he had been at

the start of the day ... how many hours ago? The OD had finally tracked him down at home. He'd come back immediately.

"That's right, Admiral," Rear Admiral Horvak said. "Last contact we had with her was the *Marvin Shields'* tracking her down to two thousand feet, and she disappeared beneath a thermocline."

He had put out the call for the admiral as soon as SOSUS Control had Bill Lane's message that the *Pogin* had disappeared.

"But it's more than that, isn't it?" Thompson said.

"I'm afraid so, Admiral. There may be some sort of trouble aboard that sub. Possibly a mutiny."

"Good Christ. What'd Lane come up with?"

Horvak handed him the message in which Lane had summarized what Newt Peters and the crew of the *John Hopkins* had told him.

Thompson read it. "He's sure about this Grichakov? Have we confirmed this with Naval Intelligence?"

"I haven't brought them into this yet, Admiral. But Bill Lane is first-class. He knows what he's talking about. In fact, if we asked our people to come up with something on this *zampolit*, their primary source would probably be Lane. And I thought we should keep this situation contained for as long as possible, so close to PIT BULL."

Thompson nodded agreement. "Do you think he's trying to break out?"

"Nothing concrete from SOSUS."

Thompson grunted. "That'd be cute, a Ukrainian sub off our Atlantic coast with a mutinous intelligence agent aboard." He shook his head. "But if he wants to sneak out into the open Atlantic there's not a whole hell of a lot SOSUS will be able to do about it. He just has to drift with the North Atlantic Current until he's clear of our sensors. And even the SURTASS unit that a ship like the *John Hopkins* tows wouldn't pick him up because of his depth."

"We've still got a chance, Admiral," Horvak said, bracing himself for the explosion.

"Not unless she comes up from beneath that thermocline."

"No, sir. The *Boston*. She's disappeared again, and there's a good chance that Armstrong is shadowing the Black Sea sub."

Thompson's face turned red. "Goddammit, Don," he barked. "What the hell kind of people do you have working for you?"

"Good ones. And if Howie does his job right, we won't lose that sub."

"But does he realize what's at stake here? They've already had firing solutions on each other. And now if this Grichakov is actually in control . . ."

"We're in for a rough time of it no matter what happens. But I'd rather have Howie shadowing that bastard. The thought of another boomer off our coast doesn't fill me with joy."

"Nor me." Thompson studied the big situation map for a few seconds. "The *Boston*—if your skipper is as good as you say he is—can just operate around the depth of that thermocline. If he's really sharp, he'll be able to duck beneath it for a look at the Ukrainian."

"That's what we're hoping for, Admiral. And that Howie will make a little noise. So our SOSUS will know he's there. If we can follow him, we'll be following the sub. One below the thermocline, and one just at its fringes."

"The problem, of course, is going to be communications with your man. If he surfaces to make contact with us, the chances are he'll lose the Alfa."

"Once they're out of the bottleneck they'll be on their own anyway," Horvak said.

"What about the *Phoenix* and *Norfolk*?"

"They know nothing about what's going on with Howie, and I think we should keep it that way."

"That's a tough call," Thompson said.

"We don't want to escalate this anymore. The three Russian subs are heading back to their own coastal patrol positions, and that fighter unit at Polyarnyy has stood down. I think we should send Deke Adams' squadron off Bear as well."

"It'll come down to one against one."

"That's right, Admiral. One of our subs versus one of theirs."

"Who's got the advantage?"

Horvak shrugged. "Probably the Alfa. She can run faster and dive deeper. But our sensors and weapons-aiming systems are better. And Mikhail Badim may not be driving his boat as hard as he might."

Thompson shook his head. "There's not a damned thing we can do about it for now, is there?"

"No, sir. Not a damned thing."

SSN *BOSTON*

It had been obvious from the beginning that something odd was going on aboard the Russian submarine. The pots-and-pans thing wasn't normal behavior. Nor was ignoring a REDFLEET ELF message.

Howard Armstrong, his executive officer, Steve McGill, and his navigation officer, Pat Williams, were hunched over a chart of the region spread out at the nav station in the attack center.

It had been Williams' suggestion that the *Pogin* had dived below the thermocline layer at two thousand feet (which put him out of range of the ELF broadcast) and that she was presently drifting silently to the southwest on the North Atlantic Current.

"That's if she's trying to break out, Pat," McGill had countered. "We just don't know for sure."

"For now we're going to go along with Pat," Armstrong said. "Let's say he is trying to break out. He wants to get past our SOSUS. He might be able to run quietly enough to slip by SOSUS, but not from a submarine above him."

"We can't go that deep," Williams stated the obvious.

"No," Armstrong agreed. "But we can get to the thermocline and then string out our SUBACS array."

On the starboard side of every Los Angeles-class submarine, a prominent fairing ran almost the entire length of the hull. It housed an advanced passive-sonar array called the Submarine Advanced Combat System, that could be towed behind the sub. The cable and winch for the assembly were fitted into the ballast tanks. Under normal conditions, nearly a mile of cable was strung out behind the sub which would move at sufficient speed to keep the sonar array at the same depth. But if the submarine stopped, the sonar equipment would sink deeper.

On the assumption that the *Pogin* was trying to break out, Armstrong had driven his boat to the southwest, stopping every few miles to lower his passive-sonar array below the thermocline and listen.

So far their search had been unsuccessful.

"He could have circled back," McGill said.

Armstrong studied the chart, where each time they had entered a tick. "I don't think so, Steve, but don't ask me why. I'm sure that sonofabitch is trying to get out."

"She's not a missile sub."

"No, her job is to attack ships. Sink them."

"Come on, Howie, this isn't war. He's not going to shoot."

Armstrong looked up. "No? He sunk the *John Hopkins*, and he was damned well close to shooting us." He looked down at the chart. "We keep going." He stabbed a finger at a spot near the extreme west-southwest limit of the SOSUS network. "Try here next."

SSN *POGIN*

Zampolit Grichakov punched the code on his handheld control unit, disarming the explosives for another four hours.

"Why are you doing this, Aleksei Mikhailovich?" Badim asked.

"Orders."

"Whose orders?"

Grichakov smiled, his face like a death's-head in the dim red battle lights he'd insisted on. "My orders come from the same source as yours."

"BLACKSEAFLEET?"

Again the *zampolit* smiled. "No, the other one. I was told to watch you."

Valeri Melnik was across the tiny attack center keeping a close watch on their depth. They were actually a little deeper than one thousand meters, right at the *Pogin*'s critical limit.

Badim studied Grichakov's eyes, trying to read a clue in them. Who was the "other one"? Could he mean General Normav? If that were the case, what game had the general been playing with him? Did he really want to know?

"Now," Grichakov said, "how soon before we're clear of the American SOSUS network?"

Badim checked the charts. "We should be able to power up within the next hour."

"Then we'll be out of their reach?"

"Yes."

"What about on the surface? What's up there now?"

"We have no way of knowing. Surface sonars cannot penetrate the thermocline beneath which we are running, nor can our sonar."

"Try."

"Do you mean go active? If there is anyone up there, they'll hear us."

"Of course not," Grichakov spat. "What do you take me for?"

Badim suppressed a smirk. "We have already established that, Comrade Zampolit." He reached up and hit the comms switch before the other man could reply. "Sonar, conn."

"Sonar, aye."

"I want you to make a careful passive sweep for anything on the surface."

"But that's impossible, Comrade Captain."

"Do it anyway," Badim said.

"Aye."

Badim stared at Grichakov while they waited.

"Sonar, Captain. I think I'm hearing something, but I'm not sure. It could be nothing . . ."

"I'll come back and listen," Badim said. He went aft to the sonar compartment, Grichakov right behind him.

The sonarman handed him a pair of earphones. At first he could pick out nothing within the mush, but gradually there *was* something. Faint. Distant. Above them. But not on the surface, he didn't think. Surface sounds, if they could penetrate the thermocline barrier, would be distorted. This was a distinct noise, though weak.

"There it is," the sonarman said.

And then Badim had it. He knew exactly what it was and what it meant.

"What is it?" Grichakov asked, his eyes bright.

Badim took off his earphones. "Put it on the speakers."

"But, Captain," the sonarman tried to protest.

"Do it so that all of us can hear your mysterious noise."

The young man complied, and the tiny compartment was filled with the rushing sea sounds. The headphones were much more sensitive, of course. And the noise they'd heard would hardly be audible on the speakers. But that's exactly what Badim wanted.

They listened for an entire minute. Grichakov finally shook his head. "I couldn't hear a thing."

"No," Badim said.

"It was there, Captain," the sonarman said. He still wore his earphones. "But it has stopped."

"You didn't recognize it?" Badim asked. "I'll tell you what it was, so you will be able to recognize it if you ever hear it again. It is nothing more than an anomaly in the thermocline. Nothing more."

The sonarman was skeptical, but he nodded. "Aye, Captain."

Badim turned to Grichakov. "As I said, as long as we run beneath the thermocline no one can hear us, and we cannot hear them."

"Very well," Grichakov said. "Very well."

SSN *BOSTON*

"We're at the edge of the SOSUS shelf," McGill said quietly. They were in the sonar compartment. "We should be turning back."

Armstrong shook his head. "If he's going to crank up his reactor, it'll be here at the edge or just beyond."

Once or twice they'd thought they heard something. But then it had faded.

Armstrong was about to pull off his earphones and head back to the wardroom for a cup of coffee when the distinctive *whoosh-whir* of an Alfa submarine came over loud and clear.

"Gotcha, you bastard," he said softly.

The sonarman looked up. "That's him, all right, skipper. She's accelerating."

Armstrong hit the comms. "Engineering, this is the captain. Dick, get us out of here. Give me three-fourths speed ahead, and prepare to firewall it. We're on to her."

"You've got it, skipper. Three-fourths ahead."

"She's making turns for about thirty knots, skipper," the sonarman said. "She's still pulling away from us, but her turns are constant now."

"Can you give me a course yet?"

"This isn't real accurate, sir, but I'd say she's on a course of about two-five-five."

Armstrong looked at his exec. "He's driving her out around the North Cape. Then he'll swing back to the southwest to intercept our coast." He turned back to his sonarman. "Haul in the towed array, but keep on it with our bow unit. Don't lose him, Lee."

"At this point, skipper, it should be easy. She's a noisy boat."

Armstrong went back into the attack center with McGill.

"We'll stick behind and above him. Chances are he's going to be busy figuring out what's ahead of him, so he won't make a turn to look back."

"We'll have to dip under the thermocline from time to time to see what's going on."

"Shouldn't be a problem. We're still within our safety margin."

"Just."

"Okay, let's not lose him, Steve. Give me turns for thirty knots, and bring us around to two-five-five."

KIEV

It was just 2:50 P.M. when General Normav's Chaika limousine topped the hill overlooking the city and pulled up in front of the Central Administration Building. The general let himself out and, briefcase in hand, strode imperiously up the broad stairs past the sentries, who came rigidly to attention, and down the broad corridor.

Admiral Ryabov had called around noon with the terrible news that Marshal Leonov had drowned in an accident at the club. It was on an open line, and the two men had lingered over the conversation, citing Leonov's many merits.

All Russian military forces everywhere in the world had gone immediately to a low-grade alert, which was SOP after the death of such a high-ranking member of the leadership.

The Americans had been warned, of course, so that they would not misconstrue what was happening. They in turn raised their DEFCON (defense condition) one notch. No one was particularly worried.

In Ukraine someone was going to have to take the blame

for Leonov's death. The fact that a high-ranking Russian dignitary died while on a secret visit to Kiev could not go unnoticed.

Normav was concerned that it might be Ryabov who would take the blame. That would make things difficult because the man was one of the key elements—if not *the* key element—in KEENSCHCAL.

There was a lot of activity in the building, and in fact all along Government row. Normav hadn't noticed it until now, when he encountered a big crowd in front of President Myakotnik's main conference room.

"Ah, General Normav, at last," Myakotnik's secretary said, extracting himself from the crowd. "We have been waiting for you."

"What is going on?" Normav asked, a little confused.

"Just inside. The foreign press and television are here already. Let's hurry."

"What are you talking about, man?" Normav demanded, pulling away from Yevgenni Soroshkin.

"It is a news conference. President Myakotnik is going to announce the creation of a new marshalship. Now, come along, General."

"I will not," Normav sneered, pulling back even farther. "This is outrageous. Since when do Ukrainians announce their staff appointments to the world? It is worse than outrageous, it is insanity."

They were attracting attention. Everyone was looking at them. The two young armed guards had stiffened, not knowing exactly what they should or could do if the situation in front of them got out of hand.

Soroshkin was unperturbed, however. He lowered his voice and stepped a little closer. "This is a direct order, General. Do you understand?"

Normav resisted for another moment, but he was an old soldier who had taken many disagreeable orders in his life. This would be no different.

He nodded finally.

"Good, very good." Soroshkin made his way through the crowd, Normav behind him.

Inside the main conference room, there were at least one hundred newspeople from all the major media—wire services, newspapers, television networks, magazines.

President Myakotnik was just finishing his statement about the untimely death of Russia's Marshal Leonov. When he was done, he started his second statement.

"Now," Soroshkin whispered, giving Normav a little shove.

"This afternoon," Myakotnik said, "I am appointing Captain General Pavl Ivanovich Normav to the position of Marshal of all Ukrainian Armed Forces. The appointment is immediate, and to be permanent until his retirement."

The connection was not lost on the crowd. Russia had lost an important figure, Ukraine was gaining one. They were thumbing their noses at their old masters.

BEAR ISLAND

The weather had closed in over the entire eastern region of the Barents Sea, with the ceiling below one hundred feet. A thin drizzle fell through a thick, cold fog.

Bill Lane stood on the deck of the *Marvin Shields* with Ryder and Peters. They had tied up minutes ago, and a jeep was waiting for Lane on the dock.

"I've recommended that you and your crew be flown immediately back to Washington," Lane said to Peters.

The *John Hopkins'* skipper nodded glumly. "Aren't you flying back with us?"

"I'm going out tonight. There's an SR-91 standing by for me. Same one that brought me up here from Andrews. See you in Washington sometime tomorrow." He hurried down the ladder to the dock and his waiting jeep.

A young Navy rating was behind the wheel. "Captain Taylor is waiting for you. He's already aboard, sir."

"Good," Lane said. "What about Deke Adams and his squadron?"

"They left about an hour ago, sir. Would you like to get a bite to eat, or something, first, sir?"

"No, thanks. I think I'd like to get this next part over with as soon as possible."

12

ALEXANDRIA

Doug Hatcher was resentful of the way Randy Turner had eased him out so early tonight. Yet, coming up the stairs to his apartment, a part of him understood that the senator's assistant was on call twenty-four hours a day. Randy complained about Wood, but working for the senator was a good job with a bright future. Something Hatcher knew he did not have, despite Randy's insistence otherwise.

"Hey, queerboy, what do you think you're doing here? Get the fuck out of here before you get hurt." He'd heard it all of his life. Even his father had turned his back when his son had come out of the closet. A Navy commission did nothing to change the man's attitude. The pain of that ostracism was almost too much to bear.

Randy Turner cared. At least for now one human being reached out a hand of love and friendship. Hatcher knew their relationship would not last. He knew that Turner was only using him for intelligence from the Joint Chiefs so that he could help his boss. But for now it was okay. There was no other alternative.

Two men in civilian clothes were waiting for him in his living room when he switched on the lights. He stepped back, his heart going into his throat.

"Where've you been, Lieutenant?" one of them said. His suit looked as if it had been slept in.

"Who the hell are you?" Hatcher said, finding his voice. "Get the hell out of my house or I'll call the cops."

The taller of the two opened his wallet and held it out. "Sterling Miller, Navy Intelligence." He nodded to the other man. "My partner, Puck Abramson."

"What are you doing here?"

"We'd like to ask you a few questions, Lieutenant Hatcher, about Operation PIT BULL. There's been a leak."

Hatcher was sick at heart. "I'm going to call Admiral Thompson."

"Your boss knows we're here."

Abramson had been looking at the books on the shelf. "We're going to be a fact of life until we find out what's going on, Doug," he said. "You can make it easy all the way around if you tell us everything."

Hatcher wanted to call Turner, but in his gut he knew it would do no good. Randy would cut him loose without blinking an eyelash.

"Somebody is telling tales out of school, and the list is short. Your name is pretty close to the top, you know what I mean?" Miller said.

"No, I . . ."

"We'll cut you a deal, Doug. Play ball with us and I think I can get you off the hook with nothing more than a bad-conduct discharge."

"I don't know what you're talking about." Hatcher's heart was hammering. He glanced toward the bathroom door down the hall from the kitchenette. The military was his entire life. A BCD would cut him off from everything he loved, from everything he'd worked for. It wasn't fair.

"We don't have a lot of time," Abramson said. "Our boss

says find the leak and plug it ASAP. He expects results. You know how it is."

"Who've you been talking to?" Miller asked. "You selling information to the Russians?"

Hatcher was appalled. "What do you think I am?" he stammered.

"We already know what you are, Lieutenant. We're trying to establish how much damage you've done so that we can try to fix it."

"I'm going to be sick—" Hatcher's stomach was churning. He held a hand to his mouth and sprinted to the bathroom. Inside, he slammed the door and locked it.

"Hatcher, you sonofabitch," Abramson shouted. He pounded on the door. "Open up!"

"I'm going to be sick," Hatcher shouted. He gagged loudly to cover the noise as he hurriedly removed the top from the toilet tank. Evidently they had not searched the apartment very well because his 9mm Beretta wrapped in plastic was still in the tank.

"We're breaking the door down!"

Hatcher fished the gun out of the water, ripped it out of the plastic bag, jacked a round into the chamber, and switched off the safety.

"Hatcher!" one of the investigators shouted, and something crashed against the bathroom door.

Hatcher turned toward the door, and as it crashed open, put the barrel of the pistol in his mouth and pulled the trigger.

OLD SENATE OFFICE BUILDING

Senator Wood parked his car in the ramp, locked up, and walked across to the elevators.

"Senator," a voice called out of the shadows behind a support column.

Wood stopped in his tracks, his heart skipping a beat. Violent crime was rampant in the nation's capital. Normally he would not have come alone, but he'd attended a last-minute meeting with some of his Senate colleagues, and his staff was already upstairs in his office to watch the President's news conference on television. The parking garage was deserted.

"Who are you?" he demanded.

"My identity is not important, Senator, only what I have to say is. It's about the Rio war games."

Wood could identify a slight foreign accent. He knew the voice from somewhere, but he could not put his finger on it. "Why don't you come out from there?" Wood started toward the column.

"Stay back," the voice warned, "or I'll tell you nothing."

Wood stopped. "I'm expected upstairs."

"You are in danger, all of you are," the voice said. "The Rio Games will be a disaster. You must call for their cancellation, or least a delay."

"That's impossible. Even if I could stop PIT BULL I wouldn't. We need the games."

"There are other ways, Senator, to accomplish what you wish to accomplish for your people. Less dangerous."

"What are you talking about?"

"We know about the money . . ."

"I've heard enough of this shit." Wood healed around the column.

A car door slammed shut, an engine roared to life, and as Wood rounded the corner, a plain blue, windowless van roared past, its tires squealing. The angle had been wrong for him to get a look at the driver, but he saw the license plate and memorized the number.

THE WHITE HOUSE

"Ladies and gentlemen, the President of the United States."

President Matthew Reasoner strode into the media-briefing room in the East Wing at precisely 9:00 P.M., prime time across much of the nation, and took his place at the podium. With him were Secretary of Defense Norbert Powers, Chairman of the Joint Chiefs Air Force General Thomas Mooreland, and Navy Vice Admiral Jeff "Deep Six" McCauley.

The room was packed to overflowing with the international press corps. Strong lights blazed at the back of the room for television cameras, and the lectern bristled with microphones.

"In six days, Russia and the United States will go to war two hundred miles off the coast of Brazil in the South Atlantic Ocean," the President began. "An American task force, under the command of Rear Admiral James P. Milliken aboard the aircraft carrier *Nimitz*, will be attacked by a Russian Federal Navy task force under the direction of Admiral Nikita Vasilievich Tulayev, aboard the just-completed nuclear-powered aircraft carrier *Kremlin*."

The room was still. He had their attention. Until this moment there had been question whether PIT BULL would come off as planned, or at all. Congress had been sniping at the President because of the cost, despite the jobs the project had already created. (Others in Congress were sniping at him because too little money had been spent.) The cold war was over, the U.S. had won, why help the former Soviet Union out of its political and financial difficulties by, in effect, shoring up its military?

Reasoner had also come under sharp criticism because of the restrictions he was placing on the Rio Games. PIT BULL was to be used to bolster *present* defense contracts, not to develop totally new-concept weapons systems.

Keeping Americans at work, while keeping the world safe for democracy, was the motto.

In Russia, President Nikolayev had come under severe criticism by the civilian population for spending precious rubles on military games when half the nation was going hungry. Only the military establishment, in some ways even harder hit than many civilians (officers to the rank of major and lieutenant colonel were housed with their families in tar-paper shacks), cautiously supported the exercise. If they went on strike it would be much worse than a coal miners' strike. The entire nation would fall into anarchy. Whose fingers would end up on nuclear triggers, if that were to happen, worried a lot of people.

"The Rio Games will become an Olympics of military strategy. Javelins will be thrown, but with blunted tips and not in anger," the President said.

"The missiles and bullets launched will be nothing more than sophisticated electronic pulses and low-power laser beams. The bombs and explosives merely computer simulations."

The President looked up with the famous Reasoner smile that got him a landslide victory from Minnesota to Texas and from Washington State to Florida. "The only reality will be the ships, the planes, the personnel, and the weather. And the benefit of easing tensions not only between us and Russia but worldwide. Benefits that will continue to pay dividends well into the twenty-first century."

Reasoner's sincere smile broadened. "A world at peace is a world in which we can start to realistically reduce the deficit. And it is a world which we can proudly leave to our children and our children's children."

Two dozen hands went up at the same moment. The President nodded toward one of the women journalists, who jumped up.

"Katherine Differding, *Washington Post*. Mr. President, can you tell us how many American lives were lost when the Russians sank our research ship the *John Hopkins* in the Barents Sea yesterday? And a follow-up question: Can you confirm that the National Security Agency sent that ship to spy on the Russian Navy base at Polyarnyy, and, if so, how that incident will affect PIT BULL?"

Oh, Christ, the President said to himself, but he maintained his composure. "You may have some of your facts distorted, Katy, but you're illustrating my point for me. PIT BULL is designed to stop any and all accidents."

"Maybe we'd better arm our ships for the games, after all," someone said, but the President, warming to his answer, ignored the comment.

PART TWO

13

RIO CENTER

The actual management of Operation PIT BULL was to be conducted from a newly-constructed, windowless cement-block building on the island of Do Pai. Despite its oriental-sounding name, the island was in Rio de Janeiro's outer bay, barely six miles from the famous beach at Copacabana.

The government of Brazil had donated the entire island to the cause of world peace (in the words of President João da Costa). PIT BULL was to be only the first of several joint military exercises between the two superpowers. And future plans even called for the inclusion of other nations' military forces, such as Great Britain, France, and Germany.

One Reuters correspondent had written that if "the U.S. and Russia are shooting at each other in mock battles, perhaps they'll never want a real war."

That was the stated hope of the politicians, though there wasn't a military man who could wholeheartedly believe in it. As one unnamed French general commented: "Sooner or later one side will perceive that it has the definite advantage, and a war will begin."

At another, more cynical level, the Rio Games were being staged for an audience of potential customers of weapons systems. Military experts from a dozen nations, among them Brazil and Chile, Pakistan, India, South Korea, and Taiwan, would watch every move both sides made. To the winner would go the spoils—billions of dollars in contracts.

A large field protected by a double row of chain-link fences, topped with razor wire, contained dozens of radio antennae and huge satellite dishes that provided the Center's communications and data links.

A half mile to the south a big generating plant had been installed, with two separate backup systems so that no matter what happened the Center would never be without power.

Armed guards were posted around the entire perimeter of the small island, whose beaches were strung with barbed wire. There were no docking facilities, and not even a spot where a small boat could land.

The only way on or off the island was from a single helicopter pad, which this morning had been busy for the past three hours, ferrying VIPs and media people across from Rio's International Airport.

Vice Admiral Jeff "Deep Six" McCauley sat behind his desk in the Center staring at his two chiefs of staff, U.S. Rear Admiral Edward Sears and Russian Admiral Ilya A. Mokretsov. In less than ten minutes they were scheduled to brief the media and representatives from the U.S. and the Russian Congresses.

"And," McCauley said, his voice rumbling in his barrel chest, "nothing will go wrong, gentlemen. Absolutely nothing."

"There has been no letup in security, Admiral," the Russian said, his English perfect.

McCauley, who had been detached from the Navy, had been posted as an undersecretary of the Navy within the Department of Defense. On the luck of the draw it was decided that for this first war game, an American would be selected for overall command. There had been little question who was right for the job.

"It'll be like sticking your hand into a hornets' nest without getting it bit," the President had told him months ago when he'd made the appointment.

"PIT BULL will come off as scheduled and as planned," McCauley had said. "I guarantee it."

This morning the entire world would be briefed.

The incident with the *John Hopkins* had so far been kept out of discussions between the officers here. But McCauley had detected the first stirring of resentment between the American and Russian teams.

"I mean to nip it in the bud," McCauley said sternly to both his chiefs of staff, who stiffened in their seats. He leaned forward. "Any officer, including you two, who shows the slightest nationalism during this exercise will find himself on the next available transportation back to his home base for court-martial. Do I make myself clear?"

Both officers nodded.

McCauley loosened up a little and leaned back. "All right, now, what is the status of our guests? Are we ready to go?"

Sears glanced at his watch. "Should be ready, Admiral. They were on the last batch of credentials. Senator Wood, who flew in this morning, was giving them a little trouble, but nothing our people couldn't handle."

Mokretsov chuckled. "Have you caught Pryakhin's act? You would think he owned our Congress."

Sears had to laugh as well. "I'd like to put those two together in a locked room for twenty-four hours."

"A rubber room," the Russian said. His idiomatic English was perfect.

"I'll calm them down during my briefing," McCauley promised. "Afterward, you're going to have to show them around. Ed takes the Russian contingent, and Ilya takes the Americans. How about the television link?"

"Looks good," Sears said. "The networks brought their own technicians."

"What about our equipment?"

"We've been in constant communication with Moscow and Colorado Springs," Mokretsov said. "They've experienced no trouble whatsoever with their real-time displays. The *Nimitz* and *Kremlin* task forces are both within three days of the staging area. In fact, they're within a few hundred miles of each other by now."

"Have the crew exchanges been made yet?"

"Should happen sometime today, depending on weather," Sears said.

McCauley nodded and got to his feet. "Now we'll see what everyone else thinks of it." He stepped into his small bathroom, where he checked his uniform in the mirror.

McCauley concealed his own grave doubts about what would happen in the coming days. Especially in light of what had happened in the Barents Sea, and what was contained in the for-your-eyes-only message he had received last night from Dave Maxwell and Horace Walker.

Technically he outranked them. But what did you say to a JC2 and a JC3? They weren't irresponsible men. He'd known and served with both of them for many years.

Nevertheless, what they were asking of him was difficult to square with his mission here, with what the President had personally asked of him.

But he was a soldier, and his job was defending his country.

Operations for the Center were conducted in what was called the Pit (after PIT BULL), which was housed in a large equipment-filled room.

Electronic consoles were arranged in a U, all facing a large three-dimensional electronic map which would show them what was happening in real time at any point beneath, upon, or above the sea.

At the opposite end of the Pit, McCauley sat with his two

chiefs of staff overseeing the actual moment-to-moment details.

Along each leg of the U, equal numbers of American and Russian technicians and officers manned their consoles that monitored, by pairs, four broad areas of the war game: air operations, which included fighter/interceptor aircraft, search-and-rescue planes, ASW units, and bombers both sides would be putting up; missile defense, which included all missiles from submarines, surface ships, or aircraft; surface operations of both the American and Russian task forces; and submarine operations, which in this case worked with an extreme handicap—they did not have the benefit of a SOSUS or a LARISSA network to help them keep track of their boats. Instead, there were several ASW frigates with powerful sonar suites, which included the SQR-18 towed arrays, ASW TDS (tactical-data system), and greatly upgraded radars.

Lieutenant Commander Lee MacArthur, the American chief of missile-defense operations, flicked a test indicator on his console.

"Shit," he swore when the red light remained on.

He flipped another series of switches to isolate the problem. He was getting an indication of an armed missile, but could not pinpoint it, not even with his test-and-search program. It was the same problem they'd had two days ago on the Russian console.

He hit his comms switch. "Georgi, what are you showing on your board? Missile-readiness locks?"

Lieutenant Colonel Georgi Borisovich Maslovski's console was on the opposite leg of the big U. He flipped some switches. "Looks like the same trouble we had Tuesday." He looked across the distance separating them and mouthed the words *fuck your mother*, and grinned. It was the Russian national expression of disgust. But profanity was forbidden on any communications circuit. During the war game the entire system would be monitored. Any conversation might be broadcast to radio and television in every country in the world.

MacArthur smiled and shrugged. "It's in my panel this time. I'll call a technician."

"It looks as if you have a reverse in polarity. My board is normal."

"Either that, or my board is normal and it's yours that's reversed."

The Russian laughed. "Mine was just fixed last week, remember?"

"Well, we'd better get on it, Georgi, because they'll all be in here in an hour for the test run."

CVN 68 *NIMITZ*

The hatch opened and the compact, well-built officer stepped through.

"Admiral on the bridge," the Marine Guard shouted, snapping to attention, as did everyone else.

"As you were," Rear Admiral James Milliken said, crossing the small bridge and climbing up into his swivel command chair with its view out across the flight deck.

"The Russian techs are on their way over, Admiral," the ship's skipper, Captain Carleton Stewart, said. He was a taller man than Milliken, and his hair had gone white several years ago, lending him an older, more studious air than the admiral, though at forty-five he was eight years younger.

The seas were starting to build again. This time the meteorologists were predicting ten-to-twelve-footers with winds above thirty knots. The flying weather was not impossible yet. In fact, there wasn't much sensation of motion aboard the huge ship, even in these conditions, but Milliken would be glad as soon as the Russians were aboard, and their chopper safely off.

Dave Maxwell had been understandably upset. They had talked last night by encrypted telephone, and Milliken had been able to hear in his voice that they were wary that the

Barents situation might only be the tip of a large and ugly Ukrainian iceberg.

"It's General Normav, Jim. That tough bastard has taken over as marshal. We're getting some pretty solid indications that Normav and his Army-Land group through Admiral Ryabov had a hand in what happened up north."

"Why, Dave? What the hell could he want?"

"We don't know yet. But you know that he had possible connections to the near miss on Ukrainian President Myakotnik. Combined with the fact he's surrounded himself with his old cronies, it all adds up to something ominous."

Milliken let it sink in for a beat. The JC3 had not called him at sea on a secure line merely to chat about the state of post-Soviet-breakup politics. He wanted something. "I'm listening, Dave."

"You're going to have to play this one by ear, but I want you to be ready out there."

"Ready for what?" Milliken had a fair idea what Maxwell was trying to say, but he wasn't going to make it easier. He needed to hear it specifically out of the mouth of his boss.

"For anything. The *Nimitz* is a valuable resource. I expect that under the circumstance you will maintain a proper defensive posture."

"Can't do much with safetied weapons systems."

"But the *Nimitz* must be protected."

"I understand, Admiral. We'll manage here. But I want to be advised of any change in your intelligence estimates."

"Will do," Maxwell said. "In the meantime, how is Carleton doing?"

"He knows his ship, no doubt about it."

"So does Borodin, the skipper of the *Kremlin*."

"What about Jeff McCauley?" Milliken asked. "Have you talked with him about this?"

"A little while ago. He'll be on the lookout from his consoles in Rio Center. But if it's going to happen, it might start up too fast for him to pull the switch. Or they might be bringing up other resources."

It was about what Milliken expected.

"What about us, Dave? Are we bringing in any resources that I should know about?"

"Not yet," Maxwell said tersely. "Keep this to yourself for now. I don't want anyone going off half-cocked."

"It's Carleton Stewart's ship. I think he should be told. And he'll want to tell his exec, Tom Mannings."

"I'll leave that up to you, Jim. But I want this kept contained."

"Right, Admiral."

Milliken hadn't got much sleep last night. Around two he had rung for his steward to bring him some tea and toast, and had spent an hour writing a letter to his wife. At six he went down to the gymnasium, where he played some one-on-one basketball with Tony Trautman, one of his Marine bodyguards, and afterward had taken a long hot shower and eaten a light breakfast.

"What's the ETA on our Russians?" he asked Stewart.

"Should be touching down in about fifteen minutes."

"Where's Tom Manning?"

Stewart looked sharply at him. He suspected that something was going on. "Back in the ASW center."

"Have him meet us in your battle cabin."

"Now?"

"On the double. I've got something to say to both of you before that Russian chopper lands."

"Aye, Admiral." Stewart called back to the ASW center and told his exec to meet him.

He followed Milliken aft, to the tiny cabin just off the bridge that he used during an actual battle. The Marine guard at the door came to attention.

"Admiral off the bridge," he intoned. "Captain off the bridge."

"What's up?" Stewart asked.

"Something that you're not going to like, Carleton."

Lieutenant Commander Tom Manning knocked once and entered the captain's battle cabin. While Stewart looked older than his years, Manning's baby face made him seem barely in his twenties. But in the parlance of some of the ratings who had come up against him and lost, he was one tough son of a bitch.

"Have a seat, Tom, the admiral has something for us," Stewart said.

Manning sat on the bunk.

"What I'm about to tell you will not go beyond this cabin except as needed to carry out my . . . recommendations," Milliken began.

With many officers such a statement was the same as saying: Here are your orders, but they really aren't orders; if you screw it up, I'll deny giving you such orders; you're on your own. But Milliken wasn't the kind of officer who would abandon his men. Stewart and Manning both knew that.

"I spoke with Dave Maxwell last night. He and General Walker are concerned about some possible dangers in PIT BULL. Concerned enough to share them with me."

Manning and Stewart exchanged a glance. "They want us to arm our weapons, just in case, is that it, sir?" Manning said. "Because of the Barents Sea thing?"

Milliken nodded.

"Begging your pardon, Admiral," Manning said, "but I think it's about time. No telling what the opposition is doing."

Milliken looked at the young officer for a moment or two and then turned to Steward. "Do you agree, Carleton?"

Stewart nodded. "Yes. But we're going to have to keep this from most of my crew, and from the Russian technicians who'll be aboard watching, I suspect, for just that— arming of weapons."

"I agree. Any ideas?"

"Well, first of all, we concentrate on our airpower. That's what we're all about here. We're going to have to rely on the ASW monitors to warn us of any new submarine resources."

"How about our Sea Sparrow missiles, or the Vulcan Phalanx guns?"

"Our entire basic point-defense missile system aboard will have to come second with those Russians aboard. We'll play that part by ear." Stewart turned to his exec. "I'll leave that up to your discretion, Tom. Just don't get caught."

"You're going to have to include Brad on this," Milliken said. Lieutenant Commander Brad Albright was the commanding officer of the three-thousand-man air wing.

"I'll talk to him as soon as we get the Russians settled in," Stewart said. "What about Rio Center, have they been advised?"

"Maxwell said he talked to Jeff McCauley. But the real decisions are going to be made by those pilots up there."

Stewart nodded grimly. "I'd take them any day in an all-out shooting war. But now we're talking about preventing one."

DOME: COLORADO SPRINGS

Physically, the DOME Control Center Link was nothing more than a jet-fighter cockpit canopy connected to an extremely sophisticated weapons-tactics trainer, in which pilots could simulate air-battle conditions, and a three-dimensional holographic battle-display system (HBDS) that would show a view outside the canopy of what was happening in a real or simulated battle.

Navy Lieutenant Luke Hardell, CO of the Stingers (UFA-113), the *Nimitz* F/A-18L Hornet squadron, zippered his flight suit, picked up his helmet, and walked out of the locker room into the main control center.

They had been training for this for the past four and a half months. And after today, they would be heading south to join their air wing aboard the *Nimitz*.

"Who are you sending up for the final flight?" Lieutenant Commander Albright had asked him by telephone last night.

"It's gotta be me, Commander," Hardell had replied.

Hardell had toyed with the idea of sending one of their

least experienced pilots (they didn't have a "worse" one) up against the Russians in this final simulation. He'd hoped that the Russians would send up one of their best, and in this way he'd be able to assess just how good or bad they actually were.

But in the end he had decided against it, for several reasons, not the least of which was his own ego. They'd been training in the DOME now all these weeks in preparation for PIT BULL, flying mostly against the computer that simulated the tactics of the Russian MiG-29 Fulcrum, which was the main aircraft aboard the *Kremlin*, and in many ways quite similar to the Hornet.

This time, at last, the connections had been made through Rio Center so that an American pilot here would be able to fly against a Russian pilot in the DOME at Moscow.

He had not been told who the Russian pilot would be, but he had a fair guess that the Fulcrum air wing CO, Captain Nikolai V. Ivliyev, would be the one, and for just about the same reasons he would be flying this furball (which was the term for an all-out dogfight).

From what he had read of the intelligence briefings, Ivliyev was damned good—one of the best of the new breed of Russian naval aviators. A couple of years ago, their Navy had developed a "top gun" program similar to the Americans'. It was producing some talented drivers.

Hardell hoped that it would be Ivliyev today.

Lieutenant Colonel Bob Wurldorf, the CO of DOME: Colorado Springs was on the telephone at one of the many consoles. He did not look happy. He beckoned Hardell over.

His wing leaders and pilots were seated behind glass in the observation center. Hardell waved as he walked to his simulator cockpit and got back the thumbs-up signs.

"Kick Ass" was their motto for this exercise. He mouthed the words and could almost hear them laughing.

Wurldorf put down the telephone and looked up at Hardell. "Sorry, Luke, but it's been called off."

"What?" Hardell asked, deflated.

"There may be a technical problem in Moscow, I don't

know, but the Russians want to call it off. They're not going to play this time. I'm going to get authorization to keep your squadron here for another twenty-four hours. Still gives us plenty of time to get you down to the *Nimitz*."

Hardell looked up at the simulator cockpit, its canopy open, another thought coming into his head. "Commander, are we still hooked up with Moscow, or did they pull the plug?"

"What have you got in mind?"

"Maybe we can shake them up a little bit."

Wurldorf grinned. "I don't know, kid. Let me check it out." He hit the comms switch, connecting him with the DOME-Rio Center liaison officer, Naval Commander Ken Adams.

"Ken, what's our link status through Rio Center? Are we still connected with Moscow?"

"Sure are."

"All right," Wurldorf said, looking at Hardell. "Stand by, Luke wants to run a . . . let's call it a link check, just to make sure we're flying over the same bit of real estate."

"They called it off, but it's your ball game."

"Go to it," Wurldorf told Hardell. "They'll probably ignore you."

"They might not respond, Commander, but I don't think they'll ignore me." Hardell climbed up the metal ladder to the platform. He stepped down into the Hornet's cockpit, strapped himself in, and pulled on his helmet, plugging its thick electronics cord into the socket that connected him to the onboard computer that operated his HMD (helmet-mounted display) system. The Lexan canopy came down and he began flipping the switches and controls to start up.

Suddenly he was on the deck of the *Nimitz*. The view from his cockpit was three-dimensional, and he could feel the pitch and roll of the deck. The twin jet engines came into the green, and a crewman outside on the deck gave him the takeoff signal. He firewalled his throttle controls, and the steam-powered catapult slammed into his back, shoving him toward the end of the flight deck: He was airborne.

A quarter of a mile out from the *Nimitz*, Hardell hit his afterburners. He hauled back on the stick, rising into the deep blue sky at a climb rate in excess of fifty thousand feet per minute, the vast basin of the ocean opening up beneath him.

There were no landmarks outside his canopy other than the empty sky and empty sea (except for the *Nimitz*, far away now to his stern), nor were any target data showing in his HMD. This time there was supposed to have been nothing in his displays except the Russian MiG-29 Fulcrum. Even that, however, was not up. The skies were his alone.

At fifty thousand feet, Hardell leveled off, did a couple of eight-points rolls—not an easy maneuver at his speed in excess of Mach 1.6— and accelerated quickly beyond Mach 2.

Seventy-five miles out from the *Nimitz*, he snapped left and dove, activating his target-acquisition radar, as his speed built up even further.

"Come on," he said to himself. "Here I am, you bastards. You're not going to leave me up here all by my lonesome, are you?"

DOME: MOSCOW

Captain Nikolai Vasilievich Ivliyev sat in the DOME cockpit simulator of his MiG-29 Fulcrum. He had powered up his systems, but all his other controls had been blocked by the technician now working on the main data-link controls for Rio liaison.

He had his helmet on, and from where he sat he could not only look out the canopy down the flight deck of the CVN *Kremlin* but could also see in his HMD that the Americans had sent up one of their Hornets despite the fact that the exercise had been postponed.

The Hornet had rapidly accelerated as it climbed to more than fifteen thousand meters. Now it was diving fifteen hundred knots, its target-acquisition radar systems illuminating an area of thousands of square miles.

Suddenly everything changed.

He leaned forward against his restraints. The Hornet had suddenly slowed down, to below Mach 1, and had made an exceedingly high-G turn to starboard. But that was impossible . . . or was it?

As he continued to watch the American plane, his mind was racing to a dozen different possibilities including equipment failure on his end. He finally centered, however, on an intelligence estimate that he'd read some months ago. The Americans, it seemed, were installing thrust-reversal systems aboard some of their naval jets. Possibly aboard the Hornets.

Was this what he was seeing?

If the Americans were able to suddenly to slow their fighter/interceptors, they would have the automatic edge in any aerial fight.

He flipped his comms switch. "Control."

"Da."

"Are you showing the American on your board?"

"Yes, we are, Comrade Captain," the controller said.

"Are we recording it?"

"Negative."

"Why not?" Ivliyev demanded harshly.

"Because it is of no value, Nikolai Vasilievich," another voice came over his headset. "Stand down now." This one he recognized as Colonel Vladimir N. Kabalin, the commanding officer of DOME: Moscow.

"Yes, Comrade Colonel, I am standing down," Ivliyev said, but his eyes lingered on his HMD as the American naval fighter/interceptor headed back to the *Nimitz*.

But it was of value, he told himself. The American pilot had made a mistake showing him this. A very large mistake.

14

WASHINGTON, D.C.

Bill Lane gained seven hours flying west in the supersonic SR-91 spy plane. They lifted off from Bear around 11:30 P.M., and, with a flying time of a little under two hours, touched down at Andrews Air Force Base at 9:30 P.M.

He watched the sun coming up in the deep blue sky and then retreat below the horizon again and disappear behind them as they screamed across the North Atlantic.

Lane managed to doze off and on in the cramped seat, but the oxygen mask was too tight on his face, and the flight was too short to get any real rest.

A dark blue Chevrolet sedan was waiting in the shadows beside the spy plane's hangar as they taxied up. The canopy opened, and Lane pulled off his helmet as the ground crewman scrambled up the ladder and helped him with his three-point restraint system.

"Thanks for the ride, Zach,"

Taylor stood up in the cockpit and stuck out his hand.

"No sweat, Mr. Lane. But can you answer me one question? Are you a spook?"

Lane had to laugh. "Nope, I'm no James Bond. In fact, I've never even seen a Walther PPK."

"Right."

Lane climbed over the edge of the cockpit and down the ladder. The rear door of the Chevrolet opened and he hurried to it. A tractor was connected to the SR-91 so they could get it inside, out of sight as quickly as possible. All the 91s were supposed to be in mothballs.

Ben Lewis was waiting in the rear seat, the stub of an unlit cigar clenched in the corner of his mouth.

"How was your flight?" the NSA Russian Division director asked.

"Amazing," Lane said.

"You did a good job for us," Lewis said. "The President sends his regards. But a lot has happened that you don't know about."

Lane looked sharply at his old friend. "Is it that Ukranian sub?"

"Apparently she's broken out into the open Atlantic. No one knows why yet. But we might get lucky. One of ours is trailing her."

"The *Boston*?"

"Yes."

"If he's not careful he'll start a shooting war up there," Lane said.

"Right idea, wrong ocean."

"PIT BULL?"

"And a lot more," Lewis said. "But you're going to hear all about it from the right people in College Park."

It was in Maryland, northwest of Washington, where the Director of Central Intelligence's house was.

Lane sat back in his seat, content to relax. Lewis wouldn't tell him anything else in any event. He also resisted the urge to try to figure out what was coming. He simply did not have the facts, except that the *Pogin* was apparently heading south, and something was up with PIT BULL. Both were scary.

COLLEGE PARK, MARYLAND

The DCI's huge home was at the end of a tree-lined driveway just off the grounds of the University of Maryland. They were stopped at the main gate, where they had to get out and submit to a body search with electronic wands. There were a lot of guards along the driveway, and, Lane supposed, in the woods nearer to the house. He had never seen such tight security around the DCI.

"It wasn't guns they were looking for back there," Lewis said as their driver took them the rest of the way up the driveway. "They wanted to know if either one of us was wearing a wire."

The implications of that took Lane's breath away. "What the hell is going on?"

Lewis sighed as they pulled up to the front entrance of the house. "We just inherited this mess. So now it's up to people like us to straighten it out."

"I'll listen to General Murphy, Ben. But that's all I'm going to promise."

"That's all we're asking."

They were admitted to the house by a civilian guard, who took Lane's overnight bag for him, and he and Lewis went back to the study in the rear. Lewis knocked and they went in.

There were two men in the large, comfortable study besides DCI General Roland Murphy, and both of them came as a disturbing surprise to Lane.

"Hello, Bill," Murphy said. "Ben." He motioned them to have a seat. "I believe everybody knows each other here."

Lewis nodded at the other two men as he sat down across the desk from Murphy. NSA Director Robert Keyes sat in a heavy easy chair, his legs crossed. The President's National Security Adviser, Bill Townsend, sat on the couch next to him. No one looked relaxed or happy.

"I thought you did a particularly good job for us up there," Murphy said. "We all do."

"Thank you, sir," Lane replied, keeping his voice even.

"How much have you been told?"

"Just that the *Pogin* broke out into the Atlantic and that one of our submarines is on her tail."

Murphy nodded. "There has been a lot going on since you left, but we don't have all the pieces yet. We think that the *Pogin*'s attack on the *John Hopkins* was just the opening maneuver by a Ukrainian military faction in an effort to wreck PIT BULL."

"Something I suggested before I went up there," Lane reminded them.

"And you also told us that you believed General Normav was behind this."

"What's happened?" Lane asked, a sudden chill passing through him.

"General Normav has been appointed Marshal of all Ukrainian Armed Forces."

"Christ," Lane said. "PIT BULL will have to be canceled."

"The Man won't do it," Townsend said. "He and Nikolayev spoke. McCauley is already in Rio briefing the media and the politicians."

"Just what he wanted," Murphy interjected.

"Yes," Townsend said. "The *Nimitz* is barely three days out, and the *Kremlin* is only a couple of hundred miles behind."

"Well within air-strike range," Keyes said, breaking his silence. "Two of the most powerful armadas the world has ever seen are in the same piece of ocean, with a madman on the loose trying to start a shooting war between us and the Russians."

Lane's brain was racing through the various possibilities. "The *Pogin* will not be able to make it that far in time. Has there been any hint from the Russians that they might want to delay the games?"

"None."

"The *Pogin* will have something more to do with this, I'd bet almost anything on it," Lane said. He turned to Keyes. "Sir, I'd like to be detached from my regular duties for the time being. I'd like to look into this."

"It's already done. You'll go through Ben Lewis so far as practicable. But you're working for the Agency now, directly under Roland."

"I'm going to need unlimited access to all our files and the Agency's archives."

"Under the circumstances I don't see how you can be denied," Murphy said. "But no one other than us in this room is to know what you're up to."

"I'll need to work with someone in the Pentagon. Perhaps General Mooreland . . ."

"No," Murphy cut him off. "I'll have someone call you."

"Who?"

"Either Dave Maxwell or Horace Walker. They want to arm our weapons systems down there without the Russians knowing about it."

It was about what Lane had expected, and it made sense. "The next question. Does the CIA have any indication that Marshal Leonov's death was *not* accidental?"

Murphy's lips compressed. "Do you think he was murdered?"

"It would fit with what Normav has been doing. Leonov may have been on to him. They were old friends."

"No matter, Normav has won."

"Unless he is caught, and the information gets out," Lane said.

Townsend nodded his approval. "This time Myakotnik would have to be convinced."

"Could lead to a coup attempt," Murphy said.

"I don't think so, sir," Lane said. "Normav and his old guard are in the minority now. Most of the Ukrainian officers' corps are satisfied to live under the rule of civil law.

Ten or fifteen years ago it might have been different, but not now."

"I agree," Townsend said. "The problem is, how do we prove Normav killed the marshal?"

"We won't know that until we go looking," Lane said. "In the meantime, all of this could be circumstantial. PIT BULL may come off exactly as planned."

"I don't think you believe that," Murphy said.

"No, sir, I do not."

CVN 68 *NIMITZ*

The weather in the South Atlantic continued to deteriorate all through the afternoon and evening, so that by 0200 some seas were breaking over the bow of the mammoth aircraft carrier.

There is not room enough belowdecks aboard an aircraft carrier to store its entire complement of planes and choppers, so fully one-third of the eighty-eight-aircraft wing had to be stowed on deck.

The flight crews worked most of the afternoon transferring the vital Tomcats, Hornets, and ASW aircraft below, leaving only the transports and AWACS and some other equipment tied topsides. There had not been room, however, for two Hornets.

Ships of the Nimitz class seldom encountered seas like this, large enough to toss them around.

It had begun to rain, and the temperature had dropped to just a few degrees above freezing. This was winter in the southern ocean.

At sunset the flight deck was placed off limits for all but essential personnel. At this hour there was no one topsides, or at least there should not have been.

A sturdy man, dressed in Navy dungarees, a watch cap, and a nylon windbreaker, emerged from a hatch in the lower deck and hurried up the ladder on the outside of the hull ten feet to the open flight deck. He had to hold on for his life.

Reaching the flight deck, he clutched a small tool kit to his chest as he ran to one of the two F/A-18A Hornets lashed down under protective canvas. He had been assured that no one would be here, and no lookouts would be maintained from the island.

All of that was not true. He was not alone.

Ducking beneath the canvas, the man quickly strapped a low-powered penlight to his forehead and hurriedly undid the fasteners that held the avionics-bay access panel in place just forward of the starboard wing.

In under a minute he had the panel dropped. Although he wore a Navy uniform, he was neither Navy nor American, but he knew the Hornet and her avionics as well as any technician aboard.

Using a tiny propane torch, and working as rapidly as he could under the conditions, he unsoldered four pairs of wires and switched their polarity before resoldering them back to their terminals.

He opened a smaller access panel on the ASQ-173 laser spot tracker and reversed the polarity of a single set of leads. He connected a tiny electronics test set to the fighter's main avionics and weapons-aiming systems bus, flipped a couple of switches, and waited for the complicated circuitry to do its job.

Moments later, three lights on the tiny panel winked green. He disconnected the set, pocketed it, and methodically rebuttoned the access panels.

He was finished within five minutes from the time he had ducked under the canvas. He slipped back out onto the open deck, the cold wind wonderful on his overheated face.

Balancing himself against the rise and fall of the deck, he made his way back to the base of the island, past one of the parked Grumman E-2C Hawkeye AWACS.

Something slammed into his back, dropping him to one knee. A deep wave of dizziness rose around him, and sparks filled his eyes.

He looked up into the barrel of a U.S. military 9mm automatic handgun, and then into a man's face.

"You," he said.

His killer nodded. "Yes," he said, and he pulled the trigger, the single shot hitting the man in the forehead, slamming him backward.

The killer threw the pistol over the side and then quickly picked up the tool kit and tossed it overboard as well.

Then he disappeared down the ladder and through a hatch into the bowels of the big ship, his part of Normav's plan completed.

NATIONAL SECURITY AGENCY

Bill Lane searched through NSA's computer-stored records at Fort Meade for Ukrainian staff realignments over the past twelve months. Not only those under General Normav but also those under Admiral Ryabov, chief of the Ukrainian Navy, and Admiral Dyukov, the commander of Black Sea Fleet, the main Ukrainian submarine branch.

It was unusual that an Army officer, even one so powerful as Normav, would have any control over the Navy, and yet it became apparent that not only had Normav been responsible for a lot of high-level naval staff appointments but had cross-serviced a number of his people—Army to Navy.

He worked through the early morning hours. He'd always had that ability (his wife would have said "curse") to concentrate.

He was tired, though, and he looked up from his computer screen as the numbers and letters began to blur, and stared for a moment at the pleasant mountain scene painted on the wall on the other side of the fake window. It had been a long time, six years now, since his divorce, and still not a day went by when he didn't think about her. More so these days, for some reasons. He would emerge from his absolute concentration and ask himself what had gone wrong.

He had been tromping around the jungles of northern Laos for three months trying to find the pieces of a NSA satellite that had gone down. When he emerged from the jungle, the divorce papers were waiting for his signature and Kitty had gone out to California to be with her brother and sister-in-law.

He'd flown immediately out to see her, but she had refused steadfastly to talk with him. And that was that.

There were no children, and she had asked for nothing except her personal belongings. He had not heard a word from her since.

Turning back to his computer, he focused again on what was scrolling across the screen. He was looking for a pattern, because behind any pattern there was human intervention of some sort.

NSA maintained not only a series of satellites, such as the KH-11, KH-12, and the latest KH-15, most of them in geosynchronous orbit over China and the former Soviet Union, but they also devised and maintained all the cryptographic equipment used by the U.S. government and military; devised codes and broke the enemies' codes; maintained telephone-intercept equipment in a dozen cities including, of course, Moscow and Kiev.

With a budget half again larger than the CIA's, the National Security Agency was in the business of collecting information by the computerful and it had not slowed down with the end of the cold war. In fact, at Fort Meade, NSA operated the most powerful combination of computers and memory anywhere in the world.

There was a pattern, of course, to Normav's moves. And it emerged in two ways. The first was the timing. All these appointments had begun about a year ago, shortly after the abortive attempt on Ukrainian President Myakotnik's life. And second, all the moves involved men loyal to Normav.

The Ukrainian KGB, from what Lane was able to gather, had remained neutral, taking a wait-and-see attitude. It was possible they thought Normav had a real chance of unseating Myakotnik. But the Military Intelligence Service, the GRU, was firmly in Normav's camp.

It was more than that, though. In the first place, they had no proof that Normav wanted to wreck PIT BULL, or worse, wanted some sort of a military incident to come from PIT BULL. Nor could he find any connection between the apparently unrelated incident of the sinking of the *John Hopkins* in the Barents Sea and the death of Russia's Marshal Leonov. But they were connected, there was no doubt of it in his mind.

He brought up a map of the South Atlantic Ocean region and punched up the latest position reports on the *Nimitz* and *Kremlin* task forces. They were barely eighteen hundred sea miles from PIT BULL's position off the coast of Brazil. Which would put them in place within seventy-two hours.

Everything seemed normal down there, not only aboard the task force ships but in Rio Center as well.

He switched his attention to the satellite link between the DOME in Colorado Springs and its Russian counterpart near Moscow. The link was open.

Lane brought the DOME training program up from memory, to analyze the data.

But there was nothing. Both DOMEs were connected, as if in the ready mode for an exercise, but nothing was running.

It was probably a test, he told himself, switching the program off. Everyone would be getting jittery now that they were so close.

He went back to a map of the world. This time he reduced his scale so that he was seeing both hemispheres of the Atlantic Ocean, all the way from the Barents Sea to where the *Kremlin* and *Nimitz* task forces were still steaming south. He brought up the available data from SOSUS Control which showed the last known position of the *Pogin* and the *Boston*, with a probable speed and course.

He then extrapolated the *Pogin*'s course, or choice of courses, to the south, assuming first that she would maintain her same speed and heading, and then in another scenario, assuming that she would soon go to maximum speed, which was nearly forty-five knots submerged.

The lines all ran out into the Atlantic Ocean, past Iceland, and directly southwest toward New York City.

Lane stared at the screen for a long time. The *Pogin* could have no real interest in New York . . . or New London. It was only a lone submarine, and U.S. naval forces were not so vulnerable there.

But in seventy-two hours, the *Pogin* could be well within striking range of the sea lanes between Europe and the U.S. east coast.

That would make some sense only if the *Pogin* were expecting a war and wanted to be in the right spot to prevent the Atlantic Fleet from bolstering the *Nimitz* task force.

He continued staring at the screen for a long time. He was missing something. The *Pogin* had broken loose either to threaten our east coast or to make us *think* she was threatening our coast.

Lane was stopped by that last notion. The incident with the *John Hopkins* had caught our attention in a large way. Enough so that we were bound to keep a close eye on the *Pogin*, and certainly notice that she had broken out.

We would be watching her. Diverting resources from elsewhere?

He expanded his map to include the Pacific Ocean and Cape Horn at the tip of the South American continent, and then picked up his secure phone and punched in a Pentagon number.

"Whiz Bang," the OD answered. It was the code name for the Command Center.

"This is Big Eye. Stand by for an operational test of Blue Horizons," Lane said. It was the code name for a NSA satellite.

The OD hesitated for a moment. "Sorry, Big Eye, I show nothing in my schedule."

"Admiral Maxwell called for it. Is he there?"

"No, sir."

"Connect me with his house, then."

"I'm sorry, sir, but . . ."

"Tell him it's Bill Lane. He'll want to speak with me."

"Yes, sir, stand by." The line went dead.

If our attention had been diverted by the *Pogin* to the North and then Central Atlantic, and if the *Kremlin* could somehow keep the *Nimitz* busy, thus diverting our attention again, what mischief could Normav be up to in the South Pacific?

What would happen if, while we were looking elsewhere, a few Ukrainian attack subs were to round the Horn into the Atlantic? They could stand by just out of detection range off the coast of Brazil waiting for the right moment to strike.

Normav was, as Director Keyes said, a madman. But would he risk war?

Was that what was happening here?

Maxwell finally came on the line. "I was expecting a call from you, Lane, but not at three o'clock in the morning."

"Sorry to bother you so late, Admiral, but I need some quick information from your people."

"Go ahead."

"That Ukrainian boomer, the *Pogin*, has broken out into the open Atlantic. Heading south."

"That's right."

"On the assumption that she is aiming for the east coast, have we put up an ASW aircraft or diverted any ASW vessels from patrol stations elsewhere?"

"Yes, as a matter of fact we have."

"A lot of ships and aircraft?"

"Enough so that we've got a real possibility of finding that bastard."

"Call them off, Admiral, because the *Pogin* isn't headed there."

"Explain yourself."

Lane did, including his fear that Normav's people may have moved a number of attack submarines into the South Atlantic.

"Whether or not that's the case, mister, I'm not going to have an attack submarine running around off our east coast undetected. You are aware of what almost happened in the Barents Sea between our boat and theirs. Howie Armstrong had a firing solution and he damned near used it. If those two come head-to-head again, especially off our coast, it's not going to be so easy to hold him back."

"Then look for him where I suggest, Admiral. Short of that, send an ELF message to *Boston*, tell her to surface for instructions."

"If he surfaces he'll lose that Ukrainian."

"Goddammit, Admiral, if I have to go over your head I will."

"Be my guest."

Lane lowered his voice. "I have no recorders on this line, and I would hope you don't."

"One moment," Maxwell said. "Go ahead."

"I know that unofficial orders were given to Admiral Milliken and Admiral Jeff McCauley. Shall I go on?"

There was a silence on the line. "We have a little time yet. Nothing is going to happen in the next few hours or so. Let's meet for breakfast." Maxwell mentioned a small restaurant in McLean. "Oh-eight-hundred. I'll be in mufti."

"Maybe you'd better bring along General Walker."

"I see," Maxwell said, finally understanding the full extent of Lane's knowledge. "He'll be there."

RIO DE JANEIRO

Copacabana had been a jewel in the night from the windows of the Presidential Suite in the Meridien-Rio luxury hotel. Standing now, looking at the gray dawn, a Bloody Mary in hand, Senator Wood was worried. When he was worried he got mad.

"Any son of a bitch thinks he can jerk me around has another thing coming. I'm a United States senator. In three years I just might become something even more powerful."

"They're playing with fire," Pamela Fisher said. "Maybe

you should fight with fire." She'd flown down from Washington with him. Tall, leggy, and blonde, at twenty-four she could hold a more intelligent conversation than most forty-year-old women Wood knew.

"I'll go to bat for my constituency any day of the week; all I ask is a little cooperation in return." Wood turned away from the window. Pamela lay naked on the big circular bed, her legs demurely crossed, her hair in disarray, her sensuous lips moist. He could not get enough of her.

"You're cochairman of the Armed Services Committee, make them listen to you."

"That's like trying to juggle with a half dozen raw eggs—out of their shells."

Pamela laughed, the sound rich. "You want to sell the military on using FUTECH hardware, but Procurements says no dice. Word has come down from the White House that there's a freeze on spending. That doesn't mean the military has stopped buying toilet paper."

"What?"

"Essentials, sweetie. No matter what happens, the military has to buy the essentials or pack up and go home. So it's simple; just make FUTECH hardware indispensable."

"Easier said than done, darlin'. Just because they're the opposition doesn't make them dumb."

"FUTECH has got the brains," Pamela said. "Maybe if the Hornet's head-up systems don't work quite up to par. Or maybe the guide-by-wire, or look-down, shoot-down, or laser-aiming subassemblies might malfunction at the wrong time."

Wood licked his lips. She was talking about sabotage.

"I'm not suggesting sabotage, sweetie. What I am suggesting is that with the right push from you, FUTECH should be able to come up with some way of ... let's say, straining those systems beyond their theoretical limits."

"You're amazing," Wood said in wonderment. He put his drink aside and went to her on the bed. She came into his arms, throwing a leg over his.

"I called Bob about that other thing," she said.

Wood stiffened. He'd told her about the warning in the parking ramp, but she had no business calling Bob Skeritt. If that bunch thought he couldn't handle the job, they would back out of their monetary arrangement with him.

"Don't worry about it," Pamela said. "He gave me the name of a man in Philly who helps out in these kinds of situations. He's expensive, but very, very discreet."

Wood rose up on one elbow. The nipples of her breasts were getting hard, and it was difficult for him to look at anything else. "Help with what kinds of situations?" he asked.

She brushed the tips of her long nails against his penis, and he flinched. "He'll find out who that asshole was in the garage, find out what his problem is, and he'll take care of it."

"When?"

"Soon," she said. She pushed him down and then straddled him. She had an amyl nitrite capsule in her hand. "Now I want to see what you're really made of, or if you're too tired to make it after last night."

15

CVN *NIMITZ*

It was eight in the morning but still dark. The storm, which the meteorologists had completely missed forecasting, was supposed to last only twenty-four hours, but in the meantime wind gusts registered fifty knots with sustained winds above forty and rising.

The giant aircraft carrier was in no danger. With a length of 1,092 feet and a beam of 134 feet she was just about impervious to anything the sea could throw at her. She displaced 90,944 tons. With a full load of stores, aviation fuel, aircraft, and men (3,300 crew and another 3,000 in the air wing) she weighed more than 180 million pounds. Her two A4W pressurized-water-cooled nuclear reactors, each capable of producing 140,000 horsepower, could push the *Nimitz* along at speeds over thirty knots, and yet she had to be refueled only at thirteen-year intervals.

Unlike most Russian ships, which fairly bristle with weapons systems, U.S. carriers lean more heavily toward complex electronic suites—although the *Nimitz* was equipped with three 20mm Vulcan/Phalanx CIWS (close-in weapons system), which were completely self-contained and automatic, and three eight-tube Mk 29 launchers for the newly retrofitted RAM Sea Sparrow close-in surface-to-air missiles. In addition, U.S. aircraft carriers always travel in battle groups from which they derive their main close-in defense capabilities.

And of course the *Nimitz* carried her awesome air wing: Twenty-four updated F-14B Tomcats; the Stingers squadron of twenty-four F/A-18L Hornets; ten A-6E Intruders, the carrier's standard heavy-duty attack bombers; four KA-6D Intruders, which were the tanker version of the bomber; four E-2C Hawkeyes, which were the AWACS (airborne early-warning/air-control platform); four Grumman EA-6B Prowlers, the standard carrier-borne electronics-warfare aircraft with its powerful ALQ-99F ECM jammer pods; ten S-3A Vikings ASW aircraft, fitted with a Univac AYK-10 to process data from its sensors; and six SH-3H Sea King helicopters, which were also used as powerful ASW platforms. Additionally the *Nimitz* carried a few noncombat choppers used mostly for transport.

Overall, the air wing aboard the *Nimitz* was as powerful as the entire air forces of most nations.

Lieutenant Tom Manning took the escalator below and went aft to the sick bay. Several medics stood around in the outer offices drinking coffee and talking.

"Good morning, sir," one of them said. "They're in the operating theater. Coffee?"

"Nope," Manning said, shaking his head. "I had the misfortune to see an autopsy about five years ago. My stomach will never forget it."

At the operating theater, he held up at the doors and looked through the windows. Dr. Dan Wilder was doing something to the head of a body lying on the gleaming stainless-steel table. Marine Captain Gregory Washington, the head of CID aboard the *Nimitz*, stood to the right.

Washington spotted Manning at the window and waved him in.

"Good morning, Commander," he said, keeping his voice low. The doctor was talking into an overhead microphone.

"Is he finishing?" Manning asked.

"Just starting, but he's come up with a few things already."

The doctor turned around. "Good morning, Tom."

"How's it look, Dan?"

"Well, he was shot twice. Once in the left shoulder, which probably knocked him to his knees, and the second time in the forehead at a slight downward angle, at point-blank range."

"Standard-issue nine-millimeter," Washington said, taking the first slug out of his pocket for Manning to see.

"We got an ID yet?" Manning asked Washington.

On any cruise of eight or nine months, there were numerous fights and usually one or two suspected homicides. Many were man-overboard situations, and usually no body was found. But every now and then tensions would erupt, possibly during a card game, and someone would pull out a knife or a gun and do his buddy in.

"We're working on it," the Marine cop said. "I've got the section chiefs doing head counts. But Doc has got something else to tell you."

Dr. Wilder, who was a Navy lieutenant and fairly new to the ship, stepped inside, giving Manning a full view of the body on the table. The chest had been partially opened. But what was worse to Manning was the head. The top had been sawn off, exposing the brain, which had been cut open.

Manning stepped back a pace, his stomach heaving.

"Oh, sorry," Wilder said. He casually draped a towel over the skull. "This kid is not an American. Bill Everett is coming down to look at the teeth. I'd say what's in his mouth was done in Europe ... possibly eastern Europe."

Manning looked at Washington. "Russian?"

"It's a thought."

"Have we got anyone of Russian or eastern European descent on the crew? Maybe someone who went back to visit?"

"I already checked. There are three possibilities, all accounted for."

"Christ," Manning said.

"Yeah. We've got six Russian observers aboard. It's going to be real interesting if this guy turns out to be one of them. Shot to death with an American military handgun."

Manning shook his head. "I'd better tell the old man. He and Milliken will want to call CINCLAN. Where was he found?"

"On the flight deck, Commander."

"This was found on his body," Washington said, taking something out of his pocket. It was a small, narrow-beam penlight, attached to an elastic head strap.

"Son of a bitch," Manning swore. "Where on the flight deck and when?"

"Around 0600, just forward of the island. About thirty feet from one of the Hawkeyes parked topsides. The officer of the deck spotted him and called me. But he'd been dead for several hours. Doc thinks sometime between midnight and 0300."

"Do you need this?" Manning asked, indicating the penlight.

"Not for the moment," the cop said. He handed it to the exec.

"Not a word to anyone outside your department, leastways not until the captain and the admiral see this."

"Yes, sir," Washington said.

Manning hurried back up to the bridge. Neither the captain nor the admiral was there. The officer of the watch said that the admiral had not been on the bridge yet this morning, and that the captain, who had been up most of the night, had retired to his battle quarters.

Manning left the bridge and knocked softly on the captain's door.

"Come," Captain Stewart called out.

Manning went inside as a small light over the captain's bunk came on. Stewart had taken off his shoes, but otherwise was fully dressed.

"Sorry to disturb you, skipper, but I thought you'd better hear what happened last night before the shit hits the fan."

Stewart picked up his telephone. "Charlie, bring me some coffee, would you please?" He hung up. "All right, Tom, what's happened this time?"

"There was a murder overnight," Manning said. "Shot in the back and once in the head at point-blank range."

Stewart nodded.

Manning pulled out the penlight and handed it to the captain. "This was found on his body. Up on the flight deck. About thirty feet from one of our Hawkeyes."

Stewart looked from the penlight to Manning. "Spell it out for me, Tom."

"Greg Washington is in on this, of course. I just left him in the dispensary with Dan Wilder, who is doing the autopsy. There was no identification on the body. But Wilder doesn't think he's American."

"What?"

"Skipper, there's a great possibility that the dead man is one of the Russians who came aboard. It's possible he was trying to sabotage one of our planes on deck, and it's likely that one of our people shot him to death, and then ran off."

"Have we started a head count?"

"Yes, sir. But it'll take some time to complete. Washington figured that we should keep this low-key."

"Yeah. Has the admiral been informed?"

"Not yet, sir."

"All right. First I want every aircraft and weapons system aboard this ship double-checked. We'll go through Colorado Springs and Rio Center as if we were making a final test on the entire system. If anything looks out of line, I want to be informed immediately."

"Aye, sir."

"Once you've got that going, I want you to have coffee with our Russian observers."

His phone buzzed. Stewart snatched it off the hook. "Where's my coffee?" He listened and then pursed his lips.

"I'll meet him in a half hour in the bridge officers' wardroom." He put down the phone.

"The Russians?" Manning asked.

"It's their team leader, Lieutenant Lemekhov. Says one of his technicians is missing."

Manning raised his eyebrows. It was obvious what was going to happen next. And it wasn't going to be very pleasant.

"I want you to get our maintenance people started on the systems checks immediately. I'd like that completed by 1200 hours. Then I want you to get back to the dispensary and have Wilder clean up that boy as good as possible. We're going to stonewall this for now. So far as we know, unless Lieutenant Lemekhov tells us different, that boy was one of ours who got into a fight over a poker game. We're going to say nothing about this thing." Stewart glanced at the penlight. "Nothing else was found on his body? Tools, anything like that? A weapon?"

"Nothing, sir. Just this."

"Whoever killed him may have taken his wallet and his money, and his tools if he had any. But why? Some sort of a cover-up?"

"I don't know, sir," Manning said.

"As soon as you're finished with that, have Washington standing by in the dispensary. I'll bring Lieutenant Lemekhov down to identify the body. And afterward . . . well, we'll just have to see what happens."

Lieutenant Viktor Ivanovich Lemekhov stood at the head of the operating table. Dr. Wilder held back the sheet so he could look at the body.

"Is this your man, Lieutenant?" Captain Washington asked.

Lemekhov nodded. "It is Gennadi Chalkin. Who has done this, and who has authorized an autopsy?"

"We thought he was one of ours, Lieutenant," Wilder said. "He had no ID and was dressed in American naval dungarees."

"Can you explain that?" Washington asked.

"I need explain nothing to you, Captain," Lemekhov said. "I must first call my captain. Investigators will have to be sent over."

"Negative," Stewart said from the doorway. "This is my ship, and my people will handle the investigation. We will find out who killed him . . . and we will find out why."

Lemekhov looked from Stewart to Manning to Washington. "Am I to be held prisoner here, then?"

"No, you may call your ship, and you and your people may leave if you wish. However, no other Russian personnel will be allowed aboard."

"At least allow me to have his body returned to his ship."

"I will speak to your captain myself. As soon as this weather abates a little, our technicians will be going over to the *Kremlin*. They can take his body along."

"That is not acceptable, Captain."

"You have no choice."

CVN 142 *KREMLIN*

The *Kremlin* was Russia's only nuclear-powered aircraft carrier. Her sister ship, the *Gorkiy*, was stalled unfinished in the yard, and would likely remain there. The Russians had no money to complete her. But President Nikolayev had wanted at least one carrier, if for no other reasons than national pride and jobs.

As aircraft carriers go, the *Kremlin* was not particularly large; at 984 feet in length and a beam of 125 feet, she displaced 75,000 tons fully loaded. But each of her two nuclear reactors were capable of producing more than 200,000 shaft horsepower, pushing the big ship at speeds over thirty-five knots. She was faster and more maneuverable than the Nimitz-class carriers of the American fleet, and much better armed.

Her weapons systems included sixty-four SS-N-12

surface-to-surface missiles (SSM), seventy-two SA-N-2 surface-to-air missiles (SAM), forty SA-N-4 SAMs; four 76mm cannons; eight 30mm Gatling guns; ten 533mm torpedo tubes; and an antisubmarine array of weapons which included a pair of SUW-N-1 missile launchers and a pair of twelve-barrel RBU-6000 (antisubmarine rocket launchers).

Her air wing was of necessity smaller than that aboard the *Nimitz*, consisting of only twenty MiG-29 Fulcrums; ten Sukhoi 27 Flankers (both of them Mach 2.3-plus fighter/ interceptors); sixteen Ka-Ag Helix ASW helicopters carrying torpedoes, sonobuoys, dipping sonars, and magnetic-anomaly detectors (MAD); and four Helix B helicopters to provide over-the-horizon targeting data in real time.

In a fight, it was believed in the West that the Nimitz-class carriers would be successful because of their superior electronics and air wing. In the East, strategists believed that the Kremlin-class carriers would win because of their superior weaponry. After all, they argued, the last carrier left afloat and operational would determine the victor. All the *Nimitz*'s aircraft would be worthless if their platform was at the bottom of the sea.

Testing the carriers was one of the reasons for PIT BULL. But that was still days away. Now there were other problems to be faced.

Admiral Nikita V. Tulayev and Captain First Rank Viktor Mikhailovich Borodin sat across the broad conference table facing the fleet *zampolit*, Colonel Nikolai S. Smolin, a husky man with a round, bald head and a bulldog face that matched his personality.

"We can force the issue, Comrade Admiral," Smolin told Tulayev.

"And just how might we accomplish that, Comrade Zampolit?" the admiral asked sarcastically. "Fire a missile across the *Nimitz*'s bow?" He was not afraid of Smolin, though in actuality the *zampolit* wielded more power aboard than did an admiral, even the flag.

Smolin thumped the table. "It is one of our boys lying dead over there, killed by a zealous American cowboy!"

Tulayev stifled a smile. The man was impossibly melodramatic. "I spoke with Admiral Milliken. They are just as interested in bringing the culprit to justice as we are. His body will be returned to us with the transfer of the American team here."

"I say we must not wait ..."

Admiral Tulayev held up a hand to silence the man. "Unless you mean to take over this entire operation, Comrade Zampolit, which would require a direct order from REDFLEET, you will hold your place. PIT BULL is the wish of our President, and nothing will stand in its way. Have I made myself clear?"

"Perhaps too clear, Admiral," Smolin said.

Captain Borodin leaned forward. "I will call Captain Stewart and lodge a formal protest. But we will not take this any further, Nikki. On this there will be no further discussion."

Smolin held himself in check.

Tulayev had closely watched the exchange. There was something between the two men, he thought. Some under-the-table agreement, some vodka-and-blini deal that excluded the chain of command. But there was nothing he could do about it. An officer's effectiveness stemmed from only one thing: his subordinates' willingness to follow his orders. He was thankful that PIT BULL was only an exercise. If this were the real thing, he would have Borodin and Smolin replaced ... if that were possible.

"We will check the air wing and our weapons system one last time," he said.

"As you wish, Admiral," Captain Borodin said. "Do you wish to go through our DOME?"

"Yes, but this time via Rio Center. It is time to have a dress rehearsal."

"I understand," the captain said. "The weapons systems will all be safetied, but not unloaded."

As much as that last part worried him, Tulayev felt there

was no way around it. A fleet so mighty as the *Kremlin*'s could not come halfway around the world without protection. It was simply unthinkable.

A lot of eyes around the world would be watching them, evaluating their performance.

Admiral Tulayev went topside to the bridge, where he got up into his swivel chair. The weather was not good, but the meteorologists promised a break sometime this evening.

Somewhere to the west, about three hundred kilometers away, the *Nimitz* and her battle group were steaming steadily south on a course roughly parallel to that of the *Kremlin* This was theoretically as close as the carriers were supposed to get to each other.

But Tulayev had a few surprises up his sleeve. He could not hope ultimately to win against the American's superior air group. But the *Nimitz* herself had a fatal weakness. One which he meant to exploit to the fullest.

He picked up his secure tactical telephone. "Connect me with Admiral Milliken aboard the *Nimitz*."

While he waited for his call to go through, Tulayev stared out the windscreen toward the bow, the huge waves now breaking over the flight deck.

When the fight came it would be awesome, whether or not it was for real. Besides the two carriers, each fleet was composed of nine ships. Under his command was a pair of Kanin-class destroyers with full armament including SAMs, the RBU-6000 systems, torpedoes, and cannons; a pair of Krivak II-class missile frigates with a multitude of missile and torpedo systems; one Kala-class antisubmarine-warfare cruiser, with her range of weapons systems as well as a Helix A helicopter; one Kirov-class battle cruiser, which could put up three Helix helicopters, which would help guide twenty SS-N-19 missiles, ninety-six SA-N-6 missiles, forty SA-N-4s, and 128 SA-NX-9s, as well as her guns; and three Sierra-class nuclear attack submarines.

They would be fighting the American force of two Ticonderoga-class destroyers, whose firepower was nearly beyond belief; one Iowa-class battleship; a pair of guided-missile frigates; an antisubmarine-warfare cruiser; and three Los Angeles-class nuclear attack submarines.

"Admiral Milliken, Comrade Admiral," the communications *michman* said.

Tulayev turned back to his telephone. "Good morning, Admiral. I wished to talk to you about a test we will be conducting through our DOME and Rio Center this morning."

"Good morning, Admiral Tulayev," Milliken said. "We will be conducting a test as well this morning. I think this is very wise ... considering everything."

16

DOME: MOSCOW

It was three in the afternoon and Lieutenant Ivliyev was in his quarters finishing his packing. He and his squadron were scheduled to leave by military jet transport in a couple of hours to Tripoli, Libya, and then across the Atlantic to the city of Fortaleza on Brazil's northeast coast. There they would be within five hundred kilometers of the fleet and would transfer to a much smaller aircraft that was capable of taking them out to the *Kremlin*.

It would be a long, tiring trip. But all of the pilots were young (Ivliyev as squadron commander was only twenty-eight) and they would have more than thirty-six hours of rest before they would fly their preliminary test sorties.

Still, he thought, they were leaving here in defeat. Or actually it was worse than that; they would be stepping away from the penultimate flight test behind the actual running of PIT BULL.

His father had never run away from a fight. Not even

when cancer had begun to eat his body. In a way, he was glad that the old general wasn't alive now to see this.

All he wanted was a chance to show those Americans what a Russian pilot could do. Especially now that he alone was privy to their little secret of thrust reversal.

Someone knocked at his door. "Come," he snapped, annoyed. It was probably one of his pilots wanting his hand held.

Colonel Vladimir N. Kabalin, the commanding officer of DOME: Moscow, came in. Ivliyev snapped to attention.

Kabalin smiled coolly. "As you were, Comrade Lieutenant," he said, his eyes going to the flight bag on the cot. Kabalin was an Air Force officer, but it was rumored that he was also GRU. He had not treated them badly during their stay here, but he was not a man filled with warmth. This was the first time he had come to any pilot in his quarters.

"You pilots are a strange lot," Kabalin said. "Prima donnas, I would say." He sighed. "But then I suppose it is the nature of your training and the way of things these days. In order to be an effective fighter pilot one must be an independent thinker. Not a team member. You're emulating your American counterparts, I suspect."

"We're better than them, Comrade Colonel."

"Yes, of course."

"And I would like to have had a chance to prove it before PIT BULL."

Kabalin waved a hand to silence Ivliyev. "Well, you have gotten your wish, Nikolai Vasilievich. I made the arrangements after I saw how excited you were to prove your point earlier. The link still exists between Colorado Springs through Rio Center. I am authorizing you to take to the skies and fight your battle."

"When?" Ivliyev felt as if he were a dog straining at a leash.

"Now. Your adjutant is calling your men."

"Is the American pilot up?"

"No, but we think that since he made the first challenge

and the Colorado Springs DOME hasn't been shut down, he'll be watching for you. Do not fail."

"I don't think I will," Ivliyev said. "No, comrade, I will not."

By the time Ivliyev had changed into his flight suit, his entire squadron had once again gathered in the observation room overlooking the simulator cockpit.

A ground crewman helped strap him into the narrow cockpit of the MiG-29 Fulcrum. He pulled on his helmet and plugged himself in. Finally he powered up his systems.

Once again he was on the flight deck of the *Kremlin*, but this time the weather was much worse.

Of course they were connected in real time through Rio Center with exactly what was happening aboard the *Kremlin*. If the weather was bad there, it would show up the same here.

This, he thought, was at the extreme limit of their operational capabilities. If the weather got worse, he would not be able to take off. Or if he got off, he would not get back aboard.

But then, he told himself, this was war.

His engines came up into the green. "Ready for launch," he said into his microphone.

"On your signal."

"Three ... two ... one ... launch."

The steam-powered catapult flung the 39,000-pound aircraft down the deck like a toy. Ivliyev slammed the throttles for both engines fully forward, his fingers on the afterburner button on the right side of his stick in case he needed the extra power immediately.

But then he was airborne, dipping down until the wings bit into the spray-laden air, and he hauled the stick back as he brought up his landing gear, and the powerful fighter shot into the morning sky and he was lost in the low-lying clouds.

He was free.

The GRU told them that the American pilots' motto for PIT BULL was "Kick Ass." They all understood the term.

This time, Ivliyev thought grimly, *he* was going to kick ass.

RIO CENTER

Lieutenant Commander Charles Poole, American chief of air group operations, rushed from the BOQ, showed his ID badge to the Marine guards at the door, and hurried inside.

Already more than half the Pit team had shown up. He was sitting at his console when he spotted his Russian counterpart, Major Aleksandr G. Lopatin, coming through the door and mounting the steps to the console tier.

Not everyone would be coming in for this limited exercise. But as the American chief of staff, Rear Admiral Edward Sears, had explained to him just minutes ago on the telephone, this would be a perfect opportunity for a spot-check of their air and missile consoles.

Admiral McCauley and the other brass were not coming in. Nevertheless there was little doubt in Poole's mind that old Deep Six would be lurking around somewhere.

His console powered up, he plugged into the three-dimensional situation display at the head of the room.

Lopatin's voice came through Poole's headset.

"Looks like one of our . . . pardon, only one Red Bandit up."

Poole had to grin. Despite the tension that the incident in the Barents Sea had caused, he and Lopatin got along. Here in Rio Center there were no Russians or Americans. No good guys or bad guys. Only Red Bandits (Russians) and Blue Bandits (Americans).

"I concur," Poole said, locking the image from a section of the big board into his own screen. He flipped switches for the SIF (search-and-identify feature) program. Instantly the data were displayed across his and Lopatin's screens.

The single Red Bandit up was a MiG-29 Fulcrum, fuselage designator 38. The aircraft being simulated at DOME: Moscow was virtually identical to the real number 38, which at this moment was aboard the *Kremlin* steaming south. The pilot was Lieutenant Ivliyev, the Fulcrum's squadron commander and reputedly one of the best.

Earlier in the day, DOME: Colorado Springs had sent up a Hornet, but the challenge had gone unmet.

Poole was hoping for some action now, if for no other reason than to cool tensions.

"I'm showing him climbing through fifteen thousand meters and passing Mach 2," Lopatin said. "Looks like he's aiming for a high arc and then a shooting run . . ." Lopatin stopped in midsentence. "Ah . . . there it is."

"I see it," Poole said. The Fulcrum's LDSD (look-down, shoot-down) radar system had just gone active. Three seconds later it was switched off.

Poole looked across at Lopatin. The Red pilot was baiting the Americans. Here I am, he was saying. Come and get me, if you can.

"Come on," Poole said to himself. "Someone, anyone, just get up there and kick his sorry ass."

Lopatin switched console communications and display to match missile defense. Poole flipped the appropriate switches when he, too, realized what else was going on.

"Lee, I'm showing a missile system armed and ready on that Red Bandit," Poole said.

"That's a roger," Lieutenant Commander Lee MacArthur said. "Looks like he means business. With any luck we'll have some action tonight."

"If someone will get one of the Blue Bandit pilots out of bed," MacArthur's Russian counterpart, Lieutenant Colonel Georgi Maslovski, said. "It may be 2330 here, but it's only 0630 at the Springs."

"All right, cut the chatter, gentlemen," Rear Admiral Sears' voice came through all of their headsets.

Poole and the others looked over toward the command console at the far end of the U. Sears and the Russian chief of staff, Admiral Ilya Mokretsov, were seated at their command positions. Only McCauley's chair was empty.

"Is a Blue Bandit scheduled to go up, sir?" Poole asked.

"I don't know, air group," Sears said. "This is an unscheduled test."

"War's unscheduled too," someone said.

DOME: COLORADO SPRINGS

"Do you think he took the bait last night, Luke?" Lieutenant Tom Cathey asked. He was one of the pilots in Hardell's squadron. He and the DOME CO, Bob Wurldorf, were waiting for Hardell to finish getting into his flight suit.

"I don't know," Hardell said, fumbling with the zippers. "And I won't know until I see how he's coming at me out of the chute. If he tries a supershot maneuver, then he's taken the bait. If not, he missed it."

In a conventional maneuver, a fighter meeting the enemy head-on would maintain a rather stable altitude. When he closed to range for his missile, he would fire, and then immediately make a high-G turn either to disengage or to come around again for a second shot.

If that were his maneuver, thrust reversal would put his enemy ahead of him before he could do a thing about it.

It was what Luke had showed the Russians the Hornet could do.

However, if the Russian understood this maneuver, then he could try a "supershot," which their intelligence believed the Fulcrum was capable of doing.

In this maneuver, the attacking fighter fired his first missile, but instead of continuing at the same speed and altitude, he made an extremely tight climbing turn to the left or right. At the top of the arc his aircraft would be in a high-speed stall—he would have traded altitude for speed—and would sideslip drastically. Even if his enemy were to use the thrust-reversal option, the Fulcrum would still be above and behind him, at a match speed, and in the perfect killing position.

It was dangerous of him to have shown the Russians the Hornet's thrust-reversal capability, but as Hardell had explained it, the Russians would have found out about it anyway within the first ninety seconds of battle.

"What I'm going to show them this time, Colonel, is going to make believers out of them," he told Wurldorf.

"You're the pilot," Wurldorf said.

In truth it was a subjective business. What the enemy "thought" might happen was often all that was needed to change the advantage.

Hardell grabbed his helmet and he and Cathey gave each other a high-five.

Colonel Wurldorf had to smile despite himself, and he shook his head.

"I don't know what the hell you've got planned, Luke," Wurldorf said. "But just kick his ass."

Hardell gazed at the cockpit simulator of his F/A-18L Hornet. "Right, sir."

He'd brought his own ground crewman, Smitty, with him from the *Nimitz*. The short, swarthy petty officer first class watched his lieutenant climb in the cockpit.

"I've been watching some of his shit up there, Luke. He's trying to goad you."

"You've been peeking again, Smitty?"

"Fuckin' A. His LDSD has been illuminated twice now. He wants you to think that he's going to come in high and fast. But I think the sonofabitch might be after an ultra-low solution." (Ultra-low-level operations were those that took place at 250 feet or less above the surface of the ground or ocean—difficult and dangerous.) "I'd bet a month of my sorry-ass pay that he's going to try a supershot on you right out of the box."

The display outside of his cockpit barely had time to settle onto the *Nimitz* mode, with its bad weather and pitching decks, when the steam catapult slammed him forward, and he hit his afterburners.

This strategy was strictly forbidden (using afterburners on deck was dangerous and destructive), but he wanted to be away from the ship as quickly as possible.

He glanced in his rearview mirror, which showed him climbing away from the *Nimitz*, and then powered up his HMD (helmet-mounted display) and his master armament panel to the left of his stores (weapons) management display readout on a small CRT.

He'd shown the Russian his thrust-reversal strategy and he knew about the Russian's supershot capability. But he had other tricks in his own bag. He wondered about the Russians.

Over the pilots' lounge door aboard the *Nimitz*, there was a plaque that someone had tacked up. He'd seen the same thing over the doors of other naval pilots' lounges.

"Fighter pilots should have an allotted area to cruise around in as it suits them, but when they see an opponent they must attack and shoot him down. Anything else is absurd—Manfred von Richthofen, 1917."

It was his turn now. He would cruise around, find the enemy, and shoot him down.

RIO CENTER

"Look alert, gentlemen," Rear Admiral Sears' voice came over their headphones. "We've got a Blue Bandit in the fray."

Poole's console locked onto that fact an instant later. "I have him at one hundred fifty nautical miles from Red Bandit," he spoke calmly into his headset.

"Confirm," Lopatin said.

"Neither bandit has target acquisition. Neither has activated his ECMs."

"That's also a confirm."

They were actually nothing more than human backup for computer control, which under normal conditions was much faster. But in case the machines went bad, or a critical decision had to be made, humans were involved.

"I'm showing Red Bandit's LDSD radar again," Lopatin said.

"I read Blue Bandit's weapons-arming controls," MacArthur, from missile defense, jumped in.

"Confirm LDSD from Red Bandit," Poole said belatedly. He punched up a higher resolution for a section of his screen. It was beginning not to make much sense.

"Air group, are you showing clutter on Blue Bandit?" Admiral Sears asked.

"Aye, command," Poole said. "What do you make of it, Aleksei?"

"He's on the deck. Under sixty meters, I would say. Ultralow-level operations."

But the Russian was high and coming on fast. If the Hornet remained that low, the Russian with his good LDSD radar would have the perfect shot.

"Come on," Poole same to himself. "Get the hell out of there, you silly bastard." He didn't know everything there was to know about the F/A-18L, except that with the right pilot she was probably as good or better than the Fulcrum.

"They have each other," Lopatin said.

Electronically they were seeing each other now. The Russian turned on a direct course toward the Hornet and kicked in his afterburners, because his speed immediately climbed to nearly Mach 2.5.

"Confirm," Poole said.

"Weapons systems on Red Bandit . . . now on Blue Bandit as well . . . fully activated," Maslovski said.

"Confirm," MacArthur said right behind him. "And now the furball starts."

DOME: MOSCOW

Ivliyev knew that he was in a simulator cockpit at the DOME outside Moscow, but all of his senses told him that he was in a real Fulcrum in the real skies three hundred kilometers off the east coast of Brazil.

Even if he turned his head to look out the side of his canopy, or checked to his rear, he would not see the DOME's darkened auditorium. He would see a three-dimensional holographic representation of the real world.

Included in that representation, though still well outside visual range, was the lone American fighter/interceptor which his radar systems had identified as an F/A-18L Hornet, the same type of aircraft that had gone up in the afternoon to challenge him. And it was probably the same pilot too, he thought.

This was to be a one-on-one fight. The Americans had no AWACS Hawkeyes up to vector the Hornet, nor did Ivliyev have an AEW&C (airborne early warning and control) Ilyushin Mainstay-A to guide him and his weapons systems. The old axiom that most pilots who are shot down never see their attacker would not apply here.

At 150 kilometers, his forward-looking search-and-identify radar had picked up a possible target inbound, low and fast.

He turned toward it, illuminating it with his LDSD just long enough for a positive identification, and then he kicked in his afterburner and headed down toward the deck.

He had to admire the American pilot for his courage. No matter how good he or his aircraft was, a thrust-reversal maneuver so close to the surface of the ocean would be extremely dangerous. At such speeds, and under such extreme stresses, neither pilot nor machine was in complete control.

Both aircraft were doing over Mach 2.3, which gave them a closure rate of more than eighty kilometers per minute.

Ivliyev did the mental arithmetic as he armed his weapons systems, which included two R-60 close-in "furball" missiles, which were actually the AA-8 Aphids, and four longer-range and more powerful AA-10 air-to-air missiles, plus a pair of 30mm rapid-fire cannons mounted in the Fulcrum's lerxes.

At eighty-five kilometers out, barely one minute on target, and a little more than forty seconds to fire, his LDSD radar was in tracking range and he was locked onto his target.

He chose a single R-60, using the selector on his stick, and then eased the safety off the firing switch.

His ECMs beeped a warning that he was being illuminated by an enemy's weapons-radar system, and with his left hand he activated a series of countermeasures that would confuse the Hornet's system into seeing multiple targets.

The instant the American hit his thrust reversals, Ivliyev would pull sharply up to the right, in a nine-G climbing turn, at the top of which he would be sideslipping in a high-speed stall, right behind the Hornet, when he would fire his missile before the other pilot knew what was happening.

Normally in an attack run like this there would be a lot of chatter between the pilots in the wing, with the AEW&C Mainstays, and with his own controller back on the *Kremlin*. Silence like now was eerie.

His IR (infrared) detectors showed the heat signature of the Hornet below and ahead of him. At five thousand meters he started to haul back on his stick. He wanted to meet the American head-to-head at the same altitude, which was barely three hundred meters.

He saw the American warplane below and coming fast.

Changing his own strategy, Ivliyev quickly switched to an AA-10 longer range missile and fired.

In the next instant, almost on top of the Hornet, he switched back to the R-60 Aphid and prepared to climb and turn to the right for his supershot.

RIO CENTER

"Red Bandit has fired an AA-10," MacArthur said, carefully monitoring the display across his console.

"I confirm," Maslovski said. "Range at firing thirty kilometers . . ."

"It's a miss, it's a miss," MacArthur reported.

"Confirm, confirm."

Everything was happening incredibly fast.

The Russian had fired his missile and then had rearmed his R-60 while jamming the American's acquisition radar.

In the next instant he had pulled up and sharply to the right, in what the book called the supershot maneuver. It was the perfect counter to Hardell's thrust-reversal capabilities which he had so amply demonstrated twelve hours ago, and which here at Rio Center they had analyzed that afternoon.

But the Hornet was not doing that this time. Hardell was definitely not going by the book.

MacArthur sat forward as Lopatin's voice came over his headset from the Russian's air-wing-control console.

"He's breaking off. The Blue Bandit is breaking off . . ."

"Negative, negative," Poole said. "He's running his own supershot."

MacArthur could see it now. The Hornet had kicked in its afterburners and was climbing, but to the left, in the perfect mirror image of the Fulcrum's supershot maneuver.

Both fighters were releasing radar-confusing aluminum chaff and IR-confusing flares.

The Russian fighter hit the top of his arc first, turned over at the top, and automatically fired his R-60.

"Missile is off, Red Bandit has released his missile," Maslovski called.

"Confirm," MacArthur said.

But the Hornet was not there, or at least it wasn't where the Russian had expected it to be. Instead he was slightly above and to the Fulcrum's right.

"Blue Bandit has released his missile," MacArthur said.

"Confirm," the Russian replied. "Red Bandit's missile is a miss. It's a miss."

"Confirm," MacArthur said as he watched the drama being played out. Both pilots were damned good. Hardell had released what looked like an AIM-120 AMRAAM launch-and-leave missile at the top of his turn.

The Russian fighter's radar systems and ECMs instantly told him of his mistake: His missile missed, and an ememy missile was tracking him. He immediately broke off the engagement, turned right again, and dove for the deck.

The AIM-120 was called a semi-smart missile, in that for the first portion of the flight it merely homed in by its inertial navigation system (thus not being fooled by chaff or flares). Once a firm radar target was acquired, however, the missile's own radar took over.

It was up to the good pilot to keep out of its radar envelope, which in this case Ivliyev was trying to do by getting down into the ground clutter.

The missile's LDSD capabilities were limited by the relatively small size of its radar antenna.

It was very fast, but at its Mach 4 speed it had a duration of only about thirty seconds, and it was not as maneuverable as either the Fulcrum or the Hornet.

Ivliyev's job now was to keep out of the missile's way until it ran out of fuel.

But he had not counted on the American pilot.

DOME: COLORADO SPRINGS

The Russian pilot was good, but he was flying by the book.

The instant Hardell released his missile, he turned back on its tail, following it to its target, so that he could get a good view of what the Fulcrum was doing, and get off a second shot if needed.

Ivliyev had gone down to the deck to confuse the

AIM-120's look-down, shoot-down radar, and then had begun a series of high-G turns, right and then left.

Each time, the slower-turning missile's arc became wider and wider, even though it was getting closer and closer to the Fulcrum.

Within the first ten seconds it was unclear. But in the next ten seconds Hardell knew for certain that Ivliyev would successfully evade, and he made his decision.

It was called kicking the poor bastard when he was down. The strategy was simple. When the enemy pilot was engaged in trying to evade your missile, you waited, knowing that he would turn inbound sooner or later. When he came in range you shot him with your gun.

The Hornet was equipped with an M61 Vulcan cannon capable of firing six thousand 20mm rounds per minute at a muzzle velocity of 3,400 feet per second.

That meant that each bullet tossed out was only thirty-four feet behind the previous one.

The Hornet carried only 570 rounds, which gave it a little less than six seconds of firing. The trick, of course, was to get your target at a ninety-degree angle. The Fulcrum, which was about fifty-eight feet long, would travel its own length at Mach 1 (which she was doing now) in about five-hundredths of a second. At that speed, if the Vulcan was aimed and fired properly, the enemy would be hit at least four times: once just forward of the cockpit, once just aft, once midway to the tail cones, and a final hit a few feet forward of the exhaust pipes.

Enough to bring the Fulcrum down in a clean kill.

The Fulcrum was four nautical miles out when she turned again to the right and almost immediately back to the left. This time Hardell was waiting at nine o'clock, one thousand feet high in a shallow dive.

The AIM-120 missed its target one last time, its engine finally flaming out, and it fell toward the sea.

Two seconds later the Russian fighter came in range, and Hardell squeezed off a series of shots. Blowby gas from the cannon shot back past his canopy.

At first he didn't think he had hit the MiG, and he made a tight turn back to the left, activating his target-acquisition radar and arming another AIM-120. But as he came around 180 degrees, he saw the Fulcrum spiraling down toward the ocean, out of control.

Immediately he shut down his radars, safetied his weapons, and did two snap rolls, before he turned back toward the *Nimitz*.

DOME: MOSCOW

The MiG-29 simulator cockpit was canted to the left and forward at an extreme angle. Ivliyev hung by his straps watching his instruments unreel, and looking out his canopy as the surface of the ocean came nearer and nearer.

It seemed real. But he did not care. In some respects he almost wished it were not a simulation.

At the moment of impact, he flinched involuntarily, and the simulator gave a big lurch. Moments later, the auditorium lights came up and the simulator rolled over to the level, all its instruments dead.

The canopy came up and his *michman* was there to help him unstrap, but Ivliyev brushed him aside, undoing his own restraints and wriggling out of the cockpit.

On the platform he yanked off his helmet and glanced up toward the observation room, but his pilots were not there any longer.

He slammed his fist into the side of the simulator, denting the aluminum skin, the noise echoing hollowly throughout the big room.

Someone below on the auditorium floor started to clap slowly, and Ivliyev turned around. It was the DOME CO, Colonel Kabalin, his uniform blouse unbuttoned, his tie loose. It looked as if he, too, had suffered through the exercise.

"Russia's greatest pilot cannot shoot down a Hornet, but

is well on his way to destroying a MiG simulator. You and I will talk. There is a story I would like to tell you."

Kabalin had the power to scrub him from PIT BULL. If that happened he would never get his revenge.

He glanced back at the simulator cockpit. Somehow, no matter what he had to do, or how much pride he had to swallow, he wanted to fly again. He now knew the Hornet's performance envelope.

He went down the stairs to Kabalin. They left the auditorium and stepped out into the afternoon, the sky clear and the weather pleasantly warm.

"The American fighter is quite a ship," Kabalin said as they headed slowly toward the officers' club.

"Yes, Comrade Colonel, and the pilot was crafty as well."

"But there will be a next time. You will be leaving here with your squadron in ninety minutes, just as scheduled."

Ivliyev wondered what the old fool wanted. The man had returned from retirement a year ago to head the DOME project. It was someone's crazy idea, probably in the Kremlin—though despite his age and his aloofness, the man had done a good job.

"Let me tell you a story, Nikki, about myself. During the last couple of years of the Great War, I was a young man serving in a tank squadron. For the first six months we fought well, although we were losing ground. This was in the winter of 1942. Stalingrad belonged to the Nazis. But for us younger men who had never felt the horrors of war, it was still a great adventure.

"Our commanding officer sent me and four of my friends into Stalingrad on a spying mission. What we saw there opened our eyes. It still makes me cry to think about the cannibalism. There was no food for Russians, so after the rats were gone, and the bark had been stripped from all the trees for soup, they began eating each other. We were losing, and badly. When we reported back to our commander we suddenly had humility and shame.

" 'Now you will be good fighters for the *Rodina*,' our commander told us. And he was correct, Nikki. Now we were fighting like men and not boys, not for ourselves, but for Mother Russia."

They stopped, the Ivliyev looked at the old man. He was correct. The lesson was the same now.

Kabalin managed a slight smile. "Your nose was rubbed in the dirt, and you came up fighting mad. But next time when you go out to do battle, Comrade Lieutenant, fight as a man and not as a prima-donna boy. The *Rodina* is counting on you."

The colonel took his arm and they continued across the quadrangle. "Now, there is another story I must tell you. But this one you must be careful about. In fact, tell no one for the moment. This story is about an old friend of mine who has a plan to save the *Rodina* once again as he and I once helped save Stalingrad."

DOME: COLORADO SPRINGS

Hardell came in low over the *Nimitz* at just under Mach 1 and executed a series of victory rolls, climbing out at the end and punching in his afterburner as he made the Hornet stand on her tail.

As he passed through twenty thousand feet, Colonel Wurldorf's voice came over his helmet radio.

"Well done, Luke. Want to try for a carrier landing? Real time."

"How's the weather?"

"Terrible. Below margins."

"If this were PIT BULL?"

"Unless you got back in one piece, your kill would be balanced out," Wurldorf said matter-of-factly.

"I've got to go for it."

"Your call, Luke. But make it snappy. You've got a squadron of pilots down here fighting each other for the privilege of buying you the first drink."

Four miles out, Hardell turned back into the wind and

started his final approach. The Hornet began to buck and heave in the uneven gusts at this altitude, and Hardell suddenly had to wrestle for control of the fifty-million-dollar airplane.

He could see through his canopy that the *Nimitz* was rising and falling on the big seas; the simulation was real enough to make him sweat.

"Come right five degrees, adjust your rate of descent to one thousand feet per minute," his controller said.

It was nearly impossible to hold any steady rate of descent. The best he could do was eyeball the carrier deck as it came closer and closer.

If he blew this landing, nothing would be hurt but his pride, of course. And yet this exercise was being evaluated and analyzed by Rio Center, which meant that the Russian pilots aboard the *Kremlin* would know exactly what he was capable of . . . or incapable of. He planted the Hornet hard on the deck, the first and second wires caught, and he was stopped.

He almost expected to see ground crewmen come running, but the auditorium lights came up, his instruments died, the image outside his canopy faded. His canopy popped open.

He could hear the cheering and whistles when he pulled off his helmet.

His ground crewman, Dick Smith, was there to help him out of the cockpit.

"Well, Lieutenant, you sure the hell kicked ass," he said.

Hardell grinned. "Did you have any doubts?"

RIO CENTER

Admiral Jeff McCauley, alone in his quarters, was gazing out his windows toward the brightly lit condos behind the beaches at Copacabana when he was visited by his U.S.

chief of staff, Rear Admiral Sears, who had a triumphant look in his eyes. "Hope I'm not disturbing you, Admiral."

"Is Admiral Mokretsov with you?" McCauley asked.

Sears shook his head, grinning. "We're clear here?"

"I just had the room swept. Well, spit it out, Ed. How'd we do?"

"We kicked ass, Jeff. It was their squadron commander. He didn't know what hit him. Our boy had about two hundred dollars' worth of simulated nosewheel damage from landing. He offered to reimburse the government."

"The hell you say," McCauley said, remembering what it was like to be young. "When can we get them aboard?"

"Within twenty-four hours. Should be a break in the weather."

"How'd Mokretsov take it?"

"I don't know, Jeff. He didn't stick around long enough for me to ask."

17

MCLEAN, VIRGINIA

Admiral David Maxwell and General Horace Walker, in civilian clothes, threaded their way through the dining room to where Bill Lane was seated by the windows overlooking the Potomac River.

It was nearly eight-thirty, they were a half hour late. Lane had been drinking his coffee and reading the *Washington Post*, wondering if he was wasting time here.

He and Ben Lewis had come up with the indexes for a hundred thousand telephone conversations from two dozen key numbers in Kiev and Moscow that NSA had intercepted over the past twelve months. They were doing a computer search under a number of references—Normav, PIT BULL, the GRU, Leonov, and others.

But that would take time. Most of the rest of the day, if he could get at it. He'd been irked with this delay. Finally he spotted the two officers heading his way.

"Sorry we're so late, Bill," Maxwell said. "Something

came up that we couldn't miss. We had to get the last of it via secure telephone on the way over here."

They ordered coffee and toast. When their waiter was gone, Walker leaned forward a little. "What did you mean about secret orders?" he asked, keeping his voice melodramatically low.

"I'm working for the President, General, but we're all on the same side here," Lane said. "I just want to get that straight from the start. I happen to agree with you that we should hold off running PIT BULL, at least until the Ukrainians are out of the picture. And I happen to agree—although I don't like it—with what you've told Milliken and McCauley."

"And what might that be?" Walker demanded.

Lane stared at him until Maxwell intervened.

"I don't think we can afford to fight among ourselves," he said. "I think we can trust Bill."

"I don't care to have civilian interference . . . ," Walker started to say, but Lane cut him off.

"That's the way we do things in this country, General." Walker sat back in his chair.

"You said something came up this morning, Admiral," Lane prompted.

"A joint exercise was conducted between DOME: Moscow and DOME: Colorado. We won decisively."

Lane thought for a moment. "Might not have been the best thing to do," he said slowly.

"What are you saying? That our win might make them do something . . . foolish?"

"It's a thought. But it doesn't matter, I suppose. We're going to be ready for them. I'm still trying to come up with something concrete on Normav."

"Well, I've got one thing for you on that score," Walker said, more cooperatively. "I called our military attaché in Kiev, an old friend. I asked him to check on something for me, which he did. It seems that Normav and Leonov were both members of the same exclusive officers' bath club in

Kiev. The club where Leonov drowned. And on that morning, Normav and his old cronies were there."

"It doesn't prove . . . ," Maxwell began.

"Hear me out, Dave. Leonov stopped going there after the breakup of the Soviet Union. But all of a sudden he shows up, meets Normav and his pals in the middle of a crisis, and drowns. That stinks."

"I agree," Lane said. "It means that Leonov was on to General Normav's plan, and he went there to try to talk him out of it."

"And Normav killed him for that?" Maxwell asked.

"Looks like it," Walker said. "Which puts us back to square one. PIT BULL should not be run. If it is, we damned well better be prepared for that old bastard."

"Evidently Leonov didn't tell anyone, otherwise President Nikolayev would have called for a delay," Lane said. But where did the *Pogin* fit, and were they going to try to bring in more resources around the Horn? "Some of the answers will be aboard the *Kremlin* and her support ships . . . ," he added, but the expression on Maxwell's face stopped him from continuing.

"There's something else, Bill. Last night aboard the *Nimitz* there was a killing. One of the Russian observers was shot dead with a nine-millimeter handgun. His body was found early this morning on deck."

"Christ," Lane said softly. "What the hell was he doing on deck?"

"Possibly sabotage," Maxwell said. "They found a penlight with a head strap. It was all he was carrying. Evidently his killer cleaned out his pockets, but missed the light."

"Wait a second . . ."

"We came to the same question: If one of our boys shot him while he was mucking around with an aircraft on deck, why take his tools and evidence of what he was doing?"

"Unless it wasn't one of our people," Lane said. "Unless it was a Ukrainian spy."

"Why?"

"He did something to one of our aircraft. When he was

finished, he was killed to make sure he didn't let anything slip. And I'll bet you anything that one of the other five Russian observers aboard is actually Ukrainian. Find out who he is, you'll have your killer."

Maxwell nodded. "What have you come up with?"

"There's no doubt now that Normav is behind some plot to use PIT BULL for his own advantage. Possibly one as extreme as starting a shooting war, which he believes Russia will lose. But he won't stop with what's been done so far. There will be another incident, or incidents."

"All designed to do what?" Walker asked.

"To provide a diversion so that he can get more resources into the PIT BULL arena. Submarines, I would guess. Maybe to bring us to a position where we'll consider shooting first. If he wants a war, he wants us to start it."

"We just might oblige him," Walker said.

"I hope not, General."

Maxwell glanced at Walker.

"I think it's time that you brief General Mooreland and the other chiefs," Maxwell said. "We can set up a conference circuit, encrypted, with Milliken and Stewart aboard the *Nimitz*, and Jeff McCauley down in Rio."

Lane looked at his watch. "At noon. I've got something else to do in the meantime."

NATIONAL SECURITY AGENCY

Ben Lewis had gone to the director first thing in the morning to get priority on one of the Cray supercomputers in the subbasement. But "Bill Lane's little project," as it was being called, was getting top billing, and the way was cleared immediately.

By the time Lane returned from McLean, the program had already been running for nearly two hours. He got himself a cup of coffee, took off his jacket, loosened his tie, and perched on the edge of the console where Lewis was watching the printout unreeling from the big machine.

"Anything yet?"

Lewis shook his head. "Nothing concrete, though there've been plenty of references to Leonov and PIT BULL."

"Nothing on Normav?"

"Not much, Bill. If he's in there, no one mentions his name. They didn't have to."

"We'll have to take a statistical sampling, I suppose, and hope for the best."

"Do you want to write the program?"

"Yeah. We'll run it simultaneously with the main search." Lane sat down at an adjacent console. His program in concept was simple. In execution it was more difficult. In effect, he was telling the computer that within the hundred thousand telephone conversations on tape, there ought to be references to General Normav, but that none were coming up. He told the computer about Leonov, PIT BULL, the GRU, and the fact that Normav had been gathering his old cronies, many of them former Soviet military men, around him in Kiev for the past year or so.

Finally he asked the computer to figure out how big a random sample of telephone conversations they would have to listen in on to have a reasonable chance of coming up with one involving Normav.

The supercomputer came back with its answer almost immediately—an answer Lane anticipated. Considering the subject matter and considering General Normav's position, any significant telephone conversations with the general would likely have been held over secure lines.

Given that negative factor, the random sampling of what they had would be divided into two sections. The first would be quite small, only one-tenth of one percent of the total calls—one hundred. If something came up in that sample, then a much larger sample, larger by a factor of ten, would have to be taken to find anything significant.

Unless they got lucky.

"All right, it wants us to take a preliminary sampling of one hundred calls," he told Lewis. "I'll start with the calls you've already been through."

"What are you looking for specifically?"

"I don't know." Lane plugged a set of earphones into his console. "But I hope to hell I'll recognize it."

He punched a few buttons, shunting a batch of one thousand telephone transcripts to his console, and had the computer pluck out ten calls at random. He put the first one up on his tape machine and hit the playback button. His screen instantly lit up with the details of the call, including the caller's number and the number called.

A clerk in the office of Russian Federal Naval Procurement on Pirogovskaya Street had telephoned the Inspector General's Office in the Ministry of Defense in the Kremlin to complain of the tardy delivery schedule of reduction valves from the factory in Moscow to the shipyards in Kaliningrad.

Another call was from a female secretary in an unidentified general's office (the number was in the blind, though the NSA analysts had given it an eighty-seven-percent probability of originating inside the Kremlin) to a male voice at a blind number outside of Moscow. The date was six weeks ago:

We've all been working twelve and fourteen hours a day ... ever since ... well, you know. It's starting to get on everyone's nerves.

The girl sounded tired. The call had been placed by her at 2145 hours. Her Russian was colloquial.

It won't last much longer. You know this, Svetlana. And then we will be free.

Or dead.

Don't say that, even in joking. If someone should overhear ...

Yes, you are correct, of course, Vasha. Will I see you tonight ...

Lane backed up the tape to "Or dead" and listened to it again. What wouldn't last much longer? And why might they be dead? Could they have been talking about the possibility of a war arising out of PIT BULL?

He shunted the tape to a specially reserved analytical memory bank. Later he would try to make some sense of the data. He brought up another call.

"Hello, here it comes again," Lewis said suddenly.

Lane pushed his chair across to Lewis' console. "What have you got, Ben?"

"Looks like some kind of a code word. I've picked it up out of a Normav reference. Hold on a second." Lewis brought the conversation up on the speaker.

The screen showed that a call had been made from the Department of Ukraine Army-Land, on an internally blind number, to another blind number somewhere on Kreshchatik Street in Kiev. The machine had picked it out on the basis of the number and the use of the name Pavl—General Normav's first name.

. . . *in the morning*, an angry voice that the computer identified as probably belonging to Normav said.

Lewis fast-forwarded the tape, finding a specific bit of the otherwise innocuous conversation.

. . . *it will go as scheduled, but perhaps not as planned. KEENSCHCAL will determine that.*

Normav? Lane wondered. The computer was assigning a ninety-five percent probability of it being he. That left fully five percent that it was not.

Lewis played that section again. "Keenschcal. Some sort of an operational code. Means 'dagger point.' Which in itself might not mean a damned thing, except it was the name of Normav's tank during the war."

"Bingo!" Lane pushed over to his terminal. "Reprogram for references to KEENSCHCAL, with crosses to Normav and all of his new staff appointments over the past year!"

THE PENTAGON

They met in the chairman's briefing auditorium, a small room just off the operations center. General Mooreland had gathered not only Dave Maxwell, Horace Walker, and the other two chiefs but also their operations officers, CINCs of all the fleets and submarine operation groups.

It was a much larger group than Lane wanted to address. Given what he and Ben Lewis had discovered, he thought the need-to-know list should have been minimum.

Mooreland had disagreed, and had decided that he did not want to run to the President with this. Not until their proof was more concrete.

Lane brought no audio or visual presentation with him, nor any notes. What he was about to tell them would be short, sweet, and to the point.

At the podium he began. "My name is Bill Lane. I'm an analyst with the National Security Agency's Russian Division. At present I have been detached from my regular duties to work with the Director of Central Intelligence, with my reports going directly to the President. This is because of the incident with the *John Hopkins* spy vessel off the Russian coast in the Barents Sea, and of course the upcoming PIT BULL war games."

He had their attention.

"Specifically I was asked by the President to investigate the possibility that elements within the Ukrainian military would try to subvert PIT BULL, change it into something else, something dangerous."

There was a stir in the audience. General Mooreland looked uneasy. "We are not here to chase gremlins, Mr. Lane."

"No, sir. A specifically engineered Ukrainian counteroperation, designed and powered by General Pavl Normav, which may be going under the code name KEENSCHCAL . . . which means 'dagger point.' Coincidentally the name of General Normav's tank in World War II."

"What is the purpose of this supposed counteroperation?" Mooreland demanded.

"To start a shooting war by provoking us into firing the first shot."

"I don't think so," the Chairman of the Joint Chiefs said angrily.

"Pardon me, General, but you're wrong. I am prepared to show you what the Ukrainians plan on doing, and perhaps how."

"And will you tell us how we can counteract this colossal bit of sabotage?"

"No, sir. Just my analysis."

"Continue, then," the chairman said. "You will be given a fair hearing."

I doubt it, Lane said to himself. But he'd promised the President.

J. EDGAR HOOVER BUILDING

"What a load of horseshit." Joseph Bishop, deputy assistant director of the FBI's Special Investigative Division, looked up from the report.

"We don't like it either, sir," Navy Intelligence Officer Sterling Miller said. "But we've run it out as far as we can without your direct help."

Bishop, forty-eight, who'd been a cop all of his adult life, smelled big trouble here. But the Bureau could not sidestep the investigation, because what the Navy had come up with seemed to be nearly airtight. "Do you know where Senator Wood is at the moment?"

"In Rio, sir. At least he was as of this morning. He's staying at the Meridien-Rio Hotel."

Bishop glanced again at the report Miller and his partner, Puck Abramson, had prepared. The trail led from Lieutenant Hatcher to Randy Turner to Senator Wood and from there it spread in a dozen different directions—to the dozen largest designers and manufacturers of military weapons systems and electronics. Worse than that, however, was a possible connection between the Senator and a Russian intelligence officer by the name of Anatoli Tumanov.

"I'll run the Russian's name through our Counter-Espionage Division, but with Senator Wood out of the country for the moment, we're going to have to bring the CIA in on this."

"Yes, sir," Miller replied.

"In the meantime we'll set up a tail on the senator's executive assistant and the rest of his staff. We can check bank accounts, birth, Social Security, and military records." Bishop shook his head. "Nobody's hands are going to come out clean on this one. Nobody's."

SSN *POGIN*

The submarine was quiet. They had settled into a kilometer-consuming sea routine of watch-on-watch, although many of the boat's functions were automatic. Badim wanted his crew kept busy.

Fortunately, Grichakov, his renegade *zampolit*, had not strutted around the boat, so tempers had not flared. But Badim was genuinely fearful of what might happen if one of his crew decided to take a shot at the man. They'd probably blow up, not only killing themselves but contaminating a huge section of the North Atlantic.

Grichakov had slept through most of the night locked in Badim's cabin, the encoding device for the explosives at his side.

They had discussed storming the cabin and taking the device away from him, but decided against it. If they made noise that woke the *zampolit*, he might feel threatened enough to blow the bomb. And even if they tortured him, they might not be able to extract the defusing codes.

Badim bunked with his *starpom*, Valeri Melnik. He got up, splashed some water on his face, and made his way forward. It was a few minutes before nine in the evening in

Kiev, which made it about 0700 here at their present position south of Iceland.

The odors of breakfast filled the confines of the submarine, but he felt queasy and the thought of food didn't help. Perhaps just a glass of tea.

A rating was seated alone in the sonar room, and he looked up as Badim stopped at the doorway. "Good morning, Comrade Captain," the young man said.

Normally there should have been two men on duty here. It was union rules. An experienced older hand and an assistant. This was a boy.

"Where is your shift supervisor?"

"Getting something to eat, sir," the seaman said uncertainly.

Badim nodded and smiled. "What's it look like out ahead of us?" he asked.

"I think I may have heard a pod of whales, sir. But that was two hours ago."

"Beautiful animals," Badim said. "Nothing else? No ships?"

"We're still beneath the thermocline, Comrade Captain. It is very difficult."

"Yes. When your supervisor returns, have him come see me, would you?"

The young man nodded, uncomfortable now that his *michman* (warrant officer) might be in trouble.

Badim went forward into the attack center and conn, where Melnik was hunched over the chart table with their navigation officer, Lieutenant Karpovich.

"Good morning, Captain," Melnik said.

Badim nodded. "Where is our friend Grichakov?" he asked softly.

Melnik glanced aft toward the hatch. "Still sleeping."

"All right, what's our situation?"

"We're still running at one thousand meters, at thirty-five knots," Melnik said.

"We've left Iceland behind?"

"Yes, Comrade Captain," Karpovich said. "We're well out into the open Atlantic now."

Badim thought about it for a moment. "All right, everyone listen." All eyes turned toward him, even those of the helmsman. "I'm going to play a little trick on our *zampolit*, and everyone here is going to have to help me. But it will be dangerous."

Melnik nodded. "What have you got in mind for that little bastard?"

"I want you to get Sitnikov up here on the double, before Grichakov wakes up," Badim said. Sitnikov was their chief engineer. "I want him to fix all of our depth gauges so that they read seven hundred meters too deep. We are going to bring the boat up to three hundred meters, but I want all the gauges to read one thousand. I think Grichakov would blow up the boat if he found out."

"That will leave us open for detection by the . . ."

"Yes, it will, and it's exactly what I want, Valeri," Badim said. "That Los Angeles-class sub is behind us, just above the thermocline. I heard him on sonar. Every now and then he dips below to make sure we're still here."

"But if he sees us getting too close to his coast, he may shoot."

"Yes, he may," Badim said, "in which case we would have to turn and fight. There would be no time for us to head to the Panama Canal, or wherever that crazy *zampolit* wants us to go. Then we must figure out what to do about him."

"What about our sonar? As soon as we go up, they'll hear the American boat and sound the alarm."

"I'll take care of that. The *michman* owes me a favor just now."

SSN *BOSTON*

"Sonar, conn."

"Conn, aye," Lieutenant Steve McGill, the exec, replied. He glanced at the clock. It was 0745 local.

"I'm getting hull-popping noises from that sub ahead of us. She's on her way up, slowly."

"Jesus," McGill muttered. He switched the comms. "Captain to the bridge, captain to the bridge, on the double."

"Her course and speed seem to be constant and I'd estimate the angle on her planes to be no more than a couple of degrees," the sonarman reported.

"Whatever you do, stay away from your active gear," McGill said. "Tell me when she passes through the thermocline." He turned to his duty crew. "Gentlemen, we're going to need fast action when the time comes. The moment that boat comes through the thermocline she'll be able to detect us. So we're going to shut down at that time and drift long enough to see what the hell she's up to."

Captain Armstrong came through the companionway on the run. "What's up?" he asked, ducking through the hatch.

"The *Pogin* is on her way up, skipper," McGill said. He explained what his orders were.

Armstrong nodded approval. "But, Steve, he might know we're back here and wants to prepare us for the fact he's surfacing. Either that or he wants to bring his boat up so gently that no one else aboard—outside the conn—will know they're on the way up. We'll find out soon enough."

GEORGETOWN

The afternoon passed with depressing slowness. The computer continued to analyze the tens of thousands of telephone calls, and Lane and Lewis had both turned their attention to the statistical sampling. By eight in the evening they had come up with no other mentions of Normav or the elusive code word, KEENSCHCAL.

"You're not doing any good here now," Lewis told him finally.

Lane looked up from his screen, barely able to focus his eyes. He had been going on coffee and adrenaline for what seemed like weeks. Combined with the time-zone changes he had suffered through, he was nearing collapse.

"Go home and get a few hours sleep, Bill. I promise that if anything comes up I'll call you."

Lane nodded. He had nothing left inside, and it was all he could do to drive back to his apartment.

Traffic was light at this time of the evening. The only pedestrians were two priests who came out of his apartment building and headed toward the church. He thought it was odd. So far as he knew, no priests lived in his building. They had probably been visiting someone.

He parked in front of his brownstone, grabbed his overnight bag, and got out of the car.

The priests stopped about thirty yards away and looked back at him.

Odd, he thought again. They stepped apart, both of them suddenly reaching inside their cassocks.

For a long instant Lane was befuddled. One of the priests drew a gun and snapped off a shot, the bullet ricocheting off the sidewalk just behind Lane. He roused himself to action, ducking behind his car.

The shot was from a silenced pistol, a fact clear as he fumbled his overnight bag open, pulled out his Beretta .380, and switched off the safety.

The second priest ran into the street to have a shot at Lane. Lane popped up and fired three quick shots, at least one hitting the man in the chest, stopping him, the last hitting him in the forehead.

Lane's unsilenced shots were very loud in the quiet neighborhood. A car screeched to a halt at the end of the block.

Lane rolled left. The second priest fired twice, both shots slamming into the side of his car.

Whoever they were, they had probably been inside of his apartment. Possibly setting a booby trap. They definitely wanted him dead.

He fired a shot in the general direction of the priest, who fired back, his silenced shot missing Lane by an inch.

Whoever the hell he was, he was no amateur. His partner had made a stupid mistake; this one wasn't about to.

In the distance, he could hear a siren. They had not counted on him having a gun. Nor had they counted on him showing up. But their orders were to kill him on opportunity.

Ukrainians. Was there any other possibility?

The siren was closer now.

"Throw down your gun, comrade, and I guarantee you will not get hurt," Lane shouted in Russian.

There was no answer. He heard the sound of someone running, and he looked over the trunk lid of his car in time to see the priest reach the corner.

The siren was right on top of him now. Lane fired two shots, one of them catching the priest in the leg and knocking him down.

Someone was behind him. "Police! Drop it! Drop it!"

Other sirens were converging. Lane slowly laid his pistol down and raised his hands. The priest got up and disappeared around the corner.

"I'm Bill Lane, National Security Agency. That man at the corner tried to kill me. He's wounded. If you send someone after him now, you'll catch him before he reaches his embassy."

"Just hold your mouth," one of the cops shouted. "We'll get this straightened out."

18

SOUTH ATLANTIC

The 1,500-ton whaler *Shibayev* plowed north through the angry seas about 150 miles south of the Falkland Islands. She was without cargo, though she was well ballasted with seawater and therefore well down on her marks.

It was nearing midnight. Captain Gennadi Roskov was on the bridge, his gaze alternating from the darkness outside to the ghostly green glow of the radar set.

Nothing was out there, either visually or electronically. Yet they were coming up on their rendezvous point.

Roskov was seventy-one. He'd been around for a long time, and often at moments like this he wondered if it wasn't time to give it up. There was an apartment in sunny Odessa, beaches, his wife and his grandchildren. They could be a comfort to an old man. And yet when his call to arms had come he could not hold back. It was duty ... honor ... everything.

"We are getting close, Comrade Captain," his first officer, Lieutenant Anatoli Seregin, said softly at his elbow.

Roskov turned sharply to him, startled out of his thoughts. "Anything on the radio?"

"Not yet. But our satellite navigator says we're within a kilometer or two of our rendezvous point."

"Yes, I know. Fuck your mother but I would have wished for better weather than this. There may be accidents."

"Yes," Seregin said with a shrug. He was young. He didn't know yet how much there was to lose. "Of course it will make it all the more difficult for the enemy to see what we are doing."

Aleksei Anosov, their radio and ECMs officer, poked his head around the corner from his cubbyhole just aft of the bridge. "We are being scanned, Comrade Captain."

"From what source, can you determine that?"

"It's definitely land-based. I think it must be coming from the south."

"Antarctica?"

"Yes, Comrade Captain. Perhaps from the American scientific installation on Graham Land."

Roskov had to smile. Antarctica was just too important and strategic to leave to chance. The Americans as well as the Russians maintained listening and watching posts there. And now it would suit their purposes just fine.

"All right," he said, girding himself. "Send it now."

"Aye, Captain," Anosov said, turning back to his radio equipment. He adjusted the frequency and keyed the microphone. "Mayday, Mayday, Mayday," he called urgently. "This is the fishing vessel *Shibayev* calling. Mayday, Mayday, Mayday!"

KING GEORGE ISLAND

The wind was up, blowing across the rocky island with gusts of more than one hundred knots. Nothing alive could be out in this weather.

Navy Ensign Don Larsen held the earphones tighter

against his head. There was a signal deep in the mush that had sounded like Mayday to him, first in English and then possibly in Russian.

"Lieutenant," he called over his shoulder.

"Yeah," Lieutenant Bob Ellis answered from across the small comms room where he sat watching several radar screens.

"Have you got a bearing and range on that last target that came around the Horn earlier today?"

"I'm scanning her right now, as a matter of fact," Ellis said. "I show a bearing of zero-one-zero. And she's just about out of my six-hundred-mile ring."

Larsen adjusted his automatic direction finder. "Well, Lieutenant, she's a Russian fishing boat . . . or at least that's how she's identifying herself. And she's calling Mayday." He could hear the ship's weak signal better now.

"Sonofabitch." They had received secret orders this morning about any activity around the Horn. The word was out that somebody might be trying to mess with PIT BULL. Ellis stared at his main search radar screen, then jumped up and went over to the KW-26 crypto machine which connected them via satellite with the Pentagon's Command Center. He opened the circuit.

"There's not much we can do for them now, from here," Larsen said.

"But if they're really in trouble . . ."

He got through to the duty operator, who sent the go-ahead signal.

SOSUS CONTROL: SOUTH ATLANTIC

There were not many underwater listening posts south of the equator anywhere in the world, except for an American-built, British-run station on Ascension Island. The seabed sensors were stretched out around the island and covered a broad area of the Atlantic as far south as the Tropic of Capricorn.

They had watched both fleets steaming south and still had them on their scopes. It was the most traffic on the sea and beneath it they'd ever seen, and they were using the opportunity to fine-tune some of their procedures, among them picking out the acoustical signatures of each ship and submarine.

The task was not easy because of the huge mass of data, and the new equipment the American Navy had installed eight months earlier. Just now there were still a few American technicians hanging around to teach their British cousins the intricacies of the new, more sensitive programs.

U.S. Navy Ensign Scott Anderson was stationed at the same console with his British counterpart, Lieutenant Trevor Probyn.

"It comes down to two major problem areas," Anderson said. "The first is identifying the types of ships and boats, and the second is the number."

Probyn did not like the younger man, whose brash and oftentimes crude manners were irritating, but he had to admit that the American knew what he was talking about. He was an absolute genius when it came to his equipment.

"Fortunate that PIT BULL is being run so timely for us," Probyn said.

Anderson did not miss the slight sarcasm, but he ignored it. The fact of the new equipment and the presence of the Americans was an open joke between them all. It was assumed, of course, that the Russians had made their own extra preparations.

"Multiple targets of the same class, for instance, give us the most trouble," Anderson said. "Just like now. We're showing three Los Angeles-class submarines heading south with the fleet. But are there really only three? Or could there be a fourth one hiding between a pair of identical signatures?"

"Can we fine-tune to that extent?" Probyn asked, impressed despite himself. He held his earphones tighter to his ears.

Anderson punched up the display of the Los Angeles-class footprint and then brought up what they were actually hearing, which was nothing but a jumble of noises and traces across their scope.

"At this point you can leave it to the computers to do the separation, or we can do it manually. Depends on the skill of your operator," Anderson said. He hit the computer analysis function, and immediately most of the trash was gone. Slowly, as the machine began to separate the individual signals, the traces across their scope began to break apart. One and then two Los Angeles-class footprints were identified, but the machine was having trouble with the third.

"Will it come up with an identification?" Probyn asked.

"Sooner or later," Anderson said. "Either that or it will tell you to go manual, that it's having a little trouble."

He switched to manual and fine-tuned a series of filters that slowly separated the final submarine from the others as well as from the tremendous amount of surface noise.

"There," he said, but he immediately switched to another channel, one with the signature of the Russian Sierra-class submarine. There should have been three of them. But he swore that he had heard something else in the mush. Another submarine, and not a Sierra. But what? Another Alfa like the one that had caused so much trouble in the Barents?

This was not the time, he decided, to take chances.

"What is it?" the Brit asked.

"Just be quiet and listen," Anderson said softly. "I think someone is trying to sneak through the front door on us."

RIO CENTER

Admiral Jeff McCauley, a dead cigar clenched tightly in his mouth, sat in his bathrobe in the command communications center just behind his quarters a quarter mile from the operations building.

He had spent much of his evening here like this, listening first to reports from their Antarctic station on King George Island (all comms and intelligence data generated from the Antarctic continent went through Rio Center), and then information-only reports from their SOSUS on Ascension.

He was starting to put it all together, and what he was coming up with wasn't very comforting.

He called on the secure line to his old friend Dave Maxwell at his home in Bethesda.

"Things are heating up around here, Jeff," Maxwell said. "But Mooreland is adamant about doing it by the book."

"It's not so quiet here either," McCauley said. He quickly explained to Maxwell what he had learned from their Antarctic station. "Could be nothing, Dave. But the timing and proximity have me concerned."

"A word of advice: Don't let any of Mooreland's people down there know the extent of your intel operations. He'll have your ass. And it goes without saying to keep the Russians out of it."

"We're going to have to call them on it, if it turns out that Ascension is correct and they're trying to introduce a fourth submarine into the fight."

"That has to come from us. But you're going to have to stay out of that side of it. At least publicly. But listen to me, Jeff, I wasn't kidding when I said things are coming to a boil up here. And I don't mean politically. Someone tried to kill Bill Lane this evening. Just outside his apartment building in Georgetown. Two of them dressed as Catholic priests came after him. He took out one and wounded the other. The D.C. police caught up with him. The likelihood is that it was a Ukrainian GRU operation."

"Which General Normav has in his pocket."

"Exactly. Lane may be on to something that Normav wants him silenced for."

"In the meantime, what are we going to do about this Russian fishing vessel—if she is Russian—that's sending out a Mayday? She's damned close. I think we should put something down there if for nothing else than a look-see."

"I personally agree, but I have to take this one to Mooreland."

"Time is short, Dave," McCauley said. "The ship could really be in trouble. The humanitarian thing to do is get down there and offer a hand."

"It may be Ukrainian, you know. You're going to have to play it carefully for the moment." Maxwell paused. When he spoke again his voice seemed oddly strained, as if he were suddenly ill at ease. "I'm going to talk to Mooreland now. I think you're going to have to be brought in no the rest of this."

McCauley stiffened. He had told them all before he accepted this assignment that he could not do so in the blind. His intelligence would have to be complete and current.

"Talk to me, David," he said coolly.

"There was a shooting aboard the *Nimitz* last night. One of the Russians was killed."

"Goddammit, why wasn't I told?"

"Mooreland wanted to hold off until Lane briefed us. Afterward he said that nothing would have to be done until PIT BULL started. Bill Lane wanted to clue you in on it, Jeff, but Mooreland vetoed him. And I can understand why. You're supposedly acting as nothing more than a referee down there. He doesn't want you contaminated."

"Crap."

"I'll talk to him, I promise you. This has just gone too far to keep you in the dark."

"All right, but you'd better get to him fast. Something is going to have to be done about that fishing boat."

"I'll get right back to you."

"Do that."

IPANEMA

The sky was overcast but the night was warm on the beach in front of the luxurious Meridien-Rio Hotel. Sitting on a lounge chair, sipping a drink with Pam Fisher, Wood was feeling good. He was finally starting to make progress.

Almost without exception every U.S. Navy officer he'd spoken with down here for PIT BULL was all for the new weapons systems that FUTECH and others were developing. "We're a twentieth-century Navy going into the twenty-first century," one lieutenant commander told him. "We don't watch out, we might get our asses shot off in some nasty little regional war somewhere."

Bob Skeritt had telephoned from Billings to ask how things were going, and told Wood that he had FUTECH's full support. "Anything you need, Senator, just give me a call and it's yours."

Skeritt had hinted that the little problem Pamela had called him about would soon be taken care of. But that had made Wood somewhat uneasy, though he wasn't sure why. It seemed like melodrama. So had the way he'd been approached in the garage.

"Tomorrow's a big day, sweetie, I suppose you'll be busy," Pamela said.

"Yes, I will. Can you manage on your own?"

She smiled. "I think so. Shopping looks good here."

Wood had placed twenty thousand dollars in her account before leaving Washington. He suspected she would have it all spent by tomorrow afternoon.

The beach was patrolled by private security guards to keep the panhandlers away from the rich guests, so Wood was not concerned when the young boy took their picture.

"You and the lady want to buy the picture?" the boy asked, grinning. "Plenty cheap."

Pamela was wearing a micro-floss bikini, and the kid, who couldn't have been more than twelve or thirteen, kept licking his lips. Wood had to smile.

"Sure, kid," he said. "Ten bucks if you get back here in the next hour."

"One hour," Pablo Pinzón told his control officer. "But given that piece he's with, he might not remember."

"He'll remember," Tony Lessing said. "At least I would." Lessing was a CIA case officer stationed in Rio. He'd gotten a look at "Wood's Goods," as the girl was being called. She was a knockout.

"Just get back here with the picture," Pablo said. "And make an extra one for me. That chick gives me a hard-on."

Lessing had to laugh. Pablo was only eleven.

19

THE PENTAGON

It was after ten in the evening EDT when Admiral Maxwell entered the Pentagon and went to General Mooreland's suite. The chairman had specified the meeting place upstairs, and not the basement operations room. That was curious.

The Marine guard admitted him to Mooreland's outer office. "The general is expecting you, sir."

Maxwell knocked at Mooreland's door and let himself in.

Horace Walker was seated across the desk from Mooreland, who was in uniform. Walker, like Maxwell, was in civilian clothes.

"Good morning, Mr. Chairman," Maxwell said, sitting down.

"It's my understanding that you have been in direct contact with Jeff McCauley, as late as this evening."

"That's correct. That's why I wanted this meeting even at such an awkward time, sir."

"Contrary to direct orders, Admiral . . ."

"General, I know how to take orders as well as any military man. But I am a member of the Joint Chiefs of Staff."

"Yes, otherwise I would have you immediately relieved of duty and court-martialed."

"If that is your wish, General, then you will have my resignation on your desk within the hour."

"It would not be accepted. Just as any deviation from PIT BULL will not be accepted by either me or the President. On that basis, which General Walker understands, let's have it out, here and now."

"Very well," Maxwell said. "In short, I agree completely with Bill Lane's assessment that under the direction of General Normav the Ukrainians plan on starting something during PIT BULL. It's my belief that we must be prepared to counter this threat."

"You base this on what, other than his briefing to us?"

"In part the attempt on Lane's life last night by two men who it is believed were Ukrainian military intelligence agents. And on a situation—two actually—that are developing in the South Atlantic."

"Go on."

"SOSUS on Ascension is reporting a possible Alfa-class submarine hiding in the *Kremlin*'s task force heading south. This would, of course, seriously jeopardize the balance of power in the operation, but it would also constitute a loaded-gun maverick situation that must not be allowed to continue."

"You're right. A message will be sent by me directly to Normav. There is still time."

"Yes, sir. But there's another situation down there. A Russian fishing boat in trouble just south of the Falklands. She has sent a Mayday."

"How do you know about this?"

"King George Island picked it up and relayed it to us. My operations officer called me with it at home."

"What does Jeff McCauley have to do with it? You did speak with him this evening."

"Yes, sir. He was also aware not only of the SOSUS report but of the Mayday as well."

"How?"

"He has, of necessity, his own intel . . ."

Mooreland slammed his hand on his desk. "I will not have it. Do you understand what this could mean if the Russians got hold of it? We would be playing right into Normav's hands. McCauley must remain scrupulously neutral."

"He is a United States fighting man, General. He must be apprised of the situation on the chance that something will actually develop."

Mooreland was fuming.

"I agree with Dave," Walker said, speaking for the first time.

"Then I will give you both a direct order. Gentlemen, Rio Center, and that includes Jeff McCauley, will remain neutral throughout PIT BULL. They will remain noncombatants. Got that?"

"Yes, sir," Walker said.

"Aye, General," Maxwell replied. "What about that fishing vessel in distress? She may actually be Ukrainian. Are we going to ignore her?"

"No. What resources do we have in the region other than the *Nimitz*'s task force?"

Maxwell glanced at Walker. "We have the *Augusta* in port at Stanley."

"A submarine in the Falkland Islands," Mooreland mused. "In contravention of our agreement with the Russians."

"She is to be cleared from the zone within the required thirty-six hours."

"I wonder," the chairman said. "What class?"

"Los Angeles."

"An attack submarine," Mooreland said. He leaned forward. "All right, Admiral. You will personally order the *Augusta* south to see what the situation is with that fishing vessel. Her orders will be top secret. She is not to reveal her position to anyone for any reason unless lives are being lost or about to be lost. She is to look for any signs that this Mayday is a ruse by the Ukrainian Navy in an attempt to sneak hostile resources into the region. In the meantime, you will contact the Brazilian Navy and request they send one of their ships to the rescue."

"Yes, sir." Maxwell was relieved that Mooreland wasn't going to hamstring them completely.

"What about Jeff McCauley?" Walker asked.

"He is to be kept out of this. His only function is PIT BULL. I repeat: His *only* function is the war game."

"Yes, sir," Walker said.

Maxwell nodded, but his thoughts were already ranging far ahead.

RIO CENTER

"Watch yourself, Jeff. He's out for blood, and you and I are first in line," Maxwell told McCauley a half hour later.

"I could go over his head," McCauley said. "I think I could convince Stoeffel." Leonard Stoeffel was the Secretary of Defense.

"The President would veto anything he said. PIT BULL is on, and you're to be the referee. Nothing more."

"Bullshit. There's nothing stopping me from keeping my eyes open."

"Not a thing at this point," Maxwell said. "But Mooreland knew more than I thought he should."

"Concerning Rio Center?"

"That's right. He's probably got his own eyes and ears down there."

McCauley sighed. "This is bad business, Dave, pitting us against each other. If it ever came to an actual war, we would be at a severe disadvantage, at each other's throats like this. I don't like it. But I've been a military man too long to be able to disobey orders."

"We're talking survival here."

"Yeah, if we're right we'll get a medal, if we're wrong a court-martial. Damned if I care for either under these circumstances."

"I know," Maxwell said. "I feel exactly the same. I'll call Milliken and Stewart. They'll have to keep on their toes."

"I'll watch from this end as closely as possible. But if something comes up I just may have to make a unilateral decision."

"I know, Jeff. You're in the hot seat."

SS *SHIBAYEV*

The weather had gotten even worse over the past few hours. The seas were monstrous, some of them over fifty feet. Captain Roskov, an old Soviet Navy man who had transferred to the Black Sea Fleet, braced himself in front of the radar set, a glass of strong, sweet tea in his hand.

So far no one had answered their Mayday, which Anosov continued to send out at irregular intervals. It was possible that they had overextended themselves, and their rescue ship would not be able to make the rendezvous in time, or they would not be able to transfer crew and do what had to be done.

But all contingencies had been planned for, had they not? That's what he had been told. But of course Roskov had been in battle situations long enough to realize that even the best plans often went awry.

"Comrade Captain, we are receiving an answer now!" Anosov called out excitedly.

Roskov stepped back to the comms room. "Is it the *Ryanny*?"

"No, sir, it is the Brazilian Navy, I think. But their English is bad, and I do not understand Portuguese."

"Well, what do you think they are saying?"

"They are unable to send an aircraft because of the weather, but they have sent a coastal missile boat to help."

"Fuck your mother," Roskov mumbled. "Are they giving us an ETA?"

"Six hours, Captain. Now they are saying that if we require help sooner than that, they have volunteers who will try to fly out to us."

Roskov shook his head in frustration. Six hours. It did not give them much time. By now the Americans knew that something was going on. Surely the Antarctic station had transmitted its data to the Pentagon, and Rio Center had been informed. The eagles would be gathering. Six hours. It would have to be enough.

"Tell them that our pumps are just keeping up with the inflow. If nothing worsens we should manage for six hours. But if things fall apart we will advise them. And Aleksei. Thank them for me."

"Yes, Captain."

Roskov went back onto the bridge. His first officer, Anatoli Seregin, returned from the galley with a fresh pot of tea, some vodka, and a few blini. "Have we made contact?"

"Not yet, but the Brazilian Navy wants to be heroes."

"They are sending someone to rescue us?"

"It would seem so."

"But, Captain, what will we do if they arrive before the *Ryanny*?"

"Then there will be an unfortunate accident. The Brazilian rescuers' vessel will sink to the bottom with a loss of all hands. There is no other way. Let us hope that the Brazilians are not efficient."

SSN *SPASSKY*

The nuclear-powered Ukrainian Sierra-class attack submarine *Spassky* ran in silent mode at ten knots on a course of zero-one-zero degrees, 350 meters beneath the storm-tossed surface.

She had passed well south of the Horn, finally reentering the Atlantic nearly ten hours earlier, where she had loitered, waiting for her diversion to show up. It apparently had.

"Conn, sonar," the comms speaker blared in the attack center.

Captain First Rank Ivan Zaytsev hit the button. "Conn, aye."

"It is the *Shibayev*, Comrade Captain," the sonarman said. "She's about one thousand meters off our starboard bow on roughly the same course as us."

"Speed?"

"Less than five knots. I'd guess she's wallowing in the seas."

They'd surfaced briefly a few hours earlier to do some ELINT gathering, and had seen how the weather was deteriorating.

"Any other surface activity?"

"There might be something behind us, making fast turns around the Horn."

"The *Ryanny*?"

"Can't say yet, sir. If it continues I might be able to identify it within the next hour."

"Good, Anatoli Nikolaievich," the captain said. He almost broke the connection but then thought of something else. "How about beneath the surface? Any other submarines in the vicinity? Especially to the north?"

"None, Comrade Captain. We are alone down here."

Zaytsev grunted his approval.

His *starpom*, Lieutenant Vladimir Myshko, turned to him. "If they even think we're here, Captain, they will send that Los Angeles-class boat."

Their ZIS-One satellite had detected the U.S. submarine's heat signature some days ago. By agreement she was supposed to be moved out of the PIT BULL operational area thirty-six hours before the war game started. But there was nothing preventing her captain from heading south, submerging, and then turning back north. If she was quiet and her skipper was good, she would do it undetected.

That was one of the reasons, Zaytsev thought, it was so terribly important that he get through undetected. "At all costs, Ivan Ivanovich," Admiral Dyukov had told him personally some months ago. (How he had known of an American submarine lurking in these waters was anyone's guess. But then, the man was CINCBLACKSEAFLEET.)

Zaytsev had not realized just what was meant by "at all costs" until he received his specific orders by radio in the South Atlantic some days ago. It was possible, even likely, that there would be a loss of Ukrainian lives before this exercise was completed.

But he was here simply to follow orders and help protect the nation. Something was going to happen. That came down from the highest levels. The Americans would possibly use the games as an excuse to "make a mistake" and introduce live weapons into the operation. A battle would take place between the Russians and Americans. Zaytsev's orders were to stand by. A battle here would very well spread to an intercontinental exchange of missiles, with Ukraine in the backwash. A very dangerous situation at best.

"So we will maintain a defensive reserve," Dyukov had told him and the other officers. "If something should occur, you will know what to do."

FFG *RYANNY*

The 3,900-ton Krivak II-class guided-missile frigate *Ryanny*, late of the Russian Federal Navy, plowed through the heavy seas around the Horn directly into the wind at better than twenty-five knots. The powerful warship rose on huge waves and then plunged down into the awesomely deep troughs.

Half the men aboard were seasick, but they all maintained

their duty stations—it was a court-martial offense to miss duty because of seasickness.

Captain Petr Yelisev was on the bridge with his *starpom*, Lieutenant Vasili Tzarov, and the ship's *zampolit*, Lieutenant Yuri Mishukov. They had just fixed the *Shibayev* with their powerful search-and-identify radar.

"The timing is correct," Mishukov said.

"In this weather the transfer operation will be precarious," the captain said.

"But necessary."

"Yes," Yelisev said. Their orders were to proceed around the Horn, where they would effect the rescue of the crew aboard the whaler *Shibayev*, after which they were to send her to the bottom, and then turn and head back around the Horn into the Pacific. They were to hide themselves in the many fjords along the Chilean south coast. If a shooting war were to develop out of PIT BULL, their coded order would be KEENSCHCAL, and they would proceed to the area of battle. Few of the crew knew that the *Ryanny* no longer sailed for Russia, but had switched allegiance to Ukraine, specifically to General Normav.

Yelisev hit the comms switch. "ELINT, bridge. Have we been detected by the enemy yet?"

"We are being illuminated by radar, Captain. I'd say King George Island, the American installation."

"Any ships or aircraft?"

"None."

"Sonar, what are you showing beneath the surface?"

"Not a thing, Comrade Captain."

The *Spassky* was evidently doing her job, or at least he hoped she was on station very near the *Shibayev*, else this mission would be for nothing.

Yelisev looked at his *starpom* and *zampolit*. He did not want an incident just yet, but it was plain they both relished the prospect. He hit the comms button again. "Comms, bridge."

"Aye, bridge."

"Are you still receiving the *Shibayev*'s Mayday?"

"Aye, Comrade Captain."

"Answer it. Find out the nature of her problem, and tell them we are in our way."

And now it would begin. Yelisev thought.

KING GEORGE ISLAND

"Holy shit!" Ensign Don Larsen exclaimed. "Lieutenant, we've got comms from that target!"

"Did she identify herself?" Lieutenant Ellis called from the crypto machine.

"Sure did. She's a Russian guided-missile frigate. A Krivak II class. The *Ryanny*."

"Holy shit is right," Ellis said.

SSN *AUGUSTA*

From the moment he got word from COMSUBPLANT, Lieutenant Commander Ed Ross had pushed his boat to her limits, making more than thirty-five knots at a depth of 250 feet.

Twenty minutes ago their BQQ-5 long-range sonar gear had picked up the Russian whaler in distress, as well as another strong signal coming up from the south at high speed, and possibly a third close to the whaler.

Earlier, before the urgent call for speed, Ross had ordered their reactor at ten percent of its rated output power, which gave them just barely enough way for steerage, but made them extremely quiet in the water.

"Bridge, sonar," the comms speaker in the attack center crackled.

"Bridge, aye," Ross answered it himself.

"I've got an ID on that strong signal. She's making turns

for around twenty-seven knots. Skipper, there's no doubt that she's a Krivak-class guided-missile frigate."

"On a rescue mission, no doubt," Ross said to his exec, Lieutenant Joseph DeLauren.

"Convenient."

"Yeah, isn't it?" Ross hit the comms button again. "What about that other target you thought you were painting a while a back?"

"Skipper, if it ever was there, it's gone or hiding now."

Ross thought about it for a moment. Frank Torrell was one of the best sonarmen in the fleet. "What's your gut tell you, Frank?"

"I thought it might have been a submarine . . . though I couldn't say if it was theirs or ours. Might even be British."

"Negative. I checked that before we left Stanley. Nothing out here except us. Leastways nothing is supposed to be out here."

"Sorry, skipper."

"What do you think?" DeLauren asked.

Ross took his time answering. He poured a cup of coffee from the pot by the navigation table. "If I was running the show, and I wanted to bring in an asset, I might try to cover it up with a rescue at sea. Meanwhile, once that frigate has done her duty, she can turn tail and hide herself in the Strait of Magellan somewhere between here and, let's say, Punta Arenas. If all hell breaks loose, she'd pop out on the run."

DeLauren smiled. "It might get a bit crowded back there with the both of us holed up."

"Yeah, but at least we're not risking lives to mask our movements. Taking people off that whaler in this weather is going to be dicey business."

"Maybe they've got more at stake."

Ross nodded. "That's what I'm afraid of, Joe. You'd better rig us for silent running. We'll hang around for a bit to see what develops. If there's no sub, we'll follow that frigate to wherever she's going. If there is a submarine out there somewhere, we'll find her and escort her the hell back into the Pacific."

"They might take exception," DeLauren said.

"We'll just have to see about that, won't we?"

"You're the boss."

"Yeah."

SS *SHIBAYEV*

The seas were truly mountainous and dangerous with no sign of letup. GRU Lieutenant Sergei Barynin and Ukrainian Marine Sergeant Oleg Golanov hung on fiercely as they powered their big inflatable across the hundred meters of angry sea.

Having launched from the downwind deck of the *Ryanny*, at least they were in the lee, the seas somewhat calmer in the ship's wind shadow.

The whaler was heaving and bucking in the big seas, however, and getting aboard her was going to be tough with the equipment they were carrying.

But they had practiced this maneuver many times in bad conditions on the Black Sea. And they were expert fighting men, highly motivated and hard as steel.

The sergeant was at the controls of the big outboard motor. As they neared the *Shibayev*, he slowed them down so that Barynin was able to raise his binoculars and study the ship. He could see two people on the bridge. A third person came to the windward rail and dumped a section of heavy netting over the side to serve as a boarding ladder for them.

The crewman waved.

Barynin waved back and adjusted the straps of his backpack. He glanced back at his sergeant, who nodded grimly. They had a job to do, orders to perform, and for the next minutes, they told themselves, they would have to close their minds to any other consideration.

"This is necessary," they had been told. "These men are expendable. They are beyond redemption."

Barynin supposed they had committed some treason

against the state and so had been condemned to death. They were all military men. They had probably been given the chance to die honorably, thus saving their families from the stigma.

That was, however, of no matter to Barynin. His discipline was total.

They reached the whaler, and Barynin managed to loop a line through the boarding net and secure their bobbing inflatable.

Sergeant Golanov left the outboard running in neutral and joined Barynin forward. Synchronizing their moves perfectly with the heaving ship, they grabbed the boarding net and hauled themselves up and scrambled aboard.

There were only four crew aboard the ship: the captain and his *starpom*, the engineer, and the communications man.

"Who are you?" Barynin shouted into the wind at the crewman on deck.

"I am Yevstigney Kormakov, the engineer. The others are on the bridge."

"Very good," Barynin said. He took out his Makarov 9mm automatic pistol and shot the man in the forehead. The body dropped to the deck.

At the angle from the bridge windows no one could have seen anything on the side deck.

"Go below, I'll take care of the others on the bridge," Barynin told Golanov.

The sergeant took Barynin's heavy backpack and disappeared through a hatch that led below to the engine spaces.

The GRU lieutenant entered a forward hatch that led up to the bridge. The odors of the electronic equipment above mingled with the diesel smells from below.

The regular crew of twenty men and officers had been taken off at Santiago. That was ten days ago, a long time for only four to run such a ship. Barynin had to admire their stamina.

At the head of the stairs, Barynin held up in the darkness to survey the situation. The hatch onto the bridge was open, as was another hatch just aft. He could hear someone inside arguing, and from the compartment just aft came the squawks and squeals of radio equipment.

Barynin moved forward swiftly.

In the radio room, the ECMs man, Aleiksei Anosov, looked up startled, his eyes wide. In one smooth movement, Barynin raised his pistol and fired a shot into the forehead just above the left eye. The man tumbled backward against his equipment.

Someone shouted an alarm on the bridge as Barynin stepped through the hatch.

The *starpom*, Anatoli Seregin, stepped back with his hand upraised as if to fend off a blow. Captain Gennadi Roskov yanked open a cabinet and fumbled for a pistol.

Barynin shot the captain first, hitting him in the side, in the neck, and finally just above his ear.

"Fuck you . . . ," Seregin called out, but Barynin calmly shot the executive officer twice, in the chest and in the face. The man was dead before he hit the deck.

SSN *AUGUSTA*

The explosion could be heard throughout the submarine.

"Sonar, bridge. What the hell was that?" Captain Ross demanded.

"Just a second, skipper," Torrell said. "Ah . . . it's that whaler. I'm still hearing the frigate. But they're close. They might have got the crew off."

Fifteen minutes earlier they had heard the screw of a small boat crossing to the whaler and, minutes later, returning to the frigate.

"She's going down, skipper," Torrell said. "I'm hearing breakup noises, machinery breaking loose."

"What happened, Frank?"

"Skipper, that was no engine room explosion. I'd be willing to bet that ship was scuttled."

"Damn." What the hell was going on up there? Ross hit

the comms switch again. "Any sign of that submarine you might have heard earlier?"

"Negative."

Ross turned to his exec. "We've got no other choice, Joe. Bring the boat to periscope depth."

RIO CENTER

The five-bell designator for a top-priority message jangled on the teleprinter in the communications center at the Rio complex.

Chief Petty Officer Tom Jarvis jumped up from where he was drinking coffee and hurried to the machine as the message spewed out. He read it with a growing disbelief. "Jeez . . ." he whispered.

Jarvis pulled the message from the *Augusta* off the machine, hit the button that automatically retransmitted it to the Pentagon, and then picked up the telephone and dialed the number for Admiral McCauley's quarters.

THE PENTAGON

At one in the morning, Admiral David Maxwell was recalled to the Pentagon Command Center, this time by Rear Admiral Harry Morrison, operations chief of Atlantic Submarine Operations, a scholarly-looking man with horn-rimmed glasses. He and Maxwell went back a long way together.

"This better be good, Harry," Maxwell said.

"Judge for yourself." Morrison handed Maxwell the message that had just come in from Rio. "Ed Ross on the *Augusta* sent this. He's good, Dave. I trust him completely."

The message was long and detailed, two pages. Ross had

given it a top-secret, top-priority designator and Maxwell could see why after the first couple of lines.

"There's only one reason why they'd sink their own ship after staging their little rescue operation, and then run back into the Pacific. They're hiding something. Probably that boomer Ed might have heard earlier."

"If she's there, she knows we're around now," Morrison said.

Maxwell was trying to think it out. The message had been relayed through Rio Center, so Jeff McCauley knew the situation. The Ukrainians apparently were trying to sneak a sub through the front door past Ascension, and now they were trying to do the same thing from the south under the cover of a noisy emergency.

"Have the *Augusta* surface and pick up any wreakage that might show the whaler was sabotaged."

"It doesn't matter . . . ," Morrison started.

"No, it doesn't. In reality, Ross is just going to bide his time, giving that boomer, if there is one there, the chance to sneak away. Ross's going to give the bastards a head start and then he's going to follow them north to PIT BULL."

"How do you know she'll head that way?

"Where else?"

J. EDGAR HOOVER BUILDING

Joseph Bishop's secretary brought the file in to him, and he opened it to the photograph on the first page. It and the fingerprints the CIA had managed to lift from a glass in the senator's hotel room positively identified the woman as Pamela Lynn Fisher, twenty-four, originally from Tampa, but presently living in Los Angeles. Her employer was FUTECH Corporation.

While attending UCLA as a mathematics major, the young woman had been suspected of operating a prostitution ring in Las Vegas in which college girls could earn money. The investigation had been dropped for lack of sufficient information, but reading between the lines, Bishop figured the district attorney in Vegas had been pressured into dropping it. The girls Ms. Fisher recruited all came from wealthy, influential families. They turned tricks less for the money than for the thrill of it.

After college, Ms. Fisher worked briefly for McDonnell Douglas until FUTECH hired her for its Los Angeles Engineering Division.

Bishop sat back. According to the report, the young woman had expensive tastes. Too expensive for an engineer's salary. Apparently she'd been given to Wood as—what? A bribe? Bishop asked himself. And if that were the case, what else had FUTECH given the senator and what were they asking in return?

20

"Are you all right?" The DCI, Roland Murphy, asked Bill Lane. It was 7:30 A.M., and the sun streamed through the seventh-floor window of the director's office.

"I got lucky, General," Lane said. "They're Ukrainian GRU. The dead man has been identified."

"A good thing you got home when you did. There was enough explosives wired to your apartment door to take out the entire floor. They weren't fooling around."

"It's Normav, no doubt about it, General. But he's got help. Right here, in Washington."

Murphy's jaw tightened. "Explain yourself, Bill."

"I made my briefing at the Pentagon, and shortly thereafter someone tried to kill me. There's a penetration agent at fairly high levels in the Pentagon. Someone communicating directly with Normav, or at least with Kiev through the head of GRU operations here in D.C."

Murphy got up. He keyed his intercom. "Have Howard Ryan come in, please." Ryan was the agency's general counsel, one of the most important people on the DCI's staff. It was he who often kept them out of big trouble with Congress. He and Murphy were close friends.

"We're going to have to go very carefully on this one, Bill. The Bureau is going to have to be brought in on it, of course. But once that happens, once we instigate an all-out witch-hunt, there'll be no turning back. A lot of people will get hurt in the fallout. I've seen it before. Not pretty."

"No, sir," Lane said glumly. Normav had done his work well. Too well?

Ryan, a pinch-faced former New York Park Avenue attorney, showed up a minute later, and Murphy quickly briefed him on what had happened last night in front of Lane's apartment, and Lane's suspicions that there was a Ukrainian agent in the Pentagon, most likely on the staff of one of the Joint Chiefs.

"Of course this has something to do with PIT BULL," Ryan said. "And you seem, at the moment, to be the key to unraveling Normav's plans."

"I think so, if . . ."

"But then, perhaps they were trying to kill you for another reason. Something completely different. Perhaps having to do with your recent work at the NSA. That's possible, isn't it?"

Lane nodded. "But the timing is off."

"I agree, it stinks." The lawyer turned to Murphy. "A witch-hunt would take too much time. The Bureau wouldn't even be started by the time PIT BULL took off. Normav, if he is indeed behind this, will be counting on that. So he's safe. But apparently not from Bill Lane here. It's why they tried to kill him. He may know something that would cause the entire plot to go sour."

"So what are you suggesting, Howard? That we stash Bill somewhere safe while we pick his brains?"

"No, that would take too long. The solution—if Mr. Lane wants to accept it—is to put him right in the middle of the fray."

"Sir?" Lane asked, already not liking the sound of it.

Ryan turned to him. "You should become one of the key players in PIT BULL. Get out of Washington and go down to Rio, where you can brief Admiral McCauley. Then you should get out the *Nimitz*. You can find the killer of that Russian technician, and you can help find out what damage they might have done. Plus you'll have a front-row seat. You might be able to spot trouble before anyone else can."

"Normav would not be expecting such a move," Murphy said. "And at least aboard the *Nimitz* you would know who your enemies were. There are only five Russians aboard. One or more of them may actually be Ukrainians, or Russians with allegiance to Normav."

And an entire task force a couple of hundred miles away, Lane thought but did not say. Both men were waiting for his reaction.

He nodded finally. "I can't do much of anything from here. When do I leave?"

"Within the hour," Murphy said. "Your old friend Captain Zachary Taylor will be standing by for you at Andrews."

KIEV

"We failed, Comrade Marshal," General Valeri Katayev said.

It was six in the evening, Kiev Civil Time, and the slanting light showed the dust motes in General Normav's office in the Council of Ministers Building.

"My order stands," Normav said. "He must be killed."

"He has disappeared. We have an unconfirmed sighting at Andrews Air Force Base."

Normav's eyes narrowed. "Did you think to check if one of their SR-91 spy planes has taken off?"

Katayev was grim. "It has. About the time William Lane was spotted there."

"Then we must assume he is off again," Normav said. "Where to?"

"We don't know that yet."

"Think, Valeri Viktorov. Where would Mr. Lane's presence do KEENSCHCAL the most harm?"

"Rio," the GRU general said. "Perhaps the *Nimitz*. But this man is no technician."

"He can still do us much harm. In Rio and aboard the *Nimitz* we have our resources. I want Mr. Lane dead before PIT BULL begins."

"Yes, Comrade Marshal."

Normav allowed a slight smile. "I spoke with General Mooreland, who called from the Pentagon. A sad man. He believed me when I denied any knowledge of Black Sea submarines heading south. But he cannot guess the half of it. Neither can Mr. Lane. Oh, Valeri Viktorov, there is much more to come."

21

RIO DE JANEIRO

The sleek, black, droop-winged SR-91 supersonic spy plane touched down at Rio's Aeroporto do Galeão two hours after she had taken off. It was 3:00 P.M. local. The cool wind that blew up from the Baía de Guanabara surprised Bill Lane for a moment until he realized that this was the southern hemisphere and it was winter.

"I'm not going to ask you what's going on," Zachary Taylor said, with his friendly smile.

"I don't guess I could tell you anyway."

"Take care of yourself. I don't know what's going on between here and Washington and Bear Island, but I hear the rumors."

It didn't matter what the Air Force pilot knew, because he did not know the truth. If he had, his life would have been in danger.

He was hustled fifty yards to a waiting SH-2F Seasprite LAMPS-I (light airborne multipurpose system) helicopter whose engine was already warming up.

He was the only passenger aboard the small chopper. They lifted off, made a sickening climbing turn to the right, and accelerated to the southeast at maximum rpm. Lane figured they wanted him down on Ilha do Pai ASAP.

RIO CENTER

Lane's first view of the Center was unremarkable. It was nothing more than a low island filled with scrub brush and a few cement-block buildings. Two stern-faced Marine guards, their M-16s at the ready, met him on the landing pad and escorted him to a back entrance into headquarters.

He was shown down a broad corridor and into an office where a dozen Navy ratings were busy at computer terminals. No one seemed to notice his arrival.

Five minutes later, one of the ratings came over. "Mr. Lane?" he said politely. "The admiral is ready for you, sir."

Admiral Jeff McCauley did not bother to get to his feet when Lane was shown into his austere office. Nor did he bother to motion toward a chair. It was clear, without a word being spoken, that he resented civilian interference in his command.

"Dave Maxwell and Roland Murphy say hello," Lane said, taking a seat across the desk from the admiral. "I've been sent down to brief you and offer any help."

"Your flight out to the *Nimitz* is about ready to take off. I wouldn't want to keep you." McCauley said, without inflection. "Captain Stewart has sent an A-6F Intruder for you."

"It can wait," Lane said quietly.

For just a moment it didn't seem that McCauley had heard him, but then his face reddened. "If you people want my resignation, you'll have it. But in the meantime allow me the room to do my job here."

"I neither know nor care what the hell you're talking about, Admiral. My name is Bill Lane. I am an analyst with the National Security Agency on special assignment to the Central Intelligence Agency, under special orders from the President."

"Exactly what is it you want?"

"I think that Ukrainian Marshal General Normav is trying to provoke the U.S. into firing live rounds in the upcoming PIT BULL games in an effort to begin a nuclear shooting war between us and Russia. Normav and his old-school cronies believe that is not only long overdue but would give Ukraine a free ride if Russia were destroyed."

"Yes?" the admiral said cautiously. "What am I supposed to do about it?"

"Be more than a referee, Admiral, unless you don't care what happens."

The admiral stared at him long and hard. Then he slowly got up from behind his desk, went to a small sideboard, and took out a bottle of Kentucky whiskey and two glasses. He poured two healthy measures and brought them back to the desk. Lane took his.

They raised glasses to each other, drank the whiskey down straight, and then McCauley sat back.

"You're making sense so far, go on," McCauley said.

Lane put down his glass. "Admiral, I'm here to warn you that there is a pattern with Marshal General Pavl Normav behind it all. First I want to know if there has been any trouble here. With equipment, people, anything."

"Nothing out of the ordinary," McCauley said. "This is a complicated setup. There have been technical glitches of one sort or another. But as of the furball between the two DOME yesterday, everything has been functioning perfectly." He sighed. "The same goes for my staff. But I can't say it's true for the media and VIPs."

"Have they all been accredited? Including the Russians?"

"Yes."

"No last-minute substitutions?"

"None that I'm aware of."

"I'd like to have a list of your staff as well as visitors before I go out to the *Nimitz*."

"You think we might have picked up a saboteur?"

"It's a possibility, not only here but abroad the *Nimitz*. Were you told about the killing?"

"I wasn't given details."

Lane nodded. "All right, Admiral, this began about eighteen months ago in Kiev when there was an attempt on President Yuri Myakotnik's life, we think by Normav and some of his old guard."

"That didn't hit the newspapers."

"No, and evidently Myakotnik and the other moderates never put it together either, or else Normav would not have been promoted. The point is, Admiral, this took place about the same time talks for PIT BULL started. About that same time Normav began gathering his old pals around him, but quietly, so no one took notice. And they are good, Admiral, some of the best."

"He's built himself a fighting machine. You actually think he means to provoke a shooting war?"

"I do."

"Who shares your opinion?"

"Maxwell and Armstrong. My boss over at NSA, and Roland Murphy."

"But not Mooreland, and not the President."

"No."

McCauley thought about it. "Puts us all in a tough spot."

Lane nodded. "You don't know how tough. Let me tell you the rest of it, including the possibility that there'll be at least two Ukrainian submarines in the equation."

KIEV

The light had finally faded. General Normav stood at his apartment window looking out over the nighttime city. It was a little after nine, and he was dead tired.

They were so close now that he could almost taste their victory. Even their error in Washington with the NSA analyst would not be fatal. Not many believed this man Lane. Certainly General Mooreland and the President were still committed to PIT BULL, the fools.

The man behind him put down the telephone. "William Lane is at this moment in Admiral McCauley's office, presumably briefing him on everything he knows."

"Everything he thinks he knows," Normav snapped peevishly. "Can we get to him there, at Rio Center?"

"It would be messy, Pavl. Besides, he's already talking to McCauley, so the damage has been done."

Normav looked at him. "But you do have the resources to handle it if need be?"

"Of course, as well as aboard the *Nimitz*."

"No one knows about your people? Not even the GRU?" It was his one big mistake, placing such total reliance on his military-intelligence people.

"We are working now to sabotage the aircraft that will take Mr. Lane out to the *Nimitz*. If that fails he will be killed aboard the carrier. An accident, perhaps, or perhaps the GRU officer will be found guilty just before he kills himself."

Normav flashed a tight smile. "We cannot lose. Before a fight, two men are boasting; afterward, only one." It was an old peasant proverb. "Indulge an old man a bit of gloating."

"Then gloat. In the meantime. I have work to do, my old friend. There have been ugly rumors that you had a hand in poor Marshal Lenov's death. Irresponsible. They will be stopped."

Normav's smile widened. "With you involved, I think anything is possible for me."

"Yes," Russian Secret Service Director Vladimir A. Krykov said at the door. "It is true."

SOUTH ATLANTIC

It seemed to Lane that he had spent a major portion of the week in very fast but very uncomfortable airplanes. He sat now in the bombardier's seat of a Grumman A-6F Intruder, the carrier's heavy attack bomber that had been sent out from the *Nimitz* to fetch him.

The pilot explained that since the Intruder had a range of only six hundred nautical miles, and the *Nimitz* was nearly twice that distance out, they would have to refuel en route.

"A maneuver second in excitement only to a carrier landing," the pilot said.

But the in-air refueling from the KA-6D tanker version of the Intruder was a relatively mild operation to Lane. They came up behind and below the KA-6D, which unreeled the umbilical hose with its parachute-like connecting end. When it was close enough, the bomber pilot maneuvered his refueling nozzle into the socket and the fuel began to flow.

It took less than ten minutes, and when the bomber pulled back, the windscreen was splattered with a few drops of the green fuel.

That had been nothing compared to what they were facing now. The ship below them looked not much larger than a rowboat that was heaving up and down on the steep seas.

The carrier had been turned into the wind. His pilot lined up on final, and the nose dropped so that they were heading right at the forward edge of the deck. If they missed, they would crash into the bow, and their wreckage would be plowed under the ship and chopped up by the propellers.

Lane could see crewmen in yellow windbreakers on deck, and other aircraft, their wings folded up, lashed down in front of and behind the island structure.

They seemed to be coming in too fast, but all of a sudden they were down, hard, and an instant later they were yanked to an abrupt halt by the arresting wires.

Lane pulled off his restraining straps as a tow unit pulled them down the deck. The canopy opened and the stiff sea breeze filled the cockpit.

Now Lane could feel that he was aboard the ship. The waves were still at least thirty-footers and the big carrier was moving up and down. He fought a brief wave of nausea.

A ground crewman with a ladder helped Lane down from the cockpit and directed him toward a hatch in the side of the island.

Lane hurried across the heaving deck to the hatch, lurching as if drunk.

A dark-haired man, lieutenant commander's oak leaves on his collar, was coming through the hatch. "Mr. Lane?"

"That's right."

"Tom Manning, executive officer." They shook hands. "The admiral and skipper are waiting for you."

"How far are we from the start?"

"We'll be in striking range in about forty-eight hours."

"It could happen at any time once we're in range?"

"Yes, sir. Now, if you'll just follow me."

On the *Nimitz*, like any other big aircraft carrier, despite her size, space was at a premium, taken up by the needs of six thousand or more men and officers, nearly ninety combat aircraft and all the fuel needed for them (that had always been a problem aboard aircraft carriers), and the stockpile of weapons, many of them nuclear.

The interior of the ship was a rat's maze of passageways, steep ladders (stairs), elevators, and, surprisingly enough, escalators to move duty crew back and forth efficiently.

"Making these ships bigger doesn't help," Manning explained. "The designers just load them with more aircraft and weapons systems."

There might be more actual crew living room, Lane guessed, aboard a modern nuclear submarine than aboard a carrier.

It wasn't that way, however, in Admiral Milliken's flag quarters. A Marine guard outside the doorway saluted and let them in. The cabin was actually a roomy suite. It was richly paneled with dark wood, thickly carpeted, and finished with expensive butter-soft leather chairs and couches.

Admiral Milliken was a small but sturdy man who looked

as if he'd spent his life in the sun. Captain Stewart, on the other hand, looked pale as a banker.

They were seated across from each other, sipping coffee, and both got up when Lane and Manning walked in.

"Thanks for coming down to help us out," Captain Stewart said.

"Did you have a chat with Jeff McCauley?" Milliken asked.

"Yes, sir. I left his office a couple of hours ago."

"Dave told me all about you," Milliken said. "Before we get started here, though, I want to establish some ground rules. What's said in this room does not leave this room. But nothing is taboo in here. I want the truth in unvarnished form. Okay?"

"Yes, sir," Lane answered.

"I have one question for you. General Mooreland and the President both feel strongly that the political ramifications of PIT BULL far outweigh any possible dangers," Milliken said. "It's my understanding that you do not share that view. Is that correct?"

"Admiral, the President asked me personally to see what I could do to make it go. That's what I'm here to do."

"Fair enough, son. Now let's hear what you've come up with that has Dave Maxwell and Horace Walker so heated up. You do know about the killing here aboard the *Nimitz*?"

"Yes, sir. That's part of it. Someone tried to kill me in Washington last night. They were GRU officers, and I suspect that someone will try to kill me here. I think I know who it is, and why."

THE PENTAGON

Admiral Dave Maxwell was on his way back up to his office in E Ring when he bumped into General Horace Walker, who was on his way down to operations. They went together to one of the coffee shops that looked out into the interior courtyards.

"He's aboard," Maxwell said, keeping his voice low.

"He's already talked to McCauley?"

"And Milliken."

"Well?" Walker asked impatiently. They both felt that a lot was riding on what would happen in the next few hours, not the least of which was their careers.

"Jeff has been angling for a bigger slice of the pie from day one. Milliken will go along with us too."

Walker looked away. "Lock and load," he said softly.

"That's what he told them, and they agreed," Maxwell said. "No matter what happens, we won't be caught with our pants down."

"But if Normav's goal is to get us to shoot first, we've just played into his hands by arming our weapons."

"Yeah," Maxwell said. "But the hell of it is, we simply don't have any other choice."

THE RUSSIAN EMBASSY

Anatoli Tumanov turned off the lights, but before he left his office he looked out the window down at 16th Street. Traffic was light. He'd never felt so strongly that he was a foreigner in a foreign land. His orders from Moscow were confusing. PIT BULL was essential to President Nikolayev, who, like American President Reasoner, was committed to easing world tensions.

The exercise was equally important to powerful men in the Kremlin and at the Lubyanka who saw it as a salvation for Russia's beleaguered economy. If Russia did well in PIT BULL it would mean billions in weapons sales.

Cutting through the doublespeak, Tumanov's orders were to stop anyone else from interfering with the exercise so that the Russians would have a clear field in which to interfere.

On the elevator, the Foreign Intelligence Service officer knew that his work was finished in Washington. He was leaving for Rio tonight to try and stop Senator Wood. No matter what happened there, he would be forced to return to Moscow.

America was foreign, but at least there was food to eat, cars to drive, football to watch, shopping at stores that had goods on the shelves, and a political system that seemed to work.

He signed out with security and outside started across the sidewalk to his blue, windowless van when a black Cadillac pulled up and a tall, thickly built man got out and came directly toward him.

Sensing danger, Tumanov stepped back. He seldom carried a weapon, and tonight was no exception.

Ten feet away the man raised a pistol and fired four shots in rapid succession, all of the 10mm bullets hitting the Russian in the chest, the second destroying his heart and killing him instantly.

From the time the Cadillac pulled up to when the shots were fired was less than five seconds. Sterling Miller and Puck Abramson, parked across the street, pulled their weapons as they leaped out of the car.

"FBI! FBI! Stop!" Miller shouted, racing across the street.

The Russian was down, the shooter was turning around, as if in slow motion, and the Cadillac raced away, burning rubber.

"Put your hands up now!" Miller dropped into a shooter's crouch, both hands on his Glock 17 automatic, the man's torso in the middle of his sights. He could see Puck out of the corner of his eye doing the same.

Still as if in slow motion, the shooter stopped in his tracks and raised his hands above his head. Traffic was screeching to a halt, and someone came out of the embassy in a dead run.

22

ANDREWS AIR FORCE BASE

They were actually on their way. The afternoon was warm
and humid after the mountains of Colorado, and where they
were going it would be winter, albeit mild.

Lieutenants Luke Hardell, Tom Cathey, and Bragg Williams stood in the pilots' lounge in the Operations Building
waiting for their KC-135 transport to come up on the apron.
It was going to be a long flight down to Rio and from there
via Grumman Greyhound out to their air wing on the
Nimitz. They were keyed very high, not only because of the
upcoming missions in which they'd be flying against real
Russian pilots, but because of what Hardell had done in the
exercise. He had become a local hero.

"He was damned good," Hardell told the other two pilots.
"He came up with that supershot just like I thought he
would, but it was crisp. His entry came sooner than ours,
and his rate of turn and climb was sharper. If I hadn't been
waiting for it, he might have had me. Your guys are going
to have to watch your asses."

"He wasn't about to back off," Williams said thoughtfully. He came from an Iowa farming family, and although he was naive, he was bright and skillful, one of the graduates of the Navy's Top Gun program (as they all were in Hardell's squadron).

"No," Hardell agreed. "But up to that point he sure as hell went by the book. The scoop is this, gentlemen. We have always been able to count on the fact that Ivan would go by the book, his book. And Ivliyev did just that, up to a point. Now all bets are off. He went to school on us, and you can be sure the lessons are being passed along."

"Then we might as well toss out everything we learned at Top Gun, is that what you're saying, Luke?" Cathey asked.

"No. All I'm saying is watch your asses. They're a lot better than we thought."

FRUNZE AIRFIELD, MOSCOW

Captain Nikolai V. Ivliyev stepped outside the pilots' lounge and sniffed the night air. It smelled faintly of fog from the Moskva River, and of Moscow itself, but there was no odor of aviation fuel.

He reached inside his tunic, pulled out a cigarette, twisted its long cardboard filter ninety degrees, and lit it, drawing the smoke deep into his lungs.

His pilots had avoided him ever since the aerial fight. Not because they were ashamed of their squadron commander, but out of loyalty: They felt he would want to be alone with his thoughts. He smiled to himself. They'd been surprised when immediately afterward he called a briefing session in the operations auditorium in which they had replayed the tapes of the fight. Following the tape he gave them a long, penetrating chalk talk.

"You had better learn by my mistakes, comrades," he told them, "or else we will look very bad in PIT BULL."

The door opened and Ensign Petr Boskritz came out.

"Pardon, Comrade Captain, but we are ready to go. Our transport has arrived."

"Nervous?" Ivliyev asked.

Boskritz opened his mouth, but no sound came out. He lowered his head. "Yes, I am."

"Well, so am I. Maybe it will make us more precise pilots."

"Do you think so?" the young man asked, looking up.

"Yes, of course," Ivliyev said.

CVN *NIMITZ*

Petty Officer Second Class Robby LePlace looked up from the scope of his electronics test set and reached into the avionics bay of the Hornet he'd been working on for the past twenty minutes. He adjusted a contact. Something wasn't right, but he couldn't figure it out.

He'd run into the same problem this morning when he checked this plane topsides, just aft of the island. They'd let it pass for the moment, but after they'd checked out every other unit he had this one brought down into the maintenance bay.

"Are you still fucking with that thing?" his boss, Chief Petty Officer Warren Bradley, barked behind him.

LePlace shook his head. "I can't find the problem, Chief, and it's starting to piss me off."

Bradley pushed LePlace aside. He flipped a couple of switches on the test set, then looked inside the avionics bay. The laser spot tracker was exposed. He checked out the leads from the test set to the aircraft. Everything seemed to be in order, and yet ...

"That's what I mean, Chief. The polarity seems to be reversed here. But when I run it through Rio Center it comes out all right."

"Then jumped-up Jesus, what's your problem?"

"It's not right."

"As long as it matches Rio what difference does it make?" Bradley checked the indication of reverse polarity on the scope once more. "All right, button it up. We've got work to do."

WASHINGTON, D.C.

Rush-hour traffic was beginning to pick up when Ben Lewis drove into Washington from Fort Meade. It had not been made quite clear to him what was going on, but it did have something to do with the Ukraine GRU officer whom Bill Lane had managed to wound, and who had been turned over to the FBI.

Lewis was met at the reception desk by a wiry man who identified himself as Special Agent Dennis Cills.

"Thanks for coming over so quickly, Mr. Lewis. I think this is something your people ought to be in on."

Lewis didn't, but he was here and willing to listen.

They went up to the fifth floor and were stopped at a bulkhead by an armed security guard, scanned with an electronic wand, and asked to sign in.

"Security is tight on this one," Cills said.

The inner corridor was dimly lit. As they passed a partially open door, Lewis caught a glimpse of a lot of computer equipment.

They entered a room and continued through to an inner office, thick curtains covering what Lewis took to be a large bay window.

"We've finished our preliminary interview with the survivor of the murder attempt on Mr. Lane," Cills began. "We've established a number of facts, but before we turn him over to the second-team debriefers we thought you might like to talk to him."

"I thought he would still be in the hospital."

Cills smiles cooly. "He never went to the hospital. We took care of him here."

"What'd you get from him?"

"Name, rank, and serial number for starts. Georgi Yevdokimovich Balan. He's a lieutenant in the GRU out of their embassy, though he was a new face to us. We watch them pretty closely. Apparently he was flown in just for this job. No time for us to make him."

"They were here specifically to kill Bill Lane?"

"No doubt about it. You know there was another shooting last night. In front of the Russian Embassy. One of their intelligence officers was gunned down by a Mafia hood."

"Any connection with this one?"

"Unknown. But something else is scaring the hell out of our boy here. Something more than going home to face the music."

"Unusual," Lewis mused.

"We took off the kid gloves with him. Still he won't break. He'll tell us about the GRU, about his boss and his boss's boss, about his communications routines and letter drops, but he won't even think about defecting." Cills shrugged. "We were hoping that you might be able to help out."

"In trade for what?"

"We'll share the product."

"What else is there?"

"The names of other GRU officers . . . on assassination teams. A list that may have at least one match aboard the *Nimitz*."

"Christ," Lewis said, his throat tightening. "Who is it? Bill Lane is aboard down there right now."

"I didn't know that," Cills said. "His name is Viktor Lemekhov. A lieutenant. He may be among the Russian technicians."

"Does the Navy know?"

"The message just went over to them."

Lewis' mind raced. Possibly it was the break they'd been looking for. Lane had said before he left that he hoped they would follow him south and try to kill him again—at least it would prove that he was on the right track.

"Is he here? I'd like to talk to him."

"In the next room." Cills went over to the curtains and drew them aside, revealing a one-way window that looked into an interrogation room.

The Ukrainian, a bandage around his right leg, sat smoking and drinking vodka across from another man.

"Armando Sanchez, my partner," Cills said. He hit the intercom switch. "Our company has arrived. He'd like to talk with your friend."

Sanchez smiled but didn't look at the glass. "Come on in. I can use the break."

Cills turned to Lewis. "Do you want to go at him alone?"

"Is he cooperative?"

Cills glanced back into the room. "Very, except on the one subject."

"You and your partner can stay in the room," Lewis said.

They went around the corner and through another door into the interrogation chamber. The Ukrainian looked bleary-eyed from the vodka but was wary nevertheless. He looked hard-used. Lewis didn't want to think about that, though; the man was an assassin.

He also didn't want to take much time here. Bill Lane would have to be warned.

"Good afternoon, Georgi Yevdokimovich," Lewis said in Russian. He was certain everything in here would be recorded.

Lewis smiled, reached across the table for the vodka bottle, and took a long swig. He shook his head. *"Fuck your mother, but you are in deep shit over this KEENSCHCAL business."*

The Ukrainian's eyes widened. He jumped up, clearing the table with one sweep of his hand before either Cills or Sanchez could react.

"Son of a bitch, go ahead and run your little games! We will see how it all turns out in the end!"

"Thank you," Lewis said respectfully.

CVN *NIMITZ*

The two messages came within minutes of each other. The first from the Pentagon to Captain Gregory Washington, head of the ship's CID detail. And the sound by high-speed encrypted teletype from NSA, for-your-eyes-only to Bill Lane.

Lane's message came in a series of code groups that he had to decrypt laboriously by hand in his own quarters. The job took nearly twenty minutes. When he was finished he hurried back up to Milliken's quarters.

"I know who the GRU agent is," he said.

Captain Stewart and Marine Captain Washington were there. Neither seemed surprised.

"We know," Milliken said. "We just got this."

He handled Lane the flimsy of the message, which was, except for the business about the Ukrainian's reaction to KEENSCHCAL, a duplicate of his message from Lewis.

"I got the same thing," he said.

"So, we arrest the bastard and hold him until the war game is over with, and afterward we try him for murder," Washington said.

"No," Lane said. "In fact, I want you to keep your people away from him."

"He's here to kill you, and by your own statement he probably killed that technician."

"But why did he kill one of his own people?"

"A cover-up of some sort," Washington said.

"That's right. And have we found what equipment the man was tampering with?"

"Not yet," Captain Stewart said.

"Pardon me, Captain, but these people are good. You may not find out what they've done until it's too late."

Washington picked up on it. "Unless?"

"Unless you let me do this my way. Let me work on him. He'll be nervous knowing I'm here now. His assignment is to kill me. Well, he's going to get even more nervous when he finds me leaning on his people."

"So he'll make a move, hopefully before he's ready, and you'll . . . we'll nail the bastard."

"Something like that," Lane said. "He's here to interfere with PIT BULL. I would like a chance at stopping him."

The skipper and the admiral exchanged glances. "Doesn't look like we've got much choice," Milliken said.

"I guess not, Admiral," Stewart said. He turned to Lane. "This is a big, very expensive piece of equipment, Mr. Lane, with a lot of good men aboard her."

"I understand exactly what's at stake, Captain," Lane said.

SSN *AUGUSTA*

"Conn, sonar. Skipper, I've lost her."

"Are you at maximum sensitivity, Frank?" Ed Ross asked.

"Aye, skipper, but she's gone. Last I heard she was still making turns for maximum speed."

"Any sign of that sub?"

"Negative."

His exec, Joe DeLauren, was at the periscope searching the waters around them. At this low latitude the sun went down early. He had been using the periscope's light-intensification circuitry for nearly an hour now.

"Anything out there?" Ross asked.

"Nothing that would do us any good. Another oil slick came to the surface a few minutes ago. From her fuel tanks probably."

Ross checked the chronometer on the bulkhead above the navigator's station. It had been a long time since the whaler had been scuttled. Time enough for the frigate *Ryanny* to head back toward the Horn, and more than enough time for that sub, if there was one there, to go a long distance north. Far enough to lose herself easily along the ragged shoreline or deep beneath a thermocline somewhere. The odds favored a submarine in the open ocean, despite all of their sophisticated ASW equipment.

That is, if he did not know where to look. The COMSUBPLANT had been very specific about that, however.

Patience, Ross told himself. He'd been taught that by his father, who had himself been a Navy captain, and of course he'd been taught it at the academy and then at sub school in New London, Connecticut. But it was tough in the real world.

DeLauren looked up from his periscope. "How about scanning the *Ryanny* with radar?"

"I don't want to light her up. She'll be expecting us to come up behind her, and I don't want to pinpoint our position any more accurately than they already have it." For all they knew, the Russian frigate was already west of the Horn.

"How much longer are we going to sit around here, then?"

"No longer," Ross said, finally making his decision. He hit the comms switch. "I want a message to COMSUBPAC. Tell him that we have found no survivors, that the Russian frigate we identify as FFG *Ryanny* has departed station toward the west, and that we are preparing to submerge and head out of the operational area. We should be in Pearl in ten days."

It was a decoy message and all the crew knew it. The hope was that the *Ryanny* would pick it up and decode it.

Now the real fun began.

"Dive the boat, Joe. Take us to twelve hundred feet."

DeLauren was startled, as were the other crewmen on the conn. That was too deep for normal operations. Such depths were used only in emergencies by American submarines.

"They won't be looking deep. Might give us the edge."

DeLauren realized the wisdom of the maneuver and he grinned. "Aye, skipper," he said. "Now let's kick some ass."

THE PENTAGON

It seemed to Admiral Maxwell that it had been weeks, perhaps even years, since he had last slept. But he felt vindicated finally.

The message from the *Augusta* had been relayed from COMCPACSUB just minutes ago. By now the Los Angeles-class submarine was on her way back north on the trail of the Ukrainian submarine. The equation down there was beginning to even up.

FFG *RYANNY*

Captain Yelsiev stepped off the bridge when the fading light made it impossible to see anything beyond their bow.

The seas were still confused, though the weather had calmed considerably. But the ocean was no more confused than he. In the hours since the whaler had blown, he had gotten no answers.

He had been standing on the wing deck with his *starpom*, Vasili Tzarov, when the big rubber raft started back. It was clear no one from the whaler was aboard.

"Where is the crew of the *Shibayev*?" Tzarov had asked.

"I don't know, Vasili," Yelisev had said. "Perhaps their ship is not in trouble, after all. Perhaps they decided to remain aboard."

At that moment a huge explosion had lifted the whaler half out of the water. She settled almost immediately with a twenty-degree list to starboard, down at the bow, and sank rapidly.

Barynin and Golanov, in the inflatable, had not bothered to turn around and look. The bastards had been expecting the explosion. In fact, they had probably set it. They had taken heavy packs across with them. They had not brought them back.

Yelisev looked through the bridge hatch. There'd been no

time to talk with the two, even if he had the desire. His orders were simply to effect a rescue and then withdraw around the Horn until they received further orders.

He sighed. If he could just understand, he told himself, it might be easier to bear.

He had watched the whaler go down. Not once had he seen the slightest evidence that any of her officers or men were attempting to abandon ship.

What had happened over there? Had Barynin and the sergeant killed all twenty of the crew and then set the explosives? It was hard to contemplate.

He continued aft, dropping down one deck and entering the officers' wardroom. Only one man sat sipping a glass of tea at the long mahogany table. He looked up with a bland expression on his face, but it gave Yelisev a chill.

"Good evening, Comrade Captain." Lieutenant Barynin said in a voice as gentle as a breeze through a wheat field.

Yelisev nodded, not trusting himself to speak. He poured a glass of sweet tea from the samovar on the sideboard and sat down at the end of the table.

Barynin stared straight ahead for a long time, noisily sipping his tea. Yelisev watched him out of the corner of his eye. Barynin seemed not to have a care in the world.

"There were only four crewmen aboard the whaler," Barynin said at last.

"What?"

"The *Shibayev's* regular crew was taken off at Santiago a couple of weeks ago. These four were merely the delivery crew."

"Where are they? What happened to them?"

"They are dead. I shot them all before the explosives blew out the bottom."

Yelisev reared back.

"They were criminals, Comrade Captain, who volunteered for this mission to save their families future trouble. Now they will be listed as Ukrainian heroes. Don't you see?"

"No, I do not . . ." Yelisev was interrupted by someone at the door.

"But *I* see, Comrade Captain," his *zampolit*, Yuri Mishukov, said. He came in and sat down. "Apparently you have orders for us," he said to Barynin.

The GRU lieutenant nodded and pulled a brown envelope out of his tunic. He handed it to the captain. "I'm sorry that you have these feelings, Comrade Captain. I am not a naval officer, but believe me, I understand the code of the sea. I did not like it myself."

"What are your orders?" Yelisev asked without opening the envelope.

Barynin shrugged. "I do not know. I was merely given this envelope and told to hand it over to you once we accomplished our objective and were safely on our way into the Pacific."

Still Yelisev did not open the envelope. It was time to shake this bastard up a little. "Does this have anything to do with the American submarine behind us?"

Barynin had no reaction. "I'm sure it does. Comrade Captain. But that part is none of our concern. All will be stated in your orders."

"Are we all to become killers, then?" Yelisev asked.

CVN *NIMITZ*

Greg Washington had arranged for Lane a naval uniform with the rank of lieutenant commander. It was agreed that he would be identified by his real name, but as a special CID investigator who had been sent down from Washington to look into the killing.

The first of the Russian technicians he called for was shown into the temporary office within the bowels of the big ship. Lane knew only approximately where he was, in a section that contained offices, one of the dispensaries, and somewhere not too far away (because he could smell the odors of cooking) one of the galleys.

"Have a seat, Yevgenni Petrovich," Lane said pleasantly.

Washington, who let the young technician in, withdrew from the inner office and closed the door.

The Russian looked uncertainly at Lane. "Why have I been brought here like this, sir? I wish to speak with my team leader."

Lane leaned forward and pretended to read something out of a file folder. "That would be Lieutenant Viktor I. Lemekhov?"

"Yes, sir."

"All in good time," Lane said, smiling. "I would like first to speak to you about your good friend Gennadi Chalkin. His death is very unfortunate. We want to discover who killed him."

The young tech, Soloviev, fidgeted. "I am sorry, Commander, but I did not know him very well. He was new to our team."

"I see. Was he sent out to you along with Lieutenant Lemekhov? Or did their transfers come at separate times?"

The kid seemed trapped. "They came together," he said softly.

Lane pretended to write something in his file. He knitted his eyebrows. "We have discovered something very disturbing, Yevgenni Petrovich. Something I will need your help with. It is possible that your friend was murdered by one of your own team members."

Soloviev's eyes widened. "What are you saying to me? This is impossible. This is some kind of a plot against us. I will not hear it!" He jumped up.

"Sit down," Lane ordered.

The kid started to back up.

Lane pulled out a 9mm military automatic and pointed it at the young Russian. "I said, sit down!"

There was a commotion in the outer office. Washington's

voice raised in anger. It was their signal that Lemekhov was on his way in.

The door banged open and the GRU lieutenant filled the opening, snarling. "What is going on here?" His eyes took in the gun in Lane's outstretched hand. "Either shoot him or put that pistol down, Commander."

Lane hesitated, then laid the gun carefully on the desk. "May I do something for you, Lieutenant?"

"What are you doing with my man?"

"Conducting an investigation into the murder of Gennadi Chalkin, also one of your men. It's my belief that one of your people killed him."

Lemekhov laughed dryly. He motioned for the young Russian to leave the office, closed the door behind him, and sat down across the desk from Lane.

"Then you and I have a problem, Commander," he said. "Because I believe the killer was one of *your* people, and I will not allow you to question my men."

Lane smiled. "You have no choice in the matter. This is U.S. territory. If I have to place you all under arrest, I will."

"I will talk to my admiral aboard the *Kremlin* . . ."

"Not unless you have your own communications facilities, Lieutenant. Ours aboard this carrier are off limits."

"You are willing to jeopardize PIT BULL over this, Commander?" Lemekhov asked incredulously.

"You can cut the act, Viktor Ivanovich. I happen to know that you are an officer with the GRU. And I suspect that it may have been you who murdered your own man."

"Why would I do such a thing?"

"Frankly, I haven't figured that out yet, except that we believe Gennadi Chalkin may have been attempting to sabotage one of our combat aircraft."

"If I had shot him, I would be a hero to Americans."

"Unless your reason was to throw us off the track. Unless you feared that he might open his mouth at the wrong time."

Lemekhov had a faint smile on his lips. "This is really

fantastic, you know. Am I under arrest, then, for the murder of poor Gennadi?"

Lane paused. "No, you are not, Lieutenant. Not yet. But I would like to speak with your people. I would like to get this settled."

"And so would I, believe me. I will talk with my men and I would like to speak with my admiral aboard the *Kremlin*. Until I am allowed to communicate with my own task force, I will not allow you to speak with my men. It is simple."

Lane sighed as if in defeat. "I will talk with my admiral. They will have to work it out among themselves."

"That is wise," Lemekhov said skeptically. He got to his feet, gave Lane one last glance, and left the office.

Washington came in and closed the door. "Well?" he asked. "Did he take the bait?"

"I think so," Lane said. "The next step is up to him."

"Yeah, it's up to that bastard to kill you."

SSN *AUGUSTA*

"Conn, sonar."

Ross hit the comms switch. "Conn, aye."

"Skipper, I've got a contact on passive about fifty thousand yards out."

"Have you got a bearing and depth, Frank?"

"She's almost dead on our bow, but well above us, running no deeper than three hundred feet."

Ross glanced at his exec and navigation officer. "Is this our boat, Frank?"

"I can't say that for sure, skipper. But she's a Sierra-class sub, making turns for thirty knots."

The Sierras were nuclear-powered attack submarines that had first showed up in service in the mid-eighties. She was slower than the Alfa class and could not dive quite as deep, but she was bigger, and her machinery spaces, including her pump rooms, were well insulated, which meant she was an extremely quiet boat.

With her powerful electronics and armaments (she was capable of launching every class of weapon left in the Russian or Ukrainian submarine service), she was a formidable weapon.

Ross was respectful of her and her captain.

"We'll stay on the same course and speed." he said.

"What if she detects us?" DeLauren asked.

"We'll either stay and fight or surface and call for help."

SSN *SPASSKY*

Captain Zaytsev, headphones clamped to his ears, stood behind the chief sonar operator and listened to the rhythmic sounds deep within the mush and roar of the ocean outside their hull.

It was difficult to pick out exactly what he was hearing. The sonar operator was watching him. He shook his head, and the young man reached over and switched in a couple of noise filters. Suddenly it was clear to Zaytsev.

"I have you now, you bastard," he said softly. "It is the Los Angeles-class boat. But his signal is strange. Range and bearing?"

"On our port quarter, same course and speed, but much deeper. Perhaps more than three hundred meters."

Odd. "How far back?"

"Fifteen thousand meters."

The captain handed the earphones to the sonarman. "Feed that information into our targeting computer."

Zaytsev hurried forward to the attack center, where his *starpom* was speaking with their navigation officer and weapons systems officer. "Time to go to work, comrades."

"Captain?" Myshko asked.

"That American submarine is on our tail. I want a continuous firing solution on her."

"Are we going to attack?"

"Only if she tries to surface and communicate with her home base or with the PIT BULL task force. That, we will not allow."

23

CVN *KREMLIN*

The weather had cleared. The Grumman C-1A Trader touched down on the deck of the Russian nuclear-powered aircraft carrier with a sharp bark of her tires, was caught by the arresting wires, and came to a neck-wrenching halt. A tow unit was connected to her nose gear and she was hauled to the far end of the flight deck.

The *Kremlin's* operations officer had requested a quick turn around, no reasons specified, though the *Nimitz* had informed them that a Russian COD (carrier onboard delivery) aircraft was incoming from Rio, and probably was bringing in the last of the *Kremlin's* air crew.

Navy Lieutenant Mark Dreyfus unbuckled his seat belt and got to his feet. He was the team leader of the six American observers sent from the *Nimitz* to monitor the Russians' actions during PIT BULL.

"All right, gentlemen, it's time for us to start earning our pay," he shouted over the noise of the engines. He was a big, rawboned Texan whose real job was CID under Greg Washington.

"They're not going to be real happy with us, Lieutenant," Chief Petty Officer Bob Schaefer said.

Dreyfus looked at the aluminum coffin they'd brought with them. He wished he could have brought the name of the killer with him, along with the Russian body. It was going to be tough for them to do their job here because of the murder.

"Keep your cool, Mark," Washington had told him. "They're probably going to try to bait you, make you blow up, so that they can send you home. Don't let them do it."

A pair of Russian deck crew approached. They looked from the Grumman's crewman to the aluminum coffin.

Dreyfus, who could speak Russian, stepped over to the hatch. "Is your officer here?" he asked in English.

A swarthy, thick-chested man appeared at the open hatch. He wore the rank of captain lieutenant. *"I am the starpom. Do you perhaps speak Russian?"* he asked in Russian.

"Sir?" Dreyfus asked.

"Sorry," Arkadi Zolkin said, switching to English. "I am the *Kremlin's* executive officer. Welcome aboard." His eyes strayed to the coffin. "This is our comrade?"

"Yes, sir," Dreyfus said. He handed his orders down to the Russian officer.

"If you and your men will come with me, I will show you to your quarters and your briefing will begin."

"Yes, sir," Dreyfus said. He turned back to his men. "Let's go."

They followed the exec across the breezy flight deck to a hatch in the island structure. The *Kremlin* was a lot different from the *Nimitz*. At 984 feet she was smaller, and she had many more guns and missile armaments aboard, which made up for the fact that her air wing consisted of only fifty planes, thirty-eight fewer than the wing currently on the *Nimitz*. In fact, to Dreyfus, she looked more like a hybrid carrier-battleship. The *Kremlin* would be a formidable opponent in a close-in fight.

There were a lot of crew on deck, and they watched the six Americans cross to the island. Dreyfus hesitated a moment before ducking through the hatch. His eyes met those of a young naval rating. The kid looked angry. He turned away as the coffin was off-loaded.

Tensions were definitely running high here.

RIO CENTER

Lieutenant Commander Paul Emanuel, the American controller for Operations, Surface, flipped his display up on the big situation board at the open end of the U.

A group of civilians had gathered around his console and he tried to answer their questions.

"As you can see, we are just now beginning to paint the fleet as it comes south," he said.

Most of them were news media people, including Yuri Vitrov from the Russian news agency TASS, Ben Brown from the Associated Press, and Stan Knightly from CBS. But standing just off to the left was Senator Pat Wood. The admiral had warned all of them about the Senator.

"How far out are they at this point?" Gordon Hawke, from Reuters, asked.

"About six hundred fifty nautical miles."

"In terms of time, Commander. How long before PIT BULL begins?"

"No way of telling that for certain," Emanuel said. "Both task forces are running at a SOA—speed of advance—of thirty knots, which will put them into the PIT BULL arena within twenty-four hours. However, the aggressor—which in this case by a coin toss will be the Russian task force—has the option to attack at any time within a twenty-four-hour window."

"The element of surprise," another newsman put in.

"Yes," Emanuel said, "although both task forces will be

at an increased state of readiness during the entire twenty-four-hour period."

"Why don't you tell it like it is, Commander?" Senator Wood asked sharply. "No matter how realistic you wish to make these . . . games, they still will be conducted under artificial conditions with obsolete equipment."

Here it comes, Emanuel thought. And there was no help in sight. "Yes, Senator, you are absolutely correct. These are war *games*, not actual war. Rio Center's existence with an emergency override capability in case something should go wrong becomes part of the artificiality, as do the unarmed weapons aboard the fighter aircraft."

"And the unarmed weapons aboard the warships," Wood continued. "And the attitudes of the fighting men who realize that no matter what happens, no one will get hurt. No side will really lose."

"Well . . ."

"Then why bother with this gross expenditure with outdated weapons?"

Admiral McCauley was suddenly there. "As I understand it, Senator, you voted for this project. And, in fact, were one of its champions in the Senate before Montana was passed over as a site for our DOME installation."

One of the journalists let out a guffaw. Wood glared at McCauley, but had nothing to say because the admiral was telling the truth.

"Now, ladies and gentlemen, if you will follow me," McCauley said, "The air crews from both task forces are arriving aboard their carriers. You will be allowed to interview them in a news conference via a video link with the *Kremlin* and the *Nimitz*."

Senator Wood remained behind. "Thank you for your honesty, Commander," he said to Emanuel.

"Sir?"

"I'm wondering if you can answer one final question for me. But I want it straight or not at all."

Emanuel noticed that his Russian counterpart, Yuri Y. Anisomov, was watching them.

"It's my understanding that a Russian technician aboard the *Nimitz* was murdered. What can you tell me about it?"

"Nothing at all, Senator."

J. EDGAR HOOVER BUILDING

"You're a patriot, that a fact, goomba?" Navy Intelligence Officer Miller asked. "Go around killing Russians? They're our allies now."

Miller was interviewing the suspect, Ernest Conito, in one of the interrogation rooms at FBI headquarters. Conito's attorney, Harvey Renfrew, was also present.

The attorney, dressed impeccably in a silk suit, leaned forward. "Mr. Conito served his country in the Army, which makes him a patriot. And there's no need for racial slurs here."

Miller glanced at Conito's file and thick rap sheet. "A bad conduct discharge after three months doesn't qualify."

"He volunteered."

"To avoid rape charges," Miller shot back, closing the file. "What we've got here is murder one in front of two witnesses. On top of that the Russians are screaming their heads off and the State Department wants to hand your client over to the Moscow district prosecutor." He turned to Conito. "You've never done hard time, Ernie, until you've done it in a Russian jail. They call them insane asylums, because if you commit a crime they figure you must be nuts."

The only words the killer had spoken after his arrest were to admit that he understood his rights under the Miranda decision and to ask for his attorney.

"Okay, get outta here," Conito said to Renfrew.

"You sure?"

Conito nodded, and when the attorney was gone, he looked across the table at Miller through lidded eyes. "I want to cut a deal."

"No deals, Ernie. The Bureau has you on this one."

"I'm not doing time in any Russian jail. Whatever it takes you got it. I'm working for some heavy hitters on this one."

Miller shook his head. FBI Special Investigator Joseph Bishop was in the other room catching this on closed circuit. If he wanted to step in and take over he would.

"Talk to your boss."

"Tell me first and I'll take it to him if I think it's worth a shit and that you're not lying to me. Convince me, Ernie."

"Gimme a cigarette."

Miller handed the killer a cigarette and book of matches.

"The Russian was an intelligence officer by the name of Tumanov," Conito said, blowing smoke. "No friend of ours. He was leaning on somebody important. Somebody else asked if I could step in and eliminate the problem."

"I want names."

Conito took another deep drag. "The Russian was leaning on Senator Pat Wood."

Miller kept the triumph off his face. "Who was this somebody who asked you to take the Russian out?"

"Bob Skeritt, a veep at FUTECH."

"He tell you what sort of an ax Tumanov had to grind with Wood?"

Conito shook his head. "We didn't get into that. The Russian was fucking with our people, so I was hired to take him out. I'll do time, but not in Russia. They can't even take care of their own people worth a shit."

24

CVN *NIMITZ*

"Squadron, attention!"

Lieutenant Luke Hardell and his Stingers squadron came to attention in the main pilot's briefing room as their air wing CO, Commander Brad Albright, strode up the aisle to the podium.

"As you were, gentlemen," he said, and the twenty-five pilots took their seats. The other three squadrons that composed the wing were not present at this briefing. They had remained aboard the *Nimitz* during her long cruise from the east coast of the United States, taking to the air in practice sorties against each other, and against imaginary over-the-horizon targets sent up by the DOME through Rio Center. The all-pilots briefing was scheduled for later today. Albright called this meeting because of what had been happening recently aboard the carrier as well as because of what Hardell had done against the Russian pilot, Ivliyev.

"I cannot say that I am happy," Albright began. He hit a switch in front of him and the auditorium lights dimmed. A screen brightened behind him. Everyone recognized the replay of the furball between Hardell and the Russian.

"We are down here, gentlemen, to show each other—us and the Russians—just what we are capable of. We are here to demonstrate to each other the futility of waging actual war. As far as that goes, I agree wholeheartedly. I begin to have problems when what we do becomes a matter of ego and/or personalities."

Luke Hardell sat ramrod-straight in his chair. Albright was one man you didn't mess with.

"PIT BULL was designed to provide, among other things, an opportunity for us to go to school on our enemy. It was understood that we would not reveal anything to the opposition unless absolutely necessary. The fact of the matter is, however, that someone does not share our idealism."

Luke Hardell jumped to his feet. "Begging your pardon, Commander, but . . ."

"As you were, Lieutenant," Albright said sharply.

Hardell hesitated for just a moment. "Aye, aye, sir." He sat down.

"Hardell, what you did against that Russian pilot was brilliant . . . and stupid!"

"They'd dominated the practice sessions, sir," Hardell called out.

"That's right, Lieutenant, thus allowing us to go to school on them without the reverse happening. By giving in to your ego, you showed them exactly the maneuver we didn't want them to see. Now they've gone to school on us over this one. It's time for us to do the same." Albright turned to the screen. The Russian fighter was just starting into its tightly controlled supershot maneuver. He stopped the film. "G-LOC . . . G-induced loss of consciousness. I think we've found a key for the moment to beating the best they've got. And Lieutenant Hardell inadvertently showed us the way."

The flight physiologists had discovered G-LOC in the mid-eighties. There was an upper limit to what a pilot could withstand in terms of high-G loads in extremely tight turns during combat situations. It wasn't quite the same as blacking out from loss of blood to the brain, though the effect was nearly the same. G-LOC was caused by a sustained high-G maneuver, or a sudden increase in the G load a pilot had to endure after going through a continuous load for some time—such as in the supershot maneuver. The pilot's body could no longer maintain a proper blood *pressure* to the brain and the man lost consciousness. But unlike blacking out because of a lack of blood to the brain—when the pilot recovered as soon as the G load was taken off him— G-LOC continued to incapacitate the pilot for thirty to sixty seconds afterward—plenty of time, at that speed, for the jet fighter to crash.

"The Russian squadron leader, Nikolai Ivliyev, we believe was on the verge of G-LOC at the time he fired his second missile in the supershot maneuver," Albright said. "Lieutenant Hardell won his furball, but Ivliyev, had he been flying a real aircraft, would have been dead before Hardell fired a shot."

Suddenly he had the rapt attention of every pilot in the auditorium.

"The name of the game is nose advantage. Keep the nose of your aircraft pointed at your target at all times. The operative maneuver is turn-shoot-go. Remain in attitude no more than one or two seconds. I want rapid, short-duration maneuvers with quick acceleration. You will thus avoid the G-LOC condition yourselves, and possibly induce the Russian pilots to blunder into the error."

"Sir, have the other squadrons been briefed to this effect?" Hardell asked.

"Yesterday," Albright said. "They all watched your furball with Ivliyev, and several of them realized what was going on. I'm surprised none of your people caught it."

The remark stung, as it was supposed to.

"Squadron attention!" the adjutant shouted.

The pilots jumped to their feet and Albright strode out of the auditorium.

Lieutenant Cathey, sitting next to Hardell, snorted. "The bastard. You won it fair and square."

"Belay that, mister. That bastard is correct. Listen to him, it might save your ass tomorrow."

CVN *KREMLIN*

The entire air wing's complement of pilots was gathered on the forward end of the hangar deck. It was the only space large enough to hold all of them at the same time. All the ground crewmen and maintenance personnel had been removed, and armed guards were stationed at every hatch and elevator to make sure no one stumbled into the meeting. The American observers at that moment were being kept busy topsides by the admiral and the captain.

It was just as well, Ivliyev thought. Were they down here, they might get torn apart. His people had just learned about the murder of the young Russian technician aboard the *Nimitz*. Feelings were running high.

But now he had other things to think about; they all did. Their air wing CO, Lieutenant Commander Mikhail Kalinin, was speaking to them. Seated next to him at the table was the *Kremlin's zampolit*, Colonel Nikolai Smolin, a pinch-faced little man with small, mean eyes.

"You have been told about this murder not to excite your emotions, comrades," Kalinin said, "but so you can better understand the lengths to which the Americans will go to make something out of PIT BULL."

"I do not understand, Comrade Commander," Ivliyev said. He knew he was speaking for all the pilots in his squadron.

"Perhaps I can explain it for our young men," Smolin said. "Simply put, Captain, it is our belief that the Americans mean to use PIT BULL as an excuse to stage . . . shall we say . . . an unfortunate accident. They mean to engage us in a shooting match out here, in which they hope to destroy our only operational nuclear aircraft carrier. It would be a great prize."

"But what about the man aboard the *Nimitz*? Why was he killed?"

The *zampolit* shook his head. "We'll probably never know that, Comrade Captain—which is a poor thing to admit, especially since we must tell his mother something. But we can guess that Gennadi Chalkin stumbled on information that would have proved what the Americans' intentions are, and he was murdered to silence him."

"Then let us turn our backs and sail away from this madness, Comrade Colonel," Ivliyev said.

"No," Kalinin barked. "We will be prepared, Nikolai Vasilievich. You will see. But first we must talk about something the Americans call G-LOC, and how they will probably try to use it against you tomorrow during the actual air battles."

Ivliyev had heard the term, as they all had. He didn't know of anyone who had experienced the phenomenon, although since the advent of high-G training maneuvers, there had been unexplained crashes from time to time. It was something the flight doctors and engineers were working on.

A screen was set up behind the head table. On it came the aerial battle between Ivliyev and the American pilot, Luke Hardell, via their DOME.

The moment Ivliyev began his supershot maneuver, Kalinin touched a control on a handheld electronic unit and the action went into a freeze frame.

"Here you were, Comrade Ivliyev, just seconds away from the G-LOC condition," Kalinin said.

Ivliyev sat forward. What was he being told now? That no matter how good he was, no matter how much he had learned, it was still useless? There had been no way for him to know about the G-LOC condition, not in a simulator.

"The American pilot need never have fired a shot," Kalinin continued. He was advancing the action of the screen frame by frame. He stopped it again at the top of the maneuver where Ivliyev had changed directions. "The problem arose because you started the maneuver not from a straight and level flight, but directly after a pair of high-G turns. The flight surgeon agrees that the conditions you placed yourself under were perfect G-LOC."

"Then, Comrade Commander, the Americans have not only their supershot maneuver in their arsenal, but they also have their thrust reversal. It is two to one against us."

"Not so," Kalinin said. "You will have two very important factors in your favor during the actual war games battles. The first will be your Fulcrum's superior LDSD weapons-radar capability. Their equipment cannot match ours, in this maneuver."

"And the second?" Ivliyev asked.

"We are expecting an accident, an incident . . . ," Smolin interrupted, but Kalinin warned him off.

"In addition to your laser targeting and scoring systems run through the DOME and computed by Rio Center, you will all carry live weapons."

Urgent whispers broke out among the pilots.

"We will not be caught shorthanded in this battle," Kalinin went on. "We will take to the skies prepared for . . . anything."

THE PENTAGON

Dave Maxwell, in his office, was on the secure telephone with Jeff McCauley when the light flashed on his other phone indicating a call from within the building.

"Hold on, Jeff." Maxwell answered the other line.

It was Horace Walker. "Mooreland just came in. He wants us downstairs on the double."

"What's up?"

"I don't think he knows anything, if that's what you mean. I hope it's just a pep talk, but you can never tell with him. One of the reasons he's chairman."

"I'll be right down."

"By the way, did you hear that one of Thompson's aides

committed suicide? He was a young lieutenant. I'm told that the FBI was investigating him."

"Anything to do with PIT BULL?"

"I hope not."

Maxwell went back to his secure line. "Mooreland just came in, wants us all downstairs."

"Does he suspect?"

"I imagine he does, Jeff. But I don't think he knows for a fact. How are things holding together at your end?"

"The senator had heard about the incident aboard the *Nimitz*. He want us to confirm or deny. Of course we're stonewalling it."

"That bastard's got spies everywhere."

"I'm telling you, Dave, if this blows up in our faces we'll be forced to retire."

"When I consider the alternative, retirement doesn't seem like such a bad deal—if we're wrong."

The others were already gathered in the chairman's office overlooking the operations room which had been set up for the start of PIT BULL tomorrow.

It was four in the afternoon when Maxwell took his seat at the command table, where he would be during the games, and where he would be in the event an actual war were to begin, and Washington were not yet destroyed.

He nodded at Walker and Marine Lieutenant General Tom Sanderson.

"Gentlemen, in thirteen hours the window of PIT BULL will open," General Mooreland began without preamble. He was worn out by the events of the past few days, yet seemed alert and capable, his voice and manner strong and decisive.

"At any time during the following twenty-four hours, we may expect an attack from the task force under the flag of Admiral Nikita V. Tulayev, who is, I can assure you, an extremely capable officer."

"I understand Jim Milliken had spoken with him." Maxwell said.

"Yes, and Milliken has given me his direct assurances that what happened aboard the *Nimitz* will in no way affect PIT BULL. Assurances I have passed on to the President."

"General, have they found any evidence of sabotage yet?"

"None, but Bill Lane is aboard at this time conducting his investigation, and a break may be coming soon."

"But there has been no evidence found that any of our aircraft or weapons systems have been tampered with?"

"None," Mooreland said. "Every weapons system aboard that carrier have been checked and rechecked—through Rio Center."

"Then we're in good shape to begin the games, General?" Horace Walker asked.

"Yes, we are. And now I shall discuss with you our conduct in the upcoming days. Because, gentlemen, the eyes of the world will not only be on the task forces, but they will be on us as well."

KIEV

It was midnight, and Marshal General Normav was having dinner in his private dining room with Vladimir A. Krykov, the director of the Russian FIS, and Valieri V. Katayev, the head of the Ukrainian GRU. It amused him to think that the head of Russia's powerful secret intelligence service was here. But they shared a common enemy.

"William Lane is not dead," Normav said. "In fact, even as we speak he is aboard the *Nimitz* with the intent of ruining all my carefully laid plans."

"It won't happen, Comrade Marshal, because Lieutenant Lemekhov is a very capable man," Katayev said.

Normav looked at him. They had gone so far together. It was a pity that the GRU chief had finally lost his usefulness. But then, nothing stayed the same. He turned his questioning gaze to Krykov.

"It will not happen, Comrade Marshal, because William Lane will be dead within the next few hours."

Katayev looked at him sharply. "What are you talking about?"

"Simply, my dear Valeri Viktorov, that I have my own resources aboard the *Nimitz*," The FIS chief said calmly.

"This is a Ukrainian matter."

"One that you have bungled because you badly underestimated Mr. Lane's capabilities and determination."

"If we had been allowed to deal with him in the first place, we would not be in this position now."

"No matter the past, it is the present we must deal with in order to live in the future."

"Save me your homespun philosophy," the GRU director growled. He turned back to Normav. "Am I to be allowed to deal with this American?"

"There has been a change of plans," Normav said quietly. "There is too much at stake for us to take any further chances."

Katayev looked from Normav to Krykov and back. "Pardon me, Comrade Marshal, but I do not understand."

"No, you do not. And that has been the problem all along. Now, different methods must be employed if we are to be successful. In fact, Valeri Viktorov, your bungling has very nearly cost us the entire operation." He nodded at Krykov.

The Russian spy chief took a 9mm Makarov pistol from his coat pocket, cocked it, and laid it on the table in front of the GRU chief.

"No!" Katayev shouted. He snatched up the pistol and pointed it at Krykov. "Fuck your mother, but I'll get a medal when I tell them what's been going on here."

He pulled the trigger, and the hammer snapped on nothing. The gun was not loaded. He turned in time to see the muzzle of the Makarov that Normav was pointing directly at his head, and an instant later a tremendous thunderclap burst in his brain.

"It was the strain," Krykov said.

"Yes, so many good officers have fallen in recent times," Normav said. He wiped his fingerprints from the gun and bent over Katayev's body. He stared down at his old friend. It was too bad. So many good and brave men, old comrades in arms, had fallen in battle. But it was war.

"Return to Moscow. I'll call the Militia," Normav said. He pried the empty Makarov out of Katayev's hand and carefully replaced it with the weapon he'd used to kill the GRU chief. So many suicides. So much death and destruction.

"Senseless," he muttered.

CVN *NIMITZ*

Something woke Lane. He flicked on the light and focused on his watch. It was ten minutes before two in the morning. He turned the light off.

His cabin, which he had all to himself tonight, was two decks below flag territory where the admiral and captain lived. It was pitch-black. Because of the upcoming battle, all the port lights on the huge ship had been blocked out. An unnecessary precaution, he thought, but then, battles had been lost for the want of less important considerations.

He sat up and swung his legs over the edge of his bunk. The window for PIT BULL opened at 0800, barely six hours away. Everyone expected that the Russians would attack soon after that, and would not wait the entire twenty-four hours.

So what had awakened him? Nerves?

He reached for the intercom phone. "It's me," he said softly.

The phone was Captain Washington's idea. It was connected directly to the cabin across the corridor where two CID ratings were on duty at all times. But he wasn't getting an answer. "Wake up over there," he said more urgently as he felt for his own pistol, a .380 Beretta automatic.

Still there was no answer. Putting down the phone, he got up and silently went to the door. He could make out the yellow line of light at the bottom. He put his ear to the wood and listened.

No sounds came from the corridor; only the distant, deep-throated thrum of the turning props came through. But someone was out there.

He went back across the room and found the ship's telephone. He punched up Washington's number, and after three rings it was answered.

"Yes?"

"He's here," Lane said softly, facing the door. He switched the Beretta's safety off.

"What?"

"There's no answer from your boys across the hall."

"Stay put, I'm on my way." Washington hung up.

The door burst open. Lane got the brief impression of a stocky man in Navy dungarees, and then the figure fired three quick shots at the bed.

Lane snapped off two shots, the first clanging off the steel bulkhead, the second hitting its mark. The would-be assassin grunted as he fell back and disappeared into the corridor.

Lane leaped for the open door, in time to see the man round the corner at the end of the corridor. But he had left a trail of blood.

Lane raced after him as a Klaxon began to sound.

Around the corner, the blood trail led to another intersection and then ended. There was nothing. Men were rushing up the corridors from their cabins, some of them with pistols.

Lane figured he had hit Lemekhov low in the right side. No way he would be able to hide that wound. It would be a simple matter now to find him.

Washington came pounding down the corridor, a pair of Marines with him.

"He got away," Lane said. "But I hit him."

"I've got someone on the way to Lemekhov's cabin," Washington said. He went to the cabin across from Lane's.

The Marines positioned themselves on either side of the door. Washington shoved it open.

"Christ!"

Lane came up behind him. Both the CID officers were dead, shot in the face. "How could this happen? They knew about him. They wouldn't have opened the door."

Washington snatched up the phone and dialed a number. "It's me. What's going on, have you got him?"

Washington listened, his eyes growing wide. "Jesus Christ, are you sure? All right, don't touch a thing, we're on our way."

Washington hung up and stood still.

"What is it?" Lane asked.

"He's dead."

"Shit. I didn't think my shot . . ."

"Wrong one. Lieutenant Lemekhov swallowed his pistol. You shot somebody else."

25

RIO CENTER

"The window for PIT BULL is open," Admiral Jeff McCauley's voice blared from the loudspeakers.

It was 0800, and Lieutenant Commander Lee MacArthur, seated at the missile-control console, was hung over. Despite all the tensions that had been building between the American and Russian teams, they had a big party last night. The bastards sure as hell could drink.

He looked across the pit at his Russian counterpart, Georgi Maslovski. He hoped that Georgi felt half as bad as he did. Half would be plenty to assure that the man was miserable.

McCauley was seated at the head of the Pit with his two chiefs of staff, Admirals Ed Sears and Ilya Mokretsov. Above and behind them, the glassed-in observers' gallery was jammed with media people and VIPs from Washington and Moscow, including a few late arrivals who had straggled in last night.

The Russian "attack" from the CVN *Kremlin's* task force

could come at any time during the next twenty-four hours, but McCauley figured that Admiral Tulayev would make his move almost immediately.

He'd explained it during their final briefing late yesterday afternoon.

"His air wing is much weaker than the *Nimitz's* so he's going to send his fighters out to occupy as much airspace as possible as soon as possible, giving himself time to bring up his stronger surface units. If he can get the *Kremlin* and his battleships into firing range, he'll win. The delay will also serve to get his submarines into position."

He had not, however, discussed with any of them his fears that the Ukrainian Navy had introduced at least one Alfa-class submarine from the north and a Sierra-class from the south. The presence of those two boats not connected in any way through Rio Center, would dangerously change the equation.

Wild rumors had swept the Center, however, and a lot of high-ranking people were holding their breath.

McCauley switched on his mike. "Radar units aboard the *Kremlin* and the *Nimitz* have just gone active. On your toes."

CVN *NIMITZ*

The gigantic aircraft carrier was headed into the wind, which this morning was blowing at a steady eighteen knots out of the southeast, the tradewinds.

They had just been lit by an OTH (over-the-horizon) radar, which even under noncombat conditions would be assumed to come from an enemy source.

Rear Admiral James Milliken raised his binoculars and watched as a light-gun signal was sent from the wing deck at bridge level aboard the battleship *Iowa*. She, too, was being illuminated by enemy radar, and was sending up a pair of SH-2F Seasprite LAMPS-I choppers to get a better look.

He turned to Captain Carleton Stewart. "Get a message off to all ships, Carleton. Tell them I think it is coming now."

"Could be a decoy," Stewart said. "They might have us at our posts so long with false alarms that by the time the real thing comes we'll be sloppy."

"I don't think so this time," the admiral said. "Tulayev will want to get in real close so he can go toe-to-toe with us." He looked out again at his task force. "The moment we launch our aircraft we'll turn this ship around, and get the hell out of here as fast as she'll go. I want some distance between me and Tulayev."

CVN *KREMLIN*

"Bridge, radar."

"Bridge, aye," Captain First Rank Viktor M. Borodin answered the comms.

"We are being illuminated by many enemy radars, sir."

"Have they put anything in the air?"

"Aye, bridge. Numerous small targets, which we are painting as LAMPS platforms for the OTH-radar systems, as well as numerous AWACS-type forward-fire-control platforms."

"Stand by."

"Aye."

"It seems they are expecting us," Borodin said to Admiral Tulayev. "Shall we stand down?"

Tulayev hesitated a beat. "No. Send a message to all units. Attack."

DOME: COLORADO SPRINGS

Navy Lieutenant Commander Kenneth Adams was the liaison officer between the DOME and Rio Center. He sat at a console that consisted of communications units and a large radar screen. He had only to look up to see their master display DOME on which was projected the three-dimensional picture of what was happening in the PIT BULL arena.

The DOME commander, Air Force Lieutenant Colonel Bob Wurldorf, was standing right behind him.

"It's starting," Adams said. He punched the comms button connecting his position via satellite with Rio Center.

"Rio Center, I am painting numerous Red bogies rising above flight level one" (one thousand feet).

"That's a roger," Rio Center confirmed.

DOME: MOSCOW

Missile Defense Service Colonel Anatoli V. Zuyev adjusted the gain on his radar screen (the twin of the one at Colorado Springs) and then looked up at his holographic DOME display.

He punched up his satellite comms circuit. "Rio Center, DOME: Moscow. Confirm numerous Red bogies rising above flight level one."

FULCRUM-38

Captain Nikolai Ivliyev touched off his forward-looking (FL) radar the instant he was up and away from the deck of the *Kremlin*. As he continued to gain height, his velocity-search range rapidly expanded to its limit of 150 kilometers. Nothing was in view yet, but the American task force was still more that 200 kilometers out.

In his rearview mirror he watched his squadron rise one by one from the *Kremlin*.

Their strategy was for each of the squadron leaders to make immediately at subsonic speeds toward their engagement area to the southeast. The rest of their squadron would line up on their wings, at which time in unison they would cut in their afterburners and go supersonic to Mach 2.3.

Low and fast to the engagement area, then a quick pull-up to allow their LDSD weapons-guiding radar system to work, and the first shots would be fired—figuratively speaking—individual laser hits recorded by the respective DOMEs and tallied by Rio Center.

Almost like the real thing.

Ivliyev's wingmen, Ensigns Petr Bosritz, Yevgenni Mikhailovich, and Dmitri Kilmov, came up from behind him on port and starboard. He waved, they waved back. For the moment they would maintain radio silence unless there was an emergency. The only voices they would hear would be those of their DOME controllers and their OTH controller, who would vector them to their targets.

Ivliyev smiled beneath his tightly fitting oxygen mask. Time now to make up for what happened between him and the American fighter pilot, Hardell.

CVN *NIMITZ*

"Many bogies, many bogies rising from Sector One-Alpha," a forward air controller aboard one of the four Grumman E-2C Hawkeyes (airborne early-warning aircraft) radioed.

"Acknowledged," the comms man on the bridge replied.

"Time to launch," Captain Stewart said.

"Permission granted," Admiral Milliken replied, tight-lipped.

Stewart nodded at the comms man, who keyed his headset.

"This is Green Light Key Seven. Launch all aircraft. Repeat. This is Green Light Key Seven, launch all aircraft."

HORNET-4231

Lieutenant Luke Hardell's Stingers squadron was the first off the *Nimitz*. They formed up and hit their afterburners and accelerated rapidly above Mach 2.

There were three defense zones around a carrier task force. The first was contained within an envelope five nautical miles in radius, where smaller missiles could be aimed visually and fired. It was called the PMDZ—Point Missile Defense Zone. In less than a minute, the F/A-18L Hornets were outside that range.

The second was the AMDZ—Area Missile Defense Zone—which was contained in a much larger envelope, this one thirty-five nautical miles out in all directions from the carrier. From this distance, enemy aircraft could launch their longer range missiles, some of them nuclear-armed, with a high kill ratio.

The third was the ADZ—Aircraft Defense Zone—which stretched out to sixty nautical miles. Ideally the carrier group's early-warning system would give the air wing time enough to launch and get out to that point where they would engage the incoming enemy aircraft.

Ivliyev and his people would be looking for blood, Hardell thought. Well, they were going to find it. But it wasn't going to be what the Russians had in mind.

FULCRUM-38

The proximity alarm on the MiG-29's forward-searching radar pinged in Ivliyev's ear at the same moment his air controller's voice came over his comms.

"Numerous targets at flight level fifteen, relative bearing of zero-zero-three, rate of closure Mach 4.6."

Ivliyev powered up his helmet-mounted display and read on his computer that at this closure rate they would engage the enemy in less than a minute and a half.

The American planes were still well above his squadron, giving them, for the moment, the advantage. Once the actual fight began, one of the biggest dangers would be midair collisions. Squadrons then did not fight squadrons. The battle became much more personal. Within seconds of the start of the engagement, the fight became one-on-one.

"I have many hard targets," he radioed, reading them on his target-acquisition radar. His infrared scanners were showing the same thing, the heat traces from the Hornets' engines strong enough at this distance for his equipment to identify the aircraft type.

He hauled back on his stick, firewalling his throttles, and his MiG stood on its tail.

DOME: COLORADO SPRINGS

The furball was about to begin, and Lieutenant Commander Adams ached to be in the middle of it. But at forty-one he was too old. Fighting in combat aircraft at Mach-plus speeds was a young man's occupation.

He glanced up at the holographic display in his master dome. Something was missing. He had practiced with the simulators for so long he knew the approximate display for the circumstances by heart.

"It's starting," Wurldorf said beside him.

The *Kremlin* and her screening task force were steaming at top speed toward Milliken aboard the *Nimitz*, which had turned tail and was running to the northeast, the American screening ships starting to scatter.

But two of the Russian Sierra-class submarines were

missing from his display. They had somehow eluded the ASW sonars aboard the *Nimitz* task force ships.

He hit his comms switch. "Rio Center, DOME: Colorado. I'm no longer painting Russian submarines one or three."

Lieutenant Commander John Hertz, who manned the submarine-control console, came back immediately. "Neither do we, DOME. Initiating emergency-search mode."

DOME: MOSCOW

Colonel Anatoli Zuyev adjusted the gain on his radar display to sharpen the images he was receiving on the impending first aerial fight. He heard the chatter between DOME: Colorado and Rio Center, but it was of no matter. Let them search for the missing submarines. The beginning fight for supremacy was going to be in the air. He understood Admiral Tulayev's plan.

The air battle would allow him time to bring his task force to bear. Then the fight would effectively be over. So much the better if a pair of Sierras acted as loose cannons.

RIO CENTER

"What are you painting from ASW one and four?" Chief of Staff Rear Admiral Ed Sears asked.

"Nothing yet," Hertz replied, frantically punching up the displays that the ASW referee ships were generating. But he was getting nothing except for the one Sierra-class sub well out ahead of the *Kremlin's* task force. Where the hell were the other two?

"Advise at acquisition," Sears said.

All the air battles in the world would mean nothing, Hertz thought, if the submarines managed to sink the *Nimitz*. There'd be no place for her aircraft to return to, and the battle would be over almost before it had begun.

FULCRUM-38

"Thirty-eight leader, you should have visuals now," the controller said.

Something flashed below to Ivliyev's starboard, and then he saw targets all around him. The two aerial forces had merged.

His warning radar was pinging steadily in his ear, and the display in his helmet visor was a jumble of images and tracks.

Coming up over the top, he hauled his stick hard to port, jamming down on the opposite rudder, placing his fighter in a high-speed slip, almost a spin. Instantly he began to lose altitude. Directly below him his LDSD radar acquired a target, then lost it, then reacquired it.

The American fighter banked sharply to the left, in what must have been a seven-G turn, and immediately banked hard again to the right. It was one of their standard maneuvers.

Ivliyev kept on him, cutting the tangents rather than making the severe turns.

He switched his air-to-air weapons selector on the left side of the grip on his stick, to an R-23 missile, and prepared to fire.

The American fighter started to climb, but he was still below Ivliyev's position.

Ivliyev banked slightly and hit the firing button, sending out a timed laser pulse that would simulate the speed of the missile he had "launched," and the kill probability based on the relative speeds and positions of the two aircraft.

He swung to the left and climbed again, searching for another target, certain that he had killed the first Hornet.

HORNET-7032

"Three-two, you have an Aphid on your tail," the Hawkeye controller's voice blared excitedly in Lieutenant Bragg Williams' ear.

"Shit." He hauled his aircraft into a tight series of spiraling turns to the right. He'd known he was in trouble from the moment he'd realized that he was being lit up from above. It was that bastard LDSD system the Russians had installed in their Fulcrums. It and the MiG's superior cannon armament were the factors that really bothered the American pilots, because they were damned superb.

He hit the activation switches for his ALE-39 countermeasures system, releasing a flare that might fool the missile's heat-seeking capability, and aluminum chaff that would confuse its radar-guidance system.

The only thing worse on his tail would be the newer and more powerful AA-9 LDSD missile system that so far had a one-hundred-percent kill ratio against any plane the Navy could put up. But it was a larger and heavier system that was reserved mainly for the larger MiG-31 Foxhound.

His rearward-looking-radar warning indicator pinged, and the red light flashed on his panel.

"Christ, Christ," he swore to himself. He wasn't going to get out of this one. The real Russian pilots were much better than he'd been led to believe in the Top Gun program. Luke Hardell was right, after all.

"Sixty, can you get on him?" It was Hardell's voice.

Williams made another violent turn to the left as he continued to accelerate. The only hope with this kind of missile was to evade by turning inside their wider return radius so you could keep out of their way until they'd exhausted their limited fuel supply. Most of them had a range of under forty nautical miles.

"He just passed over, two o'clock high," Hardell radioed.

"I'm on him! I see him!" Tom Cathey, flying 5760, replied. "Turning in now."

Williams pulled back on his stick as a warbling screamed in his ear, and his combat-laser-aiming system went dead.

"Hornet-seven-zero-three-two, this is Rio Control. You are a confirmed kill. Return to your ship. Please acknowledge."

"Seven-zero-three-two acknowledge." Williams made a wide sweeping turn, and as he headed down to below one thousand feet (their agreed lower combat level for this operation) he looked back the way he had come. Already it was difficult to pick out the warplanes because the bulk of the furball had not only spread out but had shifted downrange nearly fifteen nautical miles.

"Here are your vectors for return," the Rio Center controller told him. He could no longer communicate with the *Nimitz*, unless it was a genuine emergency, because he was dead.

HORNET-5760

Lieutenant Tom Cathey was on the tail of the leader, who had made a successful hit on Bragg Williams, when something flashed above him, and his rearward-looking radar pinged in his ear.

"He's got me on his LDSD," Cathey radioed. He hit his thrust reversal, the Hornet suddenly losing speed.

The Russian MiG again flashed overhead, but this time it was not much higher.

"I'm on a new target, new target!" Cathey shouted, arming his Vulcan cannon and switching his targeting radar to the gun-director mode. It was good only out to five nautical miles, but he was right on the MiG now. The display went from his helmet to the HUD on top of his control panel, and the aiming pipper went off for a split second as he momentarily acquired his target.

FULCRUM-62

"Six-two, warning, warning, you have an American targeting you now, below and from the rear. Very close." The controller aboard Ilyushin Mainstay-A airborne early-warning platform three circling at fifteen thousand meters was feeding him data.

But Ensign Yevgenni F. Miklailovich already knew it. The American was too close, in fact, for him to use a missile.

He turned right, then left, accelerating again through Mach 1, but his proximity-warning radar was pinging. He could not shake the bastard.

He pulled up suddenly into the start of the supershot maneuver, choosing the risk of G-LOC over a probable hit by the American F/A-18L.

HORNET-5760

The MiG suddenly made a climbing turn to the left, its speed bleeding off rapidly. It was obvious that the Russian pilot was going to try the supershot maneuver in response to his own thrust reversal.

"Die, you bastard," Cathey said, grinning, as he got his sight on the target within the narrow, 3.3-degree beam in his HUD, along the boresight axis of his aircraft.

The MiG reached the top of its arc and began to fall off, descending, as Cathey held his own altitude, into his vertical-acquisition window.

"Now." Cathey fired. Normally the M61A1 cannon would have spit out its 20mm shells at a rate of one hundred rounds per second. In PIT BULL mode, however, his laser-targeting unit took over, the computer making the decision whether or not his aim had been accurate enough to bring down the Fulcrum.

He broke off immediately and initiated a Mach 1.5 climb out of the furball so he could evaluate what had happened below, and if he had been successful, search for another target.

FULCRUM-62

"Fulcrum-six-two, this is Rio Center," a familiar voice came over Ensign Mikhailovich's helmet radio. It was Major Aleksandr G. Lopatin, who was in charge of air wing control.

He knew what was coming. "Roger, Rio Center."

"You are a confirmed kill. Return to your ship. Please acknowledge receipt of vectors as follows."

DOME: COLORADO SPRINGS

Lieutenant Commander Adams shifted his search-and–identify radar back and forth between Hornet-5760, which had just made the kill on the Russian MiG, and Hornet-4231, which belonged to the Stingers squadron commander, Lieutenant Luke Hardell.

Something was not right.

"What's up, Ken?" Bob Wurldorf asked, not bothering to hide the triumph in his voice. They might have started out badly, but they were making up for it out there.

"I don't know yet," Adams said. "But either I've got a malfunction on my monitor, or something's up with

Hardell's laser-targeting system. I'm getting an indication of a reverse polarity."

"Which means?"

Adams looked up at him. "Which means that, under other circumstances, Hardell would be firing live weapons instead of his laser-targeting system. Thank God they're not armed."

"Call Rio," Wurldorf said. "Tell them Hardell has to break off. Now!"

Adams looked at him. "I can't, Bob, you know that. He's our boy, we stay out of it."

"Goddammit, Ken, do as I say!"

"What are you telling me?"

"They may be armed!"

Adams was stunned as the realization hit him. "Damn. I can't call Rio, but I sure as hell can call Moscow, and they can warn Rio." He punched up the private liaison comms for his Russian counterpart.

DOME: MOSCOW

Colonel Zuyev stared at his holographic display in the master DOME as he listened to Lieutenant Commander Adams' warning.

It was hard to believe. He had thought for months that the Americans might be on to them. But he had never suspected that the first breakthrough would come across his console.

"You want me to inform Rio Center?" he asked the liaison officer in Colorado.

"Yes, Colonel. I am showing a clear malfunction aboard the aircraft."

"A malfunction is part of combat. When Lieutenant Hardell realizes that his weapons systems are not functioning properly, he will return to his ship."

Adams hesitated a second. "I am making a formal request

under the rules of PIT BULL engagement procedures that Rio Center be advised of the situation."

It was Zuyev's turn to hesitate. "Is there something you have not told me, Lieutenant Commander?"

"No."

"Very well," the Russian said. He broke the connection, but instead of punching up Rio Center, he picked up a special line directly to General Normav in Kiev.

"Hello," he said. "It is about to begin."

26

RIO CENTER

In real time the action was faster than in simulation.

Lieutenant Commander Hertz barely paid attention to the aerial fight going on as he continued to search for the two missing Sierra-class submarines.

Most of his work, of necessity, was passive, since he could never be in direct contact with either the Red or the Blue submarines. He was in contact, however, with his half dozen ASW surface craft (acting as his local SOSUS), and he had the direct readouts of the ASW equipment aboard both task forces.

No one was painting those two subs, although from the latest position reports he was showing for the three Blue Forces Los Angeles-class submarines, they evidently were expecting trouble.

They had originally begun to move up into an intercept position for the oncoming Red task force, but for some reason they diverted their attention to the north-northeast.

Hertz studied the board. It was possible that the Los

Angeles-class submarines had detected the Sierras trying to make an end run and were moving to cut them off. Two submarines could do a lot of damage in a short time, especially when both task forces were busy with the aerial engagement.

He hit his comms. "COS, Blue Submarine Control. I have an idea where those boats got themselves."

"Put it up on the projections board," Rear Admiral Sears said. "What resources have you got in the immediate vicinity?"

He meant, of course, referee craft.

"None."

"Send up an Orion," Admiral McCauley broke in. "I want to *know* where they are. Now!"

27

CVN *NIMITZ*

He was in the machinery spaces, deep in the ship and far aft, almost to the stuffing boxes for the huge propeller shafts.

Bill Lane had to shout over the booming rumble of the turning shafts to make Gregory Washington hear him. "Is there any way of talking to him from here?"

Washington shook his head. "All we get is the television pictures. It's a one-way signal."

Lane looked up at the monitor screens, which showed the shafts all the way from the steam-reduction machinery back to the stuffing boxes. The closed-circuit-television monitoring equipment made the engineering crew's job much easier. Rather than personally inspecting the shafts at regular intervals, they could watch from any of several stations.

No one had noticed the dim figure of a sailor in dungarees slumped in the shadows, however, until just minutes ago. Washington and his people were first on the scene. Lane had just arrived.

"Do we know yet who he is?"

Washington shook his head. "No name yet. He's not one of the Russian observers, but we do know that he's the one you wounded."

They could see the big dark stain of blood on his shirt. It was hard to tell, however, if he was dead or alive.

"I'll go in," Lane said.

"I don't think so, sir. My orders are to make sure that you keep your skin in one piece."

"Look, Greg, this one is probably a Ukrainian, though he apparently wasn't working for Lemekhov or the GRU, which means something else is going on, something we've got to know about."

"So I'll go in there and dig him out."

"I speak Russian. Maybe it'll confuse him long enough for me to disarm him, or get him to tell me something." On the screen, Lane could see the large semiautomatic Graz Buyra pistol in the man's right hand. It was the weapon of choice of the old KGB, but not the GRU.

Topsides, the war games had begun. If something was going to go wrong, it was happening now.

"You got a gun?" Washington asked.

Lane's hand went to his Beretta .380 in his pocket and he nodded. "If I have to use it, we'll lose. We need information, not his scalp."

"Watch yourself. That bastard has already killed three people, maybe four."

Lane stepped around the bulkhead, the noise of the shafts so loud he could barely think, and worked his way aft.

The thick hull was sharply curved at this point, the steel plates rising away to his left. He hesitated. The man was lying up against a thick steel projection, just below the shaft. His eyes were open. He was staring at Lane with hatred in his eyes, but he had not yet raised his pistol.

"I have come to help you, comrade," Lane called in Russian. He stepped forward a couple of paces. The man made no move. *"You have lost a lot of blood."*

"Has PIT BULL begun?" the wounded man rasped.

Lane crouched down beside him. He was just a boy, not

more than eighteen or twenty. The name tag on his dungarees read: PO 2/C OTTLEY. He had probably been aboard the *Nimitz* during her entire cruise.

"Yes, it has already started," Lane said in English.

The boy smiled. "Then you are too late, Mr. Lane," he said, his English perfect, but his voice weak and raw. "There is nothing you can do."

"You are GRU? Ukrainian?"

The boy looked down at the gun in his hand, tried to raise it, but could not.

"Why did you kill the others, your comrades?"

"My orders," the boy said. "You were getting too close."

"You knew about me?"

The boy nodded.

"How?"

"The games have begun, it does not matter. Soon we will be dead, just like that Russian pilot."

Lane saw it all. "Sabotage? One of our planes were sabotaged, right? It was fixed so we would fire live weapons in the first sortie."

The boy was still smiling, staring down at his gun hand as if trying to will it to rise.

"Which aircraft was sabotaged?"

The boy did not respond.

Lane grabbed him by the shirt and started to haul him forward, but the boy went limp, his cheek bouncing off the steel deck. His eyes were still open and he was smiling, but he was dead.

Washington came around the bulkhead. "Gone?"

"Yeah," Lane said, brushing past him. "At least one of our fighters has been sabotaged to fire live weapons. I've got to talk to Stewart or Milliken."

HORNET-4231

Against all regulations, Luke Hardell was looking for a specific Fulcrum . . . one with the number 38 on its fuselage just below its cockpit. That was Captain Ivliyev's aircraft, and he was sure that the Russian squadron commander was just as eagerly looking for him.

The furball had spread out, reducing itself to dozens of individual fights. Slowly but surely the U.S. forces were gaining the upper hand, as expected. There had been no indication from the Russians, however, that they realized something else was happening. Little by little, they were being led away from the *Nimitz* task force and being herded back to the *Kremlin* group.

It was going to come as a nasty surprise for them when they had used up all of their fighter/interceptors and had no aerial response to the Grumman A-6F Intruders waiting to make their bombing runs against the Russian fleet. It was a one-two punch.

Now that the aerial engagement was in full swing, the tactical radio channels were mostly silent. No one needed AWACS guidance anymore. And vectors back to the task forces for killed pilots were given by Rio Center over special override circuits.

Hardell reached out with his gloved left hand and switched his secondary tactical radio to the Russian frequency, which was nearly as dead as his own.

"Ivliyev," he said softly, "I am coming for you."

He was flying at eight hundred miles per hour in a long looping turn at ten thousand feet, most of the action well below him, a lot of it right at the one-thousand-foot boundary.

He kept his microphone open so the Russian AEW&C Ilyushin Mainstay-A could home in on his signal.

A second later there was a babble of Russian, which Hardell could not understand. His proximity-warning indicator began pinging in his ear.

He had been found and illuminated. Time to fight. He snap-rolled through three complete turns before turning over one last time and diving, his speed rapidly climbing above one thousand miles per hour.

FULCRUM-42

Ensign Peter Boskritz had no idea why the American had done what he had done, nor had he even recognized the gross mispronunciation of Captain Ivliyev's name. All he knew was that his Mainstay-A had given him vectors on what apparently was the squadron leader who had shot down his captain during the practice session at the DOME. He was going to pay this time.

"Five kilometers and closing," his controller's voice came in his ear. "Target is now descending through two thousand meters."

The Hornet was above and to his right, descending on an intercept course.

Boskritz strained to catch a glimpse of the American plane against the azure sky. There! A glint of sunlight off the canopy.

In a series of smooth actions, Boskritz advanced his throttles all the way, kicking in both afterburners, which dumped raw fuel into his tailpipes, and hauled back on the stick so that his MiG blasted almost straight up. At the same moment he selected two of his R-60 Aphid air-to-air missiles, and armed them (in actually his operational computer only armed and locked his laser-tracking-and-targeting device).

Seconds later the Hornet flashed past his nose. Boskritz shut down his afterburners and rolled over in a hammerhead at the top of his arc, placing him in a perfect firing position.

But the American was not there!

HORNET-4231

The instant Hardell flashed past the MiG, he pulled back on his stick, bringing it nearly to his lap, initiating a vicious nine-G-plus inside loop.

He dialed up one of the four AIM-120 AMRAAM launch-and-leave missiles, uncaged the trigger, and held his finger over the fire button on the front of his stick.

His rearward-looking radar was alarming and his proximity detectors were telling him that he was being illuminated by an active weapons-systems radar. But he was sure that Ivan hadn't a clue to where he was. This was one trick they'd not been shown.

For an eternity, the high-G turn seemed to go on, the only thing visible outside his canopy the sky. But then the earth slid into view above him and he came up over the top of his loop. His own weapons-acquisition radar pinged that he had nose authority.

The Fulcrum was below him.

Hardell hit the fire button, and his aircraft actually shuddered as if he had really launched the heavy missile instead of just a laser-targeting pulse.

He started to roll out of his loop when he saw the AIM-120 rocketing away from him on its own motor, leaving a long tail of fire and exhaust gases.

For a second Hardell was stunned, shocked.

"Control, control, I have launched a live missile! Something went wrong! That is a live bird on a Red bogie!"

He had come around in another looping turn as he followed the Fulcrum's desperate attempt to elude what the Russian surely thought was nothing more than an electronic pulse. He would be trying to elude, but not trying hard enough, because he thought only his pride was at stake and not his life.

"Pull up, you bastard! Up!" Hardell shouted.

"Hornet-four-two-three-one, say again. Say again nature of your problem."

"Something went wrong with my firing radar! I've launched a live missile!"

"Negative, negative, we're showing a normally processed laser track . . ."

"You stupid bastards, I'm watching it right now!"

The launch-and-leave missile was the latest generation in the Hornet's arsenal. After the pilot launched the weapon, he could turn away and forget about it. The beginning of its track was run under inertial guidance, and once it got within its electronics envelope, its nearly jamproof radar system took over. And it could go a long distance at a speed in excess of Mach 4 with a burn duration of more than thirty seconds.

It took less time than that. Nine seconds after launch, the missile flew right into the rear of the Fulcrum's tailpipe, exploding with a bright yellow flash that a split second later became a much larger, brighter fireball as the MiG's fuel went up.

DOME: COLORADO SPRINGS

It was the reversed polarity he had warned DOME: Moscow about. All the indications on his panel showed a normal laser-simulated weapons launch, but he had heard in Hardell's shocked voice that an actual missile had been fired.

Adams and Wurldorf both looked up at the holographic projection in the master DOME. The MiG target was gone.

There was no doubt now what had happened. For some reason, Luke Hardell had launched an actual.

Wurldorf grabbed the spare headset and shouted into the microphone: "Stand down, stand down! All units acknowledge!"

DOME: MOSCOW

Colonel Zuyev saw DOME Commander Colonel Kabalin run across the operations room, his face flushed.

"Is it true?" Kabalin was shouting.

Pandemonium had broken out on all the circuits. It was exactly what they wanted for the next critical seconds. Zuyev had Kiev on the line again.

"Green light," Zuyev said calmly into the telephone. "This is a KEENSCHCAL green light."

"Acknowledged," the voice at the other end said, and the connection was broken.

Zuyev smiled as he hung up the telephone and looked at Kabalin. "Why, yes of course it's true, my dear Vladimir Nikolaievich."

"What are you talking about?" Kabalin screamed. "Are you insane?"

"No, not at all. On the contrary. Welcome to KEENSCHCAL. That Fulcrum was fixed. And there is more to come."

"What?"

"World War III, what else? It has begun, or will with just another little push." Zuyev's eyes grew wide.

Kabalin pulled out his Makarov pistol, cocked the hammer, and without hesitation fired a round into the officer's face, driving him back against his console in a spray of blood.

They had been fearful of precisely this. But Kabalin had not believed that the opposition would be so bold. Unless it was already too late to stop it.

RIO CENTER

Admiral McCauley got to his feet and stared at the holographic display at the far end of the Pit.

"It's a confirm," came the voice of a controller from one of the Hawkeyes circling high above the area of the aerial flight.

All combat had been broken off, but the fighters were still circling like angry hawks. The CVN *Kremlin* was still steaming at full speed toward the departing CVN *Nimitz* task force—though even as he watched, McCauley realized that Milliken was turning back toward the southeast—and the two Sierra-class task force submarines were still missing. Along with the Alfa from the north and third Sierra from the south, the situation had heated up to flammable levels even before the mishap with the AIM-120.

He keyed his microphone on the master override channel. Everyone on the entire PIT BULL team, combatants and noncombatants, would hear his voice.

"Hello all stations, hello all stations, this is Admiral Jeff McCauley, Rio Center. All units stand down. Repeat, all units stand down."

For a moment the channel was silent, then a babble of voices and demands erupted.

McCauley flipped off his comms, sat down, and picked up his secure phone. "Get me the President."

As he waited for his call to go through he looked up in time to see Senator Pat Wood, an attaché case in hand, charging across the Pit toward him. He put his hand over the mouthpiece and looked over his shoulder at his two Marine guards.

"Escort Senator Wood out of here."

"What the hell is going on, McCauley?" Wood shouted. "I demand an explanation for this incredible screwup!"

"If he resists, arrest him."

THE PENTAGON

"We're going to need some more assets down there, General," Rear Admiral David Maxwell told the Chairman of the Joint Chiefs, General Mooreland.

The call, not unexpected, from the White House had come on the heels of the disaster with the Russian MiG. What was surprising, however, was Mooreland's reaction.

"I'm not going to point fingers," he said, "because for the moment we have a country to defend. There is no telling what the Russians or the Ukrainians are going to do now."

"It was probably sabotage of that Hornet's laser-arming system," Maxwell said. "We've all seen Bill Lane's report."

"Sabotage or not, it gives the Russians a reason to start a shooting match with us. Something has to be done."

"More assets . . ."

"I'm going to the President with this."

"Yes, sir."

Mooreland looked long and hard at him. "You and Horace knew this was coming, didn't you?"

"No, sir. We just had a suspicion."

Mooreland sighed. "We're meeting in the Situation Room. As soon as I'm in place, we'll open a comms link."

KIEV

Marshal General Pavl Normav put down his telephone and looked across his operations room. It was confirmed, the Hornet had shot down one of Tulayev's Fulcrums.

General Mooreland had been called to conference in the Situation Room beneath the White House. Admiral McCauley had called off PIT BULL, ordering all units to withdraw and stand by.

And by now the key submarines would be in position. It was time for the final blow. KEENSCHCAL would become an event that no one could stop—a hurricane, wide-reaching, powerful, and destructive.

And it was also time for him and his staff to descend into their emergency Command Center one hundred meters below ground level.

Just a precaution, he thought, buzzing for his chief of staff. There was no telling how fast the situation was going to heat up, or what the Americans might do.

CVN *NIMITZ*

"Shall I recall our aircraft?" Captain Stewart asked.

Admiral Milliken stared out at the sea. He was worried about those two Sierra-class subs that were missing. They were not showing up on any of their ASW detectors. And there'd been no word from their Los Angeles-class subs.

"I don't think so, Carleton. Let's leave them up there, just in case."

"They're going to need refueling soon."

Milliken nodded absently. Something else was going on here. Something sinister. "Anything from Bill Lane or our CID people on that missing Russian?"

"No."

"I see." Milliken picked up the comms phone. "Get me Admiral Tulayev aboard the *Kremlin*." He glanced over at Stewart. "Let's see if I can defuse this situation. I've known him for a few years. He's tough, but reasonable."

Stewart got on the phone to his air wing commander to order the in-air refueling operation.

Moments later the *Nimitz*'s comms man was back on the line to Milliken. "Sir, the *Kremlin* refuses to acknowledge our transmission. Shall I keep trying?"

"Negative," Milliken said, not really surprised, after all. "You'd better get me the President on the secure line."

"Aye, Admiral."

CVN *KREMLIN*

Lieutenant Mark Dreyfus was in the big ship's ECM center, where he and his five crew had been observing the battle action. All of them, along with their Russian hosts, were in a daze. But the hostility from the Russians was thick in the air, almost palpable.

"They're not real happy about this, Lieutenant," CPO Bob Schaefer said softly.

"Can't say I blame them. Did you get through to the *Nimitz*?"

"They denied me a circuit."

"All right, just hold on." Dreyfus pushed away from his console, got up, and started across to the operations chief, a lieutenant commander who seemed reasonable.

Immediately, a pair of Russian Marine guards with automatic assault rifles barred his way.

"I want to see the captain," Dreyfus said, keeping his voice even.

"You will come with us," the Marine said in poorly accented English.

"First I'll talk to my people aboard the *Nimitz*," Dreyfus said. He started away, then he heard the distinctive snicks of ejector slides being drawn back and released.

He turned again to the guards. Both had raised their rifles at him.

Dreyfus smiled pleasantly. *"Fuck your mother, comrades, but you are going to be in plenty of shit over this one,"* he said in perfect Russian.

KIEV

General Normav hurried back up to his office to pick up a few things before he and his staff descended into the Command Center beneath the Government Complex. He looked out his window down into the main courtyard in front of what used to be the Ukrainian Socialist Republic Building. He saw several long, black ZIL limousines pulling up.

Each discharged several men and women dressed in black. They hurried into the building. More limousines arrived.

It was the Congress, or at least the inner circle, gathering for the crisis.

But they were all fools, Normav thought. And besides, they were far too late. By the time they met, the war between Russia and the United States would have begun and there would be no way on earth for them to stop it. Their choice would be simple and clean. They could either go along or die.

THE WHITE HOUSE

It was 5:30 A.M. and those officials in the loop were finding it was hard to believe that they were possibly on the verge of war. But as General Mooreland explained to a stunned President and his advisers, the hardware was in place, both sides had armed weapons, and the unthinkable accident had occurred. Blood had been shed.

"Perhaps, Mr. President, it is time to call President Nikolayev and stop PIT BULL," General Mooreland suggested.

The President looked bleakly around at the people in the room, including his National Security Adviser, William Townsend.

"I don't think so, General," the President said.

"Admirals Milliken and McCauley both advised that you back off, Mr. President," Mooreland said. "I am advising the same thing. Now, sir, before it's too late."

The President shook his head. "The entire world is watching, General. We don't want to frighten and confuse everybody. Not now, when we're so close to establishing that our armed forces are controlled and cooperative."

"Then what are your orders, Mr. President?"

"Milliken and Tulayev are to iron out their difficulties, and PIT BULL is to continue."

"Suppose the Russians began shooting back at us?" Townsend asked. "One of their advisers is dead aboard the *Nimitz*, and now we've shot down one of their fighter aircraft. What if they decide to retaliate? There is the matter of those two missing Russian submarines, as well as the

Ukrainian Alfa coming down from the north and the Sierra from the Horn. Could be awfully tight for Milliken."

"What are you suggesting?"

"Let me put more assets down there, Mr. President," Mooreland broke in. "Let me even out the odds, show them that we will not be intimidated. We'll apologize, naturally, but if we're not going to back off, at least let's show them we mean business."

"What sort of assets?"

"I can have a squadron of B-1B bombers, which are already in the air over the mid-Atlantic, within striking range in two hours."

The President paused in thought. "What do you think, Bill?" he asked his National Security Adviser.

"It would send a clear signal that we mean business."

"Do it," the President said. "No action will be taken, General, unless I give the order. Clear?"

"Perfectly, Mr. President." General Mooreland reached for the telephone.

KIEV

Marshal General Normav watched the master board below him on the main floor. Six red pips appeared in the mid-Atlantic and began to arc slowly southward.

He snatched the red command phone. "What are those targets in quadrant seven northeast?"

"American B-1B bombers, Comrade General," his air controller came back.

"How long have we been tracking them?"

"Since early this morning. We have not shown them on the display because it was believed they would not participate in the PIT BULL."

Normav glanced at his chief of staff. "We're about to see it, Arkadi."

"Shall we warn them?"

Normav shook his ponderous head. "No, there will be plenty of time after the next blow. Just a little while now." Normav began to laugh, softly at first, but then louder and louder as he threw his head back.

WATERGATE APARTMENTS

Bishop sent Special Agents Bill Seagrave and John Fay to help Sterling Miller and Puck Abramson with their investigation. Although the case had broadened in scope to include Senator Wood, it had begun as a Navy matter, and until it got into the court system it would remain so.

But bringing down a U.S. senator wasn't such an easy task. As Bishop had warned them: "You're going to have to make sure that all your *t*'s are crossed and *i*'s are dotted before I'll kick it upstairs to the Attorney General."

Wood's executive assistant, Randy Turner, might have some of the answers if he would cooperate.

Miller rang his doorbell on the eighteenth floor of the Watergate Complex and took out his ID.

Turner's voice came over the intercom a few seconds later. "What do you want?"

Miller held up his Navy ID. "Sterling Miller, Navy Intelligence. We'd like to have a word with you, Mr. Turner. May we come in?"

There was a long silence. "Can you come back later? About an hour?"

"Afraid not. Will you let us in?"

"Do you have a warrant?"

"I can wait here by the door and have one delivered in about fifteen minutes, if that's what you want." Miller exchanged glances with the others.

The door was unlocked and swung open. Randy Turner, dressed in a white bathrobe, walked across the large, tastefully decorated living room and got a cigarette from a low table.

"I heard that Doug blew his brains out," Turner said, his

back to them. "I figured you guys would be showing up here sooner or later."

Miller was momentarily taken aback. He glanced at his partner, who shook his head. Turner was evidently talking about Doug Hatcher. This wasn't expected.

"What was your relationship with Lieutenant Hatcher?" Miller asked.

Wood's executive assistant turned around, a defiant look on his face. "We were lovers, of course. But the information I got from him and passed on was never meant to harm my country. Just the opposite. Talk to Senator Wood about that. We're interested in the same thing—pulling America out of its slump."

Miller was stunned. What in hell had they stumbled into?

"You say you passed information to somebody?" Special Agent Fay asked.

Turner looked at him, one eyebrow arched. "Vyacheslav Vasilyev, my Russian control officer. He's in the bedroom, unless he's jumped out the window."

28

CVN *KREMLIN*

Lieutenant Mikhail Boskritz, head of starboard-side missile defense, stood at rigid attention in the executive officer's battle quarters just aft of the bridge. His grief was turning into a bright flame of rage.

"We do not have all the facts yet, Lieutenant," Captain Lieutenant Arkadi Zolkin said.

"But my son is dead," Boskritz replied. "We do know that it was the American missile that destroyed his fighter. There was no chance for him to eject."

"I think it will be for the best if you are relieved of duty, temporarily."

"No," Boskritz blurted. "I know my job and there are not enough trained men to handle the systems. I will remain at my post."

Zolkin gazed at him. "Very well, Lieutenant. Keep alert, there is no telling what they might do next."

"Aye, aye, comrade." Boskritz rushed back to his post.

THE PENTAGON

Streams of data raced across dozens of CRT screens in the subbasement. Bells jangled their warnings that top-priority messages were coming into the nerve center. Every telephone was busy. And the main situation board was alive with the curving tracks of the battle situation off the South American coast.

A loud warbling cut through all of that, and Admiral David Maxwell looked up at the main status board in time to see it change from DEFCON (defense condition) 3, which meant war was possible, to DEFCON 2, which meant that war was likely and perhaps even imminent. The last time the U.S. had gone to such a high state of battle readiness was during the Cuban missile crisis. Only the President could authorize it.

"Still no word on those Ukrainian subs?" General Horace Walker asked, at his console.

"Nothing yet," Maxwell said. "But it looks like Milliken is turning back into the fray."

"Any word from that pilot who shot the missile?"

"No, but he should be back aboard the *Nimitz* any minute now." Maxwell hit a button on his console, and the image on his screen blanked out and was replaced by a map of the entire world on which were superimposed all U.S. military assets. "Look at this."

Walker did, and his jaw tightened. "We don't have any other choice."

"Not now."

All U.S. forces were suddenly on the move.

MOSCOW

An aide rushed down the broad corridor in the Central Administration Building and burst breathlessly into the anteroom filled with advisers and FIS guards.

"The *Amerikanskiys*," he blurted. "They have gone to DEFCON 2!"

"He must be told," someone said.

"I'll do it," Defense Minister Tsarev said, glancing at the door to President Nikolayev's office. "Inform me the moment Marshal General Normav arrives from Kiev."

"There has been no word from him, comrade."

"I want him here immediately!" Tsarev bellowed.

CVN *NIMITZ*

Lieutenant Luke Hardell's F/A-18L Hornet touched down on deck at 0821 hours, and even before he could get out of the cockpit, the aircraft's wings were folded up, and it was tractored to an elevator on the port side and lowered to the hangar deck.

Bill Lane, Greg Washington, and the air wing CO, Brad Albright, were waiting for it.

"I had a positive lock on my laser tracker," Hardell spouted as he scrambled down from his fighter. "I don't know what the hell happened. I fired and the missile launched."

Technicians were already crawling all over the aircraft, pulling its electronics access plates off as fast as they could.

"We've been through the drill so many times now we can do it in our sleep." Hardell's gaze went from Albright to his plane and then to Lane and Washington. "What happened, sir? What's going on?"

"We think someone sabotaged your aircraft's weapons-firing systems, Lieutenant," Lane said. "I found out too late."

"How, when?"

"We're not sure of the how, but it was done the other night aboard ship."

"Why would the Russians do that, get one of their own planes shot down?"

"It's the Ukrainians," Lane said. "They want to start a war between us and Russia."

"Christ, Christ," Hardell muttered, all of it coming clear to him. He turned back to his air wing commander. "I've got to get back up there, sir."

"Not until we find out what happened," Albright said.

"Goddammit, Commander . . ."

"Son of a bitch," one of the technicians said, maneuvering his test equipment around some terminals.

CPO Warren Bradley, looking over his shoulder, was the maintenance supervisor on this section. He was shaking his head. "I think it's my fault, sir. One of my boys picked up a polarity reversal on the laser-tracker weapons system yesterday."

"Why wasn't it fixed, or at least reported?" Albright demanded.

"Sir, we ran it through Rio and it check out okay. If someone sabotaged that aircraft, then they also sabotaged Rio's board."

"That's it!" Lane snapped. "Keep your people up there on standby, Commander," he told Albright. "In the meantime, I'm going to try to stop this before we get into war!"

"What about me?" Hardell shouted as Lane and Washington hurried off.

Lane never heard Albright's answer.

THE PENTAGON

"Sabotage!" Mooreland roared. "It's General Normav, after all. The bastard did it!"

"Yes, sir," Maxwell said. They were gathered in the Command Center after Bill Lane's urgent call from the *Nimitz*.

"But the Russians haven't fired back," Mooreland said. "Not yet." His eyes narrowed. "It's going to be up to us to make certain no further shots are exchanged."

"But, General, what if they fire at us? Aren't we going to defend ourselves?" Maxwell was incredulous. "You cannot mean that!"

"PIT BULL will . . ."

"Fuck PIT BULL! We're talking about national survival here!"

"At ease, mister!"

"We're at DEFCON 2, on the President's orders."

"On my advice."

"Then, General, we better be ready for war."

"We're here to prevent war."

"The only way we'll prevent it is by showing the muscle and will to fight!"

No one said anything.

"It's the only way," Admiral Maxwell repeated, quieter.

CIA HEADQUARTERS

Sterling Miller, Joseph Bishop, and Associate Deputy Attorney General Nancy Scott met in the DCI's office at Langley with Roland Murphy and the Agency's general counsel, Howard Ryan. They were tense.

"The situation in Rio is getting critical," Murphy said. "So let's get straight to the point: Is Pat Wood a threat to PIT BULL?"

"We think it's possible, Mr. Director," Nancy Scott said. She was a sharp-looking attorney. "Since the arrest of the senator's executive assistant some disturbing information has come to light."

"Spell it out," Murphy growled.

Miller leaned forward. "Sir, the man in Mr. Turner's apartment is Mikhail Vladimirovich Ustenko, a Ukrainian intelligence officer, not Russian, although where that fits I'm not quite sure. What we do know is that Turner was feeding this man intelligence from the Joint Chiefs of Staff. He was also giving the information to Senator Wood, who was passing it along to FUTECH Corporation and other electronics and weapons-systems designers and manufacturers. We discovered that in the past few days alone, FUTECH may have given the senator as much as a hundred thousand dollars, a trip to Rio, and a top suite in a luxury hotel, as well as the services of a woman."

"We know about the girl," Ryan said. "But what do you think Wood is doing down there?"

"Turner told us that before the senator left for Rio, FUTECH promised to help him in any way they could—even by somehow interfering with the war games."

"Why?" Murphy bellowed.

"Money, Mr. Director," Nancy Scott answered. "The President wants to use the war games to help Russia from falling, but Senator Wood and his backers want to use the games solely to showcase their new weapons systems. The equipment that wins down there will sell worldwide. We're talking about billions of dollars."

"We don't have much time," Murphy said. "What is the Justice Department recommending?"

"The senator should be questioned," Nancy Scott said. "If he is anywhere near Rio Center, he should be removed."

"Now, before it's too late," Miller added unnecessarily.

Sam Hanner

29

B-1B

The squadron refueled at its rendezvous point off the Grenadine Islands about twelve degrees north latitude, and quickly accelerated above Mach 1 for the rest of their flight south.

Just moments ago they had received their coded instructions over their TREES (transient response of electronic equipment and systems) hardened ASC-19 satellite communications set, informing them that the U.S. had gone to DEFCON 2. Included was the code to go active with their defensive and offensive systems. Orders to attack, if issued, would not come until the squadron was nearly on site.

They were flying at fifty thousand feet, in a formation so loose that the six bombers were spread out over an area of nearly ten thousand square miles.

None of their powerful electronic sensors was detecting any enemy electronic emissions, which meant they were actually flying through a "safe envelope" more than three hundred miles on a side. Even if they had detected enemy radars, however, the B-1B, with its specially designed non-radar-trapping titanium fuselage, was nearly invisible—both electronically and visually.

"Skipper, my board is clean," Lieutenant Albert Rondell, the defensive-systems operator, radioed.

"Roger," the pilot and squadron commander, Major Tom Donovan, said. "About thirty minutes we'll be in launch range. You ready back there, Kenny?"

The offensive-systems operator, Lieutenant Kenneth Sanders, answered: "My key is in place, skipper."

"Keep it there," Donovan said. "This is not a drill."

THE WHITE HOUSE

"There has been no communication between the *Nimitz* and the *Kremlin* since the incident, Mr. President," General Mooreland said.

The President and his advisers were once again in the Situation Room beneath the White House. Mooreland was speaking to them via closed-circuit television from his Command Center in the subbasement of the Pentagon.

"What about Rio?" the President asked. "Has Jeff McCauley been able to get through?"

"Negative. All communications down there have broken down."

"But you can still speak with Rio?"

"Yes, sir."

"And McCauley's equipment is still tied through the DOME to both task forces?"

"To this point it is, Mr. President. But there is no telling how long the situation will remain stable."

"What are *you* recommending, General?"

"Mr. President, we're already at DEFCON 2. I think we should send an *amber light* to all of our forces. That would include our on-station submarines via ELF, which will take at least a half hour."

That would be tantamount to war.

"I'll get back to you," the President said.

CVN *KREMLIN*

"NOW HEAR THIS! NOW HEAR THIS! COMRADES OF THE REDFLEET!"

The loudspeakers boomed throughout the *Kremlin* and simultaneously throughout every ship in the task force.

Lieutenant Mikhail Boskritz looked up from his console, as did the weapons specialists under his command.

"GENERAL QUARTERS! GENERAL QUARTERS! THIS IS NOT A DRILL! A FORCE OF AMERICAN B-1B BOMBER AIRCRAFT HAS BEEN PICKED UP ON SATELLITE HEADING FOR US."

He gripped the edge of his console. "Let it happen," he said to himself. He wanted revenge for the death of his son, and he didn't want to wait long.

SSBN *MICHIGAN*

The 18,750-ton Ohio-class ballistic-missile submarine was in the station-keeping mode one hundred miles off the north coast of Norway. The Russian arctic town of Murmansk was three hundred miles to the south-southeast, and Moscow was barely fifteen hundred miles to the southeast, well within the six-thousand-mile range of the *Michigan*'s Trident II D-5 missiles. She carried twenty-four of the missiles, each equipped with ten nuclear warheads in the five-hundred-kiloton range.

She was an important force in the region.

"Conn, communications," the comms speaker blared. Lieutenant Commander Roy Tanton reached up and hit the switch. "Conn, aye."

"Skipper, we're receiving a four-message group ELF."

"Have you broken it yet?"

"Just the first group, sir. It's a flash designator, for your eyes only, with a codesignator for Lieutenant Good."

Tanton looked at his second officer. Battle orders came this way. Nothing else.

"Bring it to my quarters, and have Lieutenant Good join me."

KIEV

Marshal General Normav put down his secure telephone and looked at the situation board below. He had spent the last five minutes speaking with Admiral Ryabov, chief of the Navy, and with General Ivan Voznoy, chief of operations for the Missile Service. What they had to tell him was encouraging.

"All goes as planned, Marshal?" his chief of staff, Lieutenant General Arkadi Sheskin, asked.

"Yes, it does, Arkasha. Both air wings are still over the battle area, and now the American task force has turned inward . . . toward the *Kremlin*."

"Exactly as you had expected," Sheskin said. He looked at the blastproof elevator doors that led back up to the surface.

Normav followed his gaze. "Has Moscow called again?"

"Almost continuously. It's Tsarev."

"The fool," Normav spat. "What about our own government? Has there been any word at all from President Myakotnik?"

"Nothing."

Normav grinned. "It is time for our last surprise, then. Ryabov assures me that the VOLNA is ready."

"I will order it," Sheskin said.

VOLNA

The three-ton maritime satellite VOLNA orbited in a geosynchronous orbit nearly 22,000 miles above the South Atlantic. It and a dozen others like it had been placed in orbit over the past thirty months by Ukraine's new joint space program with Russia. Advertised as surveillance and environmental-mapping birds, the satellites were in reality a part of Ukraine's still developing Strategic Defense Initiative ("Star Wars") system, which they had stolen wholly from Russia and modified.

It was an amazing piece of hardware. It had solved two technical problems on which the Americans were years behind. The first was the development of a laser system powerful enough not only to kill satellites and high-flying missiles but to do significant damage to ground or sea targets.

The second problem the Ukrainian scientists had solved was what they called "diffuse laser energy placement." The VOLNA was capable of sending a series of high-energy beams earthward in such an array that radars and even sonars would be fooled into believing that what they were seeing was a hard target, and not simply a "laser shadow," as it was called.

Even more amazing was the VOLNA's accuracy. The resolution of its laser shadow was six inches—it could project a target as small as six inches in diameter.

The Americans could only imagine such a system!

On signal from a satellite dish in Kiev, the VOLNA laser-shadow system went active.

CVN *NIMITZ*

Petty Officer First Class Jack Sokolof held his earphones tightly against his head. He could hardly believe it. "Mr. Larsen, I've got six fast-moving screws."

Ensign Michael Larsen, chief of ASW Section-Sonar, spun around. "Are we under attack?"

"Negative, negative, sir," Sokolof said. "Sounds to me like someone is attacking the *Kremlin*. I'm showing six torpedoes in the water."

CVN *KREMLIN*

Admiral Tulayev came to the only conclusion possible after the downing of the Fulcrum: The Americans wanted to create an incident. The proof came the moment Admiral Milliken turned back for an engagement. Barely eighty kilometers separated the two big flattops now, and elements of their task forces were even closer.

"I want all weapons armed and ready to fire," he said to Captain Borodin.

"Aye, Comrade Admiral." The ship's comms blared an attack warning.

"Six incoming torpedoes, range eight thousand meters across our starboard side."

CVN *NIMITZ*

"We have a confirmation from *Missouri*," Lieutenant Commander Tom Manning said.

The *Missouri*, their only battleship, was well forward in the outer screen, nearest to the *Kremlin*'s screening vessels, and therefore nearest to the *Kremlin* itself.

"Who fired?" Admiral Milliken roared.

"No one seems to know, sir."

Milliken grabbed his secure phone and was connected directly with Admiral McCauley at Rio Center. "Jeff, are your people painting a subsurface attack on the *Kremlin*?"

"Yes, Jim, six torpedoes, but no one can tell me where

the hell they've come from. One moment the sea was clear, the next moment they were there. What's going on?"

"I don't know, Jeff. But we're in big trouble here, all of us."

RIO CENTER

"Time to impact, one hundred ninety-eight seconds," Lieutenant Commander John Hertz, in charge of the missile-defense section, announced.

McCauley sat looking at the big board, which showed not only the action in the PIT BULL arena but also the squadron of B-1B bombers screaming south.

The only elements missing were the two Ukrainian submarines and now the two Los Angeles-class submarines.

"Say type of torpedo," he called out as he lifted his hot line phone to the Pentagon's Command Center.

"Standard Mark 48, Admiral," Hertz said. "U.S. torps, but my board has no effect on them."

"Roger," McCauley mumbled.

"Whiz Bang," the Pentagon Command Center duty speaker said.

THE WHITE HOUSE

It was approaching six in the morning. Everything had occurred in the last hour. Was it possible?

The President faced his stunned advisers in the subbasement Situation Room. Was this finally it? he asked himself. How often they had practiced for this moment. How often he had thought about it in the middle of a night when sleep would not come.

It was a nightmare. *The* nightmare.

The Russians had not retaliated when one of their jet

fighters was shot out of the sky. But now this torpedo attack, apparently coming from one of our submarines ... they could not stand still for it. Shots would be exchanged. Young men would die ...

"There is no other choice, Mr. President," William Townsend, his National Security Adviser, said.

The President nodded. Now barely two minutes remained before the torpedoes hit their mark.

He sat forward. "Get me Admiral Milliken on the secure line. And have General Mooreland standing by for my orders."

CVN *KREMLIN*

Lieutenant Mikhail Boskritz stared at his screens with growing disbelief and horror. It was happening! It was no mistake, the downing of his son's plane. Until this moment he had hated that American pilot, and yet he understood that the pilot was just a young boy, like his son. And it was possible, in the heat of battle, that he had made a mistake.

Boskritz did not believe that now. The Americans were deliberately trying to provoke them into an all-out shooting war. Well, he was going to give it to them.

He hit his comms. "Defensive measure, starboard missile defense."

"Defensive measure, aye," the officer shouted.

"Is that a confirm on the incoming torpedoes?"

"Roger, roger. Six incoming. Time to impact one-four-three seconds!"

CVN *NIMITZ*

The instant the torpedoes showed up on the sonars, Bill Lane rushed off the bridge and hurried aft to the Combat Information Center. The room was lit with an eerie blue light, mostly from the radar screens and CRT displays.

The big board at the head of the room showed the state of the battle.

He was working strictly on a hunch that Normav would not allow the Russians to shoot unless they were directly threatened. And that if they were not directly attacked, he would do something to make his people think they were under attack. He had already done it once by sabotaging the *Hornet's* laser weapons-tracking system. Was this a second attempt?

Lieutenant j.g. Ed Lipton was manning one of the master consoles. Lane had gotten to know him briefly over the past twenty-four hours when they had spoken about the *Nimitz'* ECMs systems.

"ONE-TWO-ONE SECONDS TO IMPACT," the speakers blared.

Lane pulled up a chair beside Lipton. "I need your help, Ed."

"How'd you get in here, Mr. Lane?" the young man asked.

"Listen to me, I want you to extrapolate back alone the tracks of those torpedoes. I want to know exactly where they came from."

"One of our L.A.-class subs."

"I don't believe it."

Lipton looked questioningly at him. "What are you talking about?"

"Project backward along their track. Let's see where they're really coming from."

Lipton brought the tracks up on his screen and put them into the computer to compare their place and time of origin. If they had come from a single submarine, they would converge in position and time.

"They're all parallel," Lipton said after a moment. "So they were launched from more than one sub."

"Six subs. We don't have that many . . ." Lipton stopped in midsentence. "Oh, Jesus Christ, look!"

The computer continued to extrapolate the torpedoes' tracks backward to their supposed origin. But the tracks cut through the middle of the fleet, through the middle of one destroyer and a missile frigate.

"Fucking impossible!" Lipton swore.

"There are no torpedoes!" Lane shouted. He grabbed a headset. "This is Lane in CIC. Give me Admiral Milliken on the bridge, on the double!"

CVN *KREMLIN*

Lieutenant Boskritz could wait no longer.

"NINE-TWO SECONDS TO IMPACT," the loudspeaker warned.

Boskritz dialed up his weapons, keying them to the Kremlin's own missile-control radar and to the real-time data link from one of their Hormone-B choppers, providing them with OTH aiming capabilities.

His actions showed up on the missile-weapons control board on the bridge.

"Starboard missile defense, what are you doing?" Captain Lieutenant Zolkin's voice screamed in his ear.

He ignored it. "I need a counterkey," he said urgently to his *michman* beside him.

The Russians used the dual-key weapons-arming system just like the Americans for safety's sake. But the Russians used officers of unequal rank very often, and naturally the higher-ranking officer could intimidate the subordinate.

"Of course, Lieutenant," the *michman* said, turning his arming key.

Boskritz did not hesitate. He hit the firing button. Two SS-N-19 cruise missiles launched from the starboard side, accelerating toward the east on long fiery tails.

BB 63 *MISSOURI*

"BB 63, this is Overlook Two," the excited voice came over Lieutenant Guy Ottinger's headphones in the battleship's defensive-systems suite.

Overlook Two was one of the Grumman E-2C Hawkeye AWACS off the *Nimitz*.

"Roger, Overlook Two . . . ," Ottinger answered, but the air controller overrode him.

"We're showing a multiple missile launch from the *Kremlin*! You are the probable target. Confidence is high. Say again, we show a multiple missile launch from the *Kremlin*."

Ottinger scanned his board, but there was only the air wing circling some miles to the north-northeast.

"I'm showing nothing, Overlook Two."

"Negative, negative, you've got two incoming missiles on your ass, Guy! Accelerating now above Mach 2!"

"Christ." Ottinger still wasn't showing a damned thing on his board. His supervisor was right behind him now. "Can you say type of missile?"

"Roger, roger. They're SS-N-19s. Should be showing up on your board any second now."

Ottinger's heart thumped. With that cruise missile they would have barely twenty seconds' warning. He hit the Klaxon, armed the automatic aiming radars for the starboardside Phalanx CIWS (close-in weapons system) cannons, and punched up the emergency comms for the bridge.

"Bridge, CIC!" he shouted. "We have two incoming Russian SS-N-19 cruise missiles. Suggest you turn immediately to two-seven-zero."

"Roger."

The turn would put them bow-on to the incoming missiles, presenting a much smaller and more armor-hardened target.

THE WHITE HOUSE

"Send the *amber light* to all U.S. military units," the President told General Mooreland.

All of them in the Situation Room could hear the sharp intake of breath from the Chairman of the Joint Chiefs. *Amber light* was the presidential code word for all military units to lock and load their weapons systems. In conjunction with DEFCON 2, the order was virtually a declaration of war.

BB *MISSOURI*

The 58,000-ton battleship made an acute hard turn to starboard at the same time Ottinger's board picked up the two incoming Russian missiles, one a half-second behind the other.

The birds, with a range of nearly three hundred nautical miles, screamed toward their targets at speeds around Mach 2.5, ten feet above the surface, which made them extremely difficult to detect, let alone shoot down, until the last few seconds before impact. They were a big improvement over the Exocet missile.

The SPS-10F surface-search radar was warbling as it activated the aiming circuitry for the two Phalanx CIWS 20mm Vulcan cannons forward of the main stack. The weapons fired nearly six hundred Mk 149 depleted-uranium subcaliber rounds per second.

Fast and accurate, their only drawback was a range of barely fifteen hundred yards. And a missile incoming at Mach 2.5 covered that distance in just over a second and a half.

CVN *KREMLIN*

Lane was immediately patched to the Russian carrier through Rio Center as the seconds ticked down.

"Have your forces stand down, Admiral," Lane shouted in Russian. It would go much faster without translators. *"My name is Bill Lane, I work for the National Security agency. Ukrainian Marshal General Normav placed spies aboard the* Nimitz, *and they sabotaged one of our aircraft to fire live weapons. Somehow they have managed to send out a bogus signal making you believe that you are under attack by torpedoes. It is not so, Admiral. Our forces will stand down. We must avoid war here, Admiral. There is no reason for it!"*

"Have you the proof of that?" Admiral Tulayev replied in English.

"Yes. If we can stabilize this situation, the proof can be shown to you. I'll come over to your ship personally to show you what we found."

Admiral Tulayev said something that Lane did not quite catch.

"Oh, shit," Lieutenant Lipton said at Lane's elbow. "I'm showing two missiles incoming to the *Missouri*! They're going to hit!"

The Russian admiral spoke. "We may not have the time, Mr. Lane. We have launched an attack on your battleship *Missouri*."

"We're showing it," Lane answered. There was no way out of this one. At any moment the fighter/interceptors circling overhead would get back into it, this time all of them using live weapons.

"This is Milliken. Admiral Tulayev, you have my word that no retaliation will be taken for your attack on our battleship. We will stop here and now."

But there was no reply. The circuit was dead.

Lane and Lipton exchanged glances. On Lipton's scope now, the pair of incoming missiles was almost merged with the *Missouri*. Only a matter of a second or two.

BB *MISSOURI*

The tactical plot on Guy Ottinger's board went to zero, and the Phalanx guns went to full automatic.

"Brace yourselves," he called into his comms set.

Topsides in the bridge, Commander John Haig and his exec, Jim Kreger, caught the flash of the cruise missiles' exhaust at the same moment Ottinger's urgent warning came over the comms speakers, and both men braced themselves.

Both forward Phalanx cannons began firing, the noise like the angry buzz of a huge outboard motor.

The first missile was hit by one round and exploded in a blinding flash.

The second missile impacted low against the twelve-inch armor plating of the *Missouri*'s hull, just seven feet above the waterline and forward of the first sixteen-inch-gun turret.

Because of the angle, it was a glancing blow, but enough of a hit so that the SS-N-19's conventional high explosive went off, shoving the 887-foot battleship eighteen feet to starboard and blowing a hole eleven feet in diameter in her side.

Sirens began to shriek as flames shot out of the gaping wound, the heat threatening the ammunition magazine where the sixteen-inch armor-piercing shells (each weighing nearly a ton and a half) were stored. The first of the screams could be heard.

"Stand by on Harpoon launch, on my command," Commander Haig shouted into his comms.

His intership communications gear buzzed.

Haig snatched up the handset. "This is Haig."

"Milliken here. You all right?"

"We have major damage and many casualties, Admiral, but we can still fight. I'm launching my Harpoons now."

"Negative, negative, stand down! Do you copy, Haig? Stand down on my order!"

"Goddammit, Admiral. I can still fight! Don't hold me back!"

"You have your orders, mister," Admiral Milliken shouted, and then he was gone.

"Goddammit!" Haig screamed.

"Harpoons ready for launch on your orders, skipper," his exec said.

SOSUS CONTROL: SOUTH ATLANTIC

Ensign Scott Anderson was technically off duty, but he had dropped back by the control room shortly before the war games began, and he and Lieutenant Trevor Probyn listened to the radio reports with a growing disbelief.

"What the hell are they doing up there?" Anderson muttered.

Probyn looked at him, with some sympathy. It wasn't so many years ago that the British Navy had its hands full in the battle for the Falkland Islands (an issue, he thought, that still wasn't resolved).

Lieutenant John Roper, the day-shift OD, suddenly sat up straight at his console. "Hello." The British officer transferred the tracks he'd picked up onto the main status board at the head of the room.

"What is it?" Anderson snatched a set of earphones.

"Many targets, heading south," Roper said. "I can't quite separate them."

But Anderson could. Even before he processed the signals through the spectrum analyzers and filtering systems, he knew what he was hearing. He knew what was happening.

He lifted the hot line telephone to the Pentagon Command Center.

"What is it, old man?" Probyn asked.

"Alfa submarines. A whole shit pot of them. Maybe a dozen, all heading south at top speed."

"Good heavens," Probyn said.

"I confirm," Roper said unnecessarily.

LARISSA CONTROL: BARENTS SEA

Lieutenant Konstantin Demin looked away from his dimly lit scope to adjust the gain control on his console. He pressed his headset tighter to his ear.

There, faintly in the mush. He flipped his comms switch for his supervisor's console.

"Captain, it is there again. Sector one-seven-alpha. The same before."

Captain Second Rank Boris Polyakov got up from his console and came over to Demin. He plugged in his headset and listened.

A moment later it came. "There," Demin said.

Polyakov could hear it now, and he knew what it was. An Ohio-class ballistic-missile submarine, just off the coast of Norway, and so damned close now if he stepped outside he could piss on it.

This was an act of war. Polyakov unplugged from Demin's console and got on his hot line direct to Moscow.

RIO CENTER

All of the Russian officers, including Admiral McCauley's chief of staff, Admiral Ilya Mokretsov, stepped away from their consoles.

The U.S. Marine guards prevented them from leaving.

"No one goes anywhere until this thing is settled," McCauley announced.

No one argued with him.

He flipped his comms. "MacArthur, was that a confirmed hit on the *Missouri*?" he asked the missile controller.

"Aye, sir. My board is showing a single hit. Missile one was destroyed just before impact. Probably the CIWS aboard."

"Damage reports?" McCauley asked Lieutenant Commander Paul Emanuel, who was in charge of surface operations.

"An undetermined number of casualties. The *Missouri* is in no immediate danger of sinking unless the fire reaches the number-one magazine."

The big board at the end of the Pit showed no further aggressive action by either side, though the jet fighters were still in the air and had just been refueled.

It would not take much to set off the powder keg.

"Command, air group," Lieutenant Commander Charles Poole said over the intercom.

"Go ahead, air group."

"We've got another problem here, Admiral. That B-1B squadron en route has just entered her strike envelope. They could launch an all-out air attack at any moment."

"Tell them to stand off."

"I've tried, sir. Their only reply was that they have been given an *amber light*."

McCauley reached for his hot line to the White House.

CVN *NIMITZ*

Bill Lane in CIC was in a three-way secure-telephone hookup with the White House Situation Room that included Admiral Milliken, above on the bridge, and Admiral McCauley at Rio Center.

The skipper of the *Missouri* was busy trying to save his ship. So far no counterattack had been forthcoming from the battleship. Nor had the B-1Bs made any aggressive move.

But this delicate teetering could not last much longer.

"Mr. President, we are going to have to back down. I'll fly over to the *Kremlin* to explain everything to Admiral Tulayev, but we must recall our aircraft and stand down with our submarines and especially that squadron of B-1Bs."

"Is that you, Mr. Lane?" the President asked.

"Yes, sir. We've tracked down the saboteur here aboard the *Nimitz* and ... neutralized him. And we've pinpointed what he did to the Hornet. We've also pinpointed the bogus torpedo signal. Mr. President, it was sent from what we believe to be a Ukrainian VOLNA satellite. Laser shadowing. Very effective."

"I hear you, Mr. Lane. But certain of my advisers here believe that the incidents prove that Russia also wished to sabotage PIT BULL."

"Not the Russians, Mr. President, nor the Ukrainian government at Kiev, just Marshal General Normav and his old guard. Rescind your *amber light*. Stand down from DEFCON 2. Recall your B-1Bs. And any submarines heading toward the Russian coast. Please, Mr. President."

"I concur," Admiral McCauley said. "Let's walk away from this one all the wiser."

"Admiral Milliken?"

"I'm a soldier, Mr. President. I'll follow your orders. But if we're going to shed blood here, let's do it decisively, hard, across the board. Or let's do nothing."

"Stand by," the President said.

CVN *KREMLIN*

Admiral Tulayev held the secure telephone carefully to his ear, as if it were a dangerous instrument. He sat on the edge of his easy chair in his battle quarters just aft of the bridge.

"I understand your situation, Comrade Admiral, and your frustration," President Nikolayev said.

"There have been at least two deliberate acts of aggression against us."

"One of which, the supposed attack by six torpedoes, you admit yourself was nothing more than some sort of an electronic ruse."

"Perpetrated by the American forces."

"Possibly, Comrade Admiral, possibly not. In the meantime your attack on the *Missouri* was successful."

"Only partially so, though she is heavily damaged, and there almost certainly are heavy casualties. Another missile or two, and she will be at the bottom of the sea, a threat no longer."

"I forbid this!" Nikolayev commanded.

"We have the men and weapons to do the job, Comrade President."

The line was silent. Then Nikolayev sounded cold and aloof. "It is your decision, Comrade Admiral. You are working for the Russian Government, under the rule of law ... *civilian* law ... or you are working for the forces against us. Only you can decide where your loyalties lie, and what home, if any, you will have to return to."

THE WHITE HOUSE

The President looked around the long table at each of his advisers and cabinet officers. All good and true men, most with military service in their backgrounds.

At this moment they were frightened; hell, scared silly, the President thought. Just like he was.

The hot line telephone to Moscow burred softly at his elbow. He looked down at it, not surprised that Nikolayev was calling.

But was it to present an ultimatum: Stand down or die?

There had been other world leaders who had come up against the United States. But none had thermonuclear weapons. The face of war had changed forever.

The President picked up the telephone. "Hello, Mr. President."

"Mr. President, we must call a halt to this session of PIT BULL."

"This session?" Relief washed over him.

"Yes, of course, Mr. President. We cannot allow a few

unfortunate mistakes brought about by misdirected ambitions to wreck all that we have worked for."

"I agree," the President said. "But there will be much for you and me to do to clean up the ... mess that has been created."

"Mr. President, we will give each other our word, and then get started repairing the damage."

"Yes, Mr. President," President Reasoner said, smiling. "An excellent idea."

KIEV

The lights in the Command Center beneath the Government Complex suddenly went out. With them the displays on all the electronic consoles died. Even the telephones went dead.

Only a few battery-driven emergency lights flickered on.

For the briefest of instants Marshal General Normav wondered if the Russians had dropped a nuclear bomb on Kiev.

"They have cut our power and comms," Lieutenant General Sheskin said, running up from the operations floor, a flashlight in his hand.

"Ah, then you must be correct, Arkasha," Normav said, feeling sheepish.

Sheskin nodded sadly. They both understood the implications. Vladimir Krykov, the director of the Russian FIS, had told him an old Russian proverb: Before a fight, two men are boasting; afterward, only one.

In the Stalinist days they might have said: "Blame the shortages on the peasants." In those days everything was the peasants' fault.

Normav glanced at his wristwatch. It was a little after two in the afternoon. "Time to go home now, Arkasha. The battle is done."

"I will dismiss the others."

Normav buttoned his coat as he left his office and crossed the Command Center floor. Someone had opened the emergency-power controls for the elevator and cranked open the blast doors.

He waved back at his men, then boarded the elevator and rode to the surface more than a hundred meters above.

Krykov was waiting for him in the corridor. He'd brought no one with him, no soldiers, no militia.

"Good afternoon, Pavl Ivanovich," the Secret Service director said respectfully.

"I am surprised that you came back to Kiev, my friend."

Krykov smiled. "It is like a second home to me. You know I was born in Ukraine."

"I have lost."

"We will go on," the FIS director said softly. He took Normav's arm and they started down the broad, empty corridor, Normav's eyes straight ahead like the good soldier he was.

He did not see Krykov withdraw the big Graz Buyra from his coat pocket with his right hand, although he caught the motion out of the side of his eye as the 9mm pistol was raised.

Krykov fired one shot at point-blank range into the side of Marshal General Normav's head, just behind his ear, the shot echoing and reechoing down the hall as the hero of the old Soviet Union seemed to fall forever.

RIO CENTER

Two Marine guards escorted Senator Wood to McCauley's conference room. "The admiral wishes to have a word with you, sir," one of them said.

"Fine, because I've got plenty to tell him." Wood pushed his way into the conference room, and the Marines closed the door behind him.

Two men, neither of them McCauley, both of them

dressed in civilian clothes, were waiting. They did not look happy.

"What the hell is this?" Wood demanded.

"Sorry to bring you here under false pretenses, Senator, but there was no other way," the smaller, older of the two said. "I'm Alex Joyce, special assistant to Ambassador Sloane."

"My name is Tony Lessing, Senator, and I work for the CIA," the other man said.

Wood's chest tightened and he felt the first stirrings of fear. Something was wrong. "What can I do for you?"

Lessing pushed a button on an electronic device the size of a television remote controller, and waved it toward the attaché case Wood held. The unit emitted a high-pitched squeal that died as Lessing pointed it away, and grew again as he pointed the detector at the attaché case.

"Senator, you're carrying an electronic device that is sending out a signal. Can you tell me why, and where that signal is being received?"

Wood was staggered. He had no idea. "I don't know what you're talking about. I'm carrying notes and files, nothing else."

"May we look inside?" Lessing asked.

"Certainly not," Wood snorted. "I demand to speak with Admiral McCauley this instant."

"Sir, I'm afraid that won't be possible," the CIA man said. "My orders are to take you immediately to the embassy. Senate Majority Leader Thayer is standing by in Washington for your call."

"Somebody explain to me what's going on here," Wood demanded.

"Sir, we know about your connection with FUTECH Corporation, and with Ms. Fisher, as well as the one hundred thousand dollars you were given last week. Your executive assistant, Mr. Turner, has been arrested and will be charged with treason. He was passing information he illegally obtained from a member of the Joint Chiefs of Staff to a Ukrainian intelligence officer who was shot to death last night in Washington by a man hired on your behalf by FUTECH."

Wood was struck dumb.

"Senator?" Lessing prompted. "Shall I continue, sir?"

"It won't be necessary." Wood handed him the attaché case. "Get me out of here now."

30

RIO CENTER

Bill Lane's helicopter was waiting on the apron to take him across the bay to the military airstrip where the SR-91 was standing by for him. They wanted him back in Washington.

As Ben Lewis said via secure phone to the *Nimitz*, "There are a few thousand questions for you up here, boy. Don't keep us waiting."

His first stop after the *Nimitz*, however, was with Jeff McCauley.

"You did a fine job for us out there, Lane, but goddamn, it was close."

"Yes, it was, Admiral."

McCauley nodded thoughtfully. "It's going to happen again. Probably within the next six to ten months, if the President has his way."

Lane looked at him in disbelief.

"Evidently you didn't see his news conference. You were en route. He told the world that the first PIT BULL was in some respects a success. There were casualties and damage because of mistakes on both sides, but that was preferable to war. And the reason for PIT BULL was to prevent war. I agree with him, one hundred percent."

"Then we'll go through this again."

McCauley nodded. "Hopefully not quite like this time. We'll iron out the wrinkles. Oh, by the way, you probably didn't hear about Marshal General Normav either. He committed suicide."

"He got his nine ounces," Lane muttered. It was a Russian euphemism for a bullet in the back of the head. "What about Senator Wood?"

"He's on his way back to Washington. There'll be charges, maybe not in court, but certainly by the Senate Ethics Committee. He's done."

"That's the difference in our systems," Lane said.

SSBN *MICHIGAN*

The second ELF message was perfectly clear in its meaning, and came as a relief. They were ordered to stand down from their *amber light* and to go back to deep station. LARISSA was rearing her ugly head in the region and it was likely that the *Michigan* had been detected.

"Leveling off at fifteen hundred feet," the helmsman said.

Lieutenant Commander Roy Tanton glanced at the depth gauge. "Come right to zero-one-zero degrees, and rig for silent running."

"Aye, skipper," his exec, Lieutenant John Good, said. "We're under the thermocline. They won't be able to hear us."

"No use in taking any chances. They might send a couple of Alfas out here to snoop around, and I want to be long lost before that happens."

"Right," Good said. "We've got another three months up here. No use blowing it now."

"I'd rather do this than fight," Tanton said. "Being bored is preferable to being dead."

SSN *POGIN*

"It is a trick," Aleksei Grichakov blustered. He was hunched in the darkness behind a maze of steam pipes just aft of the reactor.

Mikhail Badim and his *starpom*, Valeri Melnik, crouched in the passageway two meters from the *zampolit*. Badim held out the decoded top-secret message they had received more than two hours ago.

"Not a trick. General Normav is dead, PIT BULL is over. It is all over now. It is time to go home."

"That is impossible. We could not have received that message as deep as we are running."

"That part is a trick," Badim admitted. "I had Sitnikov fix the depth gauge so that it read seven hundred meters low. We have been running for the past two days around three hundred meters. When the ELF message came, we sent up a comms buoy."

"Then the Americans know we are here?"

"Yes. There is a Los Angeles-class submarine behind us now. She has been there from the beginning."

"You knew?"

"Yes, I knew. Now it is time to stop this insanity. We have been ordered to return home."

For a long time Grichakov was silent. "Where are we now?"

"Five hundred kilometers off the east coast of the United States. Just where you wanted us to be, Comrade Zampolit."

Grichakov smiled wanly. "Good. This would be a fine place to die." He held up the electronic trigger and encoding device for the explosives that had been set around the reactor cores.

Melnik yanked out his pistol and fired a shot that struck

Grichakov high in the chest, knocking him back against the bulkhead.

"Too late!" the *zampolit* cried weakly in triumph, and his thumb stabbed at the triggering button the moment before he died.

Badim held his breath. The seconds passed.

Nothing happened.

Badim let out his breath slowly, finally understanding Normav. He had wanted a safeguard, some hold finally on Badim to make certain he would take his submarine all the way south to guard the shipping lanes in and out of the Panama Canal. But in the end he did not want to actually risk the nuclear submarine's destruction, not by the hands of a mere *zampolit*.

The bomb was a dud.

"Let's go home, Valeri," he said. "It is over now."

"What about the explosives?"

"There are none. It was a ruse."

"The American submarine behind is no mirage."

"No, but he doesn't want to fight, and neither do we. When he sees that we have turned around and are heading home he will leave us."

"Are you sure, Comrade Captain?" Melnik asked.

"Yes, Valeri, this time I am sure."

COLLEGE PARK, MARYLAND

It was eight in the evening, Washington time, and Bill Lane was on his last dregs of energy. He and Ben Lewis sat across the desk from Roland Murphy in the DCI's study at home.

It had been Lewis' suggestion that they meet here away from the CIA and the NSA. On an unofficial basis. Just friends talking with each other. Congratulating each other on a job well done.

"He's determined to go on with PIT BULL," Murphy said.

"We will be at a disadvantage, General," Lane said.

"But there is no proof that there is a second spy within the Pentagon. Only Lieutenant Hatcher. And we've come up with nothing else here."

"He's there. Working for the Russian FIS. For Krykov, who is just as antireform as Normav was, but who is younger and a whole hell of a lot more subtle."

Murphy stared at him. "Then it's up to you, Bill. You and Ben here."

"Sir?"

"Well, son, I happen to agree with you. But you've got a head start on us. You've got the ball, go ahead and run with it. Ben will provide you a home base, and I'll run interference for you."

"Ten months," Lewis was saying. "It's all we've got to dig him out before the next PIT BULL."

"They won't give it up," Lane said.

"No," Murphy agreed. "And now they'll know you're coming."

MOSCOW

The bells on Spassky Tower in the Kremlin were striking four in the morning when Lieutenant General Arkadi Sheskin left FIS headquarters in the Lubyanka downtown and climbed into the waiting Chaika limousine.

"Home," he told his driver, and he settled back in his seat to think about the latest developments.

Next time, the thought passed gently through his head. Next time.